THE
UNRAVELING

Book One of the Jeremiah and Susanne Series

Max W. Justus

NEWMAN SPRINGS PUBLISHING
320 Broad Street
Red Bank, NJ 07701

First originally published by Newman Springs Publishing 2022

ISBN 978-1-63881-827-4 (Paperback)
ISBN 978-1-63881-828-1 (Digital)

Printed in the United States of America

This book is written for persons up to 108 years. After that age, you are not allowed to read it!

The characters portrayed are entirely fictitious. Any resemblance to persons living, dead, or dead and residing in a trunk is most unfortunate and very, very silly.

Anyone who says he or she is depicted here is telling a fib! So there you are.

Thank you for reading!

Contents

Preface

This is an adventure mystery about impossible happenings by improbable people, as told by an imaginary child narrator. Over generations, this family relates tales of love, kindness, attempted murder, and final comeuppance.

During the romp, the story emphasizes the value of always learning and solving problems. Past that, we see what hope, honesty, fair play, and courage can do in good times and in adversity.

Above all, this book demonstrates the value of time well spent with our children so that they may become kind and caring adults, capable of loving and having wisdom, adults whose word and whose handshake are as good as their bond. This goal is not a fantasy; it must be an objective!

Therefore, this book is dedicated to family and friends who made everything possible and dedicated to children and adults of all ages who enjoy whimsy and try to do what is right.

Those who show kindness and courage in the face of adversity do a marvelous thing.

Author's Note

Italics are used for emphasis and to express direct thoughts.

Chapter 1

SUSANNE'S VISIT

When Susanne came to dinner yesterday, she was in a reminiscent mood. We talked of old times, of our amazing and almost magical childhood together, of our many adventures in England at Nana and Papa's old house, and our adventures on this side of the Atlantic.

Stories filled our time as we compared our memories and corrected each other's recollections. I pulled out my old notebooks, each filled like a diary, a separate notebook for each of our adventures. Lost in recollections, we frequently laughed together, although a few times we almost cried. And sometimes we sat, side by side, in momentarily embarrassed silence. So many memories! So many stories! So many people!

Pointing to my pile of notebooks, Susanne said, "Jeremiah, you must publish these. Others must know. I hoped you would begin back then when it all started. That's why I teased you after our first adventure.

"But that was nearly sixty years ago. Over seventy-five years have passed since the twenty-first century began. We are getting old and won't live forever, and then the stories will be lost. I don't have your knack for writing. Promise you will start."

Beneath her thick gray hair swept up and held with an ancient stickpin, her blue eyes were pleading, her voice sincere. She fingered the long strand of large and luminescent pearls that once belonged to our great-great-grandmother. While still in their original nineteenth-century box, Nana gave the strand to her one Christmas when Susanne was a teenager, decades ago.

Back then, Susanne was a pretty girl, full of promise. She grew into a beautiful, talented, and accomplished woman. Now, as an older person, she is still striking to behold: active, vivacious, and sharp-witted. Her kind and generous personality makes me happy whenever I see my much-loved sister. And she is the fortunate one; age has been kinder to her than to me, even though I am younger.

I looked at her from under eyebrows that would make Mortimer proud, through glasses that always irritate me, and pointed my gnarled fingers at the notebooks. "At least I have something to jog my memory," I declared, thumping my hand on some of the notebooks while looking down at my hideously shaped long thumbs.

I never look at my hands or face without thinking about our grandfather, whom we called Papa. My hands, ears, and toes are shaped like his once were. And my fingers have gnarled with age as did his—more genetic gifts from my beloved grandfather.

Every time I shave, I see my dad's well-loved image peering back at me, in my eyes and my huge nose bent in the middle. But he was handsome; I am not.

And when I think of Papa and Dad, I also think of Nana, Mom, and Phoebe. I feel grateful they were in our lives and sad at their loss. God rest their souls—all wonderful people.

After a thoughtful pause under my sister's gaze, I continued, "Let me think about writing. I'll let you know."

Susanne insisted, "Please, Jeremiah, try before it's too late." She was quiet after speaking.

"Will you help me when I'm stuck or cannot clearly recall?" I inquired.

"Yes, Jeremiah, I shall."

"I feel old. But to tell the story, I would need to speak as a child. Do you think I can do that?" I asked.

"Yes, Jeremiah, you still have a very active inner child," she replied with a little smile.

"There's an obstacle I foresee," I ruminated. "Susanne, you remember that Papa, Nana, Phoebe, Dad, and Mom always spoke to us as adults, even when we were little. They were always teaching us, even when we had no hope of understanding. Give them credit for always explaining the big words they used. They simply hoped for something to stick, that we might remember the topic while they said the same things time after time. Eventually, I think we did remember most of what was said."

Susanne nodded and responded, "That was how they educated us and made learning relatively painless. It was instruction via the dinner table or family outing!"

I replied, "Yes, you are right." Quiet followed, as my mind jumped to the past and wandered from place to place.

Finally, with irritation in her voice, my sister smashed the silence and demanded, "What *obstacle*, Jeremiah?"

Roused from my faraway thoughts, I slowly answered, "Oh yes, the obstacle. Well, in my head, all those memories are piled together in a big jumble, one on top of another. How can I distinguish what a child of seven or ten or fourteen might recall? Memories don't come with a timestamp!" I paused to look intently at Susanne, hoping for help. Puzzled, she stared back at me in silence. Finally, I asked rather sharply, "Won't Jeremiah's recollections sound like an old man talking?"

Sensible Susanne appeared pensive before she eventually replied, "You cannot recollect everything. Remember that adults do talk as adults and children recall as children do, with their own unique twists and partial understandings. I think your readers will realize that you needed to piece together what adults said using later memories. Fortunately, the adults usually had their facts consistently straight."

"In other words, don't sweat the small stuff," I said with a little laugh, "even if I make the child Jeremiah sound like an old man of three hundred."

"That's right, bro. Don't sweat anything. You were a bright kid. You remembered the topics and filled the details in later. So what? I'm *so* over it!" As only she can do, her large eyes rolled before locking on mine; her mouth formed a bemused smile.

I signaled a mock salute and said, "You are a geriatric teenaged girl."

With a nod to my comment, Susanne added, "And you may occasionally add from the viewpoint of old Jeremiah reviewing the past, as it were." She smiled more broadly during a reflective pause and continued, "But try not to comment like a Presbyterian theologian."

"Thanks for the good advice. I always said you were the smart one. I feel better already," I replied gratefully.

Laughingly, Susanne said, "I'll help you with the manuscript."

"You'll be lucky if I don't make you type it!" I replied to her face, which was half smiling and half worried that I would renege. "No promises, sis. The prospect is overwhelming!"

"Think seriously about writing it all down." She fixed me with her gaze as she quietly said, "Please, share the stories." Then she gave me her intensely commanding look.

Oh boy! Bossy Boots is serious.

That was yesterday. I've spent time thinking.

Now today, after my evening meal, I sit in my study. My worn armchair is comfortable. Glancing at the notebooks, I sip a small scotch, neat in its glass. Alone tonight, my thoughts are my own. Recalling our lovely time together yesterday and recollecting her advice, I again sense Susanne's urgency. Like her, I feel the passage of time.

I think back to my first extraordinary meeting with Leila and Mortimer. Recollections of Joshua and Penelope and their undoubted love for us make me sigh deeply. I smile when thinking of the sensual Marjorie and fun-loving Bertie, and all the others of the gang. A giggle pops out when I think of Beatrice and Marcus with his sideburns. Finally, Edgar and Jemima fill my thoughts. A little prayer of gratitude forms on my lips whenever Edgar pops into my head. The older I become, the more frequently I think about those encounters. We were so fortunate to know them all firsthand. Few others have had the same opportunity. I still miss them sixty years later. Birth favored Susanne and me in ways I am still just beginning to understand.

There were others we met back then that I could gladly have missed. Even now, they make me shudder when I think of them or say their names, even though they cannot hurt me anymore.

It was Mortimer who said, "Each of our actions, for good or ill, has consequences; and the ripple effect carries far out." Susanne and I have experienced many good ripples, and some really bad ones.

I reach for my pen and a new blank notepad. While muttering, "What gnarled fingers! At least they work," I toss the pen aside and reach for my latest electronic gizmo. It will transcribe my thoughts and words, forming the first of many tales.

For you see, it is nearing the end for me. But for you, well, it is just the beginning. So let me introduce you to the world I once knew.

On one hand, that world was full of fairness, love, kindness, care, and privilege. On the other, it was full of evil and hate, mayhem, and murder! Susanne and I inherited all that and fought through together more than once.

Shall we begin the first of the many stories that Susanne and I shared?

Chapter 2

GRANDFATHER COMES TO VISIT

"Ten-minute warning. Supper is almost ready," says Phoebe's voice from the kitchen. "Wash your hands, Jeremiah. You too, Susanne." We both know that is not a request—it's a command. Phoebe, our nanny, almost always says, "Ten-minute warning," before we are required to do whatever it is that she asks.

Susanne sometimes asks, "Why do you say ten-minute warning, Phoebe?"

Always giving the same answer, Phoebe replies, "That allows you enough time to complete what you are doing or to stop at a good spot. You two leave nothing unfinished, and there's no rush—it just seems fair."

It's hard to argue with fairness. Phoebe is always fair, in everything. We don't argue much.

While I'm washing my hands in the bathroom sink, I see my reflection in the mirror. I am tall for my age, so there's a lot of skinny me in the glass. I don't mind my floppy straight sandy-brown hair, but I hate my cowlick at the back—it always stands up straight no matter what I do.

I look at my hands and my very long thumbs. They remind me of my long and ugly great toes. I think my thumbs and toes are as ugly as my grandfather's. "Thanks, Papa," I mutter without meaning it. I'm not grateful for my odd-looking thumbs and queer-looking toes, not at all.

Now, I know my blue eyes came from Mommy and Daddy. Half expecting the mirror to let me in on a secret, I ask, "But who gave me the cowlick?"

My reflection does not answer.

As I stare at my image, I mutter quietly, "Well, hello, kid. If you think the thumbs are big, look at the nose. It's a honker!" I move my face closer to the mirror. "Daddy says it could fly away by itself. He's allowed to say that 'cause his nose is the same, also a real honker!" My eyes keep looking, but nothing happens; nothing flies away.

I mutter to my reflection, "Well, Jeremiah Brian Morris. You turned seven years old on May first, and now it's mid-September. So you are really seven and a half…well, almost. And you are still ugly!" I stick out my tongue. "So there! I hate my nose more than I hate my thumbs." I gawk at my silent reflection and then demand, "Now tell me, when will this face grow enough to catch up to my ugly honker nose?"

Again, my reflection does not reply.

"Jeremiah, what are you doing? Supper is ready. Susanne and I are waiting for you," says Phoebe's voice, clear and firm.

"Coming!" I yell out as I dry my hands. I stick my thumbs in my ears, wave my hands, and again stick out my tongue at my reflection. Giggling, I say, "Nana, nana, boo-boo."

Even though my image in the mirror doesn't answer, I feel better when I joke about my ugly face. Susanne laughs at me when she catches me talking to myself.

Once, when Susanne caught me talking to my reflection, she called me Narcissus; but she refused to tell me what that meant. "You figure it out, Mr. Mirror-mirror-on-the-wall." So I had to ask Phoebe, and she explained the story.

I recollect replying, "But I'm not looking into a pond!"

Phoebe's memorable response was "Narcissus didn't happen to have a looking glass. They hadn't yet been invented. He spent his life looking at his own reflection in a still pond because he thought the image was so wonderful. Frankly, I've always thought he had an even bigger problem," she muttered to herself, "regarding his orientation."

"What does that mean, Phoebe?" I asked.

"Later, that comes later," she replied. It was a few years before I knew what *that* meant. "The implication is that he was too stupid to know it was his own face that he loved." As Phoebe finished speaking, she gave me her *look*, so I knew to cut it out or not get caught.

Anyway, my name-calling sister, Susanne Elizabeth, is not ugly like me. Instead, she's pretty. In November, she will be ten years old. She has wavy red hair that my mommy calls Titian red. It's cut short, which gives her a pixie face. She has blue eyes and very fair skin, which sunburns easily. Like me, she is tall and somewhat skinny. Lucky for her, she has a normal-looking nose, like Mommy's.

We all live together with Phoebe, our nanny, on the fourteenth floor of a building that overlooks Central Park. We can see trees from some of our windows. This is a big deal in New York City, according to my parents.

"Sit down, Jeremiah. I have already served food onto your plate while we were waiting," says Phoebe.

Susanne looks at me quizzically. "It takes you a long time to wash your hands," she says. "Talk much?"

I ignore her.

The three of us start eating after Phoebe says grace. My parents are not home, just like usual. I start thinking about everyone important to me. I often do this when I try to make sense of the world. I don't ask why our parents aren't here. I already know the answer. They are too busy to be with us. We are not clients that count.

My mommy is a lawyer just like her mother. Mommy almost never goes to court. She says she mostly advises people on how to manage their businesses or their real estate.

Like her parents, she has blue eyes. She is very tall but about two inches shorter than her mother. She always battles extra weight, but she tries to stay trim. She works out at the gym and showers afterward. She often comes home with her light-brown hair still wet and glued to her head. That's not so pretty! But she doesn't seem to mind. She says, "I just need to exercise and be clean." Practical!

Mommy works in New York City for a law firm here. Her mother, our nana, works in London, England, for a law firm there.

Nana has blue eyes and is just over six feet tall! She is taller than her husband, our papa. She has a slight stoop in her back that she calls her dowager hump. She keeps her thick and wavy gray hair cut to just below her ears. When left alone, she says it always looks like a hair bob from the 1920s. I think that means there are waves in the hair as it falls.

As I said, Nana is a lawyer like Mommy. But in England, they call her a solicitor instead of a lawyer. She never goes to court either. In England, only barristers go to court. That's how they do it in England, even though both solicitors and barristers are lawyers. Mommy explains all of this to me, over and over. It makes my head dizzy, and I don't really understand.

But next week, both lawyer Mommy and solicitor Nana will be at the same meeting! Mommy flies from New York and Nana from London, and they will meet up in Switzerland, in a city called Zurich. I think that is really cool!

When Mommy talks, she sounds almost like her own mommy and daddy. My friends say she sounds different from their parents. I guess that's her British accent. My friends also say she uses funny words sometimes. Maybe that's because she went to college in England—at Oxford. Did she learn her funny words there, at Oxford? I dunno.

But she went to law school here, in the United States. Then she did her bar exams. Why they are called bar exams, I don't know. But Mommy says, "You can't work for a law firm without passing the bar exams."

Daddy doesn't sound at all like Mommy. He was born in Brooklyn. He is six feet, five inches tall, about seven inches taller than Mommy. His eyes are a very dark blue. His nose is big and bent slightly sideways in the middle. But his nose fits his face. His dark hair is thick and straight, but it has a few gray streaks, which he hates. His arms and legs are strong and powerful. Mommy calls him her gentle giant.

He does something with money here in Manhattan. He tells us that he manages money for Americans and for people from other countries. He goes to his office near Wall Street Monday through Friday. He worries about the stock market. He worries about clients.

He worries about the money he manages. He worries a lot. I am not so sure he worries much about Susanne or me. We have Phoebe for that.

As I said, Phoebe is our nanny. She was almost eighteen when she was hired about ten years ago to look after the new baby, my sister, Susanne. Then she got more work when I became the new baby two and a half years later!

Phoebe is younger than my parents. She has a rounded build and is about five feet, six inches tall—tall for some families, but not so much when standing beside my mommy and daddy. Her short straight hair is very thick and almost black. Her eyes are the deepest brown. Her skin is darker than mine. She says her looks come from her family in Spain. She rarely gets sunburned. Lucky Phoebe! I think she is really pretty.

Mommy sometimes says, "I envy Phoebe's beautiful nails. Her lovely hands have nails that appear long even when she cuts them short. Instead of starting halfway up the end of the finger, Phoebe's nails start much closer to the last joint of her fingers. That's why they always appear long. They are very elegant, a fortunate genetic trait."

One of the times Mom said this, I asked, "What's a trait?" Then she explained.

So my traits are the horrible thumbs and toes I got from Papa, and the honker of a nose Dad gave me. But who do I blame for the cowlick?

Phoebe loves to read to us—Susanne on one side, me on the other. That's always fun. She understands and helps me with the things I fear and the things I don't like. Her room is two away from mine and one away from Susanne's. She's always close by us and does everything for us. We love her because she's almost our real mommy.

Thank goodness for Phoebe since both our parents are too busy earning money. Dad says it takes a lot of money to keep things going. I sort of understand that but not really.

Anyway, after Mommy spends a week in Zurich, she will be in London with Nana for another week. Dad will be working. We will be with Phoebe.

But our grandfather, Papa, says he will do something really awesome. Papa says that instead of being alone without Nana either in London or at their county place, he will come to stay with us.

Oh boy! This is great. We have fun when Papa is with us and plays with our toys. He gets down on the floor to play the games we are playing—even though sometimes we need to help him up afterward.

Papa is shorter than Nana's six feet by an inch or two. He has thinning gray hair and bushy eyebrows over his deep-blue eyes, which watch everything and miss nothing. His eyes twinkle when he is playing a joke or is up to mischief. Sometimes he says, "I can never win at poker!"

His face is long, with a square jaw. His ears stick out a little, like mine do. Another thing I got from him—just like the long thumbs and funky toes! He is muscular but carries a little paunch in his belly. He is very physically active and moves rapidly when he is doing things. And something is always happening when he's around!

Papa laughs every time he says, "I've never had a real job." Actually, he manages the land he owns in the country in England. Papa once told Susanne and me, "My dad gave me a lot of land and money when he died. There is a title that came with it."

I didn't understand what Papa meant about a title. I never like to seem dumb, so I didn't ask Papa to explain. Life is confusing! Mommy says the Brits fawn over titles, and Americans don't understand what they mean. Maybe that is why I get confused. I am an American.

Anyway, for all his life after schooling, Papa helped his dad run the estate. He and Nana lived with Papa's father. Then Papa inherited. That means he got the property and money after his daddy died.

He calls himself a farmer, but I've never seen him get really dirty. I've seen other people who work for him get really dirty. The last time we visited, when I was four and a half, Papa watched what the workers did and then went in for lunch.

I never met Papa's dad. He got sick and died before I was born. I never met his mother either. Papa's mommy died in a car accident when Papa was a young man, almost nineteen. He says he still misses her.

Papa once said to Susanne and me, "When I was growing up, Mom was often in the nursery even though I had a nanny like Phoebe. She always had time for me, cared about what I was doing, asked how I was feeling. During our days together, she would insist on a hug and kiss for no reason, maybe because I never had any brothers or sisters. She played games with me on the floor too. But unlike me, she never needed help to get back up! When I came home from boarding school at the holidays, she would always plan fun things to do together."

Papa's words stuck in my memory, partly because he seemed a little sad as he talked, and his eyes were too shiny. Susanne told me she also remembers what he said.

More than once, Susanne or I asked Mommy about Papa and his parents. Mommy usually replied, "Their closeness was unusual for their time, but they both loved it. Back then, a nanny usually did all the child care, leaving the mother carefree, if she chose. But Papa's mom was especially active with him and very affectionate. My dad was lucky to have such a caring and affectionate parent. Both parents, actually." She always smiled a little when she talked about this.

"But a year after Papa went to college at Cambridge, his mom died in a car crash. That made him very sad, but it was a long time ago." Mommy always lost her smile whenever she mentioned the accident. And a few times, Mommy added, "I've always been struck by my father's sadness when he talks about his mother's death, even years later. He was fortunate to have such love and closeness to both parents. That love shaped his life."

I can hardly wait for Papa to arrive! He makes me smile inside. Daddy will be preoccupied with work. Mommy, who tends to be strict, will be in Zurich. Phoebe will be Phoebe. She will look out for us and watch over us, but she will give Papa a free hand.

I finish my dinner just as I finish my thoughts. Suddenly, I realize Phoebe is watching over us right now! She says, "Each of you, please bring your plate and cutlery over to the sink. And your milk glass if you have finished. If there is any schoolwork, get it done now. Then a little playtime before bed."

Phoebe pauses and then looks at me sternly. She says, "You were rather quiet during dinner. You looked like your mind was far away, and you actually didn't answer a question I asked you. Are you ill, or in trouble, Mr. Silent-type?"

"No, Phoebe, I'm not in trouble, and I feel fine. I was just thinking about Papa coming. I can't wait!"

"I'm glad you are excited about his coming." Then she asks, "But you *do* know you can be excited about something and still have a conversation at the dinner table, don't you?"

"Yes, Phoebe." I giggle.

"Better manners tomorrow then. Dinner is a time to talk together. You were miles away," she says firmly, "but I want you here with us instead."

I nod and say, "Yes, Phoebe, I'll act better at dinner tomorrow." But I don't say anything about all the things I was thinking about. My thoughts are sometimes my own.

As I stand beside her, she fusses with plates. Suddenly, her arms are giving me a hug, and she plants a swift peck on my forehead. "I am looking forward to your grandfather's arrival too. But make the effort to be one of us tomorrow, please."

"Yes, Phoebe, I will," I say directly to her face.

I glance over to Susanne. As she hands Phoebe her plates and cutlery, she gets a quick hug and swift forehead peck as well. Phoebe is always equal and fair.

I can tell Susanne is glad that Papa is coming. He makes her smile inside too. We are going to have fun!

While we wait for Papa, Susanne and I do our usual things like going to school together. Susanne is in grade 5, and I am in grade 2. We walk home together, sometimes with some of Susanne's friends who live nearby.

I keep asking Phoebe what day it is and when Papa is really arriving even though I know that he comes on Saturday. Susanne says that I am silly to ask.

Susanne mutters, "I'm also excited that Papa's coming, but I still know the days of the week," and then she rolls her big eyes at her idiot brother.

Even Phoebe, who never seems to get annoyed at anything, quietly tells me to stop asking the same questions. Finally, Phoebe says, "Silly goose, I'm getting exasperated. Of course, today isn't Saturday. Let's turn common sense into a lesson in deduction, shall we? Were you in school today?"

"Yes, Phoebe," I reply.

Phoebe asks, "And what days do you go to school?"

I reply, "Monday through Friday."

"Can you deduce or figure out that it is not Saturday today?" she asks, looking at me intently.

I reply sheepishly, "Yes, Phoebe." And I giggle.

Phoebe often does this. She will say something like "Most people need to be taught to think logically. And even simple things can show deductive reasoning." Phoebe is very smart!

Just like Mommy and Daddy, she always explains the big words she uses with us. When we ask her why she uses big words, she always replies, "Your parents and I agree that you both need to know the value of words and how to use them clearly and correctly. You must speak lucidly, which means expressing yourselves so you will be understood. If you learn new words every day, your large vocabulary will help you to speak intelligently and to understand others easily. Call what I do an easy school lesson."

Smart parents, smart Phoebe! So with that easy school lesson, I wait.

Saturday arrives! A driver from the office picks up Papa at the airport. When he is close to our apartment, the driver telephones Phoebe. She says, "Let's head down to the lobby to await Papa's arrival." The elevator is slower than ever. The car takes ages to arrive! Eventually, a car stops in front of our building. The driver helps Papa put his luggage on the curb, checks that all is okay with his passenger, climbs behind the wheel again, and slowly drives away.

At last, Phoebe lets us loose. The two of us surround Papa. We stretch to hug him. I impatiently wait for a hug in return. I can feel the scratch of his facial stubble as he gives me a big kiss on the cheek and then rests his face against mine. Susanne giggles from the tickle of his stubble. I know he is glad to see us 'cause he holds each of us tight to him.

Mommy and Daddy come down to the lobby as the car arrives. They hold back to let us greet Papa. When she finally has a chance, Mommy gives her dad a big hug, kisses him warmly on the cheek, and begins asking about the flight over from London.

Our dad gives him a manly hug and welcomes Papa to America. They always have this running joke between them. When Papa arrives here, Dad says, "Welcome to America!" And when my dad goes to England, Papa always says, "Welcome to Britain!" And then they always laugh out loud when they say this, the sillies.

Upstairs, as the adults talk, their conversation is constantly interrupted by questions from my sister and from me—mostly from me. Papa sits on the sofa. He calls it a chesterfield. That's British for sofa. I giggle when he says that—it sounds strange. That's my new word for today. *Ta-da!* Susanne is glued to his one side, and I am glued to his other, on the chesterfield. Papa's tweed jacket has a smell of land, horse, and outdoors, a smell that makes me think about his home in the country. I feel content.

Soon, it is time for dinner. Mommy has made a stew, which we eat with bread and butter. She has purchased a pie, a blueberry pie. She warms it and serves it with vanilla ice cream. It quickly disappears from our plates!

When bedtime comes, both Susanne and I are too excited for sleep—at least, that's what we think. We kiss Mommy and Daddy good night. We clamor over Papa in our excitement to say good night. Then Phoebe directs us to our rooms.

But once we clean our teeth, do our nightly routine, and stretch in bed, sleep comes crashing down on us. I remember Phoebe's goodnight kiss on my forehead and not much more. Later, Susanne told me that she was asleep before the light was out!

Early in the morning, Mommy is already up, finishing her packing. Dad is making coffee for the adults and cooking breakfast sausages. Papa is still asleep but wakes up with the sounds and smells of breakfast in the making. He trundles down the hall in his pajamas and housecoat. His slippers clack on the floor as he walks.

The family time over breakfast is quieter than it was at the previous night's dinner. Mom says, "Everyone seems subdued this morning."

Dad replies, "I always worry about your flight."

Mom replies, "There is always quiet, unsaid anxiety about flying, with relief on landing."

Papa says, "My daughter and my wife are both flying today. I'll feel better when everyone is safe in Zurich!"

A few hours later, it is time for Mommy to go. Everyone, including Papa, is now dressed.

We go down the elevator and wait briefly at the curb. The same driver who brought Papa yesterday comes for Mommy. Phoebe quickly says her goodbyes and moves back to give the family private time.

Dad says, "I shall miss you, Constance. I always do when you are away. But I'll be busy looking after the children, and keeping up with your father!" The adults laugh.

As we say our goodbyes and hug Mommy, both Susanne and I have tears in our eyes. We see Mommy almost every day. We love her, and she loves us. We will miss her. And when you are seven, two weeks is a long time without Mommy!

Suddenly, Susanne bursts into tears, holds on to Mommy tightly, and whimpers, "I don't want you to go. I'll miss you. I need you here."

Mommy leans down and gives Susanne another hug. "You'll be okay with Phoebe here all the time. We will talk by phone every day. And you have Papa as your treat! That makes up for a lot of things."

Mom looks helplessly over to Dad, who shrugs his shoulders and says, "And I'm here, Susanne, as is Papa. We'll all miss Mommy, but she will be safely home soon."

Susanne wipes her eyes and says, "Well, okay, maybe," but she still holds on tight to Mommy's coat. I want to hold on to Mommy tight too, but Susanne got there first!

Mommy stands up and gives Papa a very big hug and kiss. She says, "I will call when I land and when I see Nana in Zurich."

Papa says, "Yes. Please do. Give my love to your mother."

Then Mommy gives Dad a really big hug and a very big kiss and holds him tight for a long time. The driver coughs slightly. Mommy breaks away as she whispers to Dad, "Love you."

We hear him reply, "Love you more." For a long moment, his hand still lingers on the back of her shoulder.

She hugs each of us again. I finally have my chance to hold her really tight. Then she gets into the car.

"Call me daily," she commands as she looks at Dad affectionately.

He nods and says, "Yes, Constance, I will." He looks pointedly at us, wiggles his fingers back and forth over our heads, and then looks back at Mommy with eyes wide open as he says, "And I'll give you a full report!"

She smiles as she waves to us all. She blows us a final kiss. Her car disappears into traffic, and she is gone.

We stand there silently for a moment. Papa begins briskly, "The day is fine and clear. The sun is shining. I think the children need a trip to the park."

"Oh yes, please!" say two voices.

Even though the bright September sunlight makes patterns on the sidewalk, there is a breeze. We head upstairs to get coats 'cause Papa insists we wear them.

Susanne asks, "Do we really need coats?"

"Yes, you do. I don't want anyone saying they are too cold to have fun," Papa replies kindly. "My tweed will do me just fine."

Who can argue with that?

Dad excuses himself, stating he has office work that needs to be done. Papa smiles and agrees.

So down the elevator, out from the lobby, and onto the street we pour. I am very happy to be walking close beside Papa. Susanne smiles as she holds his hand. As we head to Central Park, I suddenly almost don't miss Mommy.

Does Susanne feel the same?

Chapter 3

THE CONSPIRACY

Near Central Park, Papa scans his eyes along the streets. Finally, almost in unison, we ask, "What are you looking for?"

Just then, he says, "There we are. Come this way, children."

We follow him to the street along the park. There are three horses, each with a carriage, lined up in a row. Papa talks to the first driver. They exchange money.

We walk past the gray horse, her head nodding and turning to see what her blinkers are obstructing. Susanne doesn't know about blinkers and is silly enough to ask.

Papa replies something like "Blinkers are used to cover or obscure the peripheral or side vision of the horse, the vision along the edge of the visual field. Central vision remains unobstructed. That way, motion out of the horse's work area cannot frighten her and cause her to bolt. But she still can see clearly where she is going."

We both nod as he speaks. Susanne often tells me, "I always understand everything the adults say." If her brain is anything like mine, she is lying. I understand sometimes, but often I am lost.

After Papa finishes saying whatever about blinkers, we climb up onto the carriage seats. The padded bench is comfortable, and with Papa between us, we are in heaven. We spend an hour going around the park.

Both of us have been to Central Park before but never in the horse carriages that bring tourists and other people through the park. The sun is warm on our skin. The sky is clear. Papa was right; there is a chilly breeze, but we are comfy inside our coats! We snuggle against

Papa and listen to the carriage driver talk about places we pass by, feeling the autumn sun warm us through and through.

Papa says, "This was a good idea. I do love the smell of horse-flesh." His nostrils open wide as he breathes in deeply. He looks satisfied and pleased.

During a walk in Central Park after our ride, we go over a small bridge. Papa says, "What lovely ornate banisters," as he points to the fancy handrails on each side of the bridge. We wander along areas with arching trees above gravel paths with benches for people to rest. We cross over an open grassy area. It is as if we are in the country—a tamed and ordered countryside!

Papa never loses sight of me even though I run ahead time after time despite his warnings to stay together. Susanne holds his hand or walks close to him. After an hour or so, we arrive at another street. Papa guides us.

Once we are on city streets, the park seems an unreal country dream, even though it is so close. Cars rush by, horns sound, and people cross the streets. It is a normal busy day in Manhattan.

"Is anyone hungry or thirsty?" asks Papa.

"Yes," both of us reply.

"Ice cream?" suggests Papa.

We exclaim, "What a great idea!" Soon Papa finds an ice cream shop, and in we go! Inside, there are gelato, Italian ices, sorbets, and ice cream—all kinds of flavors, too many choices! The kind lady serving us sees my confusion. She says we may try a sample before purchasing. That's one way to make a decision!

Papa and I know that Susanne usually just likes vanilla ice cream and always sticks to what she knows. When Susanne orders, Papa says, "Wow! Knock me over with a feather. You ordered watermelon sorbet in a sugar cone! Are you finally becoming adventurous with flavors, Susanne?" She smiles at him over her cone, nods, and has another lick. "About time," he mutters.

Shortly, every bit of our cold dessert disappears, and our sagging energy returns. Papa insists we wash our sticky hands before going out. He washes up with me and waits for Susanne outside the ladies' washroom door.

On the street again and ready for adventure, I ask, "Where to now?"

"Follow me," he says. "We need a cab." He hails one.

Once all three are safely inside, he gives directions. When we stop a little while later and once again hit the pavement, he pays the driver and then says firmly, "Here, you each hold my hand. This area is very busy, and I don't want you lost!"

We hold on as he walks briskly. He walks fast enough that we could become separated very easily. Then he suddenly stops and says, "This is the kiosk where they sell theater tickets." He looks at each of us and asks, "Are there any plays you two especially want to see?"

We have not thought about this before. I have been to programs before—the Christmas production at Radio City Music Hall and the *Nutcracker* ballet matinee near Christmas. Susanne has gone with Mommy to the symphony to hear them play when Dad was too busy.

I am almost jumping as I exclaim, "Will we get to go to a real play? Exciting!"

"I don't know about any plays," says Susanne.

Papa looks at me.

"Dunno, I can't decide," I say as I shift my feet side to side.

Papa asks, "Shall I choose then?" He looks from Susanne to me.

We both say, 'Yes, please. We don't know."

Papa says, "I will take you to plays that I want to see. You may not understand everything. But that is what life is like. Not everything is immediately understood, but with time and experience, things you have heard about or seen in a play all begin to make sense."

And with that, he buys four tickets for three different plays and a fifth ticket for one. As he pays, our eyes bug out when we hear the total cost.

"Why so many tickets?" we ask.

Papa replies, "I think Phoebe needs some entertainment. Your father and mother have seen two of the plays but not the third, so I shall invite your father to the one he has not seen. That one is on Saturday. The other two are on weekdays. He will be too busy, and he has already seen them."

I am beyond excited that we will be going to a play with Papa and Phoebe too. Phoebe is rarely included when we go out to something unless Mommy thinks she will need help with us. I can hardly wait to surprise Phoebe! Even Susanne bounces because she is so pleased.

Then Susanne, who is older and always obeys the rules, looks at Papa. Her face saddens as she says, "We won't be able to go. Bedtime is early on school nights. The plays will keep us out too late. Mommy will say no." Her blue eyes are suddenly very shiny, and her chin jiggles just a little. Her chin always jiggles before she bursts into tears. That's how I *always* know when she is about to really cry.

"Not to fret," says Papa. "Your mother will not know until it's too late to do anything. Phoebe will help us, and I will work on your father."

Excitement rises again. Tears disappear. Chins are steady again.

Papa asks, "Did you two enjoy our outing today?"

Susanne says, "Oh yes. It was wonderful. I've enjoyed everything."

"Fantastic!" I exclaim loudly—so loudly that people walking by look at me as if something is wrong with me.

Papa says, "One play is for Tuesday night, and the others are Friday and Saturday. The last two are not a problem. Do you agree?"

We echo, "Yes."

Papa asks, "So what shall we do about Tuesday night and Wednesday?" He waits a moment, as if thinking about this for the very first time. Then he says, "You both will go to school Tuesday. You will both have a nap after school. Then we go out for dinner and the play. Wednesday, you will be sick from school—not too sick to go to a museum, though."

"But I get homework. I cannot do that and nap," says Susanne.

Papa says, "Never mind that. We'll get it done together but not on Tuesday."

Susanne looks doubtful.

Papa adds emphatically, "And I will help you with the work you miss on Wednesday."

That seems to relieve Susanne's mind.

I know I will have homework too, but I don't care! Time with Papa is everything! A thought flashes. I ask, "How will you get around Dad? He may say no."

Papa replies, "I will tell him, not ask. And I will tell him when he is distracted with work. He won't be paying attention. I am not expecting a long discussion." He smiles calmly. His blue eyes twinkle with mischief.

I know that Papa likes to have fun. Suddenly, I realize that he likes to know the rules so he can break them. Now, we have to convince Phoebe! We start our walk home.

The shadows lengthen as the sun falls in the sky. The breeze picks up, and now the temperature drops. We are really glad Papa insisted we wear our coats. Smart Papa!

Dad is still working at home when we arrive. Phoebe's wonderful dinner smells greet us at our apartment door.

Once alone with Phoebe, Papa says, "We need to talk."

She looks startled and a little afraid. "Is something wrong? Did one of the children get injured?"

He replies, "No, nothing of the sort. Nothing is wrong." Then he invites her to all three plays and outlines his plan about our missing school.

She says, "I don't think my employers will agree."

Papa simply says, "Leave them to me."

"I could get fired," she says.

"In which case, you may work for me forever," says Papa.

"If it is that important to you, then okay." She leaves a two-beat pause before she quips, "I rather like Britain!"

We give Phoebe a hug, and both bounce as we exclaim, "It's exciting to see a play with you."

As he points a finger directly at us, Papa sounds bossy and looks stern when he demands, "Both of you, say nothing to your father about our plans." We nod that we agree.

Looking serious, Papa orders, "Phoebe, you must keep it secret too."

She replies, "Mum's the word. You handle the parents."

Papa smiles.

Phoebe looks thoughtful and then smiles broadly as she asks, "Should I get my passport renewed tomorrow? I might need to fly to Britain with my new employer!" Her twinkling brown eyes look directly at Papa.

Papa laughs out loud.

The conspiracy begins. Fun times!

Chapter 4

PLAY DAYS

Monday is a normal day at school, if normal means waiting impatiently for Tuesday night and knowing we are both playing hooky on Wednesday. I expect Mommy will still stop our plans or, even worse, that Dad will. He is on this side of the ocean, and he has the final say. We keep our silence!

Dad speaks to Mommy daily at noon New York time. He says noon is 6:00 p.m. Zurich time and calls that a time zone difference.

After we return from school on Tuesday, we both do indeed have a nap. Shortly after we awaken, we see Dad working on his computer. Papa interrupts and tells him that Phoebe has prepared food for him alone because Papa is taking Phoebe and us to dinner and a play that evening. He names the play. Noon has passed. It is too late for an opinion check!

"I've seen the play with Constance. It's a good play to see but a little mature for them," he says as he nods toward his kids.

Dad is busy and does not think about the time required or about school the next day. He agrees, "Have a good time. I'm glad Phoebe will be there to help you."

Wow! Papa knows how to score on that one. And if Dad calls Mommy, we will already be at dinner and on our way.

As Papa sometimes says, "You cannot stop what has already happened!" What a smart Papa!

We dress for dinner and the theater. All four of us get into the same cab and go to Papa's favorite restaurant.

The headwaiter remembers Papa from a prior trip and makes sure we have good service. We can order anything we want!

Phoebe looks around, a little surprised at her surroundings. She orders duck. Papa has pork. Susanne has a lady's cut steak. I learn this means slightly smaller than the usual size. I have pasta with olive oil. I love pasta with just olive oil!

As Papa orders a glass of wine, he asks, "Would you care for one, Phoebe?"

She replies, "No, thanks. No alcohol. I'm with the children. That would not do." The waiter nods with a slight smile and disappears with Papa's order.

I love everything about our meal.

After the main courses, our server asks if we want to see the dessert trolley and lists other choices from the dessert menu as well.

"Yes, please," Susanne and I say in unison, "let's see everything."

Phoebe and Papa laugh at our lively interest in desserts as we view the trolley and ask to hear the menu list again.

This dinner keeps getting bunches better! Susanne's smile is big enough to burst!

I order vanilla ice cream on hot raspberry crumble. Susanne has an ice cream parfait, which is ice cream with caramel sauce. Phoebe chooses cheesecake after admiring the trolley. Papa has a glass of port with coffee.

Papa pays while Phoebe takes us to the bathroom. Outside, we board another cab to the theater. Papa hands in our tickets as we enter the fancy lobby. Then we head inside to the theater.

Everything inside is very glamorous. Fancy painted panels have wallpaper in the middle, but the wallpaper is actually cloth. Papa sees me touching the cloth wallpaper and says, "That is silk, a sign of luxury. Don't touch, please."

Along the walls there are lights shining behind ornate colored glass. There is a huge central light with colored glass hanging from the ceiling. Papa calls it a chandelier. I crane my neck to look, but I have to be careful 'cause we are still walking to our seats. Brass hardware gleams on the doors. Everything seems bright and shiny. It feels like a different world, very different from the drab streets outside. This place makes me feel elated and important. I tell Papa.

Papa replies, "That is the intended effect. Theater is a fantasy world. Very few people live in any level of luxury. But here, beautiful surroundings make you feel excited and important. And all these things let you know that even more impressive things in the show are awaiting you. But it is all fantasy, all make-believe."

Susanne and I both pay attention to Papa. I see Phoebe's faint smile as we listen.

"No wonder I feel good," says Susanne.

"That could be your dinner talking," I mutter. She is standing beside me as we search for our seats. I poke her ribs, mostly 'cause she hates that.

"Cowlick head," she mouths almost audibly. Looking grumpy, she lunges toward me. I circle to the other side of Papa to escape. Now Susanne is really annoyed 'cause she can't get me back. Success!

She says, "I'm gonna ski down your nose!"

I think she means it.

"Enough, you two!" commands Phoebe. As we find our seats, Phoebe separates us. She looks at Papa and says, "I'm just keeping the two magnets apart." Phoebe directs our little traffic. Papa laughs.

Papa's words stay in my head. I had never thought of people using their surroundings to affect how everyone feels. I know I almost always feel good at home. Often not so much at school with its drab colors and long hallways, with monotonous rows of doors marking each classroom. What Papa says makes sense. Wow, right again!

Phoebe and Susanne continue to look around, staring at the walls, the ceiling, and then reading their programs. The lights go down. The play begins.

I'm not sure I understand all of the plot and the secondary themes, as Papa calls them. Regardless, with Phoebe on my left, Papa on my right, and Susanne next to Papa's other side, I am content.

When we get home, Dad is still working in his study. He has dirty supper dishes near his computer. He almost doesn't notice our arrival. Fortunately, he also doesn't notice that it is after ten o'clock.

We enter Dad's study and give him a kiss good night. Outside Dad's study, we hug Papa and thank him for a wonderful time. Then Phoebe helps each of us get ready for bed.

I am so excited that I stay with Phoebe while she tucks Susanne into bed. Susanne's eyes close almost immediately.

Phoebe tucks me into bed and kisses my forehead while I mumble, "I'm too excited to sleep." In the morning I wonder, when did she turn off the light?

By the time I awaken, Dad has already left for work. I see Papa up and dressed.

"I got up early to talk to your father," he says. "I told him that you both were out too late last night. I said neither of you had important activities at school today, so I wanted to let you sleep. He agreed but just this once. I have called the school and said you both have tummy upsets. That usually stops a conversation cold."

"What about Mommy?" I ask.

Papa looks at me. He replies, "I'm about to call her now."

Just then, a sleepy Susanne appears wearing her pajamas. She smiles when she sees Papa.

"Papa is about to call Mommy," I say.

"Oh dear," says Susanne sadly, with a sagging voice.

Papa uses his cell phone to get the number and then picks up the house phone. Paying no attention to us, Papa mutters into the phone, "I prefer a landline for overseas calls. Seems clearer to me." As the phone rings, he looks at his watch and says, "It is 8:30 a.m. in New York and 2:30 p.m. in Zurich. I should just catch her." He connects to her quickly.

We can hear Mommy's voice. She says, "You just caught me on break time this afternoon. Is anything wrong?"

Papa replies, "Nary a thing. Just want to catch you up." After reassurances and idle banter, Papa then comes around to the dinner we had last night.

Mommy asks, "Did the children get to bed in a decent time?"

I detect *the tone* in her voice. It is a tone that usually means trouble ahead.

Papa explains that Phoebe accompanied us to a play that Dad mentioned was good.

We hear her murmur, "Yes, it is. But a little mature for them," on the other end of the line. Then he explains that he let us sleep in and miss school.

We hear Mommy's intake of air. We dread what she will say. Then suddenly we hear her roaring with laughter. We are dumbfounded! What has happened?

When she stops laughing, she says, "Do you remember your trips to my boarding school? Usually when there was a lull, never around exams. We would go out to dinner, just the two of us.

"Then the next day, you would write a note to the head mistress about my tummy troubles. And instead of school, we would go somewhere fun or see something on exhibit or just have a day to ourselves. Do you recall?"

"Of course, I do indeed. I engineered those days," says Papa.

"Did you ever tell Nana?" Mommy asks.

"Mostly." His eyes twinkle as he speaks.

Mommy continues, "I remember those times with great fondness. We had such fun! So now, it's hooky, the second generation?"

I can't believe my ears. Strict Mommy played hooky, missed school, had adventures with her father! What else has she done that maybe even Papa doesn't know about?

Our mommy continues talking to her father for a long time. They banter back and forth until we hear a buzzer. She says, "The meeting is resuming. I really must ring off. Love you, Dad. Give my love to everyone."

They finish their goodbyes.

Papa's eyes still twinkle with glee. He says to us, "I told you I could manage that problem. You see, a guilty party is not likely to complain. And your mother and I were frequently guilty parties."

We are safe!

The rest of the day is a whirlwind of a hurried breakfast and then a visit to the Metropolitan Museum of Art.

We look at the Greek and Roman statuary and the Egyptian section with its mummies until Papa insists we must see the paintings.

Here, he really is interesting! I don't remember all that he said as he explained details of the life of each painter, but I remember the effect his talk had on both of us. He described how living conditions affected the works produced. While talking about various periods of painting style, he described some of the rebellions against old styles as painters tried new forms of expression.

Although I can't remember everything he said, I do remember that his words made the galleries come alive for all of us. We saw with new and inquisitive eyes! One smart Papa!

Eventually, it is time for a late lunch at the museum. While we dig into our food, I'm surprised and exclaim, "Hey, this museum food is good! Somehow, I expected stale bread at a museum of old things." Papa laughs out loud.

When it is time to leave, Papa says we need to make a small trip. We board a cab from the Metropolitan Museum on Fifth Avenue to East Seventieth Street.

Papa explains, "This museum was once a private home where Henry Frick and his family lived. Now it is the Frick Museum."

Inside, it is quiet. The rooms are ornate but fun to see. The furniture is heavy with carvings, which people liked back then, I guess. Papa explains how rich people used to live, with the help of servants who worked in the house doing all sorts of tasks. He tells us that Mr. Frick was an art collector. We admire the paintings. I don't especially like the fancy furniture, but Susanne does.

There is a central courtyard. I say to Papa, "I think the courtyard would be a really cool place to play ball."

Papa laughs and says, "You have the most interesting ideas!"

After lots of explanations from Papa about what we were seeing, it is time to leave. We board another cab and drive along the edge of the park until we are home, exhausted from the day's excitement.

Supper slips by. I am too tired to even notice what I eat. Bedtime comes early. I barely remember Phoebe's kiss.

The next day at school, Susanne tells a friend what we did. Unfortunately, her teacher is in the hallway and overhears. We are both called into the principal's office. The tummy bug excuse is quickly unmasked, and we are in trouble deep!

The principal calls our home. Neither of us says anything about Mommy's trip to Zurich. Maybe Phoebe will cover for us. We watch as the principal dials the phone.

Dad is working at his office, and apparently Phoebe is away buying things for supper. Papa answers.

The principal comes right to the point and inquires, "Why did you keep the two children out of school when they were not sick?"

I hear Papa's voice. He is trying not to become angry. He uses his full name. Like usual, he doesn't say his title 'cause he doesn't like the name in the title. That much I know.

Papa explains, "I considered the expedition to the museums educational." He recounts a summary of the educational talks he gave us. Later, Papa tells us that he gave an executive summary because principals usually have a short attention span!

For the first time ever, I see the principal flustered. He mentions suspension for truancy. I can hear the pitch in Papa's voice go up slightly, but he stays calm.

Papa speaks sharply, with a firm edge to his voice, as he says, "Perhaps a class report to share the education received would be more to the point." Then there is silence.

The principal's eyes open wide. His face colors. It is the perfect punishment, and he has not thought of it first. He is embarrassed!

I love it! Susanne is close to tears, and her chin wobbles. I know she can't hear over her anxiety.

The principal agrees to accept a class report from each of us.

Then Papa adds, "They are in different grades, but I will help both with their report. Do you agree?"

"Yes, that's fine," says the principal, who looks like he wants to stop talking to this Englishman we call Papa.

We smile at each other. Susanne's chin stops jiggling! We return to our classes.

Chapter 5

THE WONDERFUL WEEK

Friday night, all five of us go out to dinner. Dad questions us about missing school, Mommy's response, and our talk with the principal. He asks, "When is that report due?" We answer and tell him some of what we learned with Papa. "That's all very interesting," he says sincerely.

Dad laughs about Mommy playing hooky with Papa when she was school age. He thinks everything is funny. Like Mommy, he asks, "Are we second-generation hooky players?" He looks at each of us and then directly at Papa. "Let me see. Is Papa involved in both generations? Who is really the responsible person?" Dad laughs, and so does Papa.

Surprised, I say, "Thanks, Dad."

Dad asks, "Expecting trouble from me, were you?"

"Yes," I honestly reply.

Susanne nods and declares, "So was I."

Dad responds, "All over but the report." He laughs more. Papa's eyes twinkle. Did Dad play hooky too?

After dinner, Dad says he is going home. "I've seen the production before. It's a good play, but I don't want to see it again."

He stands up, gives both of us a kiss, and waves to Phoebe and Papa as he says, "Love to all. Enjoy. See you back at the ranch."

"We don't live on a ranch. You're being funny." I giggle. Smiling at my comment, Dad waves goodbye.

Friday night's play is a musical. The plot is outlined in the program. Papa says, "Now remember, the plot may be a little thin, but the music will be fun. This is make-believe again, and critical judgment may need to be suspended to truly enjoy the festivities." Once again, Papa has it right.

The theater is different from the other one but still very fancy. There is an orchestra that plays an overture. This is a long musical number with music from the songs of the play all put together.

The curtain rises after the overture. It seems that the actors sing at any excuse! But it is fun. Papa laughs a lot. Frequently, I am not sure why he laughs. Susanne is older and understands more than I do, maybe. Sometimes she looks like she doesn't understand either.

In the cab home, Susanne asks Papa a few questions about some of the times he laughed so hard. He looks at her sharply, stops talking for an instant, and says, "Phoebe will explain that when we are home."

Phoebe sighs and then chuckles, muttering, "That was inevitable!"

At home, we give a full report to Dad who listens attentively. He asks a few questions and tries to figure out how much we really understood from the musical. Instead of a money manager, he acts like a lawyer.

Later, Susanne exclaims to Phoebe, "I felt like a witness for the prosecution under cross-examination! I'm too young for that!"

After good-night hugs to all, Phoebe guides us to bed. Phoebe takes a long time before she comes out of Susanne's room. She tells me, "Sorry that took a little while. We were talking about parts of the play that neither of you understood."

"Well, I am only seven years old," I say.

"Yes, I know." Phoebe sighs. "But sometimes you are seven going on forty." Then she laughs.

Saturday morning, Susanne and I sleep in past eight. Papa and Dad are already up and helping Phoebe to make bacon and eggs with fried tomatoes for breakfast. We have hot buttered toast with jam and several glasses of milk. My tummy is contented when we finish eating.

Papa announces, "We should go to the Brooklyn Zoo. The day is clear and warm. There is no sign of a September chill and no forecast for rain."

We have never been to the zoo. Both of us don't like the thought of animals in cages. Then Dad says, "I'd love to come along."

We could hear a pin drop after he said that. Dad wants to go to the zoo! It must be good or he would not bother. And he rarely goes with us because he is always too busy working!

"Are you sure you are not playing hooky from work?" Susanne asks.

He replies thoughtfully, "I may be doing just that. But you are nearly ten, and your brother is seven and a bit. I listened to you both as you recounted recent activities with Papa. I realize you two are growing up too fast! We need time together before you are all grown up and away. Work can wait."

Susanne smiles. Like her, I am happy and smiling inside when I hear this.

Phoebe says, "If it's all right, I could use some downtime."

"You have earned it," says Dad.

"Yes, indeed," Papa agrees.

Phoebe is alone with Susanne and me just before we leave. She looks directly at us and says, "Living near Papa is tiring! He is always into something." She nods toward Susanne. "You two need Dad and Papa time."

Off we go—Dad, Papa, Susanne, and me!

We spend hours at the zoo. We walk from exhibit to exhibit. Fortunately, the crowds are not too big. Papa says, "If you don't mind, let me tell you about the habitats of some of the animals that we see."

Dad, Susanne, and I think this is a great idea. It's clear that Papa loves animals and has concern for their welfare. He also seems to know a lot. I remember much of the kind of thing he said that day—only because he said it frequently and emphatically, on many occasions.

He said something like "The animal habitats are being encroached on by human developments—deforestation, mining, cutting rain forests for farmland. Certain species lose their food sources as their territory disappears." He looked unhappy as he explained, "Some animals can no longer live and will become extinct. That means they will be gone forever."

I remember so well when Papa said this. Decades later, his words still make me sad for the animals and sad for us.

Susanne asks, "Don't people realize what they are doing?"

Papa shrugs his shoulders as he replies, "Honestly, Susanne, I don't know. Do they even care? Money seems to be our clue. Always follow the money!"

Fortunately, Papa's comments stuck in my mind, even though I didn't fully understand them then. It took years before Susanne and I fully understood what he meant. But to this day, I still remember the comments about money, partly because the sentences were short.

Papa says, "Children, let's talk about the way some animals behave in the wild and how they respond to captivity."

"Yes, please," says Susanne. I nod.

Some of what he says is funny. Everything he says is interesting. As he speaks, other adults linger nearby to listen. Maybe they think he is our tour guide. We both notice that Dad pays a lot of attention to Papa and how he interacts with us. Is Dad taking lessons?

By midafternoon, after a lunch and then more animals, we all decide it is cab time. We need to get back home for a rest. Each of us wants a nap.

Phoebe wakes me earlier than I want and later than she wants. She sets out our dinner and theater clothes. She calls to Susanne who is already up. She calls Dad, and he wakes Papa. She also insists Susanne and I drink a glass of milk.

"You need some fluid and protein to keep going." No arguments with Phoebe!

An hour later, all of us, including Dad and Phoebe, are ready to go out to dinner.

Papa declares, "I have reservations nearby. We can walk."

The restaurant is really interesting. The waiters are professional singers in costume for the role they are singing. Our server tells us what is on the list of specials and leaves a handwritten list for us to review, in addition to the regular menu. Dad looks at the wine list.

From time to time, one or two waiters start singing a song from an opera while another plays an instrument. Papa calls their song an aria.

While our waitress sings, another waiter plays the lute. I enjoy the plucked sound. Our waitress has a thrilling voice. Even Dad, who dislikes opera, is delighted. I think the wine helps, especially since he rarely has alcohol. Papa usually likes to have a glass of wine with dinner.

I am so distracted with the singers that I almost forget what we each have to eat. But I remember that my dinner is pasta in cream sauce. The waiter called it Alfredo. I wonder about the name. I ask, "Dad, is Alfredo the name of the inventor of the sauce? Or is his name really Fred?"

The adults laugh hard, even Phoebe. When Dad can breathe again, he says, "Alfredo is an Italian name, and Fred is really not an Italian name." Once more, he laughs till he coughs. When he stops laughing, he continues, "The sauce was invented in 1914 by Alfredo di Lelio to satisfy his wife, who was pregnant and had food cravings. He used Parmesan cheese and butter in the sauce, which he served over pasta. Eventually, he started a restaurant where he served his dish."

Papa says, "I am impressed that you know this off the top of your head." They begin to talk about food and find they both like to cook—a new connection. An ocean between them leaves a gap, which they are closing!

As she keeps us entertained, Phoebe watches the two men as they talk.

The play is in another fancy theater. This one has crystal dangles on the wall lights and an enormous central crystal chandelier. "Chandelier" is my new word.

I ask, "Papa, do you see the fancy chandelier? You taught me the word at the first play. You said that a chandelier is a fancy light fixture hanging from the ceiling."

Papa smiles at me and laughs heartily as he says, "Yes, Jeremiah, I did see the lights up there in that fancy chandelier. I'm glad you remember the name. Do you remember the origins of the word? I told you that too."

What to do? I don't remember. Just then, the lights dimmed for the play to begin. Papa looks away from me and toward the stage. He puts a finger straight up in front of his lips. Saved! And he forgets to ask me later. Saved again!

The play is really for adults. I get a little lost, but it all ends happily—that much is clear. Again, Susanne seems to understand more than I do. Phoebe says she will explain things to me later.

But I sit between Dad and Papa, with Phoebe and Susanne nearby, so I don't care if the play is beyond me.

When we get home, Phoebe does explain some of the play. Some things remain unclear. She says I will understand later. While she explains, I am getting ready for bed and so tired! I don't think I can take in anything more! My head touches the pillow, Phoebe's kisses my forehead, then nothing else.

In the morning, Sunday morning, Papa is up early, as is Dad. Together they decide to cook eggs Benedict. I don't know what this is. When I ask, Papa replies, "Wait and see."

Eggs Benedict are poached eggs with thick-cut Canadian bacon on an English muffin and covered with hollandaise sauce, which Phoebe said is made with butter and egg yolks! My, it is good! With my glass of milk, I am set for the day!

And what a day it becomes! Papa says it is time to see Lady Liberty. After we dress, we bundle into two cabs since there are five of us, and we head to the South Ferry station.

Papa gets tickets, and we board the ferry. The sun brightly glistens on the water. The weather is warm for September, but there's a cool breeze when our boat moves. Our coats keep us cozy on the ferry ride. We comfortably watch the thrilling New York skyline slowly pass by. Coming up to the Statue of Liberty on its island is awesome.

Papa asks, "Do you two know the name of the island?"

I don't, so I stay quiet. I don't like giving wrong answers.

Susanne exclaims happily, "We studied this in school. It's Liberty Island."

She always loves to give the right answer. Lah-de-dah! She really annoys me sometimes.

"That's right," says Papa. "But was it always called Liberty Island?"

Smart Susanne says, "Well, since you're asking, my guess is… that it has changed names."

Papa laughs as he says, "Right you are, oh great deductive one! It became Liberty Island in 1956. Originally it was Oyster Island. Then Governor Francis Lovelace changed the name to Love Island in 1669."

I start to giggle. "Lovelace, what a name! That sounds silly."

Phoebe says, "It sounds like Governor Lovelace liked his own name very much because he called the island Love Island after himself. It sounds like he wanted people to remember him."

Papa asks, "Do either of you know what name it became after that?"

I am silent again. Susanne looks quizzical, furrows her brow as she tries to recall, and then says, "I remember our teacher saying something about another name. It started with a *B* or a *D*, but I don't remember."

Papa looks at Susanne fondly as he says, "Good girl. You are very close. In 1673, the name had a *B* for Bedloe Island, changed just four years after it became Love Island. Maybe Lovelace wasn't as popular as he wanted!"

"So how many names before the name Liberty Island?" asks Phoebe.

"Three!" Susanne and I both exclaim.

I am the one holding up three fingers, then four as I say, "Four different names total!" Susanne and I giggle. Phoebe and Dad look satisfied. Phoebe smiles slightly; so do Dad and Papa.

When we safely land and have our passes, Papa makes sure we notice the inscription at the base of the Statue of Liberty.

It reads,

> Give me your tired, your poor, your huddled masses yearning to breathe free, the wretched refuse of your teeming shore. Send these, the homeless, the tempest tossed to me. I lift my lamp beside the golden door!

Papa asks if we understand. We each give our ideas of what the words mean until we agree that in America, all are welcome. Even the poor may have a chance to achieve success by receiving fair treatment and by their own hard work.

Papa asks, "How did we get this statue?"

Susanne answers, "It was given to us by France."

I don't know anything about this. I may be listening, sort of, but I want to move. Even though I fidget, I sort of remember the next bit.

Papa says, "That's right, Susanne. The statue was given by the people of France to celebrate one hundred years of American independence from Britain. France also had a revolution and therefore felt a kinship to the people of America."

Dad asks, "Do either of you know when the statue was given?"

I am getting bored. I put my right hand on the back of one park bench and my left hand on another bench next door as I stand between them. They are the perfect distance apart. I push up with my arms. My feet are off the ground.

Susanne says, "A long time ago." I hear Dad chuckle.

I start gently swinging back and forth. I watch my toes point down as I swing backward and point up as I swing forward. It's fun. My arms feel good.

Papa says, "Yes, indeed, a long time ago. Construction started in 1875. In 1886, the statue was opened to the public and was dedicated to the American people with President Cleveland presiding." Papa glances at me as I swing. He knows that I'm not paying much attention.

"Jeremiah, any idea who built the sculpture?" asks Phoebe from right behind me. I drop my feet to the ground and turn to look at her. I shake my head and answer, "I dunno." I see her wink at Dad and Papa.

Susanne says, "The same person who made the Eiffel Tower in Paris."

Laughingly, Dad asks, "And who made the Eiffel Tower?"

Susanne ponders for a moment and then giggles as she questions, "Mr. Eiffel?" She sounds uncertain.

Hah! Smarty-pants is not so sure!

Dad says, "Yes, Susanne, it was Monsieur Gustave Eiffel who built the statue." Then he asks, "But do you know who designed the sculpture?"

Susanne is suddenly silent.

Truly bored, I hoist up again between the park benches and begin to slowly swing back and forth. Gee, my toes are interesting as they point down and then up. I really like my shoes. They are comfy, and the toes aren't scuffed yet. Papa is still talking.

I hear Papa say something like "The sculptor was Frederic Auguste Bartholdi. Did you know that the Eiffel Tower in Paris was a temporary structure for the Paris exhibition?"

Now I am interested! I swing forward too hard as I let go of the bench. I don't fall because I hit hard against Dad's thigh as he stands directly in front of me, just to the side of Papa. Without wanting to, he exclaims, "Uumph!"

As he catches his breath, he says, "Jeremiah, you are getting big. I'm glad you didn't make me topple."

Papa suppresses a giggle as he tilts his head toward me and says, "Welcome back!"

I exclaim, "The Eiffel Tower was supposed to be temporary? Wow! Why didn't it fall down?" I have a mental image of the Eiffel Tower crumbling, then tumbling down. Now, that's interesting!

Papa laughs as he says, "It was built properly, but they initially planned for its removal. But people liked it so much that it stayed."

Susanne says, "That's amazing! The people rule."

I hear Phoebe and Papa both laugh at Susanne.

"Yay, people," cheers Dad.

Papa has us stand back so we can see more of the statue. "You can't really see much if you are too close," he says. "You need perspective, as with most things."

As we look up, Papa says, "The female statue represents Libertas, a Roman goddess. Do you see her torch? The flame is a symbol for liberty. And she carries a tablet, inscribed with the date of the Declaration of Independence, July 4, 1776."

After a pause, Dad commands, "Look at her feet. What do you see?"

I say loudly, "She has a broken chain at her feet."

"What does that mean?" asks Phoebe.

Susanne asks, "Does that mean that there is freedom from chains?"

Phoebe answers, "Yes, almost there. The broken chains symbolize freedom from bondage of any kind and the right to a fair chance in America."

"Well said," says Papa, nodding at Phoebe.

"And a fair chance for all," adds Phoebe. Papa and Dad nod vigorously.

Papa states, "It was a law professor in France who inspired Mr. Bartholdi to make the statue, saying that any monument raised to American independence should be a joint project of the American and French peoples."

Whoopee, says the little voice in my head. I actually say nothing, mostly 'cause I'm not exactly sure what he's talking about. We slowly move back toward our benches.

Papa asks, "Did America have a revolution?"

Susanne answers, "Yes, it's called the American War of Independence. That's the date on the tablet that Lady Liberty holds."

"Righto," says Papa, "but do you know why there was a revolution?"

"It had something to do with the Boston Tea Party," says Susanne.

Papa says, "You are on the right track." Then he continues with something like "America wanted no outside agency to impose taxes, and King George III of England did impose taxes. There had been unrest since the mid-1750s.

"In 1773, the colonials dumped expensive British tea belonging to the East India Company from a transport ship into Boston Harbor in protest against those taxes. As a sarcastic joke, the colonials called it the Boston Tea Party."

Susanne seems to be paying attention. Does she really understand all that, or is she pretending?

We reach our benches. I have no idea what Papa just said. Bored again, I start to swing. My feet are happily off the ground as I gently swing back and forth. Once more, I sense Phoebe behind me.

Papa is talking again. I'm not sure I exactly remember what he said that day, or whether I pieced it all together from later conversations and later education drilled into my dumb noggin. The timing of this stuff gets really fuzzy. But I do remember all these topics and that Dad later said, "Papa had his facts straight."

Papa looks mostly at Susanne as he says something like "In March 1775, Patrick Henry declared, 'Give me liberty, or give me death,' which sped up the change. War began in 1775 and finished in 1783 with the signing of the Treaty of Paris."

Papa glances at me, but he doesn't tell me to stop. The movement of my toes fascinates me. They go up and down as I swing. Lah-de-dah, my shoes really are special! I hear Papa's voice going on and on.

I must have been swinging too long. Suddenly, my left arm buckles, and I start to fall backward. I feel Phoebe's hands catching me to break my fall. My head smacks into her middle, but her hands are under my arms, pulling me upright.

"Enough of that, young man!" she declares, as she stops both of us from falling backward.

Papa looks directly at his only audience, Susanne, as he finishes the topic. I'm not completely certain, but I suspect he said, "The Continental Congress in the colonial states signed the Declaration of Independence on July 4, 1776. This is the celebration date Americans have for the birth of a free America. Hence, the date on Lady Liberty's tablet."

Susanne nods back to Papa. She always pays attention, or pretends!

Dad says, "Tell us about the French Revolution."

Papa glances uncertainly at me, correctly suspecting that I am lost with all this information, and then looks at Phoebe and Dad. He sees that they both nod yes.

"All right, then." He sighs deeply.

I'm not allowed to swing anymore. While Papa talks again, I lean against Phoebe and watch boats moving along in the water.

He continues, "France had a revolution after political unrest. This began with the storming of a horrible French prison called the Bastille on July 14, 1789."

Now he has my attention! A horrible prison was taken over in a revolution. Wow! And look at that big boat!

Papa continues, "This was followed by the guillotine execution of King Louis XVI in January 1793, and later his wife, Queen Marie Antoinette, in October 1793."

The king and queen were executed. Double wow! Now I remember. Mommy talked to us about this when Susanne had a history reading assignment.

Dad glances at me as I lean against Phoebe. He decides to test if I have been listening. Looking hard at me, Dad demands, "Jeremiah, tell me about the French Revolution."

This part I do clearly remember. Why not? There were guns, violence, a revolution, and action. We boys like that kind of stuff.

I take my eyes away from the boats in the water, stand up straight, glance at Papa, and then look directly at Dad. I shrug my shoulders a little as I recite mechanically, "It started in 1789 with the storming of the Bastille. Then Louis went chop-chop in 1793. So did his wife later in the year. I once heard Mommy tell Susanne that the French peasants called him Louis the Shorter since he wasn't so tall after they chopped off his head."

Papa tries hard to suppress his laughter. Dad smiles. Susanne rolls her eyes as she says, "If you get his attention, he always remembers everything." She adds sourly, "All except instructions."

Phoebe tousles my hair as she says, "He may look like he is elsewhere. Beware!"

The history stuff that Papa said was actually more than I could remember. I know I put that part of Papa's talk together in my head much later, knowing Papa always had the right facts. But the execution of a king, the storming of a prison, a revolution—well, all that caught my attention. That I could remember!

I don't think I'm all that smart. I just have a good memory. But this was the first time I realized that the adults believe I am really smart. Oh well, no harm in that! And it makes 'em happy. Silly adults!

Dad looks at Papa and says, "You know so much about history, John. And you make it seem very real and in the moment, as if you had been there and met people from the past and seen the action. That's real talent."

Papa suddenly turns very pale and looks ill. His face becomes somber, almost grim, as he looks down, away from us. He swallows hard and clutches his stomach as his shoulders slump forward. Is he gonna get sick?

Phoebe asks, "Papa, are you feeling all right? You look unwell."

Papa glances at her, at Susanne, and finally at me with an odd, frightened expression on his face. We all stare at him with concern. Dad reaches an arm around Papa to support him so he cannot fall. When he turns his head to look directly at Dad, Papa seems a little confused.

"Sorry, I just…" His voice trails off. Suddenly, he shakes himself slightly and moves his head side to side as if waking up. He tries to laugh a little. "Oh my, how foolish of me. I was thinking of the past…the past…of one of my history teachers. That's it, one of my history teachers! Odd to think of him now." Papa gives an insincere laugh. Once again, he shakes himself slightly and glances intently at Dad. Slowly, he begins to look normal once more.

Susanne and I both saw and remembered everything. We talked about it later when we were alone together, and at other times with Dad and Phoebe. We all speculated whether Papa saw something strange or remembered something bad that happened with the teacher he talked about. We didn't believe he was physically sick. During one of the times we speculated about this, Dad said, "Papa looked suddenly ill, as if he had seen a ghost."

Phoebe replied, "He looked almost terrified, but why? There was nothing there to frighten anybody."

When Susanne and I sometimes talked together, we wondered if we would ever know what actually happened to Papa that day. Much later, I sometimes wished I had never learned the answer.

The adults keep talking. Phoebe and Dad conspire with Papa to pretend nothing happened. But I see the adults watching Papa closely. Like me, they are afraid he is becoming ill. But as time passes, it is clear that Papa is not ill. All is back to normal. We can relax again. Whatever spooked him has gone.

After listening to the adults nattering, I am bored once more. Since Phoebe won't let me swing on the benches, I use my feet instead to tap out rhythms on the sidewalk. I don't even pretend to look interested in their conversation. Not so patiently, I wait for our climb to the crown of the Statue of Liberty.

Dad says, "It usually takes months to get tickets, and they are hard to obtain. How did you get tickets, John?"

Papa replies, "I made reservations earlier, from England. I do love the internet!"

Over here, he made it seem like a last-minute decision to visit the Statue of Liberty. Sneaky! Talk about planning ahead!

Only four people can visit the crown at one time. So up we climb, Dad, Susanne, and me, with Phoebe trailing me so she can catch me if I fall when I get tired. Papa finds a bench in the sun and pulls a bottled iced tea from his pocket.

There are 377 steps from the lobby and 354 steps from the pedestal to the crown about twenty stories up. We did it! All four of us did it! Wow!

The view from the crown is spectacular. The water around the island glistens in the autumn sun. New York lies before us. Everything has sharp shadow edges in the September light.

Dad points as he names some of the skyscrapers. "There's the Chrysler Building, the Empire State Building, and the new tower, the One World Trade Center, built where the Twin Towers once stood. I think the skyline is beautiful! What a testament to hard work and achievement," says Dad in awe, as he looks at the view.

"But," says Dad, "it's difficult to feed such a dense mass of people. Food and consumables must be trucked in daily to bring food to millions of dinner tables all over the city."

I have never thought of this before. I exclaim, "You're right, Dad. There are no farms or apple orchards on Manhattan Island, no cows or pigs."

"Everything we eat comes from somewhere else," he replies.

Susanne exclaims, "What a lot of work!"

Walking down the 377 steps from the crown to the main lobby makes us tired and thirsty. Dad says, "The backs of my thighs are sore. I am out of shape!" He doesn't look happy.

We use the restroom on the main lobby level and then buy water for each of us. When we find Papa, he is excited to learn what we have enjoyed the most. Well, not the struggle up or down! But the view of New York with its rivers and bridges, that is worth the climb!

Papa seems pleased we have enjoyed the visit so much. "Just enough time to catch the ferry," he says.

We hurry along to board the ferryboat. We sit together, tired and happy, with Dad and Papa beside us and Phoebe near us. What can be better?

The rest of the week is routine—school each day, no more skipping classes. After our school day, Papa waits for us at home, eager to learn about our day. He helps us with our homework and our reports. He listens intently after he asks, "How was the report received in class?"

Susanne answers first, "Most of the kids in my class were interested in what we learned at the museum. I didn't mention the other trips—the zoo and the Statue of Liberty. A few kids seemed a bit jealous that we have a grandfather who likes to be with us and teach us."

Papa smiles, chortles happily, and asks, "What about your report, Jeremiah? Tell us all."

I reply enthusiastically, "In my class, I talked only about the museum. That took up the time I was given. My friends were fascinated, but not so much by what we saw and what we learned. They just think it is cool beans that Papa will spend a whole day, not get tired, and always be such fun. I think my classmates want a grandfather like Papa."

Papa laughs with delight as he listens to our comments.

At home, Phoebe, Dad, and Papa cook together and make wonderful meals, different from the usual good ones that Phoebe prepares by herself. The week flies by too fast.

Susanne and I dread the weekend because Papa will leave on Saturday. When we are by ourselves, we chant, "Go away, Saturday!"

Friday night, Papa takes us to an Italian restaurant. He says, "I chose this establishment because Jeremiah loves pasta so much."

After we place our orders and begin our meal, I exclaim, "I love the warm bread."

"The menu states that the pasta is homemade," says Dad. "That sounds delicious."

Dad and Papa talk a great deal. Phoebe keeps us occupied.

At some point in the conversation, I hear Papa say, "The children are growing up too quickly."

Dad responds, "I didn't realize how much they have matured. I have been too busy to notice. I have already missed a lot. I'm not going to miss the rest."

Susanne and I look, and then smile, at each other. We don't say a word. In fact, we pretend not to hear.

Phoebe wistfully looks away for a moment and then smiles at each of us. She touches my ear as she talks.

I know that I always have a fabulous time with Papa. Will I have more fun times with Dad? What if Dad becomes like Papa?

The next day, it is goodbye to Papa as the driver picks him up for the ride to the airport. He says farewell to Phoebe and slips her an envelope.

We hug him tight and kiss his cheek. I hold his coat tight until the moment he gets into the car. His eyes glisten when he hugs us goodbye, two times each. He gives my dad a big hug.

I hear Dad say, "Thank you for opening my eyes."

Papa gives him another small hug. He climbs into the cab, checks for little fingers before closing the door, and waves from the window. The driver nods and pulls into traffic. And then, like Mommy, Papa is gone.

We stand by the curb, as numb as when Mommy left two weeks ago. We are silent until Dad says, "Your mother gets home tomorrow. Are you excited?"

We say we are, but maybe we both will miss Papa more.

Chapter 6

THE TRIP TO ENGLAND

Dad calls for a family gathering in the living room. He says, "There is something that Mom and I need to share with everyone. It's something good about Nana and Papa."

Susanne says, "That sounds exciting," as she follows Mom and Phoebe to find a spot to sit. "Are they coming to visit?"

My mind flashes to Papa's last visit. Next September, it will be three years since Papa was in New York City with us. It is now May. I just had my tenth birthday, on May first.

As I walk beside Dad, he says, "Jeremiah, you are getting a lot taller."

I reply, "Yup! But my face needs to get longer. My nose still looks too big. My ears stick out, and I look goofy."

She rarely says anything, but Susanne always looks annoyed when I mention my nose. As I sit down, Susanne mutters, "You and your nose. You are always fussing about your nose. It'll still be there in the morning."

Dad interrupts, "You are just at an awkward age, and everything will be fine in a year or two as the rest of your face grows to match your nose."

I am not so sure, so I reply emphatically, "My face will need to be five feet long to look right with my nose! I have been waiting too long for something that will never happen!"

"That's hyperbole," says Mom.

"What's that?" I ask.

Phoebe explains, "The face five feet long—that's an exaggeration. That's the hyperbole. You know perfectly well that three feet long would do!" When she finishes, she smiles at me too sweetly, her eyes twinkling as she giggles slightly.

I laugh as Phoebe intended. She doesn't like self-pity.

Impolitely pointing at Dad's nose, I say, "At least mine isn't bent sideways in the middle! Not yet, anyway!"

Dad laughs heartily and replies, "Sorry you got my schnoz!"

Susanne mutters, "Your nose, your nose, always your nose. Get over it!"

Pretending my index finger is a slalom skier on the slopes, I drag the digit down my nose and ask, "Wanna ski, Susanne?" When she's mad at me, my sister often says, "I'm gonna ski down your nose!" That's her usual threat.

Susanne crosses her eyes inwards so both her eyes are looking down her own nose.

Both of us, one after the other, are now in the crosshairs of Phoebe's stare. Oops! Suddenly, Susanne looks grumpy! I ignore my sister as Phoebe and I look toward the parents sitting near each other. To be different, Susanne looks away.

Glancing at each of us in turn, Dad says, "We are spending the summer with Papa in his country house in the southwest of England."

Susanne's grumpiness vanishes. We both bounce with excitement.

After a moment, Susanne looks thoughtful and maybe uncertain. Like a lawyer in the making, she asks, "You said 'with Papa,' didn't you? Just Papa? Won't Nana be there?"

Mom, the real lawyer, says, "Nana will be there only some of the time. During the week she will be working as a solicitor in London, as usual."

"But we will see her sometimes, right?" persists Susanne.

Dad says, "Yes indeed!"

"Oh! Good," Susanne and I exclaim together.

Dad continues, "But there is some bad news."

Suddenly, we are silent. Dad says, "Mom cannot come over with us."

Dad alone is taking us to Britain!

Somewhat sadly, I say, "Sorry you aren't coming with us, Mom." Now that I am ten, I call her Mom instead of Mommy.

Susanne asks, "When are you coming over?"

Mom's face looks unhappy as she says, "I'm presenting at a conference and have a big client who needs my help in July. I'll come over later in the summer."

Trying to hide my disappointment, I say, "But I'll be really glad to see you when you arrive."

Right then, I could never guess how very glad!

Mom looks like she needs cheering up. I go over to give her a hug.

"Thank you, Jeremiah. I needed that," she says afterward.

Two voices ask, "Is Phoebe coming with us?"

Our parents nod as Phoebe replies, "Yes, indeed, I will travel with you."

"Well, that's good," I say as Susanne nods vigorously.

"But we will really miss you, Mom!" says Susanne sincerely while I nod.

Mom still looks a little sad as she realizes how much she will be missed, and how much she will miss us.

However, Phoebe looks flushed with pleasure 'cause we're so happy that she's coming with us.

Suddenly, Susanne's face looks like she is up to something. She can never leave well enough alone. She stares at my face, slides a finger down her nose, and says, "Jeremiah, stop fussing about your nose! Forget about your nose for the summer, please."

Fiddle, she's on that again!

She adds cheerily, "Look on the bright side. You have big feet. You have a big nose. Maybe someday, you will be well endowed."

Mom exclaims, "Susanne! Inappropriate!" Her voice is pitched higher than usual.

I glance at Mom. Her face is red. Is she blushing?

Phoebe is watching Mom and Susanne intently.

Dad makes a funny sound. I can tell that he is killing a laugh.

I don't understand what Susanne has said. While I look at the floor, my foolish voice mutters uncertainly, "I don't know what Susanne means. But I read the word 'endowment' in a book recently and looked up the meaning in the dictionary."

"Mr. Webster, your favorite author," Susanne chimes in sarcastically. Like I said, she can't leave well enough alone.

Phoebe coughs with purpose. Mom and Dad stare at Susanne fixedly. That's a warning anyone can see. My sister looks quickly out through the window and then down at the floor.

Because I'm actually quite stupid, I continue, "In olden times, an endowment of money was given to a daughter when she was at a marriageable age. It was also called a dowry. Everyone knew how much money she was getting. The idea was to get suitors interested, or not."

I pause to think again. My uncertain voice says, "So if someone gets money, they are endowed. If someone gets a lot of money, they are well endowed… Yeah, I guess that's sensible." To me, this seems a very reasonable way to piece things together.

As my eyes leave the floor to look up at each of them, I see four pairs of eyes staring at me as if I am from a different planet. Suddenly, I am even more confused. My eyes fix again on the floor.

Helplessly, I cannot stop myself from saying, "But I don't think, I mean, I don't know… Why would anyone give me a lot of money for having a big nose?"

A noise makes me look up. Dad is laughing so hard he is gasping for air. He coughs, tries to say something, but cannot. His gasps and coughs make him seem like he might choke, until he mumbles, "Fine, I'm fine."

Now Mom's face is actually very red. She is clutching her sides as tears stream down her face. "Jeremiah, you are…such…an innocent!" The words are hard to understand because she is laughing so hard.

Susanne is sitting in her chair, one elbow on the chair arm, her chin cupped in her hand. "You are a total idiot, Jeremiah!" she says with a surly face.

Phoebe is trying to suppress her laughter. She smiles at me, but there is a worried look on her face as well. "You are a sweet boy," she gurgles with a smile. Suddenly, the worried look returns.

The only thing I figure out is that Phoebe needs to explain something to me. She doesn't look happy about that.

"I can explain it all to him now, if you want," says Susanne flatly. She looks quizzically first at Phoebe and then toward our parents.

"Enough, Susanne. Stop!" exclaim two adult female voices in unison.

Silently, Susanne looks at them both sourly.

Dad tries to say something, but nothing comes out. He is still choking on his laughter.

"Enough damage done, young lady," adds Phoebe sternly.

Susanne glances again at Phoebe, then at me, at Dad, at Mom, and finally stares at the floor. She appears really grumpy again!

Eventually, the laughter stops, and the room becomes quiet. Phoebe continues to look directly at Susanne. Her look always rules.

Mom leans toward Phoebe and mouths, "We can talk later." Phoebe nods.

With a straight face but with eyes still watery from laughter, Dad looks at his children and asks, "Did you know that the summer nights are shorter in London than in New York?" His voice is slightly higher pitched than usual. Is he still trying not to laugh?

"Not sure about the nights," I mutter.

"Nothing like something educational to change the topic," Susanne says insolently.

"Warning!" The sharp voice is Phoebe's, and she is stern. She is always fair, but she doesn't like lip. My parents always back her up—no dissent here! By the look on Phoebe's face, I wonder if Susanne is really in trouble. Or am I? I dunno.

Ignoring Susanne, Dad says, "The earth is slightly tilted on its spinning axis. Areas far north like Britain get more sun in summer because of the tilt towards the sun. Hence, longer days in summer."

"Longer days so we can do more!" I mutter.

"The nights are longer in winter for the same reason. In winter, the north is tilted away from the sun and gets less light. The length of daylight changes every day of the year, even if we don't notice," Dad finishes.

"Longer nights so Papa and Nana can sleep through cold weather!" I interject.

"That's one way to remember how it works," chortles Dad. Probably, he is desperately hoping we are both paying attention and that maybe, just maybe, the bickering between his offspring will stop. Unlikely!

Struggling to dig herself out of trouble, Susanne says breezily, "I remember that our teacher said that even though England is much farther north, the temperature and the climate are milder than in North America. He called it temperate—it's not too hot and not too cold. He said England is subject to the moderating influence of the Gulf Stream, which is warm water in the Atlantic Ocean."

She looks around for a moment as she guesses her audience's response, and then continues, "We had a test about climate in geography class. For the test, we had to know that the Gulf Stream starts in the Gulf of Mexico and travels along the eastern coastline of North America before crossing the Atlantic Ocean."

After pausing to recall her facts, she continues, "It splits into two branches. One branch, the Canary Current, recirculates to Africa. The other branch, the North Atlantic Drift, goes to Northern Europe. This moderates the climate in Britain."

Her eyes move like she is reading an imaginary page. This is leftover test memory. Got ya, sis!

"You've got that right, Susanne," says Dad. Susanne smiles happily, hoping she has saved herself.

I didn't know all of that. But I did know about the Gulf Stream. In a singsong voice, I exclaim, "Once, Nana explained to both of us that the Gulf Stream lets her roses grow well because they don't freeze in the mild winters and they don't bake in the mild summers. Nana's explanation makes it all easy to remember. And I knew about the Gulf Stream long before Susanne's test, so there!" I wanted to stick out my tongue at Susanne to get even. I didn't dare.

Both of our parents laugh, and Phoebe smiles, her cobra-like dark eyes fixed right on me. Phoebe doesn't like competition getting mean or out of hand. She understands both of us all too well.

Dad jumps in to say, "Okay, you two, enough of the competitive bickering. Let's just say that this information shows geology and physics at work. All this is part of Mother Nature, who is smarter than we are."

I think of our summer plans time and again over the next few days. At least Phoebe will be with us. This is very important. I really rely on Phoebe. Besides being our nanny, she is my friend, and I love her lots. And I get a good-night kiss every night of my life. I need that!

As the days pass, I can tell Susanne is also excited about the trip. She's less grouchy and seems happier more of the time. That's good because sometimes her mood is like a yo-yo. My parents say that her moodiness is caused by her difficult age, thirteen in November. She has developed an interest in boys—most boys, but not her brother. I don't count because we are related. She and her girlfriends at school have lengthy discussions about which boy is cute, which one is a nerd, which one is smart, and which one is dumb. Sometimes what they say is not very kind.

Dad has overheard the nasty stuff the girls say. Occasionally, when he thinks he's alone, I've heard Dad repeat over and over, "This behavior is all part of growing up. This is all part of growing up." I guess when he is alone, he sometimes talks to himself just like I do!

Since Papa was here three years ago, we have had a real change in the household. Dad is far more attentive to us. He does stuff with us. We go places together—even if just for a walk in the park. Every day he asks, "How was your day?" and listens to what we say. I love the attention! He knows almost as much as Phoebe does about what we do.

He even changed his schedule so that he is home earlier. He is now almost always home to have supper with us, even if Mom cannot get home in time. No more dinners with children and Phoebe alone!

Mom is still very busy at work. We see her most on the weekends when the office is closed. She works on her computer in the evening, doing work related to her office.

We hear Dad say during some of their talks, "The kids are growing up too fast. I've made changes to my career to spend time with them before they both grow up and are living elsewhere. It was Papa, your father, who really opened up my eyes."

But Mom replies, "I was recently made law partner. My workload doesn't go down. It goes up. I'm doing the best that I can."

One time when Susanne and I talked together, Susanne said, "I recognize Mom is in a tough spot. She has a family and a big job. I understand, but I don't like it."

I reply, "Yeah, it's hard for Mom. I think she wants more time with us. I love Mom. Just like you, I wish we saw more of her."

School finally finishes in mid-June; and a few days later, our bags are packed, passports ready. Mom has to go to work. She says goodbye while we are in the apartment. We hug her tight, and she kisses each of us a little tearfully. Even though she works a lot, she always shows that she loves us. We stand in the hallway as she leaves with her briefcase. Her free hand waves another goodbye over her shoulder as she walks away toward the elevator.

In midafternoon, our car arrives as scheduled. The driver gets us to the airport without any problems. Traffic is lighter than expected. We arrive a little early.

Dad says, "Now stick together. The airport is huge. Here is a note with the flight information and the name of the airline we are using. Keep it with you in case we get separated." He hands a paper to each of us.

He adds, "Security clearance is a pain but necessary. No arguing and no attitude when they tell you what to do. I have your passports and tickets. Phoebe has her own, but she will also stay with us all the time. She will help me keep an eye on you both."

We check in to get our boarding passes, leave our luggage with the airline, and then line up for security. It is just as well we are a little early. The security check-in takes forever.

They ask Dad, "Who is traveling with you?" as we all line up one after another. It gets complicated.

The airport official becomes interested when Dad says, "I'm traveling overseas with my children. Unfortunately, my wife has to work, so she isn't traveling. Phoebe, our nanny, is with us."

The official says, "You are traveling with your children and without your wife—and you are traveling with another woman. We need to check a few things, sir."

The uniformed official is not so sure Phoebe is our nanny! Is Dad abducting us with another woman?

The official asks dryly, "How can we contact your wife?" Dad gives him Mom's number written on a paper scrap. Someone takes the note and disappears.

Later we learned that they called Mom to confirm she knows about the trip. Apparently, they really want to know that Dad has permission from Mom to take us out of the country! In the mean-time, they take us out of our line. They even interview Susanne and me separately.

Phoebe becomes a little nervous. Dad tries very hard not to get angry. I just hope they catch all the real terrorists and child abductors!

Afterward, we still have to be screened. They x-ray our carry-on bags. We have to take off our belts and shoes, empty our pockets, and pass through a metal detector. Susanne has braces on her teeth, but that doesn't become an issue, thank goodness. Her chin is already jiggling like Jell-O! Crikey, I hope she doesn't cry!

We finally get to the other side of security. Susanne is almost in tears. We have to hurry.

We read the screen with terminal information, locate our gate, and rapidly walk a very long way to reach the area from which we will board the plane. Over two hours have passed already. Wow! No wonder travel takes planning!

At the gate waiting area, Dad sits between us. Phoebe is on the other side of Susanne. He starts laughing about what he calls the "abduction experience." I can tell he wants to make Susanne feel bet-ter. She is still so upset that her chin is wobbling violently as she tries to prevent tears from flowing.

Dad says, "Well, that was a twist I never anticipated." He holds Susanne by the shoulder as he talks. "We must laugh about it. It is rather funny when you think upon it. And there is a point to their concern. For all they knew, this could have been a divorce situation or something else awful happening to a family." Dad pauses, laughs slightly, and continues, "Besides, we are all being abducted by Papa, sort of, for a month at least."

Tears still in her eyes, Susanne giggles a little and says, "Yes, I suppose we are, sort of, since we are spending the summer with Papa. Knowing that we can now actually travel makes me feel better. I was afraid they wouldn't let us go." Her chin jiggles more at the thought, before it finally stops.

"Silly goose," says Dad.

I laugh out loud at Dad's foolish idea. "Imagine Papa abducting anyone!" I say between giggles.

Dad calls Mom and jokes, "I wanted to let you know we are ready for boarding and no one has been abducted." She is cross with the customs officials who called her and created the ruckus. Dad persists in joking with her until, eventually, she laughs too.

We board as we are instructed. Every plane seat is filled. Every bit of storage space is used with all the carry-on things people bring with them.

"Oh boy! We are traveling first class," I exclaim tactlessly. I look at our large chairs with room to spread. Then I look at everyone else jammed into narrow seats with inadequate legroom. Some look toward our area, maybe with envy. Far too loudly, I say, "I'm glad we get to sit here!" Tact came later.

My tall dad extends his long legs straight out, stretches his arms up wide, sighs with comfort, and says, "We must give a special thank you to Papa when we see him. He bought our tickets and upgraded to first class. I thought he was being extravagant when he said, 'A first-class summer vacation starts with a first-class airplane ride.' Let him know you are grateful."

We say, "That's a great idea." Phoebe nods that she agrees.

During the flight, we are told that flying to London takes about seven and a half hours. Dad explains, "There is a tailwind that actually speeds the plane on its way to London, far to the east of New York. Tailwinds blow from behind the plane, from the west, and push it forward, to the east."

I say, "So that is like a giant hand pushing us along." Susanne giggles when I say this. I have an image in my head—a set of hands free-floating with no attachments to a body. Silly!

Dad replies, "That's the idea. But on the return flight, the same winds are still blowing from the west to the east. They now hit the nose of the plane and are therefore called a headwind. This slows the plane enough to increase flight time by about an hour."

"So now the giant hand is pushing us back," I say.

Susanne giggles again.

Dad pauses and then says, "That's not a bad way to think about it. The return trip takes about eight and a half hours—even with the exact same route. Physics in action!" He always says that, the part about physics, I mean.

Our plane prepares for takeoff, which is exciting.

I have been to England with the entire family once before. But I was very young then, about four and a half, and don't remember much of the flight. But I still remember my terror from the noise during takeoff.

The flight attendants tell everyone how to use their seat belts, about the emergency exits, and that oxygen will flow through masks if the cabin loses pressure.

Dad, the educator, tells us, "New York has the atmospheric pressure of sea level. The plane is pressurized only to the atmospheric pressure experienced at five thousand feet." He looks at both of us to see if he has captured anyone's attention.

Maybe seeing some capture, he further explains, "Ascending from sea level drops atmospheric pressure. Above ten thousand feet, some people will have medical problems and may have difficulty breathing." He pauses and then says, "Once again, physics in action."

"Is that your favorite phrase?" I ask.

"What phrase?" questions Dad as he looks at me quizzically.

"Physics in action," I reply.

Dad thinks for a moment and laughs. "Maybe." He shrugs his shoulders slightly.

It's great that Dad always wants to teach us. His favorite phrase is probably all that I will remember. But I am beginning to love the idea of physics. It explains so much. At least, that is what I am told, over and over.

The crew checks that everyone is prepared for takeoff with seat belts fastened, tray tables in their upright position, and all baggage in the overhead compartments or under the seat in front. They are satisfied and radio the pilot. The plane begins to move.

They say the plane taxies to the runway, as if it were a car. Then the engine revs, and the plane speeds down the runway and lifts off the ground. How can a huge and heavy plane fly? I decide to ask Dad after the noise of takeoff settles.

Dad answers, "That's physics in action again. The wing has a convex upper side, like an arch when the wing is viewed side on. When the plane moves fast, the wing shape causes the air above to move faster than the air below. The difference in airspeed reduces the pressure of the air above the wing, creating a relative vacuum, which gives lift to the plane."

I don't really understand. But I think I have some details right, so I say, "Do you mean it's the shape of the wing together with the speed produced by the engines that allows the plane to fly?"

"That's right," says Dad.

Don't ask me any questions. I don't understand anything more! However, while listening to Dad, my mind makes a decision. I must learn a lot about physics. It seems useful, and it might make me seem smart, even though I'm not.

Cabin staff serves a meal. It tastes good mostly because I am hungry. Then Dad suggests that we all try to get some sleep. Both Susanne and I say, "We will never be able to sleep."

Phoebe says to us, "There is a trick you can play on yourself. Pretend you are in bed. Try to stay awake in your pretend bed. If you try to stay awake when you are in a really comfortable reclining chair, sleep takes over."

We are approaching England when they wake us for breakfast before landing at Heathrow Airport. How have I ever fallen asleep? Phoebe laughs at Susanne and me as we open our eyes.

"Welcome to Britain!" Phoebe giggles. She's being silly by repeating what Papa and Dad always say.

"Phoebe, have you been to England except for the trip when I was four and a half?" I ask.

Phoebe answers, "No. That trip with the family was my first time over to the United Kingdom. As a teen, I spent a summer in Spain with relatives, so this is my third time crossing the Atlantic Ocean. I do love to travel and see things. I always learn something new." She looks at Susanne and then me. "And you both will have the chance to experience new, interesting, and exciting things too."

That turns out to be an understatement!

We eventually land. The wheels make a bump sound as they touch the ground. The engine makes a loud noise as the plane slows.

Dad explains, "Jets have reverse thrust that acts against forward motion, causing deceleration. That saves on the brakes, which would wear out quicker otherwise."

So that's the cause of the loud noise we hear. What's reverse thrust? I don't know, but excuse me, I am not asking today.

After we get off the plane, we stay together through customs. Dad tells us, "Be very serious, no joking around, and answer only the questions asked."

A customs agent looks at our passports and asks Dad questions. We all, including Phoebe, get through customs without a problem. Then we find our luggage and exit the secure section of the airport. Just at the door, we see Papa. He waves at us. Dragging luggage behind us, Susanne and I rush to greet him.

Usually, I jump up for a big hug, but I'm too big now. I could knock him over. But I do give him an enormous hug with my big feet on the ground. Susanne, who is taller than me and certainly also big enough to knock him over, gives him a big hug too.

We talk to our grandparents and see them with our computer every few weeks. Thank you, technology! But to see Papa, touch him, and sense country smells on his tweed jacket, that is heaven! And we will see Nana soon.

After greeting Susanne and me, he gives a hug to Phoebe and a big hug to Dad.

"Welcome to Britain!" says Papa as he laughs.

Phoebe glances knowingly at Susanne and me with a little smile. She's recollecting her morning wake-up with her "welcome to Britain" silliness!

Dad laughs at the long-standing joke between them and says, "Thank you, Papa."

Papa inquires about the trip and the flight. Are we tired or revved up? He listens intently as we answer.

Papa says, "I have a car waiting. There will be plenty of room."

The car is a little like a London taxi, which always looks like a black box with wheels. But this one is longer with an extra row of seats. And there is an area at the rear for luggage.

The driver stays in the car until he sees Papa approaching. Then he gets out to help Dad bundle our bags into this long taxi as we get seated.

After Papa sits inside, he continues, "I have reserved train tickets already. We embark from the station fairly soon. There is time for tea if you'd like, but I suggest we get that at the station."

"That seems the best idea," agrees Dad.

Papa says to the driver, "Paddington Rail Station, please."

The driver nods, checks again that everyone is safely inside, and wheels us into traffic.

"Do we really go to Paddington Station?" I ask excitedly.

Papa answers, "Yes. That is where we get our train."

"We must stop to see Paddington Bear," I insist. "I mean the statue of Paddington Bear, celebrating the storybook. According to the story, Paddington Bear arrived from Peru and was found by Mr. and Mrs. Brown at Paddington Station."

Probably overtired and too excited, I babble on, "Susanne and I both have a picture of us standing by the Paddington Bear statue from our last visit when I was four and a half. In the photo, my hand is near my mouth. Susanne is standing straight and looking right at the camera. But her smile misses a front tooth because she was just about seven when the photo was taken." I pause to think for a moment, but not long enough, since I keep talking. "A few years ago, Mom told me that upper-front baby teeth fall out about then," I say excitedly while recounting everything I know. Like I said, I babble when overtired.

The adults all quietly laugh. I'm not sure what is so funny. In the rearview mirror, I can see the driver's smile.

Unperturbed, I say, "I display my picture in its frame. Susanne put hers away about a year ago. The photo is in her special memories drawer at home."

Susanne rolls her eyes. "Any other details you want to share, Jeremiah? Anything you missed, like maybe where I store my under-wear?" she asks sourly.

"You sound grumpy. Are you tired?" I ask innocently.

"Enough, Susanne," commands Phoebe, "and you too, mister." Susanne still appears annoyed.

She must be tired.

I still secretly read the Paddington Bear books, but I don't tell anybody about that. I am a big boy now. But old stories from my distant childhood are still fun!

In a short time, we are taking photos with Paddington Bear! A lady stops to ask if we want a group photo. Dad says, "Thank you. That would be very nice."

The pleasant lady takes a photo of everyone with Paddington, Phoebe and Papa included. Afterward, she says, "You and your wife have lovely children."

Dad says, "Many thanks."

Phoebe looks away, turning slightly red. After the lady departs, Phoebe giggles nervously.

Dad immediately says, "Too much explaining. I decided to let it go. Mom will get a laugh when I tell her. Mistaken assumptions in New York and now London!"

Papa says, "Your dear wife is not here, and she wants to be. Maybe you should not say anything."

Phoebe adds, "That is exactly right. 'Least said, easiest mended,' as my grandmother would say."

Before he scurries over to the ticket agent, Papa states, "I'm heading off to claim the reserved tickets. Back in a moment." In a few minutes, he is with us again.

With that, we find a tea shop and have scones and tea. Before we leave, Phoebe buys a newspaper. After walking along the platform to our train, we climb on board and stow our luggage.

In our comfortable compartment, Susanne and I sit on either side of Papa. Phoebe and Dad sit opposite. Papa and Dad begin a long talk. Phoebe makes sure we are all settled and then opens the *London Times* and begins to read.

As the train jolts and then begins to move, I think about the nice lady who took our picture. Seeing us together, it was easy to make an innocent guess about us that was completely wrong. I remember Mom saying that guesses about other people or situations are called assumptions. And Dad used that word today. I begin to wonder what assumptions I have made about other people. Are any of my assumptions also completely wrong? I glance out through the window. We are now well out of London.

"Just look at the picturesque English countryside," says Dad. "Is that the M1?" he asks as he glances toward Papa.

"Yes, indeed," Papa replies.

We look at the cars and buses on the road Dad asked about. At other times, we see countryside with sheep and stone fences. The train goes on and on. Later, I look at a map and learn the train is going south and west from London—for miles and miles.

Eventually, the rocking motion soothes me enough that I nod off to sleep. I wake up as the train reaches its destination. With Phoebe's help, Dad and Papa are organizing our belongings and preparing for departure.

At the station, the train slows to a stop. Dad, Phoebe, and Papa check the compartment for any possessions left behind. As we exit the train, we wheel our luggage behind us.

A man who seems familiar approaches after he exits a funny-looking little bus-like affair with four doors. He has broad shoulders and stands very straight, but he is shorter than Papa. His eyes, short straight hair, and thin mustache are brown. Papa greets him. I vaguely remember that the man lives and works on Papa's estate.

Papa introduces us, each by name. "Do you remember Mr. Brown, the estate manager?" He pauses and looks inquisitively at his grandchildren. "He is my right-hand man, and my left as well," declares Papa laughingly.

Two kids smile uncertainly and wave.

Dad shakes Mr. Brown's hand as he says, "Hello. It's good to see you again. It's been six years."

Phoebe greets Mr. Brown and exclaims, "You haven't changed a bit, Mr. Brown. A pleasure to see you again."

He replies, "A pity about your failing vision, Miss Phoebe." She is momentarily startled, until he laughs out loud and she realizes the joke. She laughs too; it's a wonderful sound.

Papa then asks numerous questions about what has happened in his absence since yesterday when he went down to London. After the two Englishmen finish talking, Mr. Brown and Dad load the bus, which can seat nine. All of us clamber in and buckle up. Mr. Brown drives.

It seems odd to see the driver on the right-hand side of the little bus. However, this does make sense. In Britain, vehicles drive on the left-hand side of the road. In America, we drive on the right side. In Britain, turning left is easier than turning right, just the opposite of the American system. How confusing. How easy to make a mistake!

And while I wonder if it is difficult to drive in Britain, we all head to Papa and Nana's house in the care of Mr. Brown.

Chapter 7

ARRIVAL AT PAPA'S HOUSE

The little bus follows the main roads, which are narrow and winding. We go through several villages. Some old houses are so very close to the road that their doors open almost right into the road.

When we leave the villages, the roads narrow even more. There are hedgerows on each side and no road shoulder. Both Papa and Dad comment there is no place to get out of traffic if there is engine trouble or some other reason to stop.

We turn left at a village main square and several miles later take a right between hedgerows. As a driver, I would have missed that turn. There was no sign, and nothing to indicate anything about a change in direction. I guess you just have to know. As we travel, Papa points out various old buildings and taverns that we pass. He sure knows a lot about history and architecture!

Papa talks a bit more to Dad before he asks, "Susanne and Jeremiah, do you remember when Nana and Papa's house was built?"

I am drawing a big blank. Susanne saves the day as she pipes up with "Victorian period. That makes it a nineteenth-century house."

"Right you are!" exclaims Papa. After a pause, he adds, "The dwelling was built in 1870, but with the architectural style of the Elizabethan period, called Tudor, a sixteenth-century style," which he then describes in detail.

A few moments later, Papa adds, "The house is in the shape of an H, with a central block and projections toward the drive and to the back on either side. I love that the front faces south, which gives such lovely wintertime light." After a pause, he adds, "Out a few feet from the house, you will notice a walkway that goes all the way 'round. That gap of a few feet between the house and the walkway is filled down to the footers with crushed stone. Do either of you know why?"

We both say, "Not really."

"This allows drainage of water away from the house to keep the basement dry," says Papa.

This fascinates me. Physics in action again. Dad is right!

A few miles on, we take another turn, which is actually the entrance lane going to Nana and Papa's house. Through the trees, we glimpse the house.

Suddenly, we are in a clearing and drive up the left side of the wide circular driveway, past a huge cedar tree, until we finally reach the front of the house. I remember what Papa has just told us. The walls of the lower floors are made of bricks that do indeed create fancy patterns, with wood and stucco on the upper floors and gables. The house is larger than I remember. Certainly, the front parts of the house stick out forward like the top of an H seen from above.

Nana opens the door and steps out onto the stone steps. When she steps away from the house, her loose dress waves in the breeze. She waits until the goofy-looking little bus stops before her shoes crunch on the gravel. Walking quickly toward us, her hand opens a door to greet us as we disembark.

I am the first out and the first to get a big hug. Susanne races out next to hug Nana tight. Papa gives her a hug and a kiss on the cheek. Dad gives her a warm hug. She kisses him on the cheek afterward and then pulls him close for another hug. She gives Phoebe a hug too and holds her arm for a moment.

Nana inquires of everyone, "How was the trip?" She tries to listen to the chaos of the answers.

Nigel, Nana and Papa's butler, appears quietly in the background. He has been their butler forever. Papa once said, "Nigel moves so quietly sometimes that I don't even realize he is there."

Nigel nods to Susanne and me. He is about the same height as Papa, very trim, with short well-groomed gray hair above brown eyes. He has a long face with a perfect nose; but when he smiles, as he often does, everyone smiles.

Before our departure, Mom was reminiscing about Nigel and her childhood. According to Mom, he keeps everything in order, but he is nice about it. I remember when Mom said that Nigel always makes everyone feel safe and the world stable. She should know. He has been with Papa and Nana since before Mom's elder brother was born. I recall that he wears wire-framed reading glasses sometimes, but not now.

Thinking about what Mom has told us previously makes me suddenly miss her a lot right now. It's a lonely feeling.

Meanwhile, Mr. Brown and Nigel unload the car and bring the luggage into the main hall. Then Mr. Brown disappears with his burdens of baggage, trailing Nigel, who is burdened with his. Together, they arrange which baggage will go where, all because Nigel already knows.

Inside, Nana tells each of us which room is ours. Susanne is looking around, trying to recall the house from her prior visit. Since I was four at our last visit, I don't remember much.

I worry that I still haven't said a proper hello to Nigel. But later, he'll be given my proper greeting. After all, he's always somewhere in the house.

The house windows allow in lots of light. The sunshine makes the wooden paneling in the central hall glow a wonderfully faded sandy-yellow color. Warmth and comfort radiate from the old walls with wood glowing all the way to the tall ceiling. I smell old wood, with country grasses and nearby horses. What contentment! It's very like the inner peace I sense when I smell Papa's jacket.

The adults discuss the trip, the train food, the time spent on travel, and the need for tea. My ears perk up. Tea means tasty tea cakes and lovely cold milk, both of which I love.

Susanne and I follow the adults. We pass the main staircase with its heavily carved and polished newel post and spindles and continue onward.

We enter the large dining room with huge windows on three sides. Same as the hall, the ceiling is high. The furniture is very dark and heavy looking. There is a huge sideboard with large fat legs carved all the way around and ending in square feet, same as the table. The chair legs have the same carved pattern but are slimmer, to match their size. Leather seats and upholstered padding on part of the back make the chairs appear comfortable.

Nana sees me looking at the dining room furniture. I am inspecting it closely as I stand awaiting instructions on where to sit.

She says, "Jeremiah, you look like you are about to make a purchase by the way you are inspecting everything. Do you want to ask a question?" She laughs out loud, and Papa chortles.

Papa says, "The poor lad is just trying to get his bearings."

I nod to Papa and reply, "Yes, Nana, I am puzzled. Why is the furniture here so dark?"

Nana laughs as she answers, "The furniture was made for the house at the time it was built, about 1870. Is that the right date, John? I'm suddenly uncertain."

Papa replies quickly, "Yes, Iris, the house was finished in 1870. It took more than a year to build."

Nana says, "Thank you, I sometimes lose track. Anyway, this furniture is in the same Tudor style as the house. At the time, people thought antique furniture should be very dark to suggest age. Consequently, they colored new furniture dark to make it look old, even though it was newly built to match the new house."

Susanne says, "But not all antique furniture is dark."

Nana replies, "Yes, my dear, you are right. But at the time, 1870 or thereabouts, dark wood coloring was the reigning fashion, apparently designed to add richness to the décor. The overall effect is fancy carving that Queen Elizabeth I would have recognized and liked had she seen it." Nana smiles, chortles slightly, and then adds, "Of course, she had been dead for about two hundred and seventy years when this furniture was newly carved a hundred and forty-odd years ago! And the dark color to add authenticity is a lot of silliness, in my opinion. But I am fond of these now-old pieces. And the dark wood allows me to cover marks easily." Again, she chortles. "And there are plenty of marks!"

We sit as Nana directs, she at one end of the great table, Papa at the other, and all of us taking our positions along the sides. Three-tiered plates appear, each full of wonderful-looking cakes and pastries. Between them, little sandwiches without crusts arrive on flat plates. Nana pours tea from a large pot and passes cups to the adults. Magically, milk appears in front of Susanne and me. Nigel, the butler, has served it. He moves so deftly and quietly that the service could be missed.

Where is Nigel? I twist my head around. Oh, he's over there, already disappearing into the background. When I got into some sort of trouble during our last visit, Nigel covered for me. Even though I don't recall what happened exactly, Nigel will remember clearly. I catch his eye and wink at him.

Nigel forms the slightest of smiles in return and bounces up on his toes. This means that Nigel is laughing and can't show it.

Mom once explained to me that choirboys often have jokes circulating during Anglican Mass but cannot laugh. So when they are standing, they bounce up on their toes, then down, and then up again, over and over—a substitute for laughing.

That is what Nigel is quietly doing; just once, a single chuckle, a single up on the toes. I feel safe! Nigel will still have my back, no matter what mischief I do.

We all eat and drink. The adults laugh a good deal. There are comments and lively discussions about politics, both American and British. They even talk about Canada, since Dad says he works with people from Canada.

Time passes too slowly for Susanne and me as the adults chat. We do not understand all of the talk, and we both start to get bored. As usual, Susanne stays still so no one will notice her. As usual, I start to fidget.

As if by magic, a small bowl of vanilla ice cream with a dollop of butterscotch sauce appears before us.

"In case you were getting tired of the conversation," says Nigel. His eyes are bright with mischief. Both of us dive into the ice cream.

The adults giggle as they watch our ice cream disappear. "No thanks," they say when Nigel asks if they want any.

At one point, I hear that the next two days, Saturday and Sunday, will be clear. The third day, which is Monday, is forecast to have heavy rain.

Papa says, "An inside day for the children by the sounds of it." He looks at Nana. "Is that when you need to be in London?" he asks.

She replies, "Yes, it is." She looks at Dad. "I took today off and returned from London yesterday."

Dad says, "I'm glad you did."

Nana looks pleased.

Papa says, "I will need to be in London Monday, as well. Shall we go by the same train?"

"Yes. Excellent idea," says Nana. "You can buy me sandwiches." She smiles at Papa, fluttering her eyes and flirting.

"I shall count on doing so. Almost like a date out." Both of them chuckle.

"I have meetings on Monday," says Dad. "But it's all online, so I don't need to leave the house for any of them."

Susanne and I look at each other. We know that on Monday we will need to entertain ourselves.

I am filled with curiosity. I want to explore this huge old house. What will I find?

Chapter 8

THE FIRST TWO DAYS

Since it's the weekend, Nana is not working. In the morning room after breakfast, Phoebe asks if she may join us when Nana decides to take Susanne and me on a tour of the garden and grounds. As we all head out into the bright sunshine, Phoebe notices that I'm the only one without a hat. "You need protection from the sun. Go back inside and fetch your hat, mister," she demands. Within minutes, four hats begin their walking tour.

"There is a lot of property, a lot of walking, and a lot to see," says Nana as we begin. What she says is interesting. Her enthusiasm is contagious.

Wearing his hat in the bright sunshine, Papa appears from parts unknown to ask with a laugh, "May I join your tour, oh, great esteemed ones?"

"Yes, you may," say two young voices together.

Nana giggles, and Phoebe smiles as Papa tags along. Nana talks about some of the plantings and knows the dates, some several hundred years ago, when certain trees were planted and who planted them. "The trees look like they appeared randomly, but they were deliberately placed," she says.

Wow!

Papa explains to Phoebe, "Let me tell you about several famous gardening types who worked on the design and layout of the plantings and trees."

Phoebe is surprisingly knowledgeable. She listens with interest and asks our grandparents a lot of probing questions. She talks of some of the different plants that grow in Spain but which might not flourish in Britain.

I am essentially lost after a while and not paying a whole lot of attention. But I like to look at the flowers and plants. Susanne seems more interested than I am and asks a lot of questions.

Both of my grandparents appear surprised that Phoebe knows so much about plants and gardening history. They have a passion for gardening, so this forms a wonderful bond with Phoebe. Nana asks, "How did you develop this love for the land in New York City?"

"My great-grandparents owned much land in Spain," Phoebe replies, "several thousand acres. They were from a very old family. Franco took it all away." Suddenly, she appears very sad as she looks down.

With wide-open eyes, both my grandparents watch Phoebe with sad fascination and sympathy.

"Ah, before the war," says Nana.

"Yes, before the Second World War," answers Phoebe.

"Franco was a dictator and an awful man," says Papa.

"Yes, he was horrible. My paternal grandparents were both from old landed families. When Franco took their land, he killed my great-grandparents in front of their teenaged son, the person who became my grandfather. Two days later, my grandmother's parents were shot and their land taken. My grandmother, an early teenager at the time, missed their execution.

"These teenagers escaped together with nothing but their lives. They fled first to France, and then to England, until they could get to America. Eventually, they married in America." Phoebe pauses and looks down slightly. Still looking down, she adds, "Fortunately, both sets of great-grandparents were kindly people who believed in the power of education, even for the aristocracy." She looks back up at my grandparents as she finishes.

Nana's and Papa's eyes widen even more when Phoebe uses the word "aristocracy." She has never spoken to us in any real way about her family origins. Certainly, she has never used the word "aristocracy" regarding her own origins.

I suddenly realize that Phoebe's great-grandparents, and her grandparents in their early years, lived much as Nana and Papa do now, except in Spain. I can't imagine Nana and Papa, or my parents for that matter, suddenly becoming refugees because a dictator took a liking to their property.

Phoebe continues, "Both of my grandparents were multilingual. My grandfather even had an English tutor who lived with them. English was chosen because that was the language of commerce at the time. Apparently, Grandpa was teased because he was a Spaniard who spoke American English with a slight English accent. My own father has a little of his father's accent too. It's really quite charming."

Phoebe and my grandparents all chuckle. Susanne and I are too shocked and horrified by this tale to find anything funny.

After a pause, Phoebe continues, "However, in America, my grandparents and their children were confined to the Hispanic ghetto. Regardless, my grandparents drilled into my father and into me the value of kindliness, honesty, respect for persons and property, the value of education, and the power of words. Now, I am trying to instill these values into your grandchildren."

Eyes bright with tears that are nearly falling, Phoebe smiles as she recollects, "But my family has told me many family stories, over and over." She looks around and then smiles at Nana as she says quietly, "So you see, I enjoy the gardens and the land. I have heard the stories. The love of the land is in my blood."

On autopilot, Nana gives Phoebe a hug for comfort. Nana's eyes are moist as she says, "Phoebe, I had no idea your family suffered so much. And your grandparents witnessed wrongful death and became refugees. How horrible for all of them and for you!"

Trying to make Phoebe feel better, Papa says, "But you already know that you have become a very special person to us, and certainly part of this extended family."

I am glad both my grandparents have a generous heart.

Nana forges on, "But they lost so much—money, position, social standing, and privilege! What happened to them affects you directly, Phoebe."

Papa nods in agreement.

"Do you understand the full extent of the loss, my dear?" Nana asks, genuinely baffled. "Does it not make you angry?"

"Yes, Nana, I do understand; but it is what it is. I am not angry; but rarely, I feel sad, like I am grieving. But mostly, I am a happy person," replies Phoebe, "especially with my precious ones." She looks toward us. Neither Susanne nor I know what to say.

Phoebe wipes a few tears that have now fallen down her cheeks. She says, "I almost never speak of this. It hurts."

"Sorry I probed," says Nana. "The intent was good."

"*No importante*," replies Phoebe, upset enough to slide into Spanish.

"Just remember that you have our trust and love, if that is any compensation," says Nana sincerely. While Papa nods, she adds, "And remember, you really are an honorary member of this family."

Phoebe smiles as she wipes away a remaining tear. She says, "Thank you."

Neither Susanne nor I have heard this story before. We are horrified by her tale. Neither of us knows what to do. Fortunately, we are saved because general talk resumes. As the emotions settle, both Nana and Papa appear relaxed again. After a little more time passes, we are all laughing and joking, talking "thirteen to the dozen," as Mom might say. We are really enjoying ourselves as we resume walking in the garden and along the paths in the grounds. Conversation covers many topics besides gardening. Soon Papa says something that makes us all laugh out loud. That laughter reassures me that all is back to normal.

Later that morning, Papa takes both Susanne and me to the barns. With Mr. Brown, Papa shows us how to saddle a horse, get the bridle over its head, fit the bit, and handle the reins. Susanne and I both ask, "Why are the leather straps from the bit to our hands called reins?"

Mr. Brown answers, "To rein means to stop, control, or direct. The leather straps, or reins, go from the rider's hands to the horse's mouth, which holds the bit. The bit is a metal bar.

"The mouth of the horse is sensitive. With gentle motion on the rein leather, the horse feels motion against the bit in its mouth and then knows what is expected. One must always be gentle with the reins and not hurt the animal's mouth." He pauses to let this sink in.

He finishes, "Pulling back on the reins stops the horse, hence 'reining in' the horse." Mr. Brown's explanation makes sense to us.

Both of us have difficulty mounting our horses. We need help getting up, even from the mounting block. This is an elevated square stone the rider may stand upon. It is higher than the ground and allows a shorter rider to get up, whereas taller riders may step right from the ground into a stirrup and then must catapult half of themselves over the horse's back with a gymnastic maneuver. Will I ever be able to do that?

"I hope I can soon do this myself," I say as I finally land in the saddle with some help.

"Me too," adds Susanne.

Mr. Brown quietly mutters breathlessly, "Let us hope next time will be easier." He has just helped me get up. I think he had to mostly push me up.

Papa laughs. "It's hard work keeping up with children. This summer will keep us fit."

Mr. Brown and Papa have no trouble mounting their horses. They are close by us and give us instructions on how to guide our mounts to the right and the left, to slow, and to walk.

A click with my tongue causes my horse to start walking. I pull back gently, and the horse stops. I start moving far forward in the saddle because she stops quickly on command.

As Papa sees what is happening, he says, "Now you know that you must always be prepared. You and your horse were moving forward at a certain speed. You gave a command. The horse stopped as you directed. But nothing stopped you, so you kept moving forward relative to the horse. If you had been moving forward fast, you would have dismounted over her head and onto the ground. And it would not be her fault. It would be your own. Be prepared always." He pauses and then adds, "The laws of physics will always be obeyed, even if you don't know them."

My mind flashes to Dad's "physics in action" phrase. Is Papa another one hooked on physics?

"How do I stop from going forward?" I ask.

Mr. Brown replies, "Hold tight by squeezing your knees together tight against the horse. Worst case, put your arms around her neck and hold her mane if you think you are going to be thrown." Mr. Brown makes this sound easy.

I hope I never need Mr. Brown's advice.

Mr. Brown adds, "Horse riding is fun, but it can also be very dangerous."

"I'm paying attention," I say. "I don't want to be thrown."

Susanne says, "Me too! I want to stay mounted instead of on the ground beside the horse."

We all walk our horses together in the pasture, turn the same way at the same time, and walk the opposite way, two by two. The horses are full size, young, and healthy.

My horse is slow and deliberate in her movements, with dark rust-colored hair and enormous brown eyes. Her name is Rusty. I hope to ride her often.

Papa sees me pat her neck as we ride slowly.

"So do you like Rusty?" he asks.

"Oh yes," I say.

Papa replies, "She is a very gentle animal and fond of children. She probably knows you are not experienced, so she will try to protect you. She is just as gentle as Samantha, the black horse your sister is riding."

Samantha turns her head to Papa when she hears her name. This makes Susanne start, and her heels touch into the sides of the horse. This is the horse's instruction to canter; and she does, taking poor Susanne, who is totally unprepared, completely off guard. Susanne remains in the saddle, but she lets go of the reins, which fall to one side.

Samantha is now far ahead of us, still in the paddock but far away on the other side, circling at a steady but rapid canter. Bouncing in the saddle, Susanne looks terrified and cries out, "What do I do?"

Without a sound except a click of his tongue, Mr. Brown puts his horse into action. He dashes across the paddock, canters beside the dangling reins, which he gathers deftly into his hand, and utters, "Whoa." Samantha slows to a walk and then gently stops.

Susanne looks at the miracle Mr. Brown has done, smiles broadly, and then says, "That was fun even if it was scary! I won't lose the reins next time."

Mr. Brown says merrily, "I suggest you don't."

Too soon after the excitement and a good, if tame, ride, it is time to take the horses back to the barn. Mr. Brown instructs us how to remove the bridle and the bit and keep the reins from tangling.

"Ground rules!" declares Papa firmly. "If you want to ride, you must prepare the horse before and clear up afterwards." He adds, "That teaches responsibility."

Trying to please Papa, I say, "Let me remove the saddle myself."

Adult eyes watch me as I undo the belly strap buckle and step up onto the mounting block. I am barely able to lift the saddle off the horse. It is so heavy that I start to fall sideways, and down I go before anyone can do anything. Suddenly, I am sitting on the ground beside the mounting block. Luckily, I fell far enough to the side that I missed a hard hit against the mounting block stone.

The sensible horse, Rusty, has moved out of harm's way. The saddle is in the dirt in front of me. I have straw and dirt all over my legs and backside. I feel like an idiot!

Papa asks, "Are you hurt?"

I reply, "No, I am fine."

He starts to loudly laugh for a rather long time, as I sit with legs straight out in the dirt.

Enough already, Papa! I can tell my face is already red.

Papa chortles. "So you have both learned another lesson in the barnyard." He laughs heartily again as he extends his hand to help me up. "Simple fracture of the dignity!" His laugh continues. *No tea and sympathy here!*

I hear a loud chuckle coming from Mr. Brown, whose dark eyes are twinkling. "We have both done the same thing," says Mr. Brown, "and more than once."

I feel better when they both say they have done the same thing more than once. I dust myself off. I must admit, it was pretty funny.

Both insist we learn how to give our horse a quick rubdown and make sure her feet are clean. We also check that each one has enough food and water.

As he handles his horse, Papa says, "Animals mean responsibility." Papa rubs his horse with a brush as he declares, "If you want to ride, you need to care for the animal and do the things the horse cannot do for herself."

"So, Papa, is looking after animals a lot like looking after a human baby?" Susanne asks.

"Yes, m'lady," replies Papa.

"That's a clear message," I say, as I rub my sore rump.

"And a lot of work," states Susanne.

"And now we need lunch, don't we, Mr. Brown? Shall we see what Mrs. Stewart has prepared for us?" asks Papa.

Mrs. Stewart is Nana and Papa's cook. She is really good at her job! Both of us say, "We're hungry. Lunch is a great idea!"

Once seated at the dining table, we dive into the soup, sandwiches, and tasty salad that Nigel serves. We have a choice for dessert. Susanne wants blueberry pie. I decide to try Nigel's suggestion of custard, which is creamy, smooth, and sweet. I love dessert, and Nana always has a sweet after a meal. Phoebe has the custard too. It is good to see her enjoying a meal that she does not have to prepare.

Papa says he needs to go over some things with Mr. Brown, so both men leave the dining room to visit some pastureland.

After Mr. Brown leaves and when Phoebe is in the kitchen so she cannot hear, Nana tells us, "My nanny never ate with the family. She always ate from a tray in the nursery or with the kitchen staff. Wasn't that silly? But that was the rule back then."

She pauses before she continues, "I always thought the standards were shameful. Nanny was good enough to be entrusted with the care and with the education by example of one's own children but was not good enough to sit at one's table, even on informal occasions." Nana pauses, lost in thought, and looking half sad and half angry. "Utter foolishness and snobbery!" She looks at Susanne and at me. "Not in my house! Respect for all—even at table. We all have a story behind us." Lost in thought, she looks at Phoebe's empty chair. "And Phoebe is a good and strong person, worthy of trust, respect, and love."

There may be more to this quiet outburst than we know. Maybe she had to battle for the equality she wanted to see.

Susanne quietly replies, "I am glad that times have changed. We love Phoebe's company as a member of the family at mealtime."

"Yes indeed," I pipe up. "She is family now."

"Yes, she is," says Dad. "Like Susanne, I am very glad that times have changed. And I am very glad that you feel as you do, Iris."

It seems odd to hear Dad call Nana by her real name. He usually says Nana.

Nana returns from her thoughts, looks at Susanne and me, and asks, "What else would you two like for lunch?" Just then, Phoebe returns carrying a pitcher of milk, and Nigel arrives with a board laden with various cheeses and an assortment of crackers.

"More milk, please," we kids say in unison.

"I shall have some cheddar," says Nana as Nigel gently eases the board onto the table. Dad and Phoebe declare, "This looks wonderful," and sample a few other varieties, as the cheese board makes its rounds, guided by Nigel.

"Me too," I say as I reach for the cheese knife. "I'm going to try this one with blue veins."

"Me three." Susanne giggles as I pass her the knife. She also slices several hefty pieces of cheddar and a slice of Brie. Nigel leaves the board in the middle of the table.

After lunch, as they slowly nibble away at the cheese board, Nana and Dad start a long talk involving their work.

Phoebe decides we should play croquet. She knows the rules and is a really good player, as we quickly discover. Susanne immediately starts to become competitive, like usual. I love the "whack" produced when the wooden mallet hits the ball. My aim is not very good. Clearly, Susanne is a better player than I am, even though this is the first time either of us has ever played.

We have deliciously cold lemonade after croquet. We sip slowly, while Phoebe talks about England and finishes by saying, "I am so enjoying this visit."

The afternoon slips away. Soon, it is dinnertime. Even though I have enjoyed lunch and eaten heartily, suddenly I am starving again!

We clean up and meet with the adults before dinner in what Nana calls the sitting room. Americans would call it the living room or the great room. In Britain, it is the sitting room or lounge. There is an old-fashioned formal term for it as well—the drawing room. What odd words they use here! But then they do drive on the wrong side of the road…

Dinner and the sweet afterward are delicious. But soon my eyes are heavy, and I realize how very tired I am. Phoebe notices and also sees Susanne yawning.

Phoebe says, "Bed early, you two. You both had a busy day after a long flight the day before. No wonder you are sleepy!"

Nana nods in agreement.

We say good night to Nana and Papa and give them a hug. Dad holds us both tight when we kiss him good night. Phoebe directs us to our rooms and makes sure we prepare for bed properly. I am nearly asleep when Phoebe kisses me on the forehead.

In the morning, streaks of sunlight make bright marks on the carpet and furniture. I feel energized. I can't wait for breakfast!

In the dining room, we discuss the activities for the day. Nana and Phoebe have made plans for us to have a picnic lunch after church.

Nana and Papa always go to the local parish Anglican church, a pretty stone building in the village with a church graveyard nearby. This is a typical British custom. In America, very few new churches have a cemetery attached.

"My family has attended services here for about four hundred years," says Papa as he parks our vehicle.

Dad says, "By way of comparison, many parts of the States have not yet been settled for anywhere near four hundred years." After he stops to think for a moment, Dad adds, "I am fascinated by the age of British buildings and institutions. Each visit, I learn more. History surrounds us everywhere here in Britain."

Nana says, "You cannot escape history here—that's a certainty."

During the service, Susanne sits very still, listening. I watch the local Anglican priest. He is rather thin and very serious. I look at the old wall plaques with names of dead people. Some of the dates are a really long time ago.

Nana sees me looking and, after the service, points out some plaques with last names that are the same as her and Papa's last name. This is also Mom's maiden name, Wadsworth, her last name before she married Dad. It is the same name she still uses at work.

"These are some of your ancestors," Nana says, as she points to some of the many plaques with the name Wadsworth.

"It seems strange to discover that part of my family has lived in the same place for hundreds of years," I say to Nana. "Their lives can be traced through local records, all right here, and maybe from wall plaques in a church!" Reflecting, I pause before I add, "This makes me feel small, as if my story is part of a much larger story, told over generations. At the same time, I feel constancy and a sense of safety."

"Both small and constant safety are sensible responses," she replies. Then, as Nana points out the name of Papa's title on a plaque, she says, "Papa has his family name, Wadsworth, and then the name he bears with his title. There's the title!" I read the name near her finger. Nana adds with a laugh, "I joke that it's a burden that he bears."

Papa never willingly mentions it. I have heard it before, but not often. Reading the name again, I understand exactly why he feels that way! Nana sees the reaction on my face. She giggles, school-girlish.

"Remember, before I married, Papa's father carried the title. As Papa's wife, I knew the title might eventually become mine too, if my husband's father died. It is a silly name for a relative. As one's own, it is almost a deal breaker!"

My dad sometimes says "deal breaker." It doesn't seem British. I ask, "Is 'deal breaker' a British phrase?"

Nana answers, "Heavens, no. I got it from your father. But it says it all so well!" She giggles again and continues, "I do love some of the American way of speaking. So very direct."

"Aren't the British direct?" I ask.

Nana answers, almost whispering, as if she is telling me a secret, "Only if you know the subtleties. If you don't, you are lost. It makes it hard to negotiate daily life."

"Why can't they be more direct?" I ask.

This time Nana really does whisper like a conspirator, "They think they are too polite."

I really do not understand. I smile at Nana. I just hope I will catch on fast.

As we return to the house after church, Phoebe says, "I do love the English mass. It is very close to the Catholic Mass that I know so well."

Papa replies, "We would all be Catholic today if Henry VIII had not tired of his first wife, Catherine of Aragon."

I see Nana, my parents, and Phoebe all nod in agreement.

It's too nice a day to ask! History lessons can wait.

A little later, we pile into two cars. One car is laden with picnic food and drink that Mrs. Stewart prepared the previous day before leaving for her home, where she lives with her husband. On Sundays, she has the day off, so Nana makes all meals or has Mrs. Stewart prepare something ahead.

After driving for ten or fifteen minutes, we arrive at a small lazy stream with a grassy area that is flat and inviting. Nigel and Mr. Brown set out the picnic food on an enormous blanket. There is enough room for all of us to sit on folding chairs or stretch out, protected from the grass.

We have sandwiches—some with egg salad, some with ham. There is a green salad, which Nana and Phoebe particularly like. Cold chicken and slices of ham go well with sharp pickles. We have lemon pie for dessert, with lemonade to wash it all down. It is scrumptious!

I love good food! I love to eat! So does Susanne.

The adults talk for a long time. Dad, Papa, and Mr. Brown have long talks about the future of the estate, taxes, and farm management. Nana and Dad discuss law, money, and investments on both sides of the Atlantic. Phoebe and Nana discuss our schooling.

Dad adds onto some of Phoebe's answers about our education. Papa listens intently, clearly pleased that Dad is so involved.

Nigel and Mr. Brown join in the general conversation. At times, they also talk softly between themselves.

In a pause in the conversation, Dad looks at Papa and says, "Tell me a little bit about the architectural style of your house. It seems a little unusual to me. I don't know why, but there's something about it that I don't quite understand."

Phoebe and Nana pause in their conversation to listen. Nigel and Mr. Brown seem attentive.

Papa thinks for a moment and then says, "The style is a mixture of Georgian eighteenth-century architectural ideals of symmetry placed onto a Tudor-style building designed by a Victorian architect. With new construction, Victorian architects imitated and mixed older styles with modern home comforts for the rich. A motley mix."

Dad exclaims, "Talk about mixing things up! No wonder something was niggling me."

"Very true," replies Nana, "about things mixed up. And very understandable about the niggle." She laughs. "I get a niggle sometimes too, when I actually look at the place."

Both Mr. Brown and Nigel laugh and nod in agreement.

Papa looks toward Susanne and me to see if we are paying attention as he says to the group at large, "Eighteenth-century Georgian architecture prized balance and symmetry. They believed they were returning to perfect Greek ideals.

"As you know, the period is named after four kings named George, I through IV, all from the House of Hanover, who ruled from 1714 to 1830. The Georgian period includes William IV, who died in 1837.

Dad says, "I would not have remembered the dates. My hat goes off to you and your ability to remember those dates and details."

Susanne is already sitting rigidly as she always does when she is bored. By looking fixedly at Papa, she pretends to seem interested so that no one will ask her anything. My money says her mind is elsewhere, probably on some boys at school. Susanne likes boys!

I'm lying on the blanket in front of Dad, my head between his big feet. My tootsies are sticking up my full body length forward of his. I'm looking at the clouds where I see faces and mountains. I hear Papa's voice droning ever onward. I don't care if they know I'm bored.

Nodding to Dad, Papa says, "Thank you, Sam." He sighs as he sees me, but then he notices Susanne's fake interest. He is conned.

Papa's eyes glance over the others as he continues, "And you recall that the earlier Tudor period is named after the family dynasty that ruled from 1485 to 1603. Some would call this the Elizabethan period after its most famous monarch who lived from 1533 to 1603. The architecture from that time often had fancy brickwork below with stucco and half beam on the upper floors, often with gables, no symmetry required."

Dad says, "What an encyclopedia you are, Papa."

"Yes, indeed," echoes Nana. "Certainly, he has always been mine."

Mr. Brown adds, "Details don't escape His Lordship."

I wonder if the estate manager is always happy about that. Who knows?

Seeing my attention directed only to the clouds, Papa gives up educating me, at least for the moment. He looks at Susanne because she seems interested. *Silly Papa!*

Papa continues, "This house was built when Queen Victoria was queen of England. Nowadays, most of the nineteenth century gets labeled the Victorian period. Architecture and interior decoration from the time were known for mixing styles and adding to excess. The phrase 'too much is never enough' is frequently used regarding Victorian ideals of décor."

Papa pauses and then concentrates on Susanne again. "Also from the House of Hanover, Victoria reigned from 1837 to 1901. Susanne, did you know she was only eighteen when she became queen?" he asks.

Susanne's rigid shoulders relax slightly as her interest returns. She exclaims, "Wow, queen at eighteen! Not much fun after that." She giggles.

Nana says, "And probably not much fun before that either, while she was getting prepped for the role."

Susanne says, "No teenage fun."

Dad looks sharply at Susanne, but she doesn't notice, since he's a little behind her. Just as well, perhaps!

Back on the house track, Papa says, "Anyway, this Victorian house was built about 1870 on the site of a much older property owned by the family. That old house burned down around 1867 or thereabouts. But this property with some form of dwelling has been the family retreat from London for about four hundred years."

I am tracing cloud faces with my fingers. Papa appears amused as he looks at me. He probably figures I haven't heard a word. But I have been paying some attention after the topics left finances, taxes, and schooling.

Dad leans forward in his chair to look down at me. Our heads point in different directions. It's funny to see right up his nostrils into a lot of nose hair that needs a trim. Some of it has turned gray. Gross! I giggle.

With a curious tone in his voice, Dad asks, "What did you just learn about history and architecture, Jeremiah?" He sits back so I won't bang him in the face if I sit up. He waits. All eyes are in my direction.

I stop looking skyward and sit up. Looking at Papa and then twisting to look at Dad's nose, I reply, "Four kings, George I through IV, eighteenth century; add a William, ending early in the nineteenth century; all liked symmetrical architecture.

"This Georgian symmetry was placed on usually asymmetrical sixteenth-century Elizabethan or Tudor-style brick and stucco. The house was built in 1870, in the Victorian period. The house is a real combo platter. That's what confused Dad." With a thud, I plop back to my spot, satisfied.

Papa starts to laugh. I hear Nana giggle, which she suppresses quickly. Dad snorts as he tries not to laugh.

Phoebe says, "He may not pay attention, but it all goes in, almost like osmosis."

Nana says, "I noticed early on that Jeremiah has a rather unusual mind."

She hasn't figured out that I'm not very bright. I just have a really good memory!

"It's unusual, all right," mutters Susanne as she stands up quickly and starts to trot toward the stream.

She glances back and sees I've gotten up to chase her. She runs faster. I don't know why I want to chase her. Nothing will happen when I catch her. But the chase, making both of us run, is fun for me and for her. She is laughing hard when we both reach the side of the stream.

"Jeremiah, you are a kick." While she stares at the water, she says between giggles and rapid breaths, "A pain sometimes, but fun to be around."

I look back at the adults. Now that we two are out of earshot, my father leans over to Nana with his eyes directly on her, touches her arm, and talks. Nana glances toward the two of us, sees that we are far away, and then returns her attention to Dad. Phoebe appears very attentive. Papa looks unhappily straight ahead but, like Nana, is paying keen attention; and then, after listening, both Nana and Papa ask questions, or at least talk. Nigel and Mr. Brown both glance nervously toward Susanne and me. Nigel's eyes follow me; he appears either sad or worried. When he sees me look at him, his eyes flick back to Dad. When Dad talks, he says something that makes Nana nod yes and ask something else. Phoebe stands, glances toward us, turns to say something to the group, and afterward walks toward us. The two men and my grandparents look relieved after Dad says something else at the end. *What are they talking about so seriously? I'll ask Phoebe later.*

Phoebe joins us beside the stream. As we throw stones into the water, I say, "The water is moving a little too fast to allow stones to skip. Skipping stones requires still water. Otherwise, the stones just sink—but I love the clunk and splash."

"Look," says Susanne, pointing to a ripple in the water. "A fish just surfaced."

"That is fun to watch, especially when hometown is New York City! Carp in artificial pools just don't cut it," I declare.

Laughing a little as she listens, Phoebe says, "Both of you need more country time."

As we head back toward the picnic area, Susanne mutters under her breath, "I am bored with the talk."

I reply, "Me too. I don't understand the stuff about finances and taxes, so the talk about the house was actually a bit of relief. I could understand that bit."

Susanne says, "I will never understand taxes!"

Phoebe declares merrily, "I have cards. Life is good!" Back at the blanket, she brings out a pack of cards. We play an easy card game that is fun and fast moving but would be better with more people. After the first game finishes, the adults want to play. Soon, everyone is included with great silliness and laughter as the hands are dealt and played.

When we all leave for the house again, everyone is happy and tired. It is late afternoon, but the sun is still high in the sky.

After we are back at the house, Mr. Brown says good night and drives one car back to the garage. The other remains in the driveway.

In the house, Phoebe suggests a board game for Susanne and me. We play Amazing Labyrinth, one of several games Phoebe brought over to England with us.

Then we play Monopoly, a game that I particularly like. Susanne has a real winning streak, and soon I am nearly broke. Then Phoebe has a winning streak while I slowly gain back some winnings, and Susanne nearly goes broke.

Nigel appears with sandwiches for all, and with cold milk for Susanne and me. Phoebe has tea with her sandwiches. Dad, Papa, and Nana drink lemonade. After Nigel serves, he disappears.

Too soon, it is bedtime. Phoebe commands, "It's an early morning to see your grandparents off to London. No arguments from anyone."

Susanne and I say good night to everyone downstairs, with hugs and good-night kisses all 'round. Despite my excitement from the day's activities, I don't think I am sleepy. But I follow Phoebe upstairs and soon am safely tucked into bed. I feel Phoebe's good-night kiss on my forehead.

I quietly say, "Your good-night kiss is always special."

Phoebe appears surprised, smiles, and replies, "I love giving you a good-night kiss."

"Will you answer a question?" I ask.

"If I can." Phoebe laughs.

"Today, when Susanne and I ran to the stream, I looked back and saw the adults in a conversation that made them unhappy. What were all of you talking about?"

Startled, Phoebe looks at me and murmurs, "You don't miss much, do you, Jeremiah?"

"No," I honestly reply, "and I remember more stuff better than most people."

Her resigned voice says, "Yes, you do." She looks down and pats my blanket without any purpose before she quietly asks, "Do you remember when you had those doctor's appointments a few months ago? You had extensive testing, including psychological testing."

"Of course," I giggle, "I remember *everything* about that."

"What were you told?" she asks.

I reply sincerely, "The doctor said, 'Jeremiah, you have a pathologically good memory, but you don't understand people.' I asked what 'pathologically good' meant, and he answered, 'That means it's really good.' I looked up the word later. 'Pathological' can mean extreme in a way that is not normal. That's a neat way to describe my memory—it's too good to be normal. But I already knew all of that, especially about not understanding people. My meaning is that I can't read facial expressions very well." Then I add in a singsong voice, "And now I know about pathological."

Phoebe asks quietly, "What else happened between you and the doctor?"

I think for a minute before I say, "He asked, 'Do you feel emotions like sadness, happiness, fear?' and I replied that I do, the same as other people. And while answering other questions from the doctor, I also said that I usually like people, am concerned how other people feel, and never want to hurt anyone's feelings. When I told him all that, the doctor said, 'That's called empathy, which you certainly have,' and then he explained what empathy means. Afterwards, I told him I don't understand other people's emotions because I can't figure out what their facial expressions mean. Sometimes when I misunderstand, things get awkward."

"He gave you a diagnosis." Phoebe looks at me a little uncertainly and tentatively asks, "Do you recollect the diagnostic name he gave you?"

"Yes, Phoebe, I do recollect," is my quick answer before a pause. Once again, I gather up memories and put them in order. I recite, "He said I am slightly on the spectrum and have mild autism, which is more common in boys. He stated, 'About 2 percent of all boys and about 0.5 percent of all girls have some characteristics that could be considered on the spectrum of autism.' Then he carefully explained, 'Jeremiah, you must understand that this condition called autism creates your superb memory but also prevents you from understanding people's reactions and their facial expressions.' Afterward, he also said that my case was very mild, almost subthreshold autism."

"That's right." Then she asks, again very quietly, "Did he say anything else, Jeremiah?"

"He said that my mind processes more details more intently than others do, which might indicate a mild obsessive-compulsive disorder, but is more likely part of the autism," I reply.

"Anything else?" she probes.

I answer, "He mentioned a word that confused me because I thought he told me I had asparagus syndrome; and that made me afraid I'd become tall, skinny, and green." I see a smile cross Phoebe's solemn face as she clears her throat to cover up a chuckle. I continue, "But then he spelled it for me: Asperger's syndrome. That's the named part of the autism that makes me so awkward with people. If only I could easily figure out faces! But he did say my case was very mild, which he repeated several times, and then told me I'd be okay, especially as I grew older."

"You remembered all his points. Good job, Jeremiah." Then Phoebe briskly declares, "Well, your grandparents didn't know about the testing. Your father wanted to tell them when you and Susanne were not nearby. They became worried, and maybe a little upset, when they learned of your problem." In the ensuing silence, Phoebe anxiously waits for me say something.

Eventually, I pipe up proudly, "It's not really a problem because I can do things to work around what I don't understand. Since it's important to understand what another person is feeling, I pay attention to how people respond to other people, and memorize their facial movements. That's my problem solving to learn emotions, sort of like a normal person, I guess."

"You started that process long before the doctors saw you, didn't you?" asks Phoebe.

I answer, "Oh yeah. Not understanding people's feelings is confusing and makes my world difficult to understand. And I can't share what I don't know. It's also kind of scary, like being all alone. Even without understanding, for a long time now I've been memorizing people's actions along with the movements of their faces. I guess what they should be feeling and try to figure if I'm right, in order to share their emotions, and to create facial-expression pictures, all labeled in my head. The memory part of my brain has file after file, all in order. But sometimes I can't find the right memory file fast enough, and then I get lost again. That happens a lot, especially when people do new stuff."

Phoebe looks sad for a brief moment, gives me another kiss on my forehead, and says, "It will be easier as time goes by. You will see."

"Why did you look sad just now?" I ask in confusion.

"Well, mister, because you are not good at reading people, I realize how hard you labor trying to understand daily interactions among people, things that are automatic for the rest of us. The amount of work you must do inside your head just to be with other people makes me sad for you," she replies. "At times, you must feel overwhelmed."

I glance at Phoebe's solemn face and shrug my shoulders as my answer. After a silence, I ask her, "What's to say?"

She shakes her head slightly side to side and replies almost inaudibly, "Not much, I guess. It is what it is." Her shoulders shrug too, but her deep sigh startles me.

Her face remains a puzzle, so I ask, "Is your sigh a way of showing sadness?"

"Yes, dear one, it is, at least sometimes. That sigh certainly was," she answers.

I reply, "Okay. That helps." Moving on, I ask, "Why did Dad tell the grandparents right then?"

Phoebe looks directly at me as she says, "When Nana said, 'I noticed early on that Jeremiah has a rather unusual mind,' she opened up the topic. Your dad used the opportunity to give your grandparents the information they needed to know. Your parents talked before the trip. Your mom said, 'Let my parents know the test results. I'll talk to them after I arrive, after they've had time to digest the info.' And Nigel and Mr. Brown are almost family members. They needed to know as well."

Confused by a recollection, I ask, "Nigel looked at me as if he was worried about something. What was he worried about?"

Apparently surprised by my question, Phoebe answers with a quiet sigh, "*You*, Jeremiah, he was worried about *you*. He's known you all your life, and he's fond of you. He's concerned how this will affect you during your lifetime."

"Okay. Now I understand," I reply sheepishly. I look up and sideways toward Phoebe as I ask, "Is Susanne autistic too?"

"No, Jeremiah, she is completely normal in that regard," Phoebe replies.

"I thought so. Lucky her. Good night. I love you, Phoebe," I say, feeling sleepy.

"Good night, and I love you too," she replies. She stands and heads into Susanne's room.

I hear Phoebe tuck in Susanne and give her a good-night kiss as well. Our rooms are adjoining with a bathroom between. Phoebe leaves the connecting doors open.

Susanne mutters to herself as she settles into bed. I hear her breathing become slow. Susanne remains quiet as she falls asleep. In no time, I follow her into slumberland.

During the night, I waken to hear the wind whistling and the sounds made by the trees outside as their branches blow in the wind. I hear falling rain as it hits hard against the windows.

I want to explore this old house, and I'll get my wish in daylight. Will I find bodies buried in the basement, or forgotten treasure down secret passageways? Perhaps I'll find something else surprisingly gruesome or awesome. Maybe I'll find something that will make us all rich! What *will* tomorrow bring? I can't wait to find out.

I drift off to sleep again.

Later, I would remember the old saying "Careful what you wish for."

Chapter 9

THE ATTIC

During our early breakfast on Monday morning, the rain hits hard against the morning room windows. The sky's gray clouds hang low. The adults seem preoccupied on this drab day as Nana and Papa focus on preparations for their time away. Both are almost ready to take the train to London, where Nana will be until Friday. Papa returns Wednesday.

Nana is scheduled to work with her law firm. At the last minute, she rifles through files until she finds the ones she thought she had misplaced. She sighs with relief as she finds the errant pages and appears a little annoyed as she mutters, "Keep your head about you, silly girl. Misplaced is as good as lost!"

Last night, Papa said he booked several meetings with people related to the estate and later will attend a conference on animal husbandry.

When he said this, I asked, "What's husbandry?"

Papa replied, "Animal husbandry is the breeding and care of farm animals."

I answered, "That seems a good thing to learn about, Papa. After all, you *do* say that you're a farmer." Papa looked at me quizzically and then burst out laughing.

Dad looks at Papa and asks, "How are you getting to the station?"

"We are going to drive and leave the car in the car park that's not far from where we board our train," Papa replies. "Then there is a car waiting on our return."

Dad asks, "Do they charge you to park?"

Papa replies, "Oh yes, they certainly do! They just raised the rates. They went from 'ping' to 'ow.'"

With a laugh, Dad says, "I'm free this morning." He looks at his watch and mutters, "It's just before 7:30 a.m. now. Our time here is five hours later than New York. I need to be computer networking at 10:00 a.m. New York time. That's 3:00 p.m. here. There are a few hours of office work to prepare beforehand. Lots of time!"

He's quiet for a moment and then looks directly at the grandparents, one after the other. "May I drive you? And if you call me before you return, I'll be waiting at the station. You will save on parking charges."

Nana quips, "Administration accepts! That's a wonderful offer." She giggles and blows Dad a kiss.

Immediately pointing to his watch and looking toward his children, Dad says, "And I plan to stop work at 8:00 p.m., when it's dinnertime."

"Dinnertime here or in New York?" queries Susanne.

"Here, Miss Cheeky Funny Buster," replies Dad.

"Just checking," is her snarky reply. I nod and smile.

A few minutes later, Dad and my grandparents say their goodbyes to us in the morning room. After farewells, Phoebe stays at the table glumly looking out through the windows. Susanne and I follow the three adults into the hall.

Both grandparents carry a small satchel for clothes and necessities. Each has a briefcase containing a laptop. All three adults are wearing raincoats, and two are carrying an umbrella.

Nana says, "Where's my brolly?" as she searches in the umbrella stand. "Success," she says triumphantly, holding her umbrella up for all to see.

Dad says he will drive. Our grandparents walk quickly to the vehicle. Dad follows after them, but he heads toward the wrong side of the car. "Old habits die hard!" he mutters as he corrects himself.

I see Papa laughing as he reaches forward to pat Dad's shoulder when he is finally in the car. In the front passenger seat, Nana is laughing too. Someone is getting teased!

We slowly close the main door after the tires crunch on the drive and they leave the property. We return to the morning room where Phoebe is sitting, teacup in hand, looking out at the rain.

That leaves Phoebe with the two of us. We dawdle over the rest of breakfast and listen to the steady rain as it hits against the windows. Its patter makes for a sleepy sort of day.

Eventually, Phoebe's gaze returns to us as she says, "Despite the rain, I would like to go into the village to get some toiletries and to explore."

Susanne asks, "May I come along?"

"That would be lovely," replies Phoebe. "I shall enjoy the company."

I say, "I want to stay home." I look toward Phoebe as I ask, "Is that okay?"

Phoebe replies, "Well, Mrs. Stewart, the cook, is here; and so is your dad when he returns from dropping your grandparents. Mr. Brown will be out, but Nigel is on the premises. Even though you are reliable, you will be supervised." She seems satisfied.

A moment later, Nigel suddenly appears in the morning room and says, "Apologies, I thought everyone had finished."

"We have, Nigel, not to worry. And your timing is perfect." Phoebe continues, "Susanne and I would like to go to the village, despite the rain. Is there any possibility that you could drive us when the shops open?"

"Of course, no trouble at all," says Nigel with a smile.

"Thank you," replies Phoebe, brightening.

A few hours later, wearing raincoats and carrying umbrellas, Susanne and Phoebe are ready to go to the village.

Nigel says, "Now remember to call me with at least twenty minutes' notice when you want to return. Here is my cell number in case I'm out of the house." He hands Phoebe an index card with precise printing.

After they leave, I decide to greet Mrs. Stewart in the kitchen. She is a rather stout short middle-aged woman, with thin graying hair piled high on her head in a small bun, and very businesslike. Her glasses are frequently askew and always need cleaning. When anyone comes into her kitchen, she looks annoyed. She rarely speaks, but when she does, she's always loud. Busy preparing the evening meal, she gives me a glass of milk without many words, and then I am on my own.

Finishing off my milk, I decide to visit all the rooms beginning in the basement. Downstairs, below the kitchen, are the laundry, three bedrooms, two of which are used by staff members, and one other room with a locked door. Later, I discover that this is the mechanicals room housing electrical panels, furnace, water heaters, and the like. At the back of the house, there is also a window beside a locked door to the outside. I decide to enter the empty bedroom.

Despite being in the basement, the windows are large and well above ground level, allowing lots of light even on a gloomy day. The furniture is plain, functional, and in good condition. There are twin beds that look comfortable. Certainly, the armchair is very cozy when I sit down.

Nigel's room and Mr. Brown's are marked with a brass plate on each door. I respect their privacy and do not look inside.

Mrs. Stewart does not live-in. She and her husband have a house in the village. There is no door here with her name on a brass plate.

No chance of buried treasure here. No bodies either!

Up on the main floor, I look into the sitting room—or drawing room, as it is also called—the library, the dining room, the morning room used by Nana and Papa for breakfast and sometimes lunch when they are alone, and the main hall with its wonderful mellow paneling. Papa is right. The house really does have the shape of an H.

Papa keeps his compass in a table drawer in the hall. I saw him put it back, that's how I know. It's fun to check directions with a compass. He won't mind if I use it.

The compass tells me that the main, central hall runs in an east-west direction, as the middle crossbar of the H, with rooms on each side. The front of the house with its huge circular gravel drive does indeed face almost directly south, just as Papa said.

The sitting room is on the west side, and the dining room is on the east. Both rooms project forward toward the drive. This allows windows on three sides in the sitting room and dining room.

The library is behind the sitting room. The morning room is behind the dining room, with windows to the east in order to catch the morning sun. As he eats breakfast, Papa sometimes says, "What lovely sunshine in the well-named morning room." The kitchen behind, with its sitting area, looks out to the back.

Mrs. Stewart ignores me as I nip into the kitchen and through an archway into a large area off the kitchen where the family can gather after a meal and not use the fancy drawing room. There is a closet door to the left, just past the archway. Windows are on three sides, as well as a door leading outside. As I look out through the windows, I see the basement outside entrance is very near. It has a little roof to shelter its stairs against the rain.

Besides armchairs, there is a work desk with a computer on top near one wall, and a long table behind a well-worn sofa. That table is loaded with farm catalogs and binders filled with documents related to the farm. I guess this is actually Papa's real work area, and Mr. Brown's.

Acting like a nosey parker while Mrs. Stewart is occupied, I open the closet door and find it is actually the door to the back stairs. I recollect that Nana sometimes says, "Having a second stair saves wear and tear on the main staircase and is also protection in case of fire."

I glance over to Mrs. Stewart, who is doing something brutal to innocent eggs. Without any danger of being overheard, I mutter, "So *these* are the back stairs that Nana says Nigel uses to appear quietly upstairs when he's needed. I've never seen them before." Two steps up, I close the door behind me, probably just like Nigel does, and ascend these narrow steps in their enclosed tunnel.

Upstairs, I see Nana and Papa's large room with a fireplace, sitting area, and bathroom. I see Dad's room, with its fireplace and work desk. Phoebe's room is also big and comfortable. Like Dad's, Phoebe's room has its own bathroom. Her room is next to Susanne's. My room and Susanne's room share a bathroom. There is also an unoccupied bedroom with a bathroom, just in case there are more guests.

Not far from the main staircase, I notice a door. It opens to a stairwell going to the attic. This is new territory, so I decide to explore.

I didn't have any idea at the time, but this decision was the beginning of trouble big!

The stair to the attic is wide enough to accommodate guests. The stairs are not steep, like basement and attic stairs usually are. There is a landing with a window partway up. This landing allows the stairs to completely reverse direction. Walls box in the stair with a door at the top that opens into the attic.

I look at this arrangement and mutter, "Papa once said these walls prevent heating the attic in winter. An open stair would be a real problem." Smart Papa! I twist the knob on the right side of the attic door, hear it unlatch, and swing the door partway open into a room.

This attic is very different from any attic I have ever seen—not that I have seen many. There are high plaster walls going up to meet big squared-off wooden logs, spaced regularly, that cross the ceiling and meet at an angle in the middle.

Gazing upward, I mutter, "I guess those logs hold up the roof. The rough wood on top of the logs must be the underside of the roof."

Later, Papa and Dad would tell me that the long wooden logs are called trusses or rafters. But these are so old and thick that they do indeed look like squared-off log beams.

This part of the attic is one enormous space. Dotting the walls are burned-down candles in glass jars. Later I learned that these are hurricane lamps held in place by sconces. Who knew?

Papa said that the front of the house faces almost directly south. I look through a window onto the drive below. I figure the directions—this long room runs east-west. The windows opposite must face north. I don't need the compass this time, but I use it anyway and then slide it back into my pocket.

My guess is that this room is the same size as the main hall two floors below. There is a big door at each end. A row of windows runs along each side of this big room. Papa recently said that the builders liked balance—he called it symmetry. That's clear here.

On the north side, two windows are evenly placed on each side of the boxed-in stairway door that sticks into the room. On the south side, which faces the gravel drive below, a window takes the place of the door opposite. This window has more space around it so that north- and south-facing windows are exactly balanced. The windows go elegantly almost to the floor. Later I would learn that dances were held in the attic years ago.

I look at the large wooden doors with inset panels and tarnished brass handles and locks at each end of this huge attic room. Each door looks the same, except one is toward the east end of the house and one to the west.

I open the one to the east and step inside. This room runs from the front to the back of the house. It probably has the same width as the dining room far below. It is full of old furniture and old boxes tied with string. Some are labeled—textbooks, schoolbooks, baby clothes, letters, and legal papers. The boxes have remained undisturbed for a long time, leaving the air musty. There are windows symmetrically balanced on each side of the room, but they are shorter and designed for function, not for elegance. And they are dirty.

Not much here that's any use to me. Later I would learn that thought was very wrong!

Closing the door behind me, I decide to check the far western door, the one exactly like its eastern mate. Behind it is another room, a mirror image of the one I just left. Also running from the front to the back of the house, it seems to be about the full width of the drawing room far below.

Papa is right! The H shape on the main floor goes all the way from the basement to the attic. These two rooms create the sides of the H. All the rooms are enormous, but these two are very long!

There are windows balanced on each side of both of these long rooms. I hear Papa's voice from yesterday saying that this is a Georgian architectural ideal of symmetry placed onto a Tudor-style building designed by a Victorian architect. Similar to Dad yesterday, I exclaim, "Mixing things up, indeed!"

There is less junk here. For some reason, the room is cleaner, with less dust. While there is some discarded furniture, its more neatly arranged. Boxes are stacked with more care.

Nothing useful or fun here either.

Glancing out through these clean windows at the rain, I can peer through symmetrically placed windows in the room I just left on the other side of the house, past the dirty windows, and to the great outdoors on the other side of the building. *Window symmetry in action! Whatever!*

Any discoveries I expected to find with the house search have resulted in zilch. During my disappointing search, I have discovered nothing awesome, no bodies, no treasure, nothing to make us all rich. It's just an old house with junk in the attic!

Bored, I watch raindrops joining together on the windowpanes to form rivulets of water trickling down. Somewhat disappointed and disgruntled, I turn my head to inspect this room closely and ask out loud, "What's in here anyway?"

Near the door is a large trunk with a brass nameplate. But in contrast to the dull door brass, the nameplate brass is shiny and clean. Likewise, a key in the lock looks freshly polished. Its glimmer grabs my attention. I walk over to read the nameplate.

Mortimer Wadsworth, Earl
Poppycock, 1688–1750
Leila (née Smith) Wadsworth,
Countess Poppycock, 1690–1752
Both in residence

This is really odd. I saw the same names on a plaque in the church yesterday. Now, I know Papa is actually named John Wadsworth. I have heard the name of the title before and just giggled. Nana and I discussed it yesterday—the deal breaker of a name!

When Papa's father died, Papa inherited the title and became the Earl Poppycock and Nana became the Countess Poppycock. But Papa almost never uses the title's name. It's a name everyone ignores.

When I first heard the title used for Papa, I confused it with a man's given first name. Earl can be a man's first name, at least in America.

But now I see it written in brass, no less. I completely understand why Papa rarely uses the name—Poppycock. Once, I even heard Papa call it an unfortunate name! I think it's a silly name!

I glance again at the trunk as I mutter, "I wonder what's inside." I put my hand on the key and start to turn the lock.

"Don't be intrusive!" The voice is female, lightly pitched, and very articulate, with a bell-like quality that is easily understood.

I stop dead in my tracks. I look around. I see no one.

"Who's there?" I ask.

There is no reply.

I wrap my fingers about the key and start to turn the lock again.

More sharply, the female voice states, "I said, 'Don't be intrusive.'"

I release the key like a hot potato. "Who said that?" I demand.

"I did," replies the female voice.

The voice seems to echo around me. I turn again but see no one. I hear the rain outside that spatters against the windows. But I am alone.

"Who are you, and where are you?" I ask tremulously.

"I am Leila Wadsworth, Countess Poppycock. Earl Mortimer Poppycock is my husband—Lord Poppycock as he was known." The voice stops.

I declare, "Someone is playing a trick on me. Leila Wadsworth has a plaque in the church in the village. I saw it yesterday, after church. The plaque has the same dates as the brass inscription on this chest. And she was married to Mortimer Wadsworth, so it's the same person. She died in 1752."

"That's right, dear boy," comes her reply with a sigh.

"Then she's not talking to me now," I retort.

"Yes, I am," she responds cheerily.

I state firmly, "No, you are not. You can't talk to me. You have been dead for a few hundred years." I do the math. "Two hundred and sixty-five years, to be precise."

She responds equally firmly, "Well, I agree, death is a bit of an obstacle to conversation! But I am talking to you. I shall prove who I am. But before I prove anything, who are you?"

What to do? This is too weird! I think for a bit, swallow hard, and answer, "My name is Jeremiah Morris. My mom is the daughter of John Wadsworth. Papa, my grandfather, is the Earl Poppycock."

It is the first time I have ever said Papa's title. It sounds very silly!

"Very well. I will prove that I am the person I say I am," declares the voice.

I am afraid to ask, but I screw up my courage and blurt out, "How will you prove it to me?"

"Promise not to run away?" she asks.

"From what?" I ask in return.

"From me," she says.

Now, I *am* scared! I ask, "Why would I run? Are you awful to look at? Are you going to hurt me?"

She replies, "Hurt you? Oh, child, I am your nine-greats-grandmother—great said nine times. I would never hurt you. I am hoping, we all are hoping, that you can help me…err, us.

"I am about to appear if you promise not to run away. You see, I reside in this trunk, but I seep out to investigate the world and to keep up. I have a lengthy seep about once a week. It takes energy to seep out, and the more I materialize, the more fatigued I become." After a pause, she mentions, "It is hard work being visible, so if you don't mind, I shall only give you an outline!"

Poor me! By this point, I am so confused I might agree to almost anything. I hear my wobbly voice reply, "Okay." My eyes become bigger and bigger as I watch.

It starts slowly. A slight vapor rises from the trunk. Then I hear little pops and crackles as the seams in the wood let out vapor. The vapor begins to take shape until the see-through image of a fully dressed lady appears, standing a few inches above the top of the chest, suspended on…nothing!

She has the deep-blue eyes of Papa, with long lashes, a very agreeable face, and a wiry frame. She is tall, and with her oddly curved heels on her old-fashioned shoes, she looms even taller. The fact that she is floating above the trunk adds to my confusion about her height.

As I look at her, I suddenly realize I'm shaking. This is too scary! What is she? Is she dangerous? Can I believe her when she said she would never hurt me? I would run away, but my knees are frozen in place. At least they haven't buckled!

Much later, when I was calmer, I figured out her dress is from the first third of the eighteenth century with its layers of fabric and a snug upper half, which is called a bodice. The fabric is slightly shiny, light blue with beautiful dark-blue embroidery on the top half and on the sleeves, which end in delicate lace just past the elbows.

Her hair is piled high on her head, artificially high, I think. I can see right through her, clothing and all—not to her insides, but just through her image! I remember a word that Dad used and explained recently. And Mom pulled out tracing paper to demonstrate the word's meaning. Like tracing paper, she is translucent.

I rub my closed eyes with my hands. I open my eyes again. She is still there!

Confused, I ask, "I'm not dreaming?"

Leila answers, "No, dear. I'm your nine-greats-grandmother. I reside in my trunk with my husband, Lord Poppycock. He was here for two years before I died and joined him."

I glance down at the brass plaque and see again that Mortimer Wadsworth died in 1750 and Leila in 1752. And that's what I remember from the church plaque yesterday.

I am way past confused! I bleat, "But when someone dies, don't they go to heaven or to hell?"

"Usually, but not always," she replies.

"Not always? What makes the difference? I mean, why?" I ask, baffled.

Leila answers, "Our son Edgar was accused of murdering someone. It is a terrible thing to hurt and kill someone. It takes a certain type of personality, if you ask me. Edgar is not that personality. He is far too mild and very sincere. He couldn't hurt a fly. But he was hanged, very unfair. Left a wife and daughter, very unfair, very wrong. As a consequence, we all agreed to stay."

"To stay?" I ask.

"To stay," she repeats.

"As what?" I ask.

"In residence," she replies.

"In residence where?" I ask.

"In our trunk," she states emphatically, looking at me as if I am stupid. My thoughts flash to my mom who would say "thick in the head" when she means stupid.

"In your trunk?" I ask incredulously.

"Well, yes, dear boy. And I don't think you are thick in the head. But didn't you read the brass plaque?"

Surprised by her words, I look again at the brass plaque on the trunk. The bottom line does read, "Both in residence." I shake my head in disbelief, hoping to clear away what must be hallucinations.

"Do you see what we are doing?" she inquires.

"What are you doing?" I ask.

"We are waiting…," she replies.

"Waiting for what?" I ask.

"Resolution." She nods her head in satisfaction with this answer, as if she has actually explained something!

"What do you mean?" I demand in confusion.

Leila responds, "We are waiting for someone to solve the murder and apprehend the guilty. Once that is done, we can all go to our final destination." She seems even more satisfied with this explanation. She smiles and nods happily.

Bewildered, I ask, "How can you solve a murder mystery a few hundred years old?"

She looks at me very keenly and articulates clearly, "Through memory travel, learning the facts, and communication with others of the era, channeling their spirits, as it were."

I'm lost! I don't know what I am talking to, but whatever she is, she is crazy!

"I don't understand you," I say.

She begins, "Well, sorry you are lost. Let me explain. It is not that crazy. When my husband died, he refused heaven. He wanted to stay with our son." She pauses, seeing confusion all over my face.

"Saint Peter couldn't accept Edgar into heaven after his hanging in 1745 until the legal charges were modified or dropped. Saint Peter said it was such a miscarriage of justice that fixing it should not be much to do.

"He had no intention of punishing Edgar in the other place. At Saint Peter's suggestion, Edgar stayed in a trunk, here, in the attic." She stops talking. Her eyes flit side to side as if she has been caught in a lie, and then she starts up again, "Well, actually, it was a different attic, but we moved. We had to. After all, the house was sold. And we who joined him have all eternity to find the truth and modify the charges against him." Her eyes are back to normal. Apparently, she has told the truth.

"You had to move?" I ask incredulously.

"Yes, dear boy. When the London house was sold, Saint Peter suggested we take up residence here to stay with the family," she replies, nodding her head happily again. Her huge hairdo waves dangerously as her head sways.

"And you have all eternity to sort this out?" I query.

She smiles and responds, "Yes, dear boy, no time pressure."

I don't understand most of this. My poor head starts to hurt.

Leila continues, "Saint Peter, bless his soul, was having his own problems at the time. He said it would be a big help if we could solve this one, instead of requiring his intervention. Seemed a reasonable thing to request, so Mortimer agreed, as had Edgar five years beforehand.

"But really, Saint Peter could have fixed it quick as a wink! I think he wanted Edgar to show spirit and prove he was innocent. That's what I think!" She looks at me, expecting me to agree. I just stare wide-eyed. Leila adds, "When I died, I agreed with my husband, Lord Mortimer Poppycock, and took up residence with him in the trunk. We sleep a lot, preparing for visitors, looking for the one."

"The one what?" I ask.

"The one who will solve the murder mystery," she answers impatiently but sweetly.

"Oh." I cannot think of anything more in reply. I don't know what's happening. I cannot believe my eyes and ears. *Is there a name for being this far past confused, something like super-duper confused?* Finally, I ask, "Have you never been able to get someone to help? After all, you died in 1752! That was a while ago."

Leila replies, "Let me help clear up your confusion. In fact, we have talked to several descendants from time to time and relatives who were not direct descendants. It has been hit or miss for anyone to come up here.

"Attics are usually very dirty, so no one wants to come up—even though I do my best to keep the dust cleaned away." She looks around, not entirely pleased. She adds, "Some just ran downstairs. Some tried but failed. I know the last person who tried regretted his failure. That was so sad. That's why he never came back for a visit. Some refused to try to help. That became embarrassing later."

"Why?" I inquire mechanically, completely overwhelmed.

"When they died, they were given the option of staying to assist or going to their destination forthwith. And most decided to stay and help, now that they were dead anyway. But they were not a lot of help by then, being dead and all."

In a stunned voice, I ask fearfully, "You mean you and Mortimer and Edgar are not the only ones here? If there are more people, doesn't that make your trunk a little crowded?"

Leila replies happily, "No on both counts, dearest child. We are not the only ones here, and ours is not the only trunk."

What's next? I see only their trunk, and I think I have explored everywhere.

Leila continues, "Now, you must meet your nine-greats-grand-father. Mortimer, dear, wake up."

There is no reply.

"Mortimer, dear Mortimer, wake up!" Her voice is louder. She stomps on the trunk. Nothing happens.

This time, her yell rattles the windows. "Mortimer, wake up! Come out for a wee seep!" I turn my head toward the door, half expecting Mrs. Stewart to fly up from the kitchen because she actually heard something.

"Wow, that was loud!" I exclaim as I glance back at Leila and touch my poor ears.

"Not to worry, dear boy. Only you can hear us." She looks at me with a sidelong glance. "Mrs. Stewart, Nigel, and your father are present downstairs; but they cannot hear us. Remember, we are heard by invitation only, just like we are seen by invitation only."

How does she know I am worried about Mrs. Stewart, Nigel, or Dad overhearing? For that matter, how does she know who is in the house?

"Humpff. Rumpff. Yawn. Umpff." Beside Leila, vapor starts to appear, very slowly. Cracks and pops occur, but more slowly and weaker sounding.

A groggy man in early-eighteenth-century garb appears, his white wig slightly askew. Like his wife, he is translucent, almost transparent in spots. He has large blue eyes with heavy, thick eyebrows and a round face. Over his potbelly, bits of dinner appear to be glued to his waistcoat.

His pants are called breeches, which end just below the knee. His muscular legs are in skintight dark silk hose. Is he about the same height as his wife, or shorter? I can't tell.

"What has happened, my dear?" he asks.

She replies, "You must meet someone…our nine-greats-grandson."

Leila's hands separate in a sweeping gesture to display me to Mortimer. That gesture reminds me of a game show hostess. Does she also watch TV? I have an image in my head, a really odd image.

Suddenly, Mortimer's features become sharp; his eyes fix brightly on me. "You don't say! Is he the one?" His whole frame perks up, and he stands taller. Even then, he is not as tall as his spouse.

Question answered!

"I don't know yet. At least talk to the lad," she replies.

"Well, good day to you, my lad. We have not had a visitor since your grandfather John Wadsworth was here and tried so hard but… but…failed. Welcome!"

He swooshes down beside me and extends a translucent hand and grasps mine. I feel my arm moving up and down as he shakes my hand. It seems unreal since the body is translucent, but the right hand holding mine now feels like living flesh and blood and looks solid!

"Careful, dear. You will exhaust yourself on the handshake," says Leila as she arrives beside him with a quiet swoosh.

"Quite so, Leila." He releases my hand. His arm and hand become totally translucent again.

In my confusion, I almost missed what Mortimer said. When they stop babbling, I ask, "You mean my grandfather, my papa, came up here and met you?"

"Yes," replies Mortimer. "But he was just a young lad, in his teen years. He has never returned here. I suspect that his failure upset him too much. He's not the sort to accept defeat or have reminders of past failure. We were left behind and forgotten." Mortimer sighs deeply and looks down. He looks sad.

His sadness that Papa never came back for a visit surprises me. Did he want Papa's company from time to time? Or does he think that Papa doesn't lose well and is disappointed that Papa showed it by staying away from them?

Either way, I am dumbfounded.

But any chance to sort this out in my head is smashed as my thoughts are interrupted when they immediately ask me rapid-fire questions—my age (ten), about academic schoolwork (good marks), reading skills (very good). I feel as if I am undergoing a job interview at Dad's firm or maybe Mom's. Take your pick.

Mortimer says quietly, "I think he just might be able to do it."

"I agree," replies Leila.

Mortimer affirms, "He must meet Edgar."

"An absolute necessity," responds Leila.

I am overwhelmed. Before I can say a peep, my hosts ascend to the top of their trunk. Another trunk appears out of nowhere with a rumble and a pop. It also has a shiny brass plate above the lock.

Edgar John Wadsworth, 1715–
1745, Hanged for Murder
Jemima (née Downs) Wadsworth, 1719–1760
Both in residence

I point at the shiny brass plate and ask, "What does 'née' mean?" I've already heard about the "hanged" bit.

Leila answers, "It means 'born,' as in the name you are born with or maiden name."

I look at the plaque again. My heart sinks. What is going to happen next?

That question is soon answered. On the first call, Edgar responds quickly but timidly to his mother's summons. Perhaps he was already listening?

What am I thinking? How can the dead be listening? I must be having a nightmare!

Edgar has only a little vapor show before white wig, eyes, ears, and upper face pop through his trunk. Then he stops…just below his nose. Over and over, he looks side to side with big eyes wide open. He glances up toward Leila standing beside Mortimer before he seeps out a little more. He seems afraid of me as he eyes me suspiciously.

His entrance makes him look like a cartoon.

Leila coughs loudly, which interrupts my thoughts.

But after his head and neck appear, he refuses to show more. I can see that his neck is at an odd angle. Of course, he died by hanging, which broke his neck. No wonder it is twisted and tilted to the side! Some dark natural hair peeps out from under his wig. His chin is pointed, and his teeth are very crooked, in need of a good orthodontist like the one Susanne visits.

Overall, he looks weak, harmless, and useless. Later, I would learn how wrong my guesses were. Again with the assumptions!

Edgar's large dark-blue eyes are fearful and timid. "Yes, Mother?" he says with trepidation. He looks like a man afraid of being hanged again.

"Come out all the way. Seep out all the way!" demands Leila. Fixing me with her eyes, she says, "The only nightmare is getting Edgar to seep out."

That's odd. She used the word "nightmare," and I think I am having one. What's going on?

Mortimer says, "Please, son. Come along."

"I don't like to seep out. It is so tiring," whines Edgar's timid head.

"Effort, Edgar. Show some effort," commands Leila emphatically. "Even if you are sad and tired, come out, and I mean now!" She smiles at me and opens her mouth as if she wants to say something else, but she doesn't. Instead, her eyes focus on Edgar.

Slowly, and with a long-winded whine, Edgar seeps out. Like his parents, he floats a little above his trunk. He slouches, which is very obvious because his frame is so tall and thin, with very long legs poking like sticks out of his past-the-knee breeches. His hose clings to his lower legs in places; but his legs are so thin and gangly, unlike his father's, that the silk hose hangs in folds. His shirt is loose at the collar and looks far too large for him. Over his shirt he wears a vest. The large empty pockets on each side have been well used, and stretched out. Like the shirt, the vest looks several sizes too big.

Suddenly, there is a pop and swoosh! A woman of Edgar's vintage appears beside him. From the name on the brass plate, I guess she must be Jemima.

She is not wearing a wig. Her brown hair is thick and lustrous, piled high with stickpins commanding obedience. Her beautiful brilliantly green eyes peer eerily at me from her sad, finely sculpted long face. In happier times, she might have looked attractive, even beautiful, but sadness has made her face tired and lined. She seems very suspicious of strangers, maybe afraid of more hurts.

"And what do you want with my husband?" tersely demands Jemima.

"I… I don't want anything with him," I say, trying to be polite while I stare locked in an upward gaze. She scares me, which makes my head shake a little as I answer with a faltering voice.

She turns to her mother-in-law and demands, "What is this about, Leila? You know how materializing affects Edgar."

"Yes, dear. I know so well." Leila sighs heavily. Her chest and shoulders heave with her sigh as she replies.

"Well?" again demands Jemima.

Leila collects her thoughts for a moment and answers, "It's hard to say what may happen. But Jeremiah is my nine-greats-grandson and your eight-greats-grandnephew. He seems a bright lad, aged ten. We are hoping he may be the one."

"The one?" asks Jemima. Her green eyes open wide. Somehow, their color seems even more intensely green.

"Yes, the one," says Mortimer with Leila.

"Well, that would be wonderful." Jemima pauses to look more kindly upon me with her beautiful eyes.

Edgar blinks. His big eyes open even wider. "His grandfather tried so hard, but he failed." Edgar looks directly at me as he speaks slowly and sadly. His lips twist as he snarls from the side of his mouth, "How can this one do any better?"

"So Papa not only met you, but he also tried to solve the mystery?" I ask.

"Yes, dear, that's right," says Leila emphatically.

My mind asks, *Can anyone go from dumbfounded to even more dumbfounded? Am I super-duper dumbfounded?*

Leila continues, "He tried so hard but didn't succeed, and he felt ever so bad. He has never returned to the attic, even for a visit. He was heartbroken that he had not succeeded. I do know he has thought about the situation many times over the years."

"How do you know that?" I ask fearfully.

Leila looks at me from the corner of her eyes. She lowers her fluttering lashes and states, "Well, just so you understand, let me tell you. I seep out at least once a week. As an energetic person, I can stay out longer than most before I am too tired and must return." Leila pauses to judge if I have followed her words. She adds, "I check up on things—and people. I travel. I look. I listen. I learn."

"And you eavesdrop?" I ask.

Leila blushes. "Yes, I do," she says indignantly. Then she adds emphatically, "And you might as well know, when I am in the mood, I can read minds as well. It's a good way to catch out liars!"

"Good heavens!" I exclaim. It is my turn to blush. My thoughts called her crazy, among other things, and said that this meeting was a nightmare; and she knows! Oh dear!

Inside my brain, my thoughts question, *Was this what she was about to tell me when Edgar was seeping out?*

"Yes, dear boy, it was; but I got distracted by Edgar," she says all smiles. "I can do only so much at one time. And I'm sure you were right in feeling dumbfounded."

She is reading my head like a book, or maybe newspaper head-lines. Oops!

"Now, what do you think, Jeremiah?" she asks, with an odd expression on her face. "Can you tell me, or should I read the newspaper?"

I do not know what to think! But I do have a question. Actually, I have several.

I am about to speak when Leila says, "You have several questions, do you?"

I blush scarlet. She has just read my thoughts again! I am horri-fied by this, and she frightens me. I want out of here to never return, but my curiosity pushes me on. What's to lose?

To reinforce the lesson I have just learned, Leila says, "Yes, Jeremiah, do press on! You won't lose anything by trying. And there is nothing to fear." She smiles sweetly. Suddenly, I feel like she is testing me.

I hear my wobbly, faltering voice say, "How did the family get the title Poppycock? Isn't poppycock a slang word for stuff and nonsense?"

Leila glares at me, clearly offended, then calms her eyes. She answers primly, "It's a very fine name. I, for one, am very proud of it."

"But what of its meaning?" I persistent.

Leila stares directly at me. Her expression appears annoyed as she begins to answer. I remember her answer, partly because I heard the same answer a few times afterward and even looked it up for myself much later.

Somewhat flatly, Leila recites, "Poppycock, the definition: in the slang use, the word comes from the Dutch words for 'soft dung.' *Pap* means 'soft,' and *kak* means 'dung.' However, that is a mid-nine-teenth-century coinage of the term, not unlike the current American slang involving a bull.

"We had the name years before that. It was given to us by the king of England for services to His Majesty long before that horrible slang degradation."

Despite listening intently, there is something I do not under-stand. I ask, "You died in 1752. Is that correct?"

"Yes, my dear. That is when your nine-greats-grandmother died." Leila wipes away a crocodile tear as she answers.

I ask, "Then how did you know that the slang meaning of poppycock came about in the mid-nineteenth century? You were a hundred years dead by then."

Leila sounds frustrated as she answers, "Well, I have told you before, I *do* seep out."

"And?" I ask.

She continues, "Well, when I seep out, I travel to places, I see things, and I listen. I learn."

Leila pauses for a few moments. What can she possibly say next? My head is spinning already.

Then she continues, slowly and emphatically, "Just because I am dead does not mean I should be poorly informed!" With dignity, she stamps her left foot once.

I think and think. My brain is blank. I am speechless with a mouth that is hanging open.

She smiles at me and asks, "Do you have another question?"

I realize I am out of my depth and that if I tell anyone except Papa what I have seen so far, I'll be labeled as a nutty fruitcake. Considering past history, any attempt of mine to help will end in failure. Goodness, even Papa failed! And knowing him, I suspect it does indeed still bother him. That's why he never came back to visit them again, even though he lives downstairs! But curiosity gets the better of me.

Apparently, I wasn't thinking what curiosity did to the cat. Killed it, or so they say.

"What's next?" asks my wobbly voice. Did I really ask that? And why?

Am I the one who is nuts?

"No, dear boy, you are not nuts," comes a soft feminine reply, "and cats have nine lives."

Chapter 10

JEREMIAH MEETS THE REST OF THE GANG

When I ask, "What's next?" my great-grandmother Leila suddenly smiles brightly in my direction after she answers my thoughts. Great-Grandfather Mortimer asks Leila to repeat some of what was said. After hearing, he smiles broadly as well.

"Spot on! Spot on! Good boy. That's a good fellow. Now he must meet the rest," declares Mortimer.

"The rest of what?" I ask in a flat wobble.

"The rest of us," he replies.

"There are more?" I ask in total surprise.

"Of course, dear boy. We are all here," answers Great-Grandmother Leila.

My head starts spinning again. What have I started?

"Come with me, dear." Leila floats down beside me and grasps my hand. But her hand is no longer translucent. It looks like a normal hand, has a strong grip, and feels noticeably warm. All of this surprises me. Her eyes are brimming with excitement.

Mortimer trundles translucently behind her. I suspect he trundled happily behind her most of his earthly life as well.

Edgar and Jemima look at each other.

"I don't want to go out," whines Edgar.

"Suit yourself," says Jemima with a shoulder shrug. Her green eyes flash. Her forceful swoosh as she descends from her trunk tells me she is annoyed. I crank my head around to watch Jemima as she sashays beside Mortimer. I don't know why, but I really like that sway of her hips as she maneuvers past one of the trunks and walks along. Sigh! *Let me watch her forever.*

Leila starts talking almost to herself. I'm still thinking of Jemima and watching her hips, so it takes a moment before I turn my head back and realize the words are intended for me.

I finally hear Leila say, "Concentrate, dear boy," as she pokes my ribs hard with bony fingers.

That got my attention away from Jemima's swaying hips!

"I'm concentrating," I mutter as I rub my sore ribs.

Leila continues babbling, "Now, until you considered helping, you could not see the others. I allowed you to see our trunk only because I was full of hope that you would help. When I saw you arrive, I thought you were a likely one to assist."

I stop still. Our procession stops.

I ask, "You saw me arrive with the family?"

"My dear child, I did indeed," she replies.

Confused and afraid, I demand, "How?"

She continues, "I told you. I have always been high-spirited. I am an energetic sort of person. I seep out. I look. I listen. I learn things. And I sleep soundly so I am always refreshed, ready for the next day's activities among the living and the dead."

I touch my head so it doesn't go kaboom! I will never know when she is peering over my shoulder, knowing everything I do, and my every thought. Talk about living in a fishbowl! Where's the privacy?

Leila flashes a brief smile at me as I follow along beside her. She whispers, "Rest assured, I'm always discreet."

My brain says, *But I was thinking about privacy.* My mouth says nothing.

Leila murmurs, "Remember, discretion is a good second best if privacy is breeched. Be happy with that."

I'm none too happy with her way of thinking.

Leila mutters, "Pity!" Once again, she smiles too sweetly. Suddenly, she stops near the doorway to the large empty central attic room and says, "There is something I must tell you now, before we meet the others."

I nod in agreement. I say nothing about my feelings. I can't take in more information.

"Yes, I do know it is all a little overwhelming," she commiserates with a smile. She waits, maybe a tad impatiently.

I ask, "Do you always read thoughts? I mean…do you ever take a break?" My face blushes again!

Leila answers, "Well, I usually read whatever is available, unless I get distracted. As I said before, it is a gift. I had the power in life as well. Perceptive, they called me." She nods happily and wags her head a little side to side, which makes her hairdo wave like a toy boat in a bathtub. *Watch the hair!*

Leila closes the door and blocks access as she stands before me, her arms crossed. She says, "All here have known each other for a very long time. The ones who died later had little knowledge of those who lived before. But once up here, we have all talked together, exchanging our life stories. Almost everyone knows most everything.

"I was not born high and mighty like some here were. Mortimer was unusual for his day and liked someone or not, not by their title, but by their merit as a person. That was uncommon for our era.

"I had a good mother and father, but they were not rich. I was a commoner, as we were called then—no money, no title. My mother worked hard. She kept boarders, people who pay for a bed, food, and shelter in a private house. Their presence taught me how to talk to strangers and to get along with others."

I think to myself, *Leila probably could talk freely to strangers, even if she had been brought up as sheltered as the Queen of England!*

She looks at me and sighs deeply. She remarks, "That's a sweet thought, dear boy, but some here don't take kindly to spending part of eternity in a trunk next to a commoner. Some can be unkind. It's hurtful, but it's just their nature."

Imagine my surprise when I hear this. Leila says what she thinks, and she forgives people. Wow!

"Do you understand you may hear nasty things?" Leila looks at me, waiting for an answer.

"Yes, Honorable Grandmother Ninth Great."

Leila giggles. "You sound like a Chinese fortune cookie."

I am about to ask a question. Then I remember—she seeps out to travel, to look, to listen, and to learn. I ask a different question. "Do you travel to the United States?" I ask quietly while fearing her answer.

"Oh yes, dear boy. I learn so much from the colonies. And seeping out here is much the same as seeping out there."

I am not sure if I should be happy or sad. It means she can snoop on me anytime and know my thoughts—and see whatever I am doing, anywhere in the world. She is the ultimate snoop, even if she is discreet!

"Anything else, dear boy?" she quietly asks, almost smiling.

I answer, "Yes. If you were poor and Mortimer was about to be an earl, how did you become his wife? How did you meet?"

Leila seems to take delight in the question. She answers, eyelashes fluttering, "Well, my dear, it was almost as if it was meant to be!" She pauses briefly to gather her thoughts before continuing, "He was visiting a cousin of his in our village. Mortimer was a dashing young man, handsome but quiet, a bit shy. I had heard of him—all the young ladies had!" She stops to giggle.

"His family always attended Sunday services. I was ahead of him as we were leaving church," she says. "Somehow, I twisted my ankle just in front of him. He stopped me from falling, caught me close to him, and was very attentive to my injury. I was not yet nineteen and rather pretty, with a pleasant manner and good ankles."

She pauses long enough to catch her breath. She continues, "I love conversation! We had a lengthy talk, and soon, he started calling on me." She pauses and looks fondly at Mortimer.

"He was handsome, pleasant, and a good companion. In my time, a girl needed a good husband. As they say in America, he was willing to provide 'three hots and a cot,' and with the prospects of a title! He was a very good catch." She laughs.

Leila continues, "I was willing, and we fell in love. Soon, we were wed, despite his father's objections. But in no time, the whole family, including his father, liked me. He was an only living son, so when our sons were born healthy, things were right as rain. And I made sure he had a cheery and happy wife to support him. I do love him so!"

Mortimer is behind her as she says all this. He nods and says, "Ours is a kind and loving relationship. No better wife than my Leila!" He looks directly into my eyes from under his heavy brows.

She turns to her husband, smiles, and flutters her long eyelashes.

If Mom were here, about now she would make a comment about a coy flirt charming either the pants off a snake or the birds out of the trees. Personally, while I miss Mom and her quips, I do feel glad that love holds these two together.

I am still alarmed. She knows recent American slang, which tells me she travels far and wide—including America. She misses nothing. Will I ever be safe from her snooping? Has she snooped on me all along?

Temporarily ignoring my thoughts, she steps away from the door. It springs open. Previously, there was a long wide empty room. Now it is crowded with trunks, each with a bright brass plate, giving the names and dates of the occupants in residence. The door to the stairs is still partway open, just as I left it.

Leila calls for wake up, and vapor begins seeping from most trunks, followed by pops and crackles, as the occupants slowly materialize to translucency.

I am scared speechless. I want to dash to that door and run down those stairs, but fear locks my legs in place. My knees want to buckle.

Looking at me, Leila whispers, "Not to worry, dear boy. I've invited you to meet them and talk. No harm in that." I remain immobilized. "Your legs will hold you. Take my arm." I lean on her slightly till I'm steady. Between the new crowd and her thought reading, I'm freaked out.

"Nonsense, dear, you are not a freak," says Leila.

She's at it again! I exclaim irritably, "My thought wasn't that *I* am a freak. 'Freaked out' is slang Dad uses when he means 'really scared.' That's how I feel right now." After a moment, I add, "He said that the slang phrase originally came from the drug culture, something to do with LSD, whatever that is."

For a moment, Leila looks at me sharply, then her face relaxes, and she smiles reassuringly. "Not to worry, dear boy. You are with Grandmother Leila," she says kindly.

"Yeah, I know," is all I can say. I try to block the thought that Grandmother Leila is the one freaking me out.

Leila looks thoughtful as she replies to my thoughts, "Freaked out? I missed that slang. It has a good ring. I must file that one in my repertoire!"

Wisely, I think nothing. Leila glances at me. She looks a little surprised, maybe disappointed. "But I must investigate the origin of the term so I don't use it inappropriately," she murmurs prissily. She looks at the trunks with the figures forming before us, sees that some slowpokes are still seeping out, which provides her more time, and tentatively asks, "Did your father explain what is LSD? That term is something I've entirely missed." She seems faintly annoyed that there is indeed something that has passed her by.

The question surprises me, but I answer, "Dad said it is a bad medicine that some people use for fun. They put a few drops on a small piece of paper and then eat the paper. It makes them see things that aren't there. I thought that was a pretty stupid thing to do, so I stopped paying attention to what he was saying. I wasn't interested in anything that could make my head go funny, so I've forgotten whatever else he told me about it. But I remember that Dad said it is bad stuff."

Leila looks shocked as she asks, "They want to see things that aren't there? My goodness!" A moment later, she mutters to herself, "I can't imagine what that might do to my head. It's too busy at the best of times, and there is plenty to see already. I must be very careful not to use the slang term 'freaked out.' I might be misunderstood." She suddenly straightens her back rigidly and primly looks again at the forming crowd.

I stare overwhelmed. Almost every trunk has the form of a man and a woman floating above its lid. Each form is translucent, some easier to see than others. Some are really almost transparent.

I nudge Leila's arm and ask, "Are the nearly transparent ones trying to save energy? Or are they just weaklings?"

"Mostly to save energy, although for some, it's a little of both," she replies under her breath.

A scary thought crosses my mind. With a quavering voice, I ask, "Do they all read minds like you do?" Even the question terrifies me.

Leila almost laughs as she replies, "No, dear boy, I'm the only one of this crowd born that way. The rest are just like you and your family, needing to make an educated guess about the thoughts of others, all struggling without my gift. There have been very few of us in the history of the world born this way, ever. Indeed, I'm quite remarkable." She smiles happily at me and looks self-satisfied.

So remarkable she scares me. Smiling slightly in return to be polite, I almost sag with relief. *At least there aren't more snooping spooks reading my head.* Fortunately, Leila says nothing in reply.

Each couple is well dressed in the height of fashion from their time—show-and-tell Sunday-best dressing through the centuries.

"What does the upstart want?" mutters a woman in what I guess is later eighteenth-century attire, her hair piled high. She has brown eyes, which I soon discover turn black when she is angry. She is much shorter than Leila and a little chubby.

Her tall somewhat-thin husband floats along next to her, checking his wig, his leggings, and the rings on his fingers. He pays attention only to himself. He seems to disappear into the background while I look at him—all the personality of an eggplant!

Leila whispers in my ear, "That short, chubby, rude woman is Cybil. The man beside her is my grandson, named Humphrey. I love him because he is my grandson, but I have always considered him a fool. He was heir to the title, but a waste of human flesh, in my opinion.

"I was surprised when he decided to stay. Probably from peer pressure, I should think. Or maybe he knew his ultimate destination and found this preferable."

Her candor is somewhat shocking. Is there more to know?

Leila continues, "Now to Cybil. Her father was rich and had a title. She was married, no children, and then widowed. But with her husband's title, and her own, she was a countess in her own right before she married my grandson, Humphrey.

"She was always a spoiled one, a snob with a sharp tongue. She doesn't have a kind bone in her body. She's not to be trusted." Leila almost hisses as she says this close to my ear. "And Humphrey was a perfect choice in a husband for her. Besides being heir to a title, he's compliant, and his personality is almost…invisible. That suits Cybil just fine. She likes to have her own way and to wear the breeches."

I am surprised how much she dislikes her grandson and his wife. Wow! But I must ask, "Are Cybil and Humphrey my seven-greats-grandparents?"

Leila nods. "Right you are!"

That's disturbing news, but I say nothing.

Too sweetly, Leila says to the crowd, "This upstart wants to introduce her nine-greats-grandson, Jeremiah Morris. We are hoping he may be the one."

A murmur of excitement rises from everyone.

"His mother is the present Earl Poppycock's daughter. His father is an American from Brooklyn."

Mutterings about my origins in America and comments regarding Brooklyn race through the crowd. Leila looks pointedly at Cybil, whose expression changes from bemused annoyance to real interest.

"This boy may be the one?" quizzes Cybil. "An American? From Brooklyn?"

"We are hopeful," says Leila as she smiles at Cybil and speaks a little more slowly and with very distinct emphasis to correct her. "*He* is from Manhattan. His *father* is from Brooklyn."

I see that Leila's smile is forced. At least Leila is not good at hiding her feelings, even if she is good at detecting lies.

Suddenly, Cybil is very attentive to me, asking rapid-fire questions about my plans to solve the case, none of which poor me has any hope of answering.

I stammer something incoherent. Cybil looks annoyed. Her face resembles a thundercloud! Those dark eyes turn black!

"Really, Leila! Must you? Raising false hope. Too unkind." Cybil looks around, expecting sounds of approval. She is met with stares and stony silence.

Near the back, an elderly man stands beside an equally elderly woman. They are dressed in mid-nineteenth-century clothes. He is a little overweight, with a receding hairline offset by large sideburns down to the angle of the jaw on each side. She is thin and reed-like, with a long and pointed chin. Mischief dances in her kindly eyes.

His clear voice commands, "Enough, Grandmother Cybil. We have had enough of your nastiness." As Cybil pouts, he asks me, "Have you been told anything yet about the case?"

I recite, "I've been told that Edgar was hanged after he was found guilty of murder. But he is innocent. Direct-line family and others have stayed behind in their trunks to prove his innocence. More than 272 years have passed. The case has still not been solved.

"Saint Peter knows Edgar is innocent but asked the family to solve the murder case. My grandfather was the last to try, but that attempt also flopped." I stop. I look at the old man and the old lady beside him.

"What you have said is very true. You have your facts correctly stated," the elderly man says as he looks around at the group.

He continues, "Let me explain some things to you. First, I shall introduce myself and my wife. We are your five-greats-grandparents. My name is Marcus Wadsworth. This is my wife, Beatrice. Like your papa and nana now, we were known as the Earl and Countess Poppycock.

"In life, we only knew of Edgar as a black sheep, hung for murder, never discussed. Hence, we did nothing to help during our lifetime.

"But when I died, I met Leila, who gave me the facts as she knew them, with the benefit of her frequently seeping out to explore. Like others before me, I decided to delay my final resting place until this was solved.

"When my wife died, she was reunited with me and then met Leila. She agreed to stay as well."

Marcus and Beatrice look at each other and nod in agreement. With her hands beside her, Beatrice touches the side of her husband's thigh with the back of her one hand. The hand stays tight against his thigh.

There is an odd glint in her eye as she gazes at her husband. Marcus has a momentary peculiar expression on his face as he smiles slightly and nods to Beatrice while he stares intently at her.

What was that about? What does that mean? I don't understand their glances or why her hand is pushing against his leg.

As his eyes move away from his wife's, Marcus looks directly at me and adds, "And I must say, Leila has been the only one with enough gumption to right a wrong, to work to clear the family name. Admittedly, Edgar is her son. But she believes he is innocent and not able to clear his own name. It has become her cause. I can only admire her determination," he says, finishing with a smile.

I look around. I don't know what to do next.

One trunk very near me remains without sketchy, translucent figures floating above it. I look at it, wondering. I see the names.

"Oh, all right. I see you gawking. I'll come out," says a female voice. "Bertrand, you come out too."

"Bertrand? What sort of a name is Bertrand?" I mutter to Leila.

She mumbles from the side of her mouth, "That's your great-great-grandfather's Christian name. But he has a nickname that fits him better. The name Bertrand belongs to someone who is sedate and dignified, but Bertie is the name of a party boy."

As an afterthought, Leila whispers in my ear, "Your great-great-grandmother is named Marjorie." Leila moves away as she mutters almost inaudibly under her breath, "Sexpot."

I don't know what a sexpot is, and I don't dare ask.

Leila's eyes flash at me. Her face is stern as she says, "Someone else can explain that later, not now." Her fingers stand straight up in front of her mouth to hush me up.

Leila has read my thoughts again!

She mutters, "Yes, dear boy, I have. But you don't understand these things yet."

She knows me better than I know me. That's really busted!

"Ber-tie!" exclaims the female voice. The second syllable of his name is pitched much higher than the first. It sounds like the lady yodels. And a yodel fits the name Bertie.

Slowly, languidly, vapor stirs. With stretches, a form appears and stands on the floor facing Leila. Marjorie is like no person I have ever seen! She is lovely to look at, dressed in a shockingly aquamarine tea gown of the roaring twenties. Her blonde hair is bobbed, and so blonde that I wonder how she got it that way. She has a feather, held by a band, sticking up from her forehead.

The thin straps of her shiny gown let everyone see a lot of her upper half, front and back, while the rest of the dress drops loosely to the floor around her lovely form, clinging in various places. She carries a lace-edged handkerchief made from the same vividly aquamarine-colored cloth as her tea gown. The handkerchief runs through her hands periodically and then flutters open. Her big blue eyes are both bored and full of questions.

One hand cradles a cigarette holder. She opens a small gold-colored clutch purse, pulls out a cigarette, which she puts in the holder, places the holder in her mouth, and prepares to strike a match as she waits for Bertie to appear.

Leila yells, "No smoking in the house, Marjorie! None of it, you hear! You risk starting a fire!" Leila is almost screaming.

Marjorie inquires, "What's the difference?" Sulking, she glances at Leila and mutters, "We are all dead anyway."

"Well, you may be dead, but the current owners are not. I don't want them burned up in their sleep." Leila watches Marjorie closely until the cigarette and matches disappear.

When Leila sees that she is being obeyed, she turns to me again. "Like I said, this is your great-great-grandmother, two greats as we say. She had three sons. The eldest was your papa's father, Joshua." Leila pauses before she adds disdainfully, "Marjorie was an actress before she became the Countess Poppycock."

Leila's jaw snaps shut. She grits her teeth. She leans to my ear and whispers, "Smoking in a trunk, indeed! Are there no limits to what an actress will do?"

Leila turns her head to Marjorie and smiles too broadly. I think Leila hopes Marjorie has not heard her unkind whisperings.

From a fleeting expression on her face, I think Marjorie did hear, but she forgivingly pretends that nothing was said. She asks, "So you are our hope, Jeremiah?" Marjorie looks at me with a question in her eyes and then asks, "What are you, age-wise, about ten?"

The pitch at the end of her sentence rises as a lazy question.

I stare at her. She is very beautiful, very fancy, and makes me feel that there is a part of life I don't know about yet, just like Leila said.

"Yes, that's right. I am ten," I reply breathlessly.

"A smart ten?" Marjorie asks.

"I do well in school," I respond honestly.

"Well, I can see why Leila chose you." Bertie has not yet appeared. Suddenly, Marjorie jams her hand hard against the trunk. The whole room including the windows shake when she shrieks, "Ber-tie! Get up now!"

The crowds of ancestors cover their ears or look away, pained in their ears, and embarrassed at her screaming yodel. I giggle.

"Not to worry. Mrs. Stewart cannot hear us," says Leila, reassuring me once again that we are all safely hidden.

All of this by invitation only. What an invite! Lucky me.

Finally, Bertie appears, tall and slender with dark hair slicked back. He has attractive features, sports a mustache on his upper lip, and has eyes as blue as his wife's. His loud and ugly sports jacket has wide vertical stripes of several tan shades alternating with a cream color. Some of the tan colors of the jacket stripes match the tan color of his trousers. His shoes have two colors, tan and brown, matching the colors in the jacket and pants. Like his wife, he is dressed in the smartest fashion of the roaring twenties.

He also reaches for a cigarette before he sees Leila's glare and puts his silver cigarette case away. He declares, "Spot on, Leila. No smoking in the house." Smiling while pointing his index finger at Leila, he states flatly, "Dead right." He looks at me and laughs.

Bertie sizes me up and says, "Well, he looks smart enough to help." He laughs again. "Smarter than his two-greats-granddad, at any rate." He is the only one roaring with laughter at his own wit.

I am not so sure about Bertie. I just hope he is really not the village idiot that he pretends to be. It's just as well that his nickname is Bertie. That name fits. He seems too foolish to be called by his Christian name, Bertrand. Leila is right. Bertrand ought to be the name of a statesman, and Bertie certainly does not seem like one.

Leila looks around. There remains one trunk without its figures above it. It is on the opposite wall, a bit by itself. I follow her gaze. When I walk over and see the brass plaque, my heart skips a beat.

Joshua Wadsworth, Earl Poppycock, 1922–1999
Penelope (née Winter) Wadsworth, 1924–1969
Both in residence

I realize these are Papa's parents. I see the death date of Great-Grandmother Penelope, who didn't live long enough to become Countess Poppycock. She was forty-five when she was killed in a car accident. Papa was a young man at Cambridge.

I know she must have been special, for Papa still frequently talks about her fondly. Joshua, Papa's dad, must have been very special too, for Papa sometimes speaks of how well he ran the estate and how very good he was at taking the time to explain things well, even complex things, so that they were easily understood. Papa says that takes a wise, kindly, and calm person.

With a wobble in my voice, I stand in front of the trunk and quietly ask, "Will you come out now?"

Slowly, the two figures appear. My great-grandmother has an oval face, kindly hazel eyes, and brown hair with streaks of gray, cut just past her ears. She is tall and trim, but her muscles are well defined. I remember Papa saying she would get down on the floor to play and have fun with him and that she liked to have adventures with him. That fits. From her appearance, she has obviously been a sportswoman and physically active.

Penelope says, "We don't seep out much. I have not seen you for a long time, Jeremiah. You are quite the young man now." Her mellow voice is soft, but the words are very distinct.

Surprised, I ask, "When did you see me before?" I steadily look up at their forms floating above their trunk.

She replies, "At your birth. We all tend to gather for a birth, and during your visit to England a few years ago. You were four and a half years old then." She smiles down at me as she speaks. "It is worth the effort to see a great-grandson growing, especially one who is so much like his papa."

There is a lump in my throat. I step toward her. She floats down beside me. She fully materializes briefly to give me a warm hug that I feel deep into my bones. It is wonderful to feel that much love! When she releases me, she slowly floats up beside her husband and becomes translucent again. Her eyes glisten.

When I look at my great-grandfather, Joshua Wadsworth, I realize he looks the same age as his wife; but he died thirty years later! Joshua is clean-shaven with piercingly blue eyes, a long straight nose in a rectangular face, and a square jaw. He has a shock of silver running through the front of his thick dark hair. Altogether, his face is unforgettably handsome! He is slightly taller than his wife, and although he is taller than Papa, he is thinner and less muscular. Like his wife, he is dressed in fashionable clothes of the early 1960s.

Joshua asks, "You look like you want to ask me something, Jeremiah. Is that so?"

"Yes, I do, Great-Grandfather. Great-Grandmother died thirty years before you, but you look the same age. How is that possible?"

They both laugh, as do any number of the crowd, who also murmur, "Well said, perceptive lad, not missing anything."

Joshua responds, "We are given a choice to decide what age our image may look like. Regardless of the age we choose, we still retain our lifetime of knowledge, information, and experience that we accumulated, even though we may decide to look like we are thirty."

That gets my attention!

He continues, "Some still want the trappings of youth even though they have knowledge of old age. Others want to look as they did when they were older."

Without thinking, I ask directly and somewhat tactlessly, "Why did Edgar choose to look like a hanged man?" I hear gasps from some ancestors during the stony silence after my question.

Joshua's eyes open wide in shocked surprise. Penelope looks startled. Her mouth opens slightly and then closes. She glances anxiously toward Joshua and touches his arm.

Joshua closes his eyes for a moment. He looks lost in thought. When his eyes open to focus on mine, he answers slowly and quietly, "Part of Edgar's penalty, besides being hanged for murder, was to lose the ability to make that decision. He must appear as he did the day he was hanged." Joshua looks directly at me.

I gulp. "Sorry, I mean, well…sorry," I stammer.

Jemima interrupts, "He was quite different in life before the charges were laid. He was never wildly handsome, but he was a very good man. In jail, he lost weight and became very shy, fearful, and withdrawn. The threat of hanging can do that to a person. But buried underneath all that, he is still my beloved Edgar." She appears angry and near tears.

Joshua looks at Jemima sympathetically and then down at me. He turns back to Jemima and says, "The boy meant no harm."

Looking at the floor, Jemima quietly says, "I know. The child's question was innocent." She appears sad.

Joshua's gaze rests on me as he asks, "You don't miss much, do you, son?"

"I try to pay attention," I answer.

Joshua looks at Leila. She takes her cue.

"Does anyone else have questions for Jeremiah?" She looks pointedly at Cybil, who is still pouting.

There is a growing murmur as people turn to each other to speak, wave hello across the room, and float to each other to talk. For a few minutes, there is the chaos of many conversations, most of which have nothing to do with the topic at hand. Do they never get to talk to each other? The buzz of many conversations, all colliding together, sounds like bumblebees gathering pollen or maybe wasps.

Leila says, "Now, please give me your attention." She is ignored, so she repeats herself slightly louder. No one pays her any attention.

I know what earth-shattering sounds are coming next. Perhaps Mrs. Stewart would never hear her, but I can. I want to protect my hearing. My hands tightly cover my ears, just in time.

Leila yells, "Attention, now! Look sharp!"

Every conversation stops in midsentence.

"Jeremiah is willing to investigate the mystery of the robbery and death that caused Edgar's execution. Are any of you willing to help?" she asks.

Some members of the crowd murmur, "What could I do?" and others, "What is to be done?"

I look at Leila and whisper to her, "Leila, will any of them help?"

Leila whispers back, "Good question, Jeremiah. Some want the benefits without effort." She looks sad and maybe disappointed as she says this.

Several clearly state they want to help. They say they just need to be told what to do.

Grandfather Marcus and his wife, Beatrice, say almost in unison, "We are in for whatever you need."

With dark eyes flashing black, angry Cybil declares loudly, "Well, we will have nothing to do with this nonsense!" Cybil looks down at me with contempt. "He is just a commoner and a child. An American! His father is from Brooklyn! He is no use to us."

She looks sharply at her husband, Humphrey, who says nothing. He adjusts his wig, checks his reflection in the windowpane, and then docilely follows her. With Cybil muttering, "Brooklyn indeed," both of them swoosh back into their trunk, which disappears with a loud, indignant pop.

"Goodbye," sighs Leila. "Good riddance to that Poppycock," she mutters under her breath.

Despite everything, I giggle.

Bertie and Marjorie look at each other with affection. "It might be fun." Marjorie giggles.

"I think it would be just ripping," declares Bertie.

"Maybe even scare-making," murmurs Marjorie.

"Certainly fun-making," adds Bertie.

"No downside. We are already dead!" Marjorie laughs.

"And I'm dying for a cigarette," says Bertie, looking at Leila.

"Not possible," responds Marjorie.

"What do you mean by 'not possible'?" questions Bertie, almost pouting, with his eyes narrowing.

"You are already there, dead, flatline." Marjorie's giggle sounds like a series of little bells. What a lovely sound!

They both laugh out loud at Marjorie's joke. Bertie has a harsh, barking laugh. Marjorie's full laugh is actually quite deep, almost like a man's baritone. It surprises me. It's very different from her bell-like giggle.

"We are in for the chase," they say in unison.

Leila looks worried. "All right then," she answers flatly.

Oh dear, the two-greats both want to help! I am as disturbed by this as Leila. They don't seem reliable.

Later, I will realize this is another time I am wrong in my assumptions. Once again, I am too quick to judge!

Jemima, who has been mostly quiet throughout, suddenly says, "I will do whatever I can. Leila, you know what Edgar is like. I will talk to him."

I look at Papa's parents. Penelope motions to me. She and Joshua float down to stand beside me.

Penelope says, "Jeremiah, you are my son's grandson. You are very special to me. I will do everything I can to assist you, but I am not as worldly as Leila. I have not seeped out like she has to keep up with changes in society. But I am a quick study." She looks at Joshua. They nod in agreement. She continues, "Joshua agrees... We are both in."

Joshua's hand fully materializes to touch my shoulder and tousle my hair. Penelope materializes just long enough to enfold me in a tight hug. They become translucent again as they float back up over their trunk.

"We worry about your safety," states Penelope while still looking at me intently. She utters nothing more.

Leila tells everyone, "I shall be in contact, but please think how you might help Jeremiah if we summon you." They all agree. With that, there are popping noises everywhere as translucent figure after translucent figure seeps back into a trunk, which then disappears with a pop.

As the trunks disappear, I realize what Leila meant when she said seeing them is by invitation only. When she needs me to see them, they appear. I guess that's okay, since she is the guardian of the doorway to another world. That probably means Leila must be with me to make them visible.

Marjorie, late to arrive, is in no hurry to go. "See you around, kiddo," she says in my direction. She blows me a kiss and winks.

Face-to-face with Bertie, Marjorie looks at him very intensely, wide eyed. Then she grabs Bertie's right hand with her left and says to him in a sultry, low voice, "Hello, sailor!"

Using her free right hand, she slowly fingers the top of his left jacket lapel. Her eyes focus on his.

Bertie glances down at her elegant hand with its well-manicured and shiny nails. He wraps his free hand around hers and presses her hand against his chest, over his heart. He returns her intense gaze.

Her upper eyelids close ever so slightly. Her lips part a tiny bit. They look only at each other. Both they and their trunk rapidly disappear with a resounding pop!

What was that look about? Was Bertie a sailor in the navy? Was he an officer? My mind is confused.

There were a few more pops as a few tardy ancestors and their trunks disappear with each pop. Finally, Leila, Jemima, Mortimer, and I are alone. Through the doorway, I can see Edgar floating morosely above his trunk, his face twisted to the side on a tilt. A broken neck will do that to you.

"We must start planning," says a tired-looking Leila.

I look quizzically to Mortimer, Leila, and Jemima. I want to ask questions, especially questions about *the look*.

Each has eyes elsewhere. I guess that they haven't seen a thing! Why didn't they notice what happened between Marjorie and Bertie? Each of them, especially Mortimer, appears tired. He appears so tired that his eyes are closed, avoiding my gaze. How odd!

"Just whipped, my dear. So very tired," whispers Mortimer. I look again at my nine-greats. They both seem worn out.

Do they tire so quickly? Really? Do they know I have questions? Are they afraid of something I may ask? Why? What might I ask that could frighten them into pretending they are too tired to answer?

"We are off to rest," says Jemima. Her eyes say, "No questions!"

I nod that I understand, but I don't! I decide to leave all my questions for now.

We all watch as Jemima floats ahead into the next room, grabs Edgar's hand, and seeps into the trunk with him. Their trunk suddenly disappears with a pop.

Leila watches Jemima. She says, "I give her credit. She has been faithful in all ways to her young husband. She loves him deeply. She will help you if she can. I hope she can persuade Edgar to help." She pauses and then adds, "He was once so very different, a truly commanding presence. You would never guess that by his manner now." Leila sighs deeply with a momentarily sorrowful face.

She looks at me pointedly. With forced cheeriness, she asks, "Will you come here tomorrow?"

She waits until she sees my nod of agreement. Then she looks at Mortimer with genuine fondness, touches his face gently, and says, "Come along, dear." His eyes remain closed. They float into the next room and then slide into their trunk slowly, as if melting into sleep.

I look around. The only remaining trunk belongs to my nine-greats-grandparents. The brass plate gleams brightly in contrast to the battered and worn trunk. There is no sign of what happened.

I shake my head. Was this a dream about ghosts residing in trunks? Did I really just meet my ancestors? Everything is far too unreal. Common sense says this was a dream.

The great long room in the center of the house is now empty of all trunks. The room looks undisturbed. The door to the stairs remains ajar.

Out loud, I exclaim, "Everything was just a foolish dream." My little laugh echoes in the attic room while the rain pelts against the windows. Loudly I say, "Impossible!" With less confidence a moment later, I declare quietly, "Nothing happened up here."

As I turn to leave, something catches my eye. I look closely. Startled, I gasp!

On the floor near where I imagined Marjorie and Bertie's trunk lies something vividly aquamarine. It is a handkerchief, edged with lace, aquamarine in color just like I remember it, matching Marjorie's tea gown. It is a folded handkerchief with a cigarette holder lying on top!

I pick them up. The cloth of the handkerchief is real, with a faint odor of lovely perfume. The cigarette holder is solid. There are marks from use. It looks old.

Looking around at the empty room, I ask, "If it was all a dream, how do I have these?" My eyes search everywhere, but there is no answer.

Was it all a silly dream? Or…did everything I remember actually happen?

Confused and uncertain, I hear my voice cry out, "I need help!"

Chapter 11

JEREMIAH TALKS TO SUSANNE

I close all doors so no one will know where I have been. By the time I am downstairs, it is almost teatime.

Through the open front door, I see Phoebe and Susanne as they return from the village and drop parcels in the hallway. They chat away about what they saw and what they purchased. Each has something she almost bought and now thinks she should have. They sound like they have enjoyed themselves.

Phoebe asks, "And what did you do?"

Thinking quickly, I answer, "Oh, I was just exploring this old house. There are so many nooks and crannies. It's fun to explore."

"We had fish and chips for lunch. What did you have?"

Just then, Mrs. Stewart appears, wiping her hands on her apron, her smeared glasses slightly askew. Looking at me, she says loudly, "Oh, there you are. I looked for you at lunch but couldn't find you. You will all want your tea. I will bring it to you shortly." She disappears without waiting for an answer as she yells over her shoulder, "In the morning room. Nigel is occupied elsewhere. Nothing fancy!"

"Didn't you have lunch?" asks Phoebe.

"I forgot," I reply.

Snarky Susanne says, "You forgot to eat lunch! That takes a special kind of stupid."

Phoebe stares at Susanne. Wordlessly, her facial expression silently screams, "Warning!"

Susanne sees Phoebe's look, as was intended. She glances everywhere else except at Phoebe and scampers off silently to the morning room. Clearly, point taken.

Trying to sidestep any discussion of what might have happened in the attic, I ignore Susanne, fix my gaze on Phoebe, and say, "I think I may have fallen asleep."

"Well, it's that sort of day, rainy and dreary, sleeping weather." Phoebe now uses her age-old tactic. She ignores my sister's comment since her own displeasure has been registered and now brightly and cheerily follows Susanne into the morning room. By the time I tag after, she and Susanne are sitting in front of the first volley of sandwiches and tea cakes Mrs. Stewart has presented. They are already discussing some of the lovely village houses and buildings that they saw today.

I realize how very hungry I am. My tummy rumbles, and my hands automatically reach to cover my front. As they move, my hands also feel the compass in my pocket.

Phoebe requests, "Before you sit down, would you please call your father for tea, Jeremiah? I forgot to call him. He's probably in the library." With a nod, I head out to find him as she utters a delayed and distracted, "Thank you." Passing the hall table, I return the compass and then find Dad in the library. He appears among the others in the morning room a few minutes later.

Tea includes milk for the children, a great pot of steaming tea, sandwiches of several varieties, scones and tea cakes, biscuits, jam, and a custard for dessert. Food doesn't need to be fancy to be good. I dig in with gusto.

Phoebe looks directly at me as she says, "I can see you slept through lunch. But remember supper is at eight. Don't eat too much, for you won't be hungry."

I reply, "I won't neglect my supper."

Dad watches me with curiosity as he says, "Do we never feed you? I marvel at how much you tank away with real zeal and pleasure. You will be inches taller by summer's end at this rate." Dad laughs to himself, for I am already tall for my age and rather lanky. "You need meat on your bones though," he adds.

After tea, Phoebe says she is tired and thinks she will follow my example and have a rest. Dad states he needs to work a little longer. "I'll be in the library if you need me."

After they both disappear, I say to Susanne, "I have something I must tell you."

Susanne pays no attention as she looks through some of her purchases, including a few souvenir books and a souvenir cup and saucer. This purchase especially pleases her because it pictures Papa and Nana's house.

"Please, Susanne, pay attention. I need your help," I plead.

"What have you done, Jeremiah, that you need help?"

"Nothing," I honestly reply.

"Then you don't need help," Susanne states flatly.

"It is not what I have done. It's what I am about to do," I reply matter-of-factly.

That gets Susanne's attention. She asks, slightly alarmed, "And what are you about to do?"

"I don't know yet," I answer lamely.

"Make some sense, please." She looks annoyed, but at least she's waiting for me to talk.

Now I know I have her attention!

As we sit at the table and look out through the east windows at the rain, we pick at the remainder of our sandwiches and scones. It takes me a moment to figure what to say. Trying to sound casual, I cough slightly and begin, "Today, I met the ghosts of some of our dead ancestors who reside in the attic. They need our help."

She drops the scone fragment she was eating. Her face spells disbelief. "Yeah, *sure* you did. And the dead need help? You're a joker," she replies glibly, "but you're not going to pull my leg."

"No, Susanne, I'm serious. Please just listen," I plead.

She sees my earnest face, looks at me squarely, and says, "Okay, I'll listen. That's all I promise. This ought to be good."

"The voice of Leila came from a trunk in the attic. She and her husband, Mortimer, are our nine-greats-grandparents. She frequently watches what we are doing and thinks that I can help her clear the name of their son Edgar. He was wrongly hung for murder in 1745," I state slowly.

"Of course you can. One pardon coming right up." Susanne laughs, who now sounds like a short-order cook.

"Please, Susanne, just listen," I beg. "Marcus and Beatrice, our five-greats; Bertie and Marjorie, our two-greats; and Joshua and Penelope, our great-grandparents, are all truly ready to help. Other ancestors are in the attic, all *supposedly* ready to help. Each married pair resides in their own trunk. But Leila is the cheerleader for the cause!" I exclaim.

Susanne says sarcastically, "It's always good to have a cheerleader. Does she dance with pom-poms?"

"No, Susanne," is my brisk reply. I avoid taking her bait. "She dresses as she did in life, in early-eighteenth-century clothes. Please hear me out," I plead again.

"Oh, all right. It just gets better and better," she says with fake enthusiasm, clapping her hands together and wiggling her fingers in pretend anticipation.

She should develop those strong acting skills!

Redirecting my thoughts from acting back to ancestors, I explain, "The trunks are not usually visible. If a person thinks about helping, Leila lets them hear what the ancestors say and see what they do."

I mention Cybil, our seven-greats-grandmother, and her husband, whose name, Humphrey, I recall with difficulty. "She is nasty, and her husband only thinks of himself. And Leila really dislikes Humphrey—and Cybil, come to think of it—even though she does love Humphrey because he is her grandson," I add.

Appearing thoughtful for the first time, Susanne says, "It is possible to love someone and not like what they do." She seems solemn while she speaks and looks down. Then she looks at me and asks more brightly, "Are you telling me they are not all roses and sunshine?" She giggles.

It's my guess she is not expecting an answer to that question.

I tell her, "Edgar is a frightened and timid soul. Jemima, his wife, is his defender. He is our eight-greats uncle, and she our eight-greats aunt by marriage.

"Leila wants to clear Edgar's name. The family, as requested by Saint Peter, must make this happen. Ancestors have willingly stayed as a married couple in an attic trunk so that someday they might help Edgar."

I pause to let Susanne understand this before I add, "You probably remember that our Episcopal priest talked about purgatory in his sermon a few months ago. Susanne, our ancestors are really in a form of purgatory. Each couple is in a box for two, and for all eternity, or until the case is solved. Okay, the box is actually a trunk, big deal. According to our priest, purgatory is someplace that you don't want to be for any reason. Two people residing in a trunk, it's awful! Presumably, they could be in heaven, whatever that is, but they put up with a trunk in order to possibly help." We are silent for a moment. The boxed-in idea sits heavily on my shoulders. "They deserve credit for that," I almost whisper as an afterthought.

Back on track after a lengthy pause, I try to tell all that I know. I begin again, "Marjorie wears a vividly aquamarine dress with a matching handkerchief and carries a small gold purse. Her husband, Bertie, wears an ugly jacket. Leila stopped Bertie and Marjorie from smoking." After I tell Susanne all the details surrounding Marjorie's look when she called Bertie a sailor, I say, "I don't know if Bertie was ever in the navy."

I spend time talking about Joshua and Penelope. "They were Papa's parents. They made me feel good because they care about me. It was wonderful." Everything comes tumbling out, including the story of Papa's failed attempt to help. "Leila and Mortimer both said that his failure bothers him still. Leila mind-reads, so she should know."

This whole conversation sounds weird.

Susanne listens and then says, "Your brain was collecting the family tree and fell asleep exhausted. Simply put, you have seen too many memorial plaques in the church and were putting them together in a bad dream." Susanne is smugly laughing at me.

I say, "I didn't fall asleep. Sleep was an excuse to cover my tracks with Phoebe. I didn't know what to say to her about my visit with our ancestors."

Susanne quips, "If you lied about your nap, maybe you are lying about this just to see if I take your bait. That would be pretty funny, wouldn't it?"

Showing annoyance in my voice, I exclaim, "Then explain this!" I dig into my pocket. Out comes the vivid handkerchief and the worn cigarette holder. With a raised voice, I utter, "I'm not lying to you! Marjorie had these in her hands when she spoke to me. She must have left them on the floor near their trunk before it popped and disappeared. Explain that!"

I am trying to convince Susanne when I am not sure myself. Have I just been dreaming?

Susanne stares at me and then looks away for a moment. She looks back and continues somewhat more kindly, "There is an obvious explanation. It was on the floor when you were first there. The house is new territory. You cannot notice everything the first time 'round."

"That's a very bright color to miss," I say.

Susanne answers, "Well, you are a boy. You were probably searching for pirates' treasure, so not likely to notice."

I honestly say, "It is true I was looking for fun and exciting things to find, perhaps to use for play; but right now, I don't know what I saw. I'm not sure about anything."

Susanne glances at me sharply and says, "Jeremiah, do you truly mean you actually don't know if you saw anything or if you just had a dream during a nap?"

I exclaim with a quavering voice, "I really don't know!"

Susanne pauses and looks thoughtful as she mutters, "You seemed genuinely concerned that the ancestors gave up something wonderful in heaven to stay here and help. While everything you say may be stuff and nonsense, that kind of response is vintage Jeremiah."

I'm about to say I don't quite understand *her* reaction since heaven is supposed to be pretty good, but her raised palm silences me. She asks quietly, "You really don't understand Marjorie's comment about a sailor and *the look*, do you?"

"No, I don't," I reply. "Why?"

Susanne replies, "That's the one thing you have said that makes me think you are not a complete liar, a liar who is just trying to pull my leg. You aren't there yet."

Perplexed, I ask, "Where should I be?" When she remains silent, I state truthfully, "I don't get it, and I don't understand you."

She laughs as she steadily ignores my question. She says, "Someday soon you will understand." She laughs again. "But it's not my responsibility to provide instruction to a ten-year-old. No one could possibly pay me enough to take on that job. Not even the Feds print that much money!" Something strikes her as funny as she laughs to herself, pauses for a brief thoughtful silence, and then mutters, "Just like the ancestors, I don't want to explain."

"But I'm still lost," I mutter. She shrugs her shoulders and continues to ignore me.

Wisely, I don't say, "Oh, to be nearly thirteen! To have such knowledge! I can't wait till I am thirteen and know all about the Feds, whoever they are!" My brain is really busy, but my wise tongue remains motionless. Fortunately, Susanne isn't Leila, and she can't read minds.

Finally, she says, "I tell you what. Tomorrow, Phoebe is going to London to run errands for Dad. We'll be getting more rain. Dad will be busy. We are to amuse ourselves for the day. Mrs. Stewart won't pay us any more attention than she did to you today. That means she is out of the way. Mr. Brown will be working, but not inside the house. Nigel will be occupied with his duties.

"We'll go to the attic. You will call on Leila and explain that I am here to help. We'll see if you fall asleep or if Leila wakes up again!" Susanne chuckles. After a bit, she continues, "You said she was very tired after her exertions. I wonder if she can wake up again, 265 years dead and all!" Susanne thinks this is very funny. She laughs and laughs till she almost coughs, and then she whispers loudly, "A ghost, a phantom, will she wake up? Ooooooh!" She wiggles her fingers in front of her face at a pretend spook. She laughs so hard that tears stream down her face. "You are too funny, Jeremiah."

Since I've been sitting beside her like a stick, I don't think she is correct that I'm too funny. She's been amusing *herself*. Wisely, I don't challenge her.

"I am to return tomorrow anyway. We'll do it together," my little voice says. I don't like Susanne's laughing at me. But at least she will come to the attic.

I still am not sure what really happened. Was it a dream? Did everything I remember so vividly actually occur? What will tomorrow bring?

I remember Marjorie's comment, "Maybe even scare-making!"

Chapter 12

THE SECOND ATTIC TRIP

Dad and Phoebe are down for breakfast earlier than usual. They have finished eating and now sip their coffee. Dad is explaining which papers he needs to have delivered by hand to one office and which papers are to go to another office, to a different solicitor who also assists his firm in overseas operations.

Dad says, "Every file is separated and labeled. There is a typed note to keep things straight in case I am not clear. You should have no trouble. Both offices are close together, within easy walking distance."

Phoebe is smart. She rarely makes mistakes. Phoebe reassures him as she says, "I'll get everything to the correct lawyer, or rather solicitor, as they call them here. Big question: do you need me right back?"

Dad replies, "No, of course not. I'm here with the children. Mrs. Stewart is here. Nigel is here. Mr. Brown is here, but I doubt we will see him. Papa and Nana are in London, but no matter. The children will be fine. Please, enjoy the rest of the day in London."

He adds, "There is a lot to see—museums, art galleries, shops. Try the Silver Vaults if you like. It's another rainy day, forecast to be so all day. Don't forget your brolly."

"And a brolly is what exactly?" asks Phoebe.

"British slang for umbrella," Dad glibly replies.

"I missed that e-mail," she says. "What date was it sent?"

"The first of whenever," Dad replies with a wry smile.

They both laugh.

Together they discuss the address of the Silver Vaults. I eavesdrop, intrigued. Very curious, I ask, "What are the Silver Vaults? It sounds like a place to store silver."

Dad answers, "Initially, this address in Chancery Lane was a safe deposit area. It opened in 1876, renting out rooms to hold household silver, jewelry, or anything else that needed to be stored safely. The vaults were originally giant safety deposit boxes, like we have at the bank. But they were rooms, not just a box. Later, they converted to shops. With that history, most sell silver. Some sell antiques, art objects, and other high-end items. The shops are mostly underground in the old vaults."

Susanne also looks interested, which I think is really cool. She can be a quiet bore sometimes! She says, "Phoebe, you've really got to check that out, just to say you did. I mean, silver shops in old vaults! That really does sound nifty."

"We shall see," replies Phoebe with a shrug.

Shortly afterward, Dad tells Susanne and me that he is driving Phoebe to the rail station. She has on a raincoat and is carrying her umbrella and a briefcase.

"I've got a brolly," she says.

"Your new word," Susanne exclaims.

"One I rather like." She hugs us both and tells us to be good. She dashes to the car, waves her hand to us, and blows each of us kisses. I pretend to grab mine from the air and plant it on my cheek. Susanne waves her hand.

Dad gives us both a quick hug and says he will be back after he drops Phoebe at the station and runs a few errands. "And what will you two be doing?" He looks at his offspring, his eyes a question mark.

"Jeremiah is going to show me the house, as he explored it yesterday," answers Susanne truthfully.

Dad says, "Well, don't disturb anything. And don't move things about. Misplaced is as good as lost in a house this size."

He smiles, dashes through the rain toward the wrong side of the car, catches himself midway, glances toward us, and laughs. "I keep forgetting we drive on the wrong side over here. Old habits!"

What would Nigel say to that? I say nothing. The thought continues, *Over there in America, you drive on the wrong side.* I am sure that would be Nigel's response—and Mr. Brown's.

We wave goodbye from the doorway, watch the car disappear down the gravel drive, and then close the massive front door slowly so it doesn't bang. We look at each other.

Laughing at me, Susanne asks, "Are you ready to find out if you were dreaming?"

I answer honestly, "I'm ready to find out the truth: dream, no dream, hallucination, or reality. I need to know!"

When we go back to the morning room, we finish the last of our breakfast and drink an extra glass of milk. As we finish, Nigel returns. He asks, "Do you mind if I clear away breakfast debris?"

Preoccupied, he begins clearing dirty dishes from the far end of the table before Susanne answers, "Go ahead, Nigel. We have finished."

Wordlessly, we head upstairs. When we arrive at the attic stairs, I am nervous. What if it was a dream? What if the dream is real? What's the meaning of speaking to my dead ancestors? My whirling brain is confused.

"This is the attic door," I say stupidly. I look at the door. For a long moment, I don't move, paralyzed with fear.

Susanne's face looks annoyed; even autistic me can tell. In a pretend heavy Brooklyn accent and with a falsely low voice, she says, rather unkindly, "Dah! It's da attic door, moron! Ain't we going to da attic?" Smirking, she laughs at me.

I'm scared. She is not sympathetic. Now, *I'm* getting annoyed! *I hope she notices.*

Forcefully, I pull open the door. Everything is exactly as I remember. The stair is wider and more graciously built than a usual attic stair. It is designed for visitors to ascend up nine, landing, then up nine more steps. The window allows lots of light on the landing and lets us hear the rain spatter vigorously.

After we open the door at the top of the stairs, we are in the middle of the wide, long room that runs the width of the main hall two floors below. Through the five south windows we see the gravel drive at the front of the house. The windows paired on each side of the room, north and south, reach nearly to the floor, just like yesterday.

The stairwell still pokes into the room. The old candle tapers are still in the hurricane lamps and wall sconces. The big doors at each end, east and west, remain closed as I remember leaving them.

I notice one of the glass jars over its candle is badly cracked. Another is missing altogether, details I missed yesterday. The room is essentially bare, its plaster walls reaching high to the roof above.

"This is odd," says Susanne. "This attic is never used, but it seems clean."

I reply, "Leila told me yesterday she tries to keep the area swept clean."

"Our dead great-granny is a clean freak! Wow!" Susanne starts laughing again.

I open the east door, the first side room I explored yesterday. Just like yesterday, it is filled with boxes, broken furniture, and unused but kept bric-a-brac. My goodness, the room is long!

Dust is everywhere, and today I see cobwebs, which I missed yesterday. Susanne touches a box, blows off dust, and reads the label, "School papers, Marcus Wadsworth, 1814 to 1818."

"Five-Greats-Grandfather Marcus," I say.

"Oh yeah, I almost forgot. You were talking to him yesterday! What an imagination you have!" says Susanne as she looks at me.

She motions to the dirty room around her with a wide-open arm gesture. In a singsong voice, Susanne chants, "You must tell Great-Granny…what's her name…oh yeah, Leila, that she missed a spot!" She laughs loudly. She thinks she is really funny.

I ignore her. "Yesterday, I didn't think that there was much in here for kids. I still don't," I say.

"Unless you need dust and dirt, plenty of that here. Just like an attic should be, don't you think?" is her reply.

I don't answer.

Much, much later, we discussed how wrong we were! But at the time, we didn't know how to put the facts together.

Susanne comments, "The windows are evenly spaced and balanced on each side of this room. They are shorter here, unlike the long windows in the huge central hall. Why did they build them different lengths here?"

"Dunno," I reply.

Seeing that I have no answer, she shrugs her shoulders. "Who knows?" she mutters.

We leave the room as we find it. I close the door firmly. The long central room is unchanged. Not a sign of the multiple trunks that littered the entire floor yesterday. Not a phantom in sight!

Nervously, I say, "Now I will show you the room where I met Leila."

"In your dreams," replies Susanne.

"I don't know. Let's go to the west door," I command with false bravado. My annoyance with my sister is being overtaken by fear of what's next.

I lead the way. My heart is pounding. I am not sure what I hope for, yesterday as a dream or yesterday as reality.

The west door opens easily. Susanne notices immediately that this room, like the central hall, is clean. "Even the windows have been washed! Who comes up here to sweep? I'll bet whoever sweeps up here was playing a trick on you. Someone probably used a hologram to trick you. Yesterday, they probably laughed themselves silly." She sounds slightly anxious and a little uncertain.

I ask, "Who would do that?" I look at Susanne intently, trying to make her answer. "I can't see the American side of the family, Phoebe, or our grandparents organizing that. I can't imagine Mr. Brown, Nigel, or Mrs. Stewart coming up with that plan." When Susanne still ignores me, I eventually demand angrily, "Miss Smartie, tell me exactly. Who arranged a hologram for my entertainment?"

"Well, I don't know. I'm just guessing at possibilities," she retorts. Susanne scans the room, deliberately ignoring me as only a big sister can do. And then she continues absentmindedly, "The windows are the same size here as they are in the room on the other side." She glances around again and mutters slowly and thoughtfully, "But this room is tidy and clean. Why?" She looks at the neatly piled boxes and crates. She pokes her nose behind the open door and exclaims, "Look, here is a broom and dustpan, along with paper towels, brass polish, and window spray. Someone does sweep and clean up here!"

I glance around. The trunk is still here, exactly as it was yesterday.

"Look at the brass plate, please," I say, pointing impolitely.

Susanne sees the gleaming brass plate. "Besides sweeping, someone cleans and polishes. This brass has been polished," she says as she touches the brass plaque and the key in its lock.

She reads the nameplate on the trunk.

Mortimer Wadsworth, Earl
Poppycock, 1688–1750
Leila (née Smith) Wadsworth,
Countess Poppycock, 1690–1752
Both in residence

"What a name!" Susanne begins to laugh loudly.

Oops! I forgot to remind Susanne that Papa's title is Lord Poppycock and that our direct ancestors also carried the title Earl or Countess Poppycock.

"Someone is pulling your leg. Poppycock!" Susanne says with a smirk.

I become really annoyed and bark at her, "You know better than that! You saw the plaques in the church with the name Poppycock. And you know Papa's full title is Earl Poppycock. Nana is Countess Poppycock."

Susanne says, "Oh, I suppose I do, but that name is such a gas! It sounds ridiculous." She laughs so hard that her words are difficult to understand; she wipes her eyes as tears slide down her cheeks. "And they…are…in residence, here, in…a wooden trunk!" Eventually, after she gains control again, she utters bluntly, "Now, *that's* poppycock!"

Susanne looks directly at the nameplate. Her hand is near the key. I am just behind her when she startles. We both hear a clear, bell-like female voice.

It says, "I beg your pardon?"

Susanne's gaze is still stuck on the nameplate. Her hand drops as she asks, "What did you say, Jeremiah? Your voice sounded funny."

"Nothing. I said nothing," I reply.

"Now you are teasing me." She turns her head and fixes her gaze directly on me. We both hear the clear, bell-like voice again.

"I beg your pardon. What did you say about the name Poppycock?"

Susanne sees that my face doesn't move to say anything. She looks around. She sees only me. "Who are you, and where are you?" she demands.

"Leila Wadsworth, Countess Poppycock. You are looking at our residence. Didn't you read the nameplate? More importantly, I want *you* to tell *me* who *you* are. That's just a courtesy, and I demand to be treated with courtesy!" Leila sounds miffed.

Susanne suddenly looks confused. She looks at the trunk. She reads the brass nameplate again. She looks at me, doubt written all over her face. She faces the trunk and touches the inscription.

Like a schoolmistress, Leila commands, "Answer the question, young lady."

"Better answer her, Susanne," I say.

"I am Susanne Morris. Jeremiah is my brother," answers Susanne's quavering voice.

"Did he tell you the name of the family title?" demands Leila.

"I know it already. I've always thought it sounded silly. Papa doesn't use it unless he has to. But what am I talking…to…today?" She pauses as thin vapor starts seeping from the trunk.

Slowly and with great dignity—or with as much dignity as seeping from a trunk allows—Leila stands, floating above the trunk, translucent just like yesterday. "Have you come to help?" she demands.

With confusion and fear on her face, Susanne stares first at me and then points at Leila. Looking like she cannot believe her eyes and ears, Susanne asks, "What is this? Is this the thing that talked to you yesterday, Jeremiah?" Susanne involuntarily reaches for my hand and holds it tight.

I murmur a quick yes just before Leila bursts out, "Thing? Thing? You are calling me a thing! I am your nine-greats-grandmother. I am a person, not a thing! A little respect, if you please!"

Susanne appears confused. Her chin wobbles fiercely. She is nearly in tears. Her grip hurts my poor hand.

Leila looks at her with indignation, angered by the mockery of the family name. Calling Leila a thing has not helped matters.

I don't know what to do. Finally, I say, "Leila, dear nine-greats-grandmother, Susanne is just overwhelmed. She didn't believe the story of our meeting yesterday, so she is a little confused just now." I watch Leila to see her response; none, so far.

Quickly, I add, "She thought you were a trick being played on me, that maybe you were a computer-generated hologram. But you are not. Give her a little time. She is trying to understand."

Suddenly, Leila's indignation melts. She says, "Oh, my poor dear! I hadn't thought of that. You live in such a technological age that you need to be a little skeptical." She looks at Susanne sympathetically.

"What's 'skeptical' mean?" I ask.

"Showing doubt," answers Leila absentmindedly, almost under her breath. She continues in her usual voice, "But we don't allow holograms here. They are easy enough to create, and they can resemble us at partial materialization. That would result in complete confusion!"

Suddenly, Susanne looks angry. Her chin becomes still. She drops my hand like a hot potato. Her ears turn red, and a red color flashes on the back of her neck—that means she is really mad. She appears very calm.

Susanne's cold voice says, "You must be a phony. Your brass plate says that you died in 1752. There were no holograms then, computer generated or otherwise. How do you know about holograms? What sort of a trickster are you?"

Leila's face flashes relief as she cheerily answers, "If that's your worry, let me explain."

Susanne bravely looks at her nine-greats-grandmother with angry curiosity, but she also seems a little scared.

Leila continues, "Well, my dear, it takes energy to seep out of our trunks to materialize. But I have always been a high-energy person, and also a very inquisitive one. I am always looking for new information to keep up to date. About each week, I seep out and listen to what people are saying, watch what they are doing, listen in on conversations. I travel. I look. I listen. I learn."

She pauses before she adds, "And I do so want to clear Edgar's name. My hope is that maybe someday, something overheard will help. Anyway, new information is always very interesting, and helps me keep up with the world."

Leila scrutinizes Susanne's face, pauses again, and then states emphatically, "Even the dead need to be properly informed!" Leila flutters her eyelashes expectantly. Susanne remains stone faced. Leila appears disappointed.

Ignoring Susanne's lack of response, Leila continues, "I can seep out here or anywhere on the globe. Fortunately, I started this early, so there is not much that I have missed. And I love computers! They are so handy. I have watched people hacking other computers. So clever! Too bad the hackers do not try an honest occupation. They would be so very successful. Instead, those good minds are wasted as criminals. But to answer your question, that is how I know about holograms."

"In what year did you die?" asks Susanne.

"In 1752," Leila says sadly as an incongruous tear trickles down.

"What year is it now?" demands Susanne.

Leila answers correctly, very happy to give the right answer.

Susanne pulls out her cell phone and demands, "What kind of phone is this?"

"Oh good, a quiz. I love puzzles!" Leila appears delighted to look at the phone. She glides down beside us.

Susanne pushes the phone toward Leila. I recognize the trap. If Leila drops it, Susanne will insist she is a hologram. I am just about to say something when I realize what is actually happening.

Without paying any attention, Leila lets her hand and arm materialize completely. She takes the phone handed to her and brings it to her almost-transparent face, all the while using an arm and hand that look as solid as Susanne's.

Leila exclaims enthusiastically, "Oh! This is the one I wish I had money to buy. But none of us have any money, or rarely do, something to do with being dead! What a nuisance! But on the other hand, there is no one I could call!" Her laugh sounds like little bells ringing one after another. Then she names the type and model of phone. She tells Susanne its good attributes and mentions a few drawbacks that this model has. Susanne looks stunned.

Still talking, Leila hands the phone back to Susanne. As she stares at Leila, Susanne fumbles and drops it. Leila's hands materialize just below the phone to catch it. Wow! She's fast! Leila giggles as she catches the phone, hands it back, and says, "Care, dear. Phones can break, you know."

In a faltering voice, Susanne says, "You picked up the phone and moved it. And you were ready to catch it when I fumbled. You are not a hologram. What *are* you really?" Genuinely confused and appearing dazed, Susanne puts her phone safely back into her pocket.

Leila suddenly realizes she has just been tested. She smiles broadly and flutters her lashes as she looks toward Susanne and exclaims, "What a clever test! What a very clever girl!" She pauses and looks again at Susanne affectionately as she declares, "I know this is difficult. Let me try to explain.

"I am your nine-greats-grandmother, Leila Wadsworth, née Smith, which means 'born Smith.' Née is from the French. My father's surname was Smith. I married Mortimer Wadsworth. He later became Earl Poppycock, and I became Countess Poppycock." Leila glances around her, eyes wide open, and lashes fluttering.

"Let me introduce Mortimer, your nine-greats-grandfather. Mortimer, please come out." Leila floats up above her trunk again.

Nothing happens.

Louder, she repeats her call, "Mortimer, come out now." Despite her attempt, again nothing happens.

She stomps her foot on the trunk lid and screams, "Mortimer!"
Did the windows rattle?

Leila looks directly at me and mouths the word "no."

I have got to be more careful! Thoughts are hard to control.

Slowly, Mortimer's translucent vapor appears, and soon he floats beside his wife. Susanne's eyes scan from his wig, in proper place today, to his deep-blue eyes under thick brows, further south to his belly paunch, and finally down past his thick muscular legs in dark hose beneath his breeches, the height of fashion in his day. Her eyes return to his face, then glance at Leila's before resting on Mortimer again.

I notice he still has dried food, but different, on his waistcoat. Did Susanne notice that stain too?

With a hand extended down to display my sister, Leila says, "Mortimer, this is Susanne, our nine-greats-granddaughter."

"Is she here to help?" he asks, his eyes gazing downward at my sister.

"I don't know yet, my dear," says Leila truthfully.

Looking down directly at Susanne, he asks, "Are you going to help clear Edgar's name?" As he stares intently at Susanne, his eyes plead. He seems emotionally connected to what he is asking, for he bends slightly to stoop down toward Susanne. His body becomes increasingly opaque, as if his emotions are forcing him to materialize. He is almost solid looking by the time he says, "We need help."

No one says anything as we all look at each other. Without moving, Mortimer slowly becomes translucent again. His eyes never leave Susanne's face. Does he realize he nearly fully materialized? The silence continues.

His tone, his concern, and his intensity are very convincing. Will Susanne believe that there is no trick and that she is talking to her nine-greats-grandparents?

I don't say anything, but I'm getting a crick in my neck from looking up to the grans as they float above their trunk. Is Susanne getting a crick too?

I'm about to ask when Leila breaks the silence and says, "Come down, Mortimer. Susanne has to stop craning her poor neck. Soon, she won't be able to move her head at all! Poor Jeremiah too. They've both got kinks." She touches Mortimer's hand as they both float down beside their nine-greats-grandchildren. "And maybe if she can see you better, she won't be so confused and frightened."

Poor Susanne looks even more bewildered. She stammers, "How did you know my neck was kinked? How did you know I felt confused and scared?" Susanne turns her head toward me and asks,

"You didn't tell her, did you, Jeremiah? I didn't hear you say anything about your neck. And how would *you* know how I feel, Jeremiah? You can't ever figure anything about anybody's feelings."

That comment hurt, even though she is correct. I watch people closely and catalog reactions, but sometimes I just don't understand what other people feel or why they react the way that they do. But I keep trying to figure it all out, even though, for autistic me, life is a giant and difficult puzzle.

Susanne turns further toward me, leans in, and mouths, "How does she know? No one said anything! Right?"

I shrug my shoulders and shake my head while I say, "I said nothing."

Leila looks at Susanne. "Not to fret, dear. I have the knack of reading thoughts. In life, they called me perceptive!" She smiles at Susanne, who turns away from me to look in utter confusion from Mortimer to Leila as they stand beside her.

I can tell Susanne is still doubtful as she looks directly at Leila and says, "I can't see how you knew that looking up made my neck sore. But it did. I don't know how you know what I felt. But you were right. Maybe you do mind-read," Susanne states in an uncertain and slightly anxious tone. I can tell that my sister would really prefer to get out of here fast.

She looks directly at Mortimer. Quietly and slowly, she articulates, "There is something about the way that you talked that makes me believe you, despite my confusion. Somehow, I *do* think you are both real. Without understanding anything, I believe you. I'm not sure why."

Susanne's words are spoken so softly that I strain to hear. I can scarcely believe she is saying them. Her head swivels side to side, over and over, as she looks from Mortimer to Leila and back again.

This is worse than watching tennis!

"And now I believe the story Jeremiah told me of his experience yesterday. If Jeremiah is going to help, then I will too. But I do not know how. I do not know what we can do."

She gazes helplessly at me as she finishes by asking, "Jeremiah, what are you going to do? Will you try to help?"

I know the answer from deep inside my gut. I have known since yesterday. If this meeting is not a dream or a nightmare, then I must help, if only for Papa. "If you are in, so am I, Susanne," I reply.

"I am in," she says. "I am not sure exactly what we have agreed to do. You told me that Papa tried and failed and that the failure bothers him. I guess that makes it a worthwhile cause." Susanne still looks doubtful as she stops speaking.

"We are both in," we repeat in unison.

And Susanne mentioned Papa!

Chapter 13

What Is Next?

Susanne and I continue to look at each other for a long time. Susanne looks as blank and befuddled as I feel. Neither of us knows what to do or what to say. For that matter, I don't understand how we can talk to and see dead ancestors. It's not as if we are dead too! I touch Susanne's arm. Yup, it's warm. Yup, I can feel my heart pounding. Yup, we are still alive. Like I said before, I have no clue what to do next. From her expression, neither does Susanne.

For their parts, Leila and Mortimer look happily at each other, then at their nine-greats-grandchildren, and then back at each other.

"What is your plan of action?" queries Leila. She smiles at us but then looks straight at me.

"Huh?" I stammer. "I have no plan. I don't know where to begin." My head is spinning again!

I look at Susanne. She looks totally bewildered.

In confusion, Susanne asks, "What to do next? What *do* we try next?" She looks from one to the other, still befuddled. Then she is silent; minutes pass. With an edge to her voice, Susanne finally declares, "Both of us are new to all this. You two have been thinking for a few hundred years." Susanne changes tactics and demands, "What plan have *you* devised?" She looks directly at Leila, and then at Mortimer. Her gaze returns to Leila and stays there, which makes Great-Granny cough uncomfortably.

Surprised, Leila says, "Perhaps you need more information." She waits for our answer. She gets no response, just awkward stares. She begins resignedly, "Well then, let me try to fill in the blanks."

Leila clears her throat and slowly starts, "Let me see. Edgar was hanged in the early '45. That is 1745. The alleged incident happened in September of '44, I mean 1744. It happened in London, which is where Edgar and Jemima were living.

"There was a break-in of a home, a wealthy home. That was always a risk. We had no security systems as you do now. And finding a policeman was difficult. During the robbery, silver was taken."

Leila continues, "But the owner awakened. Presumably, he heard a noise. We don't know if one of the burglars was upstairs. For whatever reason, a fall or a push, the house owner tumbled down the stairs, hit his head, and was later found dead at the bottom.

"The owner's wife was away at their daughter's home. And some of the servants went with her. The rest slept through. I always suspected that the wine cellar was not as locked up as the owners supposed."

As she pauses to gather her thoughts, Leila's eyes flit from side to side. She seems to have trouble knowing what to say.

Slowly and quietly, Leila says, "You dears know nothing about the time. I must fill in all that is well known to us, extraneous details, things you could never know without being told." She pauses even longer.

Susanne and I can only wait. Susanne stands stock-still. I start to fidget. I shift from foot to foot as I stand quietly and listen none too patiently.

Finally, Leila recommences, "We knew the owners. He was the same age as Mortimer, a very rich man. She was five years my junior. He was connected to the East India Company, which did trade with India. His name was Walter Johnson. His wife was Abigail.

"They had only one daughter, no sons. Abigail frequently went to stay with her daughter's family. As I said, that is where she was the night of the robbery. Both Walter and Abigail were devoted to their grandchildren. Walter was to join his wife the day before he died." Awash with sadness, Great-Granny pauses yet again.

She continues in a soft voice, "I often wondered if the thieves knew he was to be away and thought the house would be empty. Servants always talked too much, sometimes had improper connections, and other times were careless about where they spoke and who might overhear."

In a somewhat more businesslike tone, Leila says, "But the afternoon before his departure, Walter was requested by his business to stay in London to entertain a few men just returning from India. These men were to address the House of Commons. They arrived the day Walter was found dead. From Walter's letter to Abigail, we learned why Walter delayed his trip and that he planned to join his wife and their daughter's family in a few days after entertaining his guests." Again, her face fills with sadness and regret.

She stops to think. Now near tears and with a rather wobbly voice, she continues, "Our son Edgar was very fond of Walter, who was another father figure to him." She glances toward her husband and adds, "We both thought Walter was a fine man and a good example for our sons." Mortimer's head nods in agreement. She controls her emotions before she adds, "Like Edgar, Mortimer and I were also very fond of both Walter and Abigail." A few very real tears fall down her cheeks.

She stops crying, sniffles, and then says more brightly, "Edgar was our second son but the heir apparent. Stephen was our first child, our first son. He died just a few days before his sixth birthday. He died of a fever—a severe sore throat and fever."

She looks down. Tears start again. "I can't think of him without crying. But he is happy where he is, staying with my extended family. And he has a friend of the same age for company. The other little boy died of the same fever as Stephen. Inseparable friends in life, they have always remained together. That's why I couldn't ask him to come to stay with us here. Everything is too complicated for a child to understand. But we visit regularly. Even after all these years, it's still hard for a mother to separate from her child."

Susanne and I stare at each other in stunned confusion, both of us silent and bewildered.

Will our jaws ever close?

After another pause, Leila says, "Two other children followed after Edgar." As she dabs her eyes and wipes her face, she adds, "The next child was James, born before his brother died. Then Sebastian arrived a number of years later. James produced Humphrey, the one with Cybil." She looks at me knowingly while she wipes her nose with a handkerchief.

"Because Edgar was hanged, James assumed the title after Mortimer's death." She stops again to gather her thoughts. "James was always getting into some mischief or other," she says with a slight laugh, amused at the recollection. She blows her nose on her handkerchief, dabs her eyes again, and looks at Mortimer as he gently touches her shoulder.

It is a little while before Leila adds, "James was reckless and didn't seem to care what anybody thought about him. He was a hard one to understand. He and his wife always looked after themselves first." She stops talking and then stays silent.

Giving Leila a chance to rest, Mortimer adds, "Sebastian was a few years younger. He was not quite twenty when his brother was hanged, a hard blow for him. Like a lot of younger sons, he went into the clergy." Mortimer looks around absentmindedly and then focuses again on us. He adds, "Sebastian decided that he knew nothing about what happened in any real sense. He didn't think he could help. He and his wife took their eternal reward. But like with Stephen, we visit regularly."

No, our jaws will never close!

Leila quietly starts up again, "Now, where was I? Oh yes, the death. Edgar had visited Walter the day before he was to leave. The police knew that. They knew we were all social friends.

"But you see, one piece of the silver that was stolen turned up in Edgar's possession. He said he didn't know anything about it. They blamed him anyway."

With curiosity, Susanne asks, "How did they know it was Mr. Johnson's silver? Could there have been a similar piece but not Mr. Johnson's?"

Mortimer answers, "No. It was Johnson's, all right. There were two silver objects. One was a rabbit, and the other was a frog. They were a pair presented together. I think Walter's name was on the frog and Abigail's on the rabbit. They were silly sentimental pieces, a joke between the two from early in their marriage. They found the rabbit in Edgar's possession."

"Oh." There is nothing else she can say. Looking thoughtful, Susanne watches everyone silently.

Mortimer continues, "Edgar was in town when the robbery occurred. He went for a long walk alone that night and was reported as near the Johnson residence. That was to be expected. He and Jemima lived nearby. They said that he had access. That was enough for the police."

Susanne turns toward Mortimer and asks, "What of motive? Surely such a trinket would not be so valuable that they would think he would steal or kill for it." Susanne sounds frustrated as she speaks.

Mortimer answers, "They insinuated he was infatuated with Abigail, who was younger than her husband. Stuff and nonsense! He had Jemima, and she was as much as he needed."

I cannot stop myself. I exclaim, "You mean what they said was poppycock?"

Leila looks at me severely, does a quick read, and realizes I am trying to lighten the sadness she feels from recounting the events. She smiles. "Yes, Jeremiah, it was all truly poppycock!" she says sadly. She is near tears again.

I'm having trouble focusing on this rambling tale. There's too much information to keep any of it straight the first time around, and it goes everywhere, all at once.

While Susanne continues to look quietly baffled, I ask, "When was the last time Edgar visited Walter Johnson?"

"Two days before he died," Mortimer replies.

"Was Abigail there?" I ask.

"No, she was with her daughter," responds Leila.

"Did he visit alone?" I persist.

"No, James was with him. They seemed close then and were often together," answers Leila while Mortimer nods.

"What else can you tell us?" I ask.

Leila appears to think but remains silent.

Mortimer says, "Not much. The police investigated, said some-one had seen a man of Edgar's description entering the house just about the time of the murder, and saw him leave with a sack after-wards." He pauses before he bitterly adds, "The witness was very vague in court, but they allowed the testimony."

I probe, "Edgar is tall and very thin. I suspect he became thin-ner in jail? Is my guess right?"

"Yes," says Leila.

"How much thinner? How much weight did he lose?" I ask.

"About two stone," says Mortimer.

"What?" I am confused about "stone."

"Two stone," repeats Mortimer.

Baffled, we both ask, "What is a stone?"

Leila looks at Mortimer and then answers for him, "Sorry, dears. You don't use stone as a weight measure anymore. A stone is 14 pounds, or 6.3 kilograms. Two stone is 28 pounds. That showed on a fit young man."

"Were all three of your living sons tall?" Susanne asks.

Leila replies, "Why yes, my dear. Edgar was the tallest, but at maturity, all were tall, well-muscled, but never heavy. They were all vigorous, right to the end. Our sons looked like brothers, similar features. And in later years, Sebastian and James had heavy brows like their father." She pauses and then adds, "Edgar, like Stephen, never had a chance to show if he favored his father like that too." Overcome with memories, she bursts into tears at the thought of the early deaths. Mortimer touches her shoulders in a futile attempt to console her.

Ignoring Leila's tears as best she can, Susanne mutters almost to herself, "But in the dark, any tall man could look much like another."

I hope I can remember everything they recount.

"Can you tell us anything else?" asks Susanne when Leila stops crying.

"I don't know what to tell you," Leila and Mortimer say together.

I have a sudden thought that I have no intention of sharing yet.

I ask, "Did James, your third son, stay behind in the attic to help?"

"Oh yes, he did. But what could he do?" questions Leila.

"Where was he in the crowd that I met?" I inquire.

Mortimer answers, "Now, let me see. James and Barbara have a trunk a little out of the way against the back wall, discreet and a little more private, just behind Cybil and Humphrey's. James became a little reclusive after his brother was hanged. That was such a burden to bear in society." Mortimer seems downcast as he answers. My guess is that he recalls how the hanging burdened *him* in society.

"May we talk to Edgar and Jemima?" I request quietly.

Susanne flashes me a look that says, "What are you doing, you idiot?"

"Certainly, you may," says Leila.

Mortimer asks, "What do they want?" Mortimer seems a little lost in old memories.

Leila speaks up clearly and a little louder. "They want to talk to Edgar."

Mortimer nods. He flushes slightly and mutters, "A little trouble with the ears."

"Hard of hearing," I murmur.

"Yes, I am." Mortimer heard that!

Maybe he is not so very hard of hearing. I think maybe he is hard of listening instead.

Leila calls to Edgar. The trunk magically appears beside the one shared by Mortimer and Leila. The brass nameplate shines despite the gray skies and the rain seen through the windows. Susanne rubs her eyes in disbelief when the trunk appears. She stares wide-eyed, mouth open.

Leila says, "Edgar, Jemima, you have guests." There is a vigorous swoosh as vapor pours out and Jemima appears. Her face is bright with anticipation until she sees Susanne.

Jemima's green eyes glare at Susanne as she demands forcefully, "And *who* is this stranger?"

Poor Susanne is quite taken aback. Taken together, both the glare of the green eyes in her translucent face and her raised, demanding voice are really scary!

Susanne looks at me. I nod for her to speak. Obviously frightened, she says in a quiet, quavering voice, "My name is Susanne...

Susanne Morris. My mother is John Wadsworth's daughter. I am Jeremiah's sister." She stops.

Susanne looks from person to person before her. Then she turns away from the others to glare intently at me. She silently mouths, "What are we doing here? Are we idiots?" Her eyes shift back to stare fixedly at Jemima. Susanne seems terrified by the face before her. She moves a bit away with knees slightly bent, as if she might need to dodge a blow.

Jemima's expression softens. "Constance is your mother?" inquires Jemima sweetly, almost smiling.

Susanne nods. Her knees unbend a little bit, and she shifts a little closer.

Speaking softly and wistfully, Jemima says, "I remember watching your mother play in the yard, often with her brothers, when she was a wee thing. She was a smart and funny little girl, who reminded me of our own daughter, all grown, and now resting with her husband's family."

Susanne appears astonished. Her mouth opens to speak. Nothing comes out. Her mouth closes again. Susanne's mouth opens again to ask Jemima something. Susanne misses her chance.

Jemima says rapidly and emphatically, "Edgar almost never seeps out. But I do regularly."

Silently, Susanne's mouth closes a second time. I can see her finally relax as she realizes that no blows are coming from Jemima.

With glee, Jemima adds, "I walk on the grounds, get some air, and watch whatever the family is doing. It takes energy, but it is a little diversion. I'm not so adept at travel as Leila, but I know more of the modern world than you would expect."

Susanne seems both surprised and confused by this news. I wonder if all these phantoms seep out for a look-see. And what have they seen?

"You have decided to help?" asks Jemima.

"Both of us have," replies Susanne cautiously.

"May you succeed!" exclaims Jemima.

Susanne looks flustered and seems uncertain what to ask. I come to her rescue.

I say, "We got some information from Leila and Mortimer."

Jemima says, "Leila will be correct in her recollections. She never gets confused. Mortimer hears poorly." Jemima looks toward her in-laws with true affection. They nod back in agreement and smile slightly.

I continue, "But there may be other bits of information that we may be able to use. Some of the information may seem trivial. We want to ask questions."

"Whatever helps. Let me rouse Edgar." Jemima taps on the trunk and says, "Edgar, please come out. We have company, and they want to help."

Edgar's wig and dark-blue eyes appear. He looks frightened. He and his vapor stop after his head is exposed. His eyes dart side to side, again like a cartoon character. At least he didn't stop at his nose!

"Make an effort, Edgar," Leila says with irritation. She adds with singular emphasis, "You *really must* overcome your depression."

So that's his problem? He's a depressed ghost? Understandable, maybe, but after a few hundred years, he's holding on to his depression too long; time to let go. Maybe he needs meds?

"Come out now, Edgar. Stop dallying." Jemima's voice is authoritative.

Slowly, deliberately, and with great care, Edgar appears, still very thin, with sticks for arms and legs. His wig is askew, which he ignores. His own dark hair pokes out from underneath. His neck remains tilted at a very odd angle so that he has to twist his body to the side to look anyone in the face straight on. His eyes dart everywhere, looking for dangers that are lurking. Overall, he looks a right mess, skinny see-through legs and all.

Jemima says, "This is Susanne, Jeremiah's sister. They are both going to help." She looks at her husband expectantly.

"They need to ask questions," she declares.

Edgar says nothing.

"You will answer, Edgar," Jemima commands firmly with a stern voice.

Edgar nods that he will try.

While I feel sorry for my multiple-greats-uncle, I am also getting frustrated. Why should Edgar be afraid of new hurts? After all, he is already dead, and for a few hundred years. *Enough already! Buck up!*

Susanne looks from me to the ancestors and back again with her mouth slightly open. She appears so uncertain and confused that I'm not surprised she doesn't say anything. I guess I'll be the one to start with questions.

"You were accused and hung for the murder of Walter Johnson. Is that right?" I ask.

"Yes," responds Edgar softly and hesitantly through his crooked teeth.

"He was your friend?" is my next question.

"I considered myself a friend to all of the family," he answers in his deep and clear voice.

"Mortimer told me that you saw him two days before he died. Is that right?" I inquire.

"Yes, I did see him then," replies Edgar.

"You invited James to accompany you?" I ask.

"No," states Edgar.

"No?" I exclaim, sounding surprised.

"That's right. No." Edgar looks me in the eye.

"But he came with you?" I ask.

"Yes," he replies.

"How?" Now I am confused.

"He invited himself," answers Edgar.

"Why?" I ask pointedly.

Edgar looks bitter as he responds, "I don't know. Perhaps he wanted to be amused."

I question, "Was Mr. Johnson amusing?"

Edgar replies, "I thought so. He talked about horses, the races, his estate, and farm improvements. That is where we had the most in common. He had advanced agricultural views and read extensively. He was a great teacher who could explain things so that I would understand." He pauses and looks down to the floor. Edgar continues sadly, "And he explained so kindly. I still miss him and his kindness." He looks slightly animated, and his eyes glisten. He seems both tired and very sad.

"Was James interested in farming?" I ask.

Edgar answers, "Not then. He liked to be entertained in society. He liked to have fun at the horse races. Barbara had recently married him. She was fashionable, and he liked that."

I say, "He sounds very superficial."

Edgar looks at me sharply and then looks at his mother. Leila nods that he can answer as he wishes. "He was," is his reply.

I hear my own intake of air. I take a moment before I continue, "So why did he want to come with you? What was he after?"

Edgar answers, "I never thought to ask. My brother James was fun to be with. He was witty and handsome. He could find humor in everything. I was the serious one, not endowed with my brother's fine features. I enjoyed his company whenever he decided to give it to me."

He stops talking and looks at Susanne. His eyes scan to me, and then to Leila and Mortimer. Finally, his gaze shifts back to me. Jemima is almost hidden behind him, looking around and through Edgar, watching us all somewhat anxiously.

Edgar continues, "My older brother was the heir apparent, but he died young. Mother never got over it in some ways. But she was always cheerful, despite the emotional pain of a lost child.

"Knowing the inheritance was to be mine, I watched carefully and learned from my father as he worked tirelessly to increase production for the benefit of the estate. He was always reading whatever journals or periodicals he could on the topic of agriculture. I had to be the one who helped my father, for later the full weight of the estate would be mine. I carried the burdens. James was allowed to play."

There is a moment of silence before I ask, "Did James have a conversation with Mr. Johnson on the day you both visited?"

Edgar answers, "There was the usual preliminary social banter. But was there real conversation? No, not really. He watched as we talked. He was absent for a time, using the facilities, I think. Tea was served. And then we left. I never saw Walter alive again." His brow furrows in sadness.

He misses his friend.

I ask, "Was there anything unusual about that afternoon?"

"No. Nothing. Walter and I had a discussion, like so many others beforehand. James was in high spirits, but I was never sure why."

I ask, "Was James often in high spirits?"

Edgar replies, "Usually if he was up to mischief. But there was no mischief that day. Everything was very ordinary. Very ordinary indeed."

"What happened after the visit?" I ask.

Edgar replies, "We took the carriage back to my residence. Eventually, James took his horse and went home. At least, that is what he said he was about to do."

I ask, "Did you see Walter or James the next day? Or have any communication?"

"No," replies Edgar.

"Did James come into your house the day of the visit?" I ask.

Edgar states with certainty, "Yes. He came into the library. I left to attend to Jemima, to let her know I had returned."

I ask, "This means he was alone in the library?"

"For a few minutes," he answers.

"Where did they find the silver rabbit? The one engraved with Abigail's name?" I almost shiver with anticipation awaiting the answer.

Edgar responds, "Behind the books in the secretary's upper shelf, in the library."

I inhale deeply as I ask, "What do you mean by 'secretary'? I am a little confused. Was another person also present?"

Edgar looks at me in confusion. Jemima's head twists 'round past Edgar to get a good look at this family descendant asking silly questions.

Leila understands my concern immediately. She stifles a giggle and explains, "In Edgar's usage of the term, a secretary is a piece of furniture, not a person. There are lower drawers, a midportion that is a desk, and bookcases above the desk. The bookcases usually have glass doors. There were three shelves in this one, and they said the rabbit was behind books on the upper shelf."

Edgar nods in agreement.

"There wasn't another person present?" I persist.

"No. Why do you ask?" demands Edgar.

I reply, "Nowadays, 'secretary' means a person, not furniture. Just checking. James was alone in the library, at least briefly?"

Edgar answers almost automatically, "Yes, he was. No matter."

I ask again, "James was absent, somewhere else in Walter's house, for part of the visit?"

Edgar is bored with my questions, and it shows. "Yes, he was. You were told that previously." His voice is flat, and the words are clipped. He sounds irritated, but that is better than hiding away. At least he is responding.

I have to ask my next question, but I am afraid of the reply. Trying to hide my feelings of fear, I ask with bravado, "Do you think that James could have taken the rabbit at Walter's house and put it in the secretary while you were out of the room?"

Edgar, Jemima, and Susanne all look stunned.

Leila exclaims, "What?"

Mortimer misses the question.

"What are you suggesting?" ask Jemima and Edgar.

Susanne looks at me in disbelief. She mouths, "How did you get there?" She looks baffled.

Mortimer asks Leila, "What? What did he say?"

Leila explains to him. He appears deep in thought as he listens and finally hears.

Mortimer murmurs, "Oh, that *is* an interesting thought!" He looks solemn and more thoughtful while saying this.

"What did you say?" Susanne asks Mortimer in surprise. Her eyes glance at me after she poses the question. "I'm not sure I heard you correctly," she adds. Now, her face looks keenly interested instead of confused.

In a slightly louder voice, Mortimer replies, "I said, 'That is an interesting thought.' And it is."

Susanne asks, "Why do you say that, Grandfather Mortimer?"

Mortimer looks at Leila, pauses in his thoughts, and then continues, "I think James never did anything that was not for his own benefit." He stops talking for a moment. His eyes look to the floor.

There is sadness in his voice when he continues, "He flirted with a young woman before Barbara. She had a child by him. He did nothing because she was not wealthy enough. I paid the hush money and a stipend that cared for the child—our grandson."

As Mortimer speaks, I glance at Susanne who looks solemn. Susanne and I both realize that this was another child that they lost. Leila looks at Mortimer, sharing his sadness. As she touches his arm, his large hand covers hers completely. He holds her hand tightly and looks straight ahead.

Mortimer continues, "He met Barbara, very wealthy, titled, and spoiled she was. She would do anything that came into her mind to get her way." He pauses, his eyes scanning as he gathers his thoughts.

He adds, "She wanted a handsome and sporty man with a title. He wasn't heir to the title when she married him. But if anything happened to Edgar, she would have what she wanted. And James loved her enough to try to please her."

Everyone is surprised and slightly horrified by Mortimer's statements. Leila looks down sadly. Jemima looks at her father-in-law with surprise.

Jemima says, "You have never said anything!"

Mortimer replies, "I have never been asked."

Unfortunately, that statement is probably very true. Anyway, that's my take.

I continue, "We have a motive for James to plant evidence. And we have opportunity. But we don't know how the robbery happened. If James was responsible, I suspect he didn't do it himself. And I can't imagine that death was part of the plan."

I feel all eyes on me. I glance back at Susanne's shocked, wide-eyed stare. She looks frozen in place.

I continue, "The family was supposed to be away. Walter's unexpected change of plans was the only reason he was there. Did James know that Walter would be home the day of the robbery?"

Edgar replies, "When we said goodbye late in the morning the day before his death, Walter was to leave early the following day." He pensively continues, "So far as James knew, both owners, Walter and Abigail, would be away the night after.

"Subsequently, we learned that later in the day Walter received a message to stay in town in preparation for his guests. But he died the next night or rather, early morning of the following day, before any of that." Suddenly, Edgar's face appears even more solemn and sad.

I say, "If James had arranged the robbery, he had no reason to change his plans. Did the police ever find any other pieces of the stolen silver?"

"No," answer Leila, Mortimer, and Jemima.

Edgar shakes his head to answer. He remains quiet, eyes shiny.

"Doesn't that strike you as odd?" I ask.

Edgar stays silent, lost in sad thoughts.

Covering for him, Leila answers, "The time was eighteenth-century London. There was great wealth. There was also great poverty, more poverty than wealth. The rich were targets, with very little protection. Just walk in the wrong laneway at the wrong time of day, and the results could be robbery or robbery and death. Most stolen goods were never recovered. And many robbers were never punished. There was a veneer of gentility and a chaotic undercurrent."

Like me, Susanne seems fascinated by the response. Leila's description sounds like the Wild West—the Wild West in eighteenth-century London!

Breaking her silence, Susanne asks, "And what would have happened if Walter had not died? I am trying to understand the system back then." We both glance at Mortimer. Susanne appears to be putting pieces together.

Mortimer answers with surprising vigor, "If there had been a robbery only and the stolen property was found in Edgar's possession, he could have been charged with the robbery. If he was found guilty, he would have ended in jail and perhaps still have been hung. Really a most difficult situation."

I am appalled.

"You mean he could swing for theft?" Susanne asks.

"If you mean that he could be hung, then yes," answers Mortimer in a somber tone.

I think out loud, "If only we could figure how this was all planned." My mind is racing as I exclaim, "I wish I could hide and eavesdrop on conversations between Barbara and James before Walter's death."

From the corner of my eye, I witness Leila's downward gaze. But she doesn't say anything about my wish, at least not yet.

Suddenly animated, Susanne asks, "Did James or Barbara have anyone they could trust with a dirty secret?"

Leila looks up and answers, "Barbara would trust her lady's maid. Her name was Eliza. She came from nothing. We always suspected she had a criminal background. But Barbara raised her up in status. Eliza was fiercely loyal to Barbara, her benefactress. I sometimes wonder if Eliza didn't procure stolen merchandise for Barbara on the side. Stolen would be cheaper, and Barbara had very expensive tastes." Leila is silent and appears full of regret at the accusation she made by speaking the truth.

In a matter-of-fact tone, Mortimer adds, "James had a valet who came to him when James was in his teens. He was just a year or two older than James—he could have been an older brother. He stayed with James until they both died."

"What was his name?" Susanne asks.

"Emmett," replies Mortimer. He pauses briefly, so we wait until he continues, "Emmett liked to know the city. I am not sure he didn't explore the worst side for his own amusement. We sometimes questioned his honesty, but he was devoted to James. He would only protect James, never harm him."

Leila is suddenly very solemn, quiet, and thoughtful. She glances at each of us. Then she says, "There may be a way to find out more. But there are risks."

She looks down and then says, almost just to herself, "Indeed, Jeremiah, you might be able to listen to Barbara's own plans, just as you wished."

Everyone suddenly stares at Leila.

She will need to explain. I'm totally lost!

Chapter 14

THE PLAN

Jemima looks at her mother-in-law with concern on her face. "What do you mean?" she demands.

"That is too dangerous," says Mortimer.

Alarmed, Edgar asks, "What scheme are you up to, Mother?"

Susanne and I look at her, eyes wide open as we say in unison, "Talk to us, Leila." We wait for her answer.

Leila glances back at us, gathers her thoughts slowly, and then hesitantly says, "Well, my dears, you know…your phone can transmit ideas electronically. And you know I can read thoughts—my gift, I call it. The mind is like a computer or smartphone. If you sleep deeply enough, your body is on autopilot; and your mind, your computer, can travel with me. We can go back and act together."

Both Susanne and I look at her in disbelief. It is hard to reconcile early-eighteenth-century attire on an early-eighteenth-century person who discusses the latest technology—especially since none of it was available until two hundred or more years after her death!

While I am dumbfounded that we are talking to the dead about technology, I am actually more astounded that we, the living and the dead, are discussing travels back through time. I've read science fiction books about time travel, but to actually go back! Well, that's awesome, and more than a little scary, especially when the travel is with the dead.

Despite my fear, curiosity gets the better of me. I ask, "How deeply must one sleep for this to happen? Or is medication needed?" The thought of time travel is sure on my bucket list. It's the kind of adventure a boy wants to have. I feel equal amounts of fear and excitement. I suddenly feel very alive!

Leila smiles knowingly at me and says, "I used a lovely herbal remedy when your papa went back. It worked well and just long enough."

Equally astounded, Susanne asks, "You have done this before?"

Leila answers, "Yes, but it didn't work as planned. When your papa was a teenager, John went back in time with me. To remain safe, he needed connection to my thoughts or those of some other ghost from the present who also traveled back. He found a clue to follow and then pursued an investigation with another phantom from the attic but without me. Long story short, we lost contact. But the other person couldn't mind-read, so they had to be close by one another for John to be safe. Even minor physical separation risked danger. I'm not sure he believed that.

"He was on his own, in the wrong century with another person, and not visible. It took all my effort to find him and bring him back, against his own will I might add! He was very upset and never came to see me again. I think he was angry that I pulled him back. And he thought himself a failure and didn't like that feeling. He simply tried to forget us, to pretend nothing happened. I know because I snooped by reading his thoughts when he didn't come to visit. But we will meet again. I'm sure of it."

Her comments about Papa fit him like a glove. No wonder he never visited again. But I suspect he regrets the failure and might like to change the outcome.

I ask, "Let me see if I understand. I take a sleeping potion and go into a deep sleep. My mind follows you back in time. While we are together back in time, we solve the murder. Then we return. Do I understand clearly?"

Leila exclaims, "Yes, dear boy! You have it."

Susanne's head is swiveling between us, first looking at Leila and then at me. Her mouth opens and closes repeatedly. Jemima, Edgar, and Mortimer remain silent, listening.

"And if we separate in the past?" I ask.

Leila adds thoughtfully, "You are not seen in the past unless you are thought-connected to a phantom from the here and now, our present time within this attic. However, this present time here and now is the future when you are back in time."

That seems redundant, but later I found out it's a key point!

She continues, "I will go back with you. You cannot move things or handle things without exhausting yourself unless you are thought-connected to someone else in the past, a phantom like me." She looks at me to see if I understand before she adds, "When you and I are in proximity, meaning close together, you will feel and appear like you do now, fully materialized, but only to those with whom you are connected in thought. Otherwise, you are invisible and inaudible." She pauses to see if I am following her.

She almost laughs as she says, "One basic rule: you must not move things about while you are invisible to others. An observer might see the objects move but will not see you. They might think they were going mad!" She chuckles again.

Naturally, I imagine plates and cutlery moving alone.

Leila laughs. "Good imagining, Jeremiah."

I blush scarlet since she has again read my noggin out loud.

She continues, "We can actually separate a little. I read minds, and with that thought connection, you can go somewhere else and remain invisible and inaudible. Separated from me, you will be able to seep through things. My mind reading will keep you safe! But if you are thought-connected to anyone else, you will be visible and audible to that person, real flesh and blood as it were, but only when you are near!"

The near bit turns out to be vital! I learned that later, the hard way.

She gazes at me briefly and probably does another quick mind read, to ensure that I comprehend. "Remember, you cannot change the past, only observe!" continues Leila emphatically.

Everyone is silent after this. We anxiously look at each other. Leila's head turns slightly side to side as she gathers her thoughts, and maybe ours. Finally, she says, "But if our minds get separated, you are on your own." After a pause, Leila's insistent voice urges, "If that happens, you must have thought connection quickly to another phantom. If our connection is severed, someone from this attic must go back in time to fetch you. It can get complicated." She looks very serious.

I see Jemima and Edgar nodding vigorously in agreement when I'm told things could go wrong or get complicated. They look downwards, anxious and somber. Slowly, their eyes return to Susanne and me. Mortimer remains silent. His face registers concern.

"If we go back, will you and I be able to communicate?" I ask.

Leila answers, "When your papa and I tried, I entered the mind of the living Leila. She went to sleep, as it were; and I, the future Leila, took over. Your grandfather and I could be physically separated, but because we had the mental connection from my mind reading, he was safe. We talked together just as we do now.

"When your papa decided to strike out on his own investigating with someone else, their thought connection kept him temporarily safe. But that other person could not mind-read, so any unexpected physical separation could spell disaster. It was too dangerous. That's why I declared a halt."

I say, "I do not quite understand, but I have a vague idea of how this works."

"Yes, I know," replies Leila with a sigh.

Susanne asks with dignity, "And what about me?" Looking squarely at my face, she challenges, "Are you planning to go without me?"

I haven't thought about this. My mouth opens.

Leila answers immediately, "I think you should be backup." She is quite firm. I cannot tell if Susanne is relieved or annoyed.

I ask, "So when do I join you in the past?"

Cheerfully, Leila answers, "No time like the present."

"What happens if I wake up?" I ask.

Leila sounds hesitant as she replies, "I think you are back here. But that has never been adequately tested." She clears her throat slightly.

"What happens if I get caught in the past?" I inquire with concern.

Leila answers with conviction, "You remain deeply asleep here. Your body is here, but your mind is not. When your grandfather wandered off in the past, it took me a few days to get him back safely from his other guide. He slept for nearly a week at home. The doctors thought he was a juvenile who suffered a stroke, until he woke up moving all parts. I never want to repeat that episode!" She stares solemnly at the floor.

I exclaim, "I need to think. I don't know what to do. Give me a few hours."

Susanne looks at me like I'm nuts, but she doesn't say anything.

Edgar and Jemima remain silent and thoughtful. They wave goodbye and return to their trunk, which disappears with a pop.

Susanne asks, "Why does each trunk pop when it disappears?"

Mortimer answers, "That pop happens whenever we shift from one time, such as the present, to another time, such as eternity. I'm not certain *why* that particular sound, but that's what happens when time bends."

Susanne mutters under her breath, "Who knew?" Leila smiles despite the sarcasm of my sister.

I mutter a question, "Time bends?"

Both ancestors momentarily ignore my question in silence until Leila finally answers, "You have heard of airplanes making a terribly loud sound when they break the sound barrier. They call it a sonic boom. Think of the pop as a break in the time barrier, a time pop, but not a boom." She smiles at us, but neither of us is really any the wiser. Neither of us pushes the question any further.

Leila and Mortimer return to their trunk, wave farewell, and seep into the cracks. The attic looks quiet and serene. There is no indication of any travel plans with phantoms.

Susanne follows me as we troop downstairs together. I say quietly, "I just don't know what is the best thing to do." I repeat this to myself over and over. We end up sitting in the morning room.

Finally, Susanne emphatically and very clearly states, "Let's just put this all into perspective, please. Going back is dangerous. You could get stuck back there. And you may not succeed." She tries very hard to convince me to do nothing. She finally asks, "What do you gain by doing anything?" Her caution and that question backfire.

I reply, "But if I do nothing, then our ancestors are stuck where they are." With a laugh, I add, "I do think a few are hoping to postpone the trip to their final destination, an ugly and eternal destination—the opposite place from heaven. Papa thought this was important enough to try. He likes to succeed. He has probably always regretted what he considers his failure. Both Mortimer and Leila think that. Leila knows he has tried to forget it ever happened." I look at Susanne. "Perhaps if I solve this, Papa will feel better about his attempt. Anything I do is more for him than anyone else."

Trying to figure what to do, I am silent until my thoughts gel. Finally, I continue, "These are our ancestors, suspended eternally between heaven and hell. Like I said before, it's a form of purgatory for all of them. Leila watches over us as she keeps up with the world. She wants us to do well. How can we not help someone who watches out for us? What sort of cowardly and lazy person would I be if I couldn't be bothered to help my own ancestor correct a wrong done against my own family? I believe Edgar is innocent, so clearing Edgar's name and our family name is the right thing to do, if only for my own self-worth. It's my duty to Leila, to Edgar, to Papa, and to me."

"But something could go wrong. This could be the end of you!" exclaims Susanne.

Thinking for a moment, I finally reply, "And it could be the end of me as a worthy person if I don't. We've both heard our parents talk about moral high ground. Maybe this is what they mean. And if I don't do this with your help, then *who* will help our ancestors?"

It's a moment before I add, "If I go back to the time before the robbery and murder, I might be able to eavesdrop on James and Barbara. Even though they are our eight-greats-grandparents, they seem suspicious to me. But I probably won't find anything—just playing a hunch."

Looking at me strangely, Susanne says, "Are you going by a hunch only?"

"I need to pay attention to my gut. It will guide me. My gut feeling is worth a lot." After a pause, I grin and eventually continue, "I also need to be in Walter's house the night of the murder. I need to know what actually happened."

Susanne looks alarmed and exclaims, "Oh, that is also not a good idea! No! No! No! Not a good idea!"

I reply, "Actually, sis, it's the best." Inside my head, I know what I must do. There is really no choice except the right one. I start walking.

She follows me toward the attic again. I can tell Susanne wants to pull me back downstairs and lock me in my room.

The trunk is still there. Translucent Leila appears almost immediately. She doesn't bother calling Mortimer.

I ask, "Is tonight a good night? Papa returns Wednesday, and Nana arrives home Friday, after time in London. Phoebe and Dad are here, but we can work around them. It might be harder when more people are home."

Leila smiles happily as she says, "I was planning for tonight. I was just waiting for your agreement. I have prepared your sleeping draft. Here it is. Drink it all when it's your bedtime."

Susanne bursts out, "Not so fast, Granny."

Leila and I stare at Susanne. Her usually pleasant voice is shockingly hard in tone. She demands, "I need to know a backup plan in case things go wrong."

Leila placates soothingly, "Nothing will go wrong."

Susanne replies acidly, "Yes, it will. It did before! You said you lost track of Papa in the past, and with persons unable to fully protect him because they couldn't mind-read. Isn't that something going wrong?"

Leila thinks for a moment, then sighs, "Yes, you are right. I'm not thinking clearly." She pauses, looks at us intently, and then whispers, "I so badly want resolution for Edgar!" She looks sad as she gathers her thoughts and murmurs, "I remember that after your papa tried and failed, I realized how risky it all had been. It took me some time, and a lot of introspection, but I eventually realized then that my wishes for Edgar were blinding my judgment." She pauses and then murmurs almost to herself, "And now I am doing it again. I am such a fool to expect his charges might be cleared. We three must stop now. We phantoms can manage in our trunks."

She glances side to side absentmindedly and adds, "If we stop trying to clear Edgar's name, some ancestors may appeal to Saint Peter to go to their final destination instead of staying here. That would be good for them." Leila suddenly looks overwhelmed with sadness, and a very real tear trickles down each cheek. "But, children, I have very truly tried hard to clear my son's name." She wipes each cheek with the back of her hand and snorts slightly because she has a runny nose as she cries.

I hand her a Kleenex from my pocket. She honks her nose as she blows. She hands the used Kleenex back to me. "I don't have any pockets," whimpers Leila with a shrug, and a wry half-smile, "and thank you."

"Okay," I reply, as I stuff the wet debris back into my pocket. *Yuck! Leila's ghost sure had a lot of snot.*

Susanne looks at the sad face of Leila and asks, "Your present plan was to go back too. You planned to guide him through the city of London in 1744, right?"

"Yes," answers Leila, "of course."

Susanne persists, "If he gets stuck, or in trouble, you will stay by him, no matter what?"

"Why yes, I shall," agrees Leila.

Susanne continues, "And if he is stuck in the past, he won't wake up here, will he?"

Leila replies, "No. He will remain asleep, unconscious."

"What if you get stuck in the past too? What's the answer then?" demands Susanne's very anxious voice.

Leila looks shocked and dismayed at the thought. "Oh my! What a clever girl! I hadn't thought of that." Leila is suddenly near tears and nearly sobs, "We can't do it. We mustn't. It is really too risky. I am a foolish old woman."

Susanne looks at me. She sees that I want to help. She says resignedly, "I didn't say he couldn't go back. We just need better planning. Jeremiah needs to be safe. You are already dead. He isn't!" She pauses to catch her breath.

Lordy, she has a way with words!

My sister continues, "Who is next in line in authority here?" Now she sounds like a true lawyer, age thirteen!

"Mortimer," Leila replies, pauses, and then continues, "if you can rouse him up. But he might come with me."

"And if waking Mortimer fails, or he goes with you?" demands Susanne.

"Well, next are Marcus and Beatrice," our granny replies.

"Will they respond to me?" inquires Susanne.

"I will arrange that they do," responds Leila.

"And after them?" persists Susanne.

Leila thinks and finally answers, "Then Joshua and Penelope. And of course, Jemima, maybe even Edgar, if he agrees to seep out." She pauses and looks around vaguely, scanning again with her eyes. She finishes her thought with "If only we could motivate him, he would be the most help. He was so different before—before the murder charge, before they hanged him."

Dah!

Leila adds as an afterthought, "We mustn't forget that Bertie and Marjorie want to be included. I think they just want a day trip."

Susanne asks, "You mean, some would help just for entertainment?"

"Quite so," replies Leila, "that's my guess."

"I've met them, Susanne. I agree with Leila," I add.

Much later, I would say, "Again with the assumptions, Jeremiah, you idiot!"

Susanne asks, "Will I be able to get their attention? Will they come to help me if I ask?" She sounds worried.

"Let's ask them now," replies Leila.

"Let us ask them all," adds Susanne.

"Let me get Mortimer." Leila looks down at the trunk lid.

With thumps and bumps on the trunk and some yelling, Mortimer arrives as translucent as Leila. He floats beside his wife. She tells him our plan. He listens intently.

"Did you hear, dear Mortimer?" asks Leila.

"Of course," he replies.

There is no "of course" about it. I glance toward Susanne, who does her famous eye roll just for me. We say nothing.

I state, "I want to see James and Barbara. Point them out to me. I don't want any of them to know what we are planning, only that they may need to partially materialize to talk to Susanne or me when we request it. Can you do that, Leila?"

"Yes," Leila answers promptly.

I state, "If we get into trouble, maybe even Papa will need to be involved."

Susanne and Leila exclaim, "Papa!" Mortimer inhales deeply.

I say, "Yes, Papa. He was here before to help Edgar. He would want our plan to succeed. If I get into trouble, he needs to know." I look directly at Susanne as I add, "If you need, show Papa the handkerchief and cigarette holder that belong to Marjorie. I'll bet he will recognize them. That way, he will know what is going on and what to do."

Susanne looks amazed as she says, "You seem to have a plan deeply organized in your own head. What else have you planned?"

I have nothing thought out and no plan at all.

"Dunno." That is my truthful reply.

Looking directly at me, Leila murmurs, "We'll think of something."

With hindsight years later, Susanne and I discussed that neither of us ever considered what would happen to the family when one of their children remained unconscious in his bed while his mind was actively traveling back in time. It was much later that Susanne and I discussed what Mom might have said if she discovered our plans. The words "No way!" leapt to mind, followed by threats. Ditto for Dad, but louder. But as it happened, the rest of the family knew nothing of our activities. They could not understand what was actually happening. They could only fear the worst. But those sensible thoughts were for later. Perhaps all that was just as well. If I had once thought that I might never see my parents again, I might have lost my nerve.

Later I realized that none of the risks I was undertaking with Susanne's help ever crossed my childish mind. If Susanne thought it out, she never said anything either. I think she was as empty headed as I was. The groundless confidence of children that all will be well because that is what they want—all of that is universal foolishness and universal selfishness!

As Leila calls our ancestors, the trunks appear followed by translucent couples that seep out and float above each one.

Susanne's mouth gapes at the sight. She glances at me and then looks from Mortimer to Leila. I can tell that she remembers what I told her yesterday. No sound crosses her lips; her eyes say it all. She almost slobbers from her open mouth as she stares from one translucent ancestor to another.

Cybil looks like she is still pouting. She's probably still angry with Marcus after yesterday's rebuke. Humphrey looks distracted. Does he understand anything? Is he the real village idiot?

Leila introduces Susanne and explains, "The children might need to interview some of you or ask for your help as they investigate."

Mortimer loudly asks, "Will you all help with whatever is needed?"

Most agree they will respond to a call and will help however they can. Some are very enthusiastic in their reply. Some agree but are uncertain what they can do. Jemima is very enthusiastic. Edgar looks terrified. Some are silent. It's hard to read Mortimer's facial expression as he listens to the responses, or lack thereof.

As requested, Leila nods to the back wall, just behind Cybil and Humphrey's trunk, where the two translucent forms of James and Barbara look at the group with curiosity. When they learn Susanne and I may call for help, both watch us suspiciously and warily with slit-like snake eyes. Creepy!

Susanne touches my arm, discreetly points a finger to James and Barbara, and murmurs in my ear, "Those two give me the heebie-jeebies."

James looks about thirty-five. Although not so tall as Edgar, he is well over six feet with a muscular frame. Since he is not wearing the wig he holds clutched in his hand, thick dark hair falls over his ears.

He has light hazel eyes above his rather large nose, which is almost the size of Dad's. And like Dad, he has a very strong jawline. Despite the nose, he is a handsome man. His clothing is in the latest fashion of mid-eighteenth-century attire.

With a slight build and wiry frame, Barbara looks slightly younger than her husband as she stands beside him. Even with her wig hair piled high in an enormous hairdo and wearing her heels, she is far shorter. Her brown eyes peer out from her long face with its square chin. Under her long straight nose, her mouth is a thin, selfish slash. Her dress is a beautiful deep blue, fringed with lace at the low collar and at the cuffs, probably highly fashionable for her time. The dress and its skirts are heavily embroidered.

Both James and Barbara focus keenly on Susanne and me. They smile slightly, a smirk really. When they return to their trunk, they both momentarily glance at us with contempt. They say nothing.

Marcus and Beatrice greet Susanne affectionately. Beatrice says, "We have watched you growing up. I am glad we are meeting properly." Susanne looks too disturbed by this comment to respond.

Covering, I say, "Yes, that *is* good."

Joshua and Penelope descend from above their trunk to give Susanne a hug. Susanne responds mechanically. I can tell my sister is undergoing information overload and system meltdown despite the loving kindness offered.

Bertie and Marjorie say a special hello by asking, "When do we start? When do the games begin?"

Susanne looks at me to answer. I smile at them and shrug my shoulders. "Dunno," I reply.

Through the doorway, Jemima waves, and Edgar shows only his head and twisted neck. Susanne seems able to cope with that.

All of these unknown but attentive people overwhelm poor Susanne. After all of them have gone, she says, "That was psyche overload."

I whisper convincingly to Susanne, "I think our eight-greats-grandparents are guilty parties."

"Well, they creep me out. But then, they all creep me out," replies Susanne.

Leila hears me and immediately asks, "You think James and Barbara were somehow involved?" We both see Mortimer's face register genuine concern at Leila's question.

"Yes, I do," I reply quietly, with my eyes leaving Leila and glancing toward Mortimer.

Leila poses a profound question, "Has one of my sons been responsible for the death of another?" I can tell my words have caused her emotional pain. Despite being near tears, she grits her teeth and says, "Justice must be done. I will support whatever you find that is true and whatever you do that is good." She stares blankly into the distance, lost in the past. Mortimer suddenly appears lost as well. His face registers profound regret, perhaps caused by more than my words.

Forgetting about Mortimer and Leila's sadness, and Susanne's overload, I focus on the next big event, time travel. I ask, "Leila, how do I find you after I take the sleeping potion?"

"Pardon, dear boy?" Lost in recollections from long ago and far away, Leila muses absentmindedly. "Oh yes, the time travel. Sorry, I was miles away, in another time." She visibly gathers her thoughts, shakes off her web of sadness, and finally answers briskly, "The very last thing before sleep, you must think about this trip through time. That way, your mind will be ready. I will be watching for you. What time do you go to bed?"

"During vacation, usually around ten o'clock." Susanne nods agreement.

Leila appears excited as she says, "Right. I will be awake. I will start thinking of you just after that."

"When I see you, what happens then?" I ask anxiously.

She laughs. "The time travel is easy. We touch hands and foreheads so we mentally and physically connect."

Leila looks very serious as she slowly continues, "There is one thing I want you to understand. I will be more use to you if I can do things with a living body and not just as a phantom. When we go back, I will be in my body as it was then. I will mind-read to keep you safe. But you will need to focus on my physical person, not this phantom, in order to keep in contact."

Connecting eyes with Leila, I ask, "Let me see if I've got this right." I try to make the distinction as I repeat, "I need to get the attention of the physical Leila and not the spirit of Leila."

Susanne sternly interjects, "How does *that* happen?"

Without missing a beat, Leila answers, "When I was alive, I enjoyed certain things with gusto. Food was one. Wine was another, in reasonable quantities only. If you think of food and drink, you will have my attention." Mortimer starts to laugh a little, as if he has a hidden joke.

"If you enjoyed food and drink so much, how did you remain so trim?" asks Susanne.

Both Leila and Mortimer laugh. Leila nods to us both as she answers, "I exercised daily, long before others knew it helped. I rode horses most days and walked wherever I could. And I kept portion control. But I really enjoyed what I did consume." Her eyes open wide, and her long lashes flutter as she says, "I am a woman of strong appetites."

In later years, when we were much older and worldly-wise, Susanne and I discussed how very much we believed her as we speculated about her appetites, food being only one of them. It was Susanne who said, "I suspect Mortimer was one regularly satisfied fellow most nights." But like I said, that was years later, when we *both* finally understood much more about life and sex.

Despite her odd request, I agree, "Okay. I will think of food and drink to get your attention."

"Yes, dear. That's a good boy," she says.

"I think I am ready," I say uncertainly.

Leila hands me a small bottle containing liquid. "This will let you sleep deeply enough to allow your mind to find me here. Drink it all when you go to bed. Then come to the attic tonight after you are asleep."

How very silly that sounds! I say nothing as we descend the stairs.

"Not silly at all," says Leila's fading voice as she disappears with Mortimer into their trunk.

Near our bedrooms, I mutter, "See you downstairs. I need to hide this." My finger points to the little bottle of liquid.

Downstairs, Susanne and I are both excited and anxious. I want to start this adventure, but I am afraid. What if something goes wrong?

Phoebe arrives back from her trip to London. Near the end of supper, Dad asks what she did and if she made any interesting purchases.

Phoebe details a few things she did. "I made some purchases, a few minor things. But I did find the most interesting trinket in the Silver Vaults."

"You did get there. Wonderful! Tell us all about it," requests Dad, just as we finish eating.

Susanne appears interested and says, "Do tell all."

I am not paying much attention to their talk. My mind is elsewhere. Suddenly, I am aware of everything around me. The hairs on the back of my neck are standing up straight.

"The Silver Vaults were fascinating to see. There were wonderfully beautiful things everywhere, most well beyond my reach. I was ready to leave when I saw one little shop tucked out of the way. I decided to explore, and I came across this cute little thing. It just spoke to me as a gotta-have. I rarely feel that way about anything. But it called to me," says Phoebe quietly.

"Well, let's see your gotta-have," says Dad, looking curious.

Phoebe goes to collect a little parcel from the hall and returns with it to the dining room.

She mentions, "The shopkeeper said it is old. And it is engraved."

Wildly curious, I ask, "What did you get?" I'm barely able to contain my excitement.

"Yes. Here it is," says Phoebe as she pulls her purchase partway from its bag. She struggles to read from the bottom of the object, which is still partially covered. "Ah yes, 'Abigail, from Walter' is the inscription."

Phoebe hands the object to Dad, which he holds in the palm of his hand. "Why, Phoebe, it is actually quite lovely." He flips it over. "This looks like high-quality silver. 'Abigail from Walter.' I wonder who they were."

Dad carefully inspects the item in his hand before he continues, "I am no expert, but I suspect this is entirely hand done. The workmanship is superb. And it is quite heavy. I hope you didn't need to rob someone to get it."

Susanne and I startle when Dad says this. Then we hear Phoebe laugh and say, "Actually, the shopkeeper was very sweet. He saw I was quite taken with it. He said to me, 'This is not a popular item. Rather, it is an unusual artifact really intended for a small clientele.' That is what he said—'an artifact for a small clientele.' What an old-fashioned thing to say! Anyway, it was very expensive. I put it away and was about to go."

Phoebe pauses in thought and then continues, "But the dear man said, 'You really do like it, don't you?' When I replied that it was calling me and I didn't know why, he said, 'Then it must be yours.' He named a price no one could refuse and which I could afford. So I bought it." Phoebe smiles happily at this.

Dad sets the silver rabbit on the table, one paw up over its nose, one ear up, one slightly down, and looking relaxed, fat, and happy. The head is turned slightly as if looking to the left.

Almost shaking with excitement, I can't speak because my voice will crack, and I could never explain why. Those beans might spill. Claiming to talk to deceased ancestors who told me about the stolen bunny will label me as a nutcase.

With my muddled thoughts and the anticipation of time travel, it never occurred to me that a kind and loving son should be spilling the beans and right now! What a selfish boy! Susanne likewise said nothing. I guess she was as callous as me.

Susanne sees my burning curiosity. She asks to see the rabbit and picks it up carefully. It is longer than her palm. Her hand drops down a little under its surprising weight. "The workmanship is fine, very detailed, perfectly done." She turns it over and sees the engraving. "Wait a minute. I think I see something else just above the inscription. It's not clear."

Dad finds a magnifying glass and hands it to Susanne. She struggles for a few moments. "Oh, here it is—'On the occasion of our first anniversary, 1716.' Wow!"

196

Dad looks at it next and then Phoebe before he says, "Phoebe, it seems you have the eye to pick a real winner." Dad chortles as he speaks.

Phoebe replies, "And what's really funny—the man in the shop looked just like that man with his wife in that painting over there. He even had the white forelock." She points toward the wall near the sideboard.

I race over and read the label on the frame, although Susanne and I have already met them both.

The painting depicts Joshua and Penelope Wadsworth as a couple aged about thirty-five or so. Penelope smiles down at me, hazel eyes watching. Joshua is beside his wife, almost smiling, with a shock of white through the front of his otherwise thick dark hair.

"Those are Papa's parents," I say. I look back at Phoebe and Dad. I don't dare look at Susanne.

"Then he wasn't your salesman," says Dad, laughing. He smiles broadly at Phoebe.

"I certainly hope he wasn't. I could never explain that one!" says Phoebe with a chuckle. "They say everyone has a double somewhere."

"Yes, a doppelgänger," adds Dad.

I stay silent, like a fool.

Actually shaking, I look back again at the silver rabbit on the table.

Chapter 15

A Trip through Time

Before bed, in the few minutes Susanne and I have alone in my room, she asks yet again, "Are you sure you want to do this?"

"No. But I think I must," I reply.

"It frightens me. Suppose something bad happens," says Susanne.

"Then you will need to ask for help," I reply.

Susanne is near tears. Her chin jiggles wildly as she says, "Suppose I mess up."

I reply, "Or maybe I mess up. We must do the best we can. And remember, Papa can help if you need."

Susanne's face screams *annoyed* as she says, "He is not here!"

She is right about that.

I reply, "He comes home Wednesday night, two days before Nana. He went back once, so if something goes wrong, he will know what to do."

Later, we would realize we were naïve fools, both of us! But we had to learn for ourselves.

I ask, "Do you have Marjorie's handkerchief? And the cigarette holder?"

Susanne replies, "Yes. They are in my room. I hope I don't need to bring them out." Susanne thinks for a moment. Suddenly, with some urgency, she commands, "Make sure you have clean clothes on tonight—just in case you fall asleep for a few days. You want everything clean, at least at the start."

"Clean underwear in case I am exposed in the hospital after an accident?" I laugh out loud. "Well, they do say that for a reason!"

After a pause, I add, "It is just as well that I am taking a sleeping potion tonight. That rabbit showing up was too much! Do you think it is the same one that was used as evidence to hang Edgar?"

Susanne answers, "Well, the date is right. It's made from silver. That's the correct metal. The inscription is the same. The rabbit was stolen and became police evidence. If the family didn't claim it, then it remained with the police. Who knows what happened after that? Eventually, it may have been tossed, or taken and sold. Funny that it showed up just now. But I think it has to be the same one especially since it was one of a kind. Too many coincidences!"

"What do you think about the person who sold it to Phoebe?" I ask excitedly.

Susanne says, "Phoebe said he looked like Joshua Wadsworth. I didn't pay enough attention to him. My brain was snowed from so many people! But I suspect it was just someone who bore a superficial resemblance to him."

I reply, "I don't think so. Penelope said they don't seep out much. But Joshua looks like a man who would do whatever is necessary to accomplish what needs to be done. I think he materialized in that shop just to sell that rabbit to Phoebe."

Susanne looks at me and says, "Oh really, Jeremiah? Are you nuts? Your imagination gets the better of you sometimes. You are going around in circles. In fact, you are so far ahead of yourself that you will soon catch up to yourself."

I reply, "That doesn't make any sense."

"Neither do you," Susanne quips back.

Susanne stays in my room. I go to the bathroom to get into clean underclothes and pajamas. I clean my teeth, and when I finish everything, I return to my bed and sit down beside Susanne.

She says, "Those vertical red and white stripes on your pajamas always make me think of peppermint sticks." She laughs nervously.

I nod in agreement and chuckle quietly. I'm too nervous to laugh.

"Oh well, at least they are clean," I reply, shrugging my shoulders.

At that moment, Susanne began to say, "And what about our parents…" but fell silent as Phoebe came in. Fortunately or not, Phoebe didn't hear her. We missed our chance to inform the adults. For my part, I was so wrapped up in the adventure of time travel that I was not thinking of anyone else at all.

We all go through our evening going-to-bed ritual as if nothing is amiss. Phoebe kisses me good night. Just before she leaves, Susanne gives me a hug, which is not usual. Phoebe looks a little surprised and mutters, "The vacation in England is bringing you two closer together. Good!"

As soon as Phoebe leaves, I look at the time. Nearly ten o'clock. I take the bottle out of my night table, get a glass of water from the bathroom, and nip back into bed wearing my slippers. Sitting up, I drink down the liquid given to me by Leila. I expect the draft to taste awful, but it is sweet and fruity. I drink down the water and lie back.

Nothing happens for a few minutes. I am comfortable, oh so comfortable. I stretch and then startle, panicked. "What about Leila! I need to think about her. I need to imagine…food and…drink," I mutter as my eyes close, my breathing slows, and deep sleep overtakes me.

Just after ten, I am walking upstairs to the attic. Well, my mind is, because my body is sleeping soundly in bed.

I reach the attic door and can't open it. I look at my hand; it is translucent. I look like Leila does! Nearly transparent! Partly materialized! Not part of this world! I think of what Leila would do. I walk through the solid door, which offers no resistance. "Nifty!" What else can I say?

I quickly find Leila and Mortimer's trunk. They both respond immediately to my soft voice. She motions for me to speak quietly. Mortimer remains silent, worried-appearing, and mostly watches while Leila and I talk.

"I have a few questions, Leila. Did Great-Grandfather Joshua seep out today?"

"Whatever for, dear?" she asks, avoiding my gaze.

"Leila! Truth please," I demand dryly.

"All right, then. Yes, he did. We overheard that Phoebe would be going to the Silver Vaults."

I ask, "Did you seep out and listen?"

"Yes, dear boy," replies Leila in a flat, matter-of-fact way. She looks away and then directly at me again as she recites, "I have followed the whereabouts of that rabbit for years. For a while, it was a job to keep up with that bunny after it was stolen from police evidence. Each sale meant it hopped from one place to another! It is small enough to be a trinket and not so remarkable as to draw universal attention. Initially, it had a series of rather colorful, if brief, owners. But I followed it as it hopped here and there, until it finally settled." She stops talking and appears to be lost in thought. A momentary smile crosses her lips.

Leila continues, "A few years ago, I informed Joshua where it was, so he followed its path after it was part of an estate sale. Back then, he told me he hid the rabbit in the shop and then said, 'The owner won't mind, probably won't even recall, and it might be useful to us someday.' I hope he is correct, on all counts."

She pauses for a moment and then says, "Joshua agreed to materialize to make the sale after he put the rabbit back on the market today."

I ask, "Why was it on the market again, I mean before today?"

She replies, "It was from the dispersed estate of an old lady who owned it last. She was a relative of Penelope's who bought it years ago. She recognized the inscription when she made the purchase."

I am fascinated. "How could some old lady know that?"

Leila answers sharply, "Well, for one thing, she wasn't always some old lady. In her youth, she also tried to help, before Papa. You won't remember her. She was older than Papa and died when you were about five."

"What was her name?" I inquire.

"Emma Winter."

I ask, "Was she a relative?" I see Mortimer nod yes.

Leila replies, "She was a cousin of Penelope's, a lovely girl who came to visit for a few weeks one summer when she was in her early twenties. She came to the attic on a whim."

Curious, I ask, "Did you guide her up here?"

Mortimer nods again while Leila answers, "Yes. She was the sort of person who would help. But nothing went right, and the plan failed. The next to try was your papa."

I must ask the next question, "Where is Emma now?"

"She rests with her husband. They were both good people. She knows that we remain here. She and her husband have visited occasionally."

Astonished, I ask, "She does what?"

"Visits," replies Leila, while Mortimer tilts his head slightly and smiles.

I am dumbfounded. "How does she do that?"

"She thinks of me, so we have contact, and our thoughts arrange the meeting."

There is much I simply do not yet understand. But I try to remember what is said. That turns out to be a good thing.

"I need to know something else, and it is very important. Did James and Barbara stay at your house or visit with any servants after the robbery, perhaps during the trial, Leila?"

"Yes. Why do you ask? What is the significance?"

"Tell me all," I demand flatly.

Leila says slowly, "My, it is hard to recall the details. It was so long ago. They visited about a week before the robbery, just for dinner." She thinks for a moment and then says, "I had a few others over the night of the dinner party. I remember because I became ill that night or maybe a few nights later. I'm not sure about the date. For some reason, the memory remains unclear. It was a few days before I felt clearheaded after the illness, I do recollect that." She pauses again, looking down, lost in her memories. Leila resumes, "It's unusual for me not to recollect the exact date. But I do recall that they came for a lengthy visit during the trial."

"Tell me about that stay," I request.

She looks at her husband for reassurance. Perhaps he is recollecting too and cribbing her as she reads his thoughts.

A neat party trick if it's yours!

202

He nods slightly as Leila slowly says, "It was early 1745. The rabbit had been found in Edgar's secretary. They came to visit during the trial to help me through. Some servants were with them, including James's valet, Emmett, who was very close to James. They stayed throughout the trial. Frankly, I wish they had stayed in the country."

"Why did they not stay in their own house in London?" I ask.

"Who knows? They could have stayed away so far as I was concerned. They really were no help to me. And I needed help desperately then."

Concentrating, Leila continues, "The excuse was that their whole place was being repaired and repainted after a roof leak. The house was not habitable, at least that is what she said."

"Why did they choose that time to repair the house?" I ask.

Leila looks suddenly baffled as she answers, "That is a question I failed to ask. Barbara started the repairs and repainting immediately after the roof repairs. Barbara always wanted her wishes granted immediately. And she certainly never liked to be inconvenienced!"

On the spur of the moment, I say, "We need to go back a week or so before the robbery. You need to get me into James and Barbara's residence."

Leila responds, "Do you think there is something there that will help?"

"I don't know. But there may be information to be seen or heard. Nothing ventured, nothing gained. But I am totally guessing," I reply.

Leila nods. "Are you ready?" she asks.

"I scarcely know, but we shall try." I smile at Leila uncertainly.

Leila says, "When we arrive, you will think of me with food and drink, and I will think of you. We will have easy communication. Not to worry." Leila tries to make me feel safe. I don't feel safe at all.

I say, "I will think of good food and drink to get your attention. I'll practice that."

"Practice till perfect. That is a good plan," Leila replies.

She fully materializes as she reaches toward me. "Take my hand," she commands.

When I take her hand, I fully materialize as well. Instead of looking translucent, my hand, and the rest of me, looks like solid flesh and blood again.

"Now then, let us touch foreheads. Please, hold tight while we travel."

I look at Mortimer and declare, "See you when I return." I hope he has heard everything. Then I ask, "Or are you coming too?" I try to laugh. I fail 'cause I'm too scared.

With a nod, he replies quietly, "I'll follow after." Mortimer still looks anxious and worried.

I look at Leila and do as I am told. As I take her hands, I feel their warmth. As our foreheads touch, the room begins to spin. I close my eyes tight. I feel movement. There is a large pop and an enormous flash of light.

When my eyes open, we are in a different place. It looks like an eighteenth-century bedroom in a prosperous house.

Candles burn in their holders. There is a massive four-poster bed with drapes hanging from the rails, waiting to be drawn around the bed at night to protect the sleepers from drafts. A fancy chest with gold metalwork on the legs stands against a wall. Against another wall stands a huge armoire with an open door, from which clothes peep out everywhere. Near the bed, a very ornate wooden screen hides one corner of the room.

I look toward Leila. She is sitting on an ornate bench in front of a matching dressing table that has the same gold metalwork as the chest against the wall. The dressing table is at an angle from the bed and free standing in the room. She is gazing into her mirror that is anchored on the underside of the midsection of the dressing table-top. Hinges on that section allow the mirror to pull up and lock for use and then push back down to hide away. Nifty!

"There you are," I comment happily with a smile. Then I pose a cheerily redundant question, "Have we both arrived safely?" My smile freezes as she makes no reply. It takes a moment before I realize she cannot see me! She cannot hear me! I feel slowly rising panic, which I do my best to suppress. I utter anxiously, "Maybe if I just watch, everything will be okay. Give it time, Jeremiah! Give it time."

Meanwhile, Leila remains oblivious! Candles burn brightly from their fancy candlesticks sitting on each end of her dressing table. Leila, my only contact, remains seated still checking her reflection in the pull-up mirror framed by the candlesticks. Nothing is nifty anymore!

While thinking of good things that I like to eat and drink, I exclaim loudly, "Sure, Leila, that foldaway mirror is great; but I have a problem! Come on, Granny, talk to me. Enough with the mirror! Show me you know I am here." Despite my best efforts, my panic level is rising. I can hear my voice. Can anyone else? Hello!

My frantic voice whispers, "What to do? Details, pay attention to details! And watch! Give her time. Learn from the details. Things will be all right, Jeremiah. Just keep things in order in your head. This is just a bump in the road. She'll notice your clues of food and drink. Don't panic!" My head frantically repeats, "Watch! Don't panic," in my desperate effort to make sense of everything around me and to reduce my rising tidal wave of fear.

To calm myself with ordinary stuff, I notice that she is dressed differently than when we departed. Her gown is a dark purple, with heavy embroidery on the top and the skirt. She is wearing dangling diamond earrings and a similar-patterned diamond necklace.

As I watch her, I realize that she is in the process of preparing for dinner. Her lady's maid knocks on the door, enters when told, and says, "I am so sorry, but I've looked everywhere, and I cannot find the color of ribbon you mentioned. Apologies."

"Not to worry," replies Leila, "it was just a passing fancy. I can easily do without. Now that you've returned, help me finish." They chat as the maid starts fussing with Leila's massive hair held artificially high. I hear the conversation between the two, comments about one person after another—who became betrothed to whom, local gossip—and then James is mentioned. Apparently, her lady's maid does not have a favorable opinion of Barbara. She is concerned that Barbara leads James by the nose.

Leila says quietly, "Oh, Marie, we must remain quiet outside this room. We cannot give vent to our views." Leila looks at her maid knowingly with a tight little lip curl and adds, "Even should those views be correct."

"Yes, ma'am," replies Marie obediently with a wry and knowing smile.

When Leila is dressed, her maid asks, "Anything else, m'lady?"

"Thank you, Marie, but nothing for now. I will see you after dinner," replies Leila as she turns on her bench toward Marie who leaves by a door that opens to a wide hallway.

Leila is alone, except for me. But there's a problem. She still thinks she is alone! She doesn't seem to know that she's responsible for the care of a panicking grandson who is running out of food and drink ideas. Why didn't I ask, "What's your favorite food?" Wine, I already figured. She turns back, again facing the vanity, and once again regards her reflection in the looking glass. She checks for any errors in dress. She scans her hair held massively high, and her ears and face to ensure all is ready for company at dinner.

Once again, I think about food and drink to get Leila's attention. I just hope it works this time. My thoughts add wine, lots of wine. I exclaim frantically, "Please, Leila, don't forget about me!" I'm losing my battle against a rising tsunami of panic. What if I'm left here alone, invisible, inaudible, unrecognized, without help, and in the wrong century? There's not much future in that!

Leila asks, "Why do I keep thinking of the name Jeremiah?" She says to her reflection, "I don't know anyone of that...name... Oh my, so tired! Oh, for a good red...wine. Very...soon."

She closes her eyes and then seems to fall into a deep trance. Her head slumps forward till her chin rests on her chest, with her mouth slightly open. A few moments later she opens her eyes, shakes her head slightly, and then asks, "Jeremiah, are you here?"

"Yes," I exclaim loudly with waves of relief flooding over me.

"There you are. I see you now. Did you travel well?" she nonchalantly asks my image in her mirror.

I look at Leila with amazement and demand sharply, "What just happened?" I shake my head side to side, wipe away a little sweat, and add, with rapid speech showing my anxiety, "I couldn't get your attention. I was terrified."

Leila answers slowly and articulately to her mirror, "The real Leila who lives here does not know you. By happenstance, I was required to wait till Marie left before I dared to enter my living mind. I had no way to tell you, without causing a mishap, that there was an unavoidable delay. My deepest apologies, dear boy."

Totally relieved, I babble in a high-pitched voice, "Okay. It's all okay. I'm fine." My breathing slows as I mutter hurriedly, "It was a little scary, but I'm fine."

"Not yet, dear boy. You're not fine yet—that I can tell. But you will be soon recovered," she responds knowingly, her eyes both concerned and amused. "Now, back to what happened. You saw living Leila fall asleep momentarily as I took over. I will manage things for the foreseeable future and then return her to her former state. I won't make any embarrassing social mistakes." Leila takes a final swift look in the mirror and says, "Satisfactory." Still sitting on her bench, she swivels toward me.

I heard what Leila said, but it seems unbelievable. I am curious, so I ask, "Will the living Leila remember anything at all from this visit from you, the future Leila? Or will everything be a blank?"

Leila thinks for a moment and then replies, "We cannot leave a blank. That's unfair. But she will have only a superficial knowledge and vague remembrances of routine activities and interactions that involve future Leila while present Leila sleeps. She will not recollect anything related to time travelers who visit. Those recollections will be blocked. Her intuition about certain things will be stronger and more accurate, subliminal memories only, memories in the unconscious mind."

"And you can see me?" I ask, looking for safety and reassurance as my panic slowly recedes.

"Oh yes, dear boy. I see you clearly. Remember, no one else but Mortimer and I will be able to do so." She looks at me quizzically as she asks, "You know he decided to come along too?"

"Yes, he said he would follow." I ask anxiously, "Does the same sleep thing happen to the living Mortimer so that Mortimer's ghost and I can see one another?" I need details to understand everything about me and to create stability and peace in my head. *Stay calm!*

"Yes, on both counts. While my Mortimer will definitely be able to see you, in 1744 London he will wonder about a ten-year-old American boy in pajamas and slippers, looking like a peppermint stick. Are you hungry?"

"No. But I need to pee," I say. "No panic, but I *really* need to pee. Fear does that to me, makes me need to pee, I mean."

"The pot is under the bed on the far side," replies Leila casually.

"The what?" I ask.

She answers, "The chamber pot. We do not have modern bathrooms. They have not been invented yet." She sees my confusion. "You can take it behind the screen."

"Take what?" I ask again in total confusion.

She repeats patiently, "The chamber pot. Go behind the screen where you can do your business."

I look again at the beautiful carved wooden screen. I find the pot and copiously tinkle into it after the screen discreetly hides me. "What do I do with this?" I point to the pot containing lots of yellow liquid.

"Back under the bed," replies Leila in a matter-of-fact voice.

"Where do I wash my hands?" I ask.

"No need. Germ theory has not yet been invented." Leila laughs at her own joke.

"What else have you not told me?" I ask with a sigh.

"Much! But you are a quick study, and I cannot recall everything. The more something is done commonly, and without thought, the fewer comments one thinks to make." She glances into the mirror again, nods in approval, and adds, "The assumption is that everyone knows the same material as oneself. That is a dreadful but common mistake." Leila seems satisfied that her statement is enough.

All this is true. Once again, I feel very scared and alone. I cannot manage in eighteenth-century London as a twenty-first-century American in pajamas and slippers without my nine-greats-grandparents!

"Where is Mortimer? We need to make sure he can see me," I plead as my panic rises unnecessarily again.

Leila leaves her bench, walks over to the mantelpiece, and pulls a long narrow embroidered cloth that is hanging nearby. As far as I can tell, nothing happens.

Confused by her actions, I ask, "What did you just do?"

"I pulled the bell cord which rang the bell," Leila replies.

"I heard nothing," I say.

"Of course not!" exclaims Leila. "The master and mistress do not want to be disturbed with every bell that rings! It rings in the servants' quarters. These are not yet in widespread use and won't be till the end of this century. Bell pulls will be common by the mid-nineteenth century in upper-caste houses."

She continues after a momentary pause, "But Mortimer is handy and tinkered with a system that he created. It works well. Each bedroom has one. We are really very avant-garde. We put this in when another relative was visiting from the future and talked about bell pulls. He was here long enough to help Mortimer get it right!"

"What is 'avant-garde'?" I ask.

"It means ahead of our time," Leila answers.

"Okay." I am fascinated that Leila has no problem stealing from the future to make her present more comfortable and avant-garde! But *what else* have we borrowed from the future, and *how* did we borrow? Curious, I ask, "Do a lot of people time travel, Leila?"

"What an odd question, Jeremiah. I don't think so, but I might not know it is happening. That is a question for another day." After a slight pause, she adds, "I hope Marie cannot see you. Now don't move anything that she might see in motion. That would cause confusion and possible upset."

"Okay, Leila." I'm still wondering if other people are regularly borrowing ideas from the future to improve their lot in the present. My wandering thoughts are cut short by a discreet knock.

"Enter," says Leila from near the mantelpiece.

Marie reappears and questions hesitantly, "Yes, ma'am?"

Leila glances at me standing in the middle of the room in my red-and-white vertically striped pajamas and my slippers. She casually says, "Marie, please find Lord Mortimer. I need to converse with him here, as soon as possible. Just make sure Clive has dressed him completely before he arrives. We will leave from here to dinner."

She stands behind me.

"Yes, ma'am," she says attentively.

"Very good. One other thing," asks Leila, "is my appearance satisfactory, Marie?"

As Leila stands behind me, she slowly turns for inspection. I block the view of her skirts.

I am anxious. What if Marie sees me? I start to fidget as more panic sets in again. Accidentally, I step on the back of Leila's skirt when my restless feet shift. The skirt pulls down a little. I move my foot away fast!

"Oh yes! That dress is very fetching. But the hem is slightly longer in the mid-back. I noticed as you turned. I will attend to that tomorrow. No one will notice tonight, no need to worry. I wish I had noticed earlier."

My mouth is silent, but my thoughts say, *You couldn't have noticed earlier. I wasn't stepping on it then!* Leila glances at me with a smile. Oh dear, she is reading my thoughts again. *It's as if my thoughts are pasted on a billboard!*

"Thank you, Marie. Tell Lord Mortimer that I shall wait here," states Leila.

"Very good, m'lady." Marie looks back quizzically, wondering about Leila's persistent smile. Marie disappears, silently closing the door to the hallway after her.

"Good. She didn't see you." Leila is happy with this.

"Sorry I stepped on your dress. My foot pulled the hem down," I say apologetically.

"Not to worry, dear boy. I do so love your most interesting mind," replies Leila, "so much like mine. Really, a billboard! Did you know the first billboard was at the Paris Exposition in 1889?"

Once again, I blush scarlet because she knows my every thought. She sees me shake my head no about the Paris Whatever. She shrugs her shoulders slightly and then quietly but sternly says, "Paris Exposition, not the Paris Whatever. Details matter, dear boy." She sees me go a deeper red, which I didn't think possible. She adds, "Well, never mind for now. You have had too much new information after a bad scare, dear one. But I must tell Marie not to bother with the hem. Goodness knows, I don't want it riding up!"

In about ten minutes, Mortimer arrives. He knocks and then comes in through a different door from the one Marie used and closes it, muttering, "My dear, what is troubling you?"

"Do you know anyone by the name of Jeremiah Morris, Mortimer?" asks Leila in a girlish voice.

"Of course I do, silly girl." Mortimer laughs. "I left our trunk shortly after you did. I arrived not ten minutes ago. The living Mortimer was all fussed with your message, so I simply occupied his mind. He slept almost immediately. I do wonder if he remembers a little of the last few times." Mortimer taps the abundant midsection of his waistcoat, looks down at a new food stain, and mutters, "Oh dear, I've slopped again." He glances up at Leila and adds, "Anyhow, young Jeremiah is in his pajamas right beside you. And a very nice peppermint stick pattern they are!" Mortimer chuckles to himself.

I wish very hard that I went to bed in shirt, jeans, and shoes instead of red-and-white vertically striped pajamas and my slippers. At least I remembered the slippers!

"Marie didn't see him, so we may be safe," Leila says quietly. She giggles and then adds, "Yes, Jeremiah, the slippers were a very good idea."

Mortimer ignores her comment about my slippers as they both smile at me. Leila continues, "He will need to eat. How will that be managed? The servants will wonder if I order a tray."

Mortimer asks, "Clive is such a reliable valet, and he helped last time. Should we include him?"

Leila taps her foot hard in frustration, just once, as she replies, "Oh, I wish I had thought of that before now! That would be most wise, Mortimer. And Jeremiah says he may need to watch Barbara and James at their house. It will be difficult for us to get him there." Her eyes search her husband's face. She adds, "You are right, Mortimer. We need another agent working with us. Pity I didn't think ahead."

I feel a little confused as I frantically ask, "But how will he see me? He died well over two hundred years before I was born. How do we make contact?" The pitch of my voice rises with anxiety and confusion.

Leila smiles knowingly as she says, "Well, actually dear, he resides in our trunk. Mortimer wasn't sure he could manage without him. Clive was always devoted to Mortimer. When he died shortly after my husband did, he requested to stay with us. He doesn't leave our trunk when we are called out. He is a good servant and appears only if specifically requested. But he keeps the trunk very tidy and helps me with cleaning the attic." She pauses long enough to nod and smile happily before she adds, "And he does windows!"

I am astounded at the loyalty, but not surprised that Leila has someone to do her work. She always knows how to get what she wants and so very agreeably that no one seems to mind!

"Where is Clive now?" I ask.

"In my dressing room," Mortimer replies. "Before I left the attic, I asked Clive to come back through time with me."

"Quite the best idea, Mortimer," says Leila with a sigh of relief as she smiles at him proudly. "You are always good at thinking things through. And you avoided an extra trip to fetch him." Affectionately, she touches his face with her hand and bends to kiss his forehead.

"Shall we speak to him now, Mortimer?" asks Leila. Her eyes glance to the door that Mortimer closed. My guess is that's the door to the dressing room.

"Excellent idea, my dear," replies Mortimer, as he opens the dressing room door.

Right guess!

Leila's high hair stretches toward the ceiling while her fancy dress nearly sweeps the floor. Beside her, Mortimer is in his wig, fancy coat, breeches, and leg hose. Together they walk ceremoniously into Mortimer's dressing room.

I tag behind in my peppermint stick pajamas and fleece slippers. Looking at the pair in front of me, I almost giggle. Leila barefoot is taller than her rotund husband. With her heels and her hair piled high, she towers over him. *Side by side, they look ridiculous!*

Leila turns her head sharply to sternly look at me. I quickly glance away.

We enter the dressing room. It is a large square room with its own fireplace. Lined against the walls, there are several chests and tall cupboards for clothing storage. There is a bowl and shaving mirror on a round spindly three-legged table. In the middle of the room, two work chairs are pulled up to a large sturdy worktable piled high with clothes waiting to be folded or repaired. A single bed occupies the wall opposite the fireplace.

Clive is sitting at the central table, mending some shirts that need new buttons. "Ma'am, sir," says Clive as he stands and nods his head. They all wait silently until the door shuts, and then Clive asks, "This must be young Master Jeremiah?" He extends his hand in greeting and says, "Welcome, sir."

Shaking his hand, I ask excitedly, "You can see me?" My words spill out rapidly. I still have fear and panic hiding just below the surface.

"I took the liberty of coming prepared," Clive answers, seeming to understand my anxiety. He laughs a little as he bows slightly.

Clive sizes me up. I look closely at him.

Much shorter than his master, he is a powerful-looking man who certainly is not handsome. His eyes are almost black, peering out from coarse features. Dark stubble pokes through the olive skin of his face. I suspect his beard grows quickly and requires frequent shaving to remain clean looking. His face is square, with round cheeks and a cleft chin. He has unbelievably muscular arms, broad shoulders, heavy pecs, and muscle-bound legs as thick as tree trunks. I am really glad he is a friend. His muscles alone would make him a terrifying enemy.

Clive says, "Master Jeremiah, I must confess. I have watched you with your nine-greats each time you have visited England. It is a pleasure to see you again."

Once more, I am discombobulated. Is someone watching all the time?

Leila states, "Jeremiah needs to be fed. We must be down with our guests." She looks at Clive expectantly and commands politely, "Can you arrange something?"

"Of course. I will say the tray is for me so that I may continue working here. No one will question that."

"Excellent," says Leila as Mortimer smiles broadly at Clive.

Leila and Mortimer both appear satisfied. Each wishes me, "Good night," as they touch my shoulder when they pass. And with that, my nine-greats exit the dressing room and disappear along the wide hall, down the wide and graceful stairs, and enter one of the huge staterooms where folks are gathering before dinner. I can hear rising clatter and see candles burning, but the house is so large I don't smell food cooking.

Clive arranges for the tray, which arrives eventually. His dark eyes focus on me. His head moves slightly side to side, and then his chin tilts up a bit as he quizzes, "Do you yet have any plan?"

Knowing I'm safe with him, I talk about eavesdropping on James and Barbara in their house. "Maybe I'll get lucky and overhear their plans," I say quietly.

It was much later in recollection of all events that I would say, "Once again, Jeremiah, careful what you wish for. It might happen."

Clive says with satisfaction, "That may be easier than you think. There is a lady's maid there who would like a better acquaintance with me. Let's see if we can arrange a meeting. You will be invisible to her. Once in, you will be fine.

"I will need to follow up with the visit I arrange, but that will be the end of it. She is Lady Barbara's personal maid. Her name is Eliza. I know she has criminal connections, and I don't trust her. I happen to know that she uses her connections to secure stolen goods safely and cheaply to satisfy Lady Barbara's expensive tastes. There is nothing I can do about that. She is protected by the rich and powerful. But her actions allow me to feel no concern whatsoever when I use her for what we need."

He sees anxiety on my face. "Not to worry. She has criminal connections, but she is not violent," he adds.

"Is she dangerous?" I ask, concerned about dealing with a criminal.

"Not unless cornered," Clive replies with a smile, "and you won't be cornering her." He smiles reassuringly, "Nor shall I." He laughs softly.

I am not so sure that anything will be as easy as Clive said, especially when I am alone in a strange residence with a criminal. And if Barbara hires Eliza to procure stolen property, what else might either of them do? Everything is getting too scary. But fortified with tea and good food, which tastes wonderful, I suddenly find I am very confident and rather sleepy.

Clive sees me yawn several times in a row.

"Come along into bed, my young friend. The day has been too much, and you traveled at night. You have a big day ahead. Let's get you some rest."

I can only follow Clive's advice. Fortunately, Mortimer's dressing room also includes a single bed, in case Mortimer wants to sleep there if Leila is indisposed. I climb in when Clive says I should. The bed is comfortable and very soft. I comment, "I like the bed."

"Nothing like good feathers," answers Clive as he smiles.

"Wow! This is a feather mattress," I exclaim. "Another new experience!"

"The chamber pot is to the right side of the bed, fresh and rinsed. I will bring in water in the morning to let you wash hands and face. I know how you colonial Americans are." He smiles a crooked smile. I trust him.

I watch Clive as my eyes almost close.

I hear him say softly, "This youngster has the right heart. But he will need help. I had best start planning."

His words make me feel glad.

Clive sits down and looks seriously worried. "Yes. This will require planning, and care."

He seems genuinely concerned about my welfare as he returns to his mending. For the first time tonight, my panic and my fears disappear.

And with that, I fall deeply asleep.

Chapter 16

CLIVE'S PLAN

In the morning, I become accustomed to the chamber pot for all duties and the lack of cleanup afterward. They don't have toilet paper here! There is no shower or bath. In 1744 England, people believe bathing in water will cause illness.

Why did I ever quibble when Phoebe told me to wash my hands?

I am wearing the same pajamas. Susanne was right about clean clothes before departure!

But when breakfast arrives on a tray, destined for Clive as far as the cook knows, I am ready to eat. Ham, two eggs, bacon, scones, preserves, and tea—I manage it all and feel satisfied. When I finish about ten o'clock, Clive returns. Leila appears from the doorway that connects to her bedroom. Mortimer appears from somewhere unknown.

"May I speak?" Clive remains silent, awaiting their response.

Leila and Mortimer agree.

Clive says, "This is the first time Lord James and Lady Barbara have been suspected. Thanks to Jeremiah's probing questions, Mortimer gave information that Jeremiah used to explain their possible motive. Since James and Barbara are now suspects, Master Jeremiah wants to overhear them as they plan. That can be arranged. I have an acquaintance at James's residence. A visit would provide access to the building. If it doesn't look safe, I will have Master Jeremiah return with me."

Almost as an afterthought, Clive adds, "If all goes well, Master Jeremiah will remain there alone, but I will ensure that he knows how to get back here. He doesn't need the doors to be opened for him. He can seep through if he does not materialize. We just need to know when he will return. If he is late, then we will need to take some form of action."

Leila's and Mortimer's faces look blank as they think about this but say nothing for a long time.

Finally, Mortimer asks, "What action would we take? Let us list all the things that could go wrong." Is Mortimer taking stock of inventory? He continues, "He could fall and get hurt—most unlikely, especially since he is not corporeal." Mortimer seems satisfied that my translucency is protection from all injury.

Later, I would think, *Boy, that turned out to be the wrong answer!*

Leila says, "He could see something awful and panic. That could happen. He is only ten." She sounds worried.

More reasonable!

Very slowly, Clive says, "He could be recognized." He appears grim as he speaks.

Mortimer says, "Nonsense, that is not likely. Only we know he is here." He looks at Clive as if he has lost his senses.

Clive remains focused as he continues, "If any of the others overheard us at the trunks, they could be planning. At our trunks, all of us were told that Jeremiah and Susanne were investigating. We were asked to assist the children if needed. That alone may have been enough for Barbara to believe that we had shown our hand. We shall need to be very careful."

I really listen and pay attention. Inside my head, my mind yells, *Oh! Oh! Clive knows what he's talking about. This could develop into a very serious mess. I must be very careful!*

Suddenly, stray thoughts take over. *I wish Papa had warned Susanne and me never to go into the attic. But why would he warn us? Warning us to stay away would spur a lot of questions he would not want to answer and maybe make us very curious to see for ourselves. A no-win for Papa!*

"Not to worry, dear boy," says Leila. She pats my arm.

Foolishly, I ask, "Did you read my head just now?

She nods and then says, "Yes, I did do a quick read. You are right about taking care. Now about Papa. Remember, Papa never suspected we would meet. That's why he didn't warn you off. After all, he has done his best to forget all about us. But deep down, I suspect he actually might like to see you have a go at clearing Edgar's name. He hated his failure, but he is a big-enough person to be happy if you succeed where he failed. And I know he thinks you are a very special person, and very capable." She smiles happily as she tells me *her* thoughts.

I'm glad those thoughts make her happy, but I don't find them helpful, regardless of what Papa might think.

Finally, we all agree on a plan. I shall eavesdrop on James and Barbara in their home after Clive gets me access. My nine-greats outline a general floor plan of the residence of James and Barbara.

Focusing directly on me, Clive takes over and says, "James's house was originally built at the time of the Reformation, although it has been substantially modified since. Before the Reformation, there was only the Catholic Church in England. The Catholic Church has allegiance to the pope in Rome, Italy."

My mind silently asks, *Where is this leading?*

Leila looks at me sharply.

"The Reformation made Tudor England Protestant with the king of England, Henry VIII, as the head of the church. It was a bloody time in our history." Clive looks at me again to see that I am paying attention.

Clearly, Clive must be driving to some point. I am all ears, but please drive faster.

Leila chuckles slightly.

I hear Clive's voice continue, "The family was once Catholic and had to hide priests who conducted Catholic services after the country became Church of England. Catholic services were illegal, with severe punishment for conducting them. There are secret passageways and staircases that once provided escape for visiting priests. Remember, if anyone in the house becomes aware of your presence, these secret areas might allow you to be observed and followed without your knowledge." He looks intently at my face.

Pay dirt! Message received.

Leila nods to me in silent agreement with a slight smile.

I ask, "Do you mean other phantoms or time travelers might be watching?"

Clive appears uncertain how best to answer. Seeing Clive's sudden hesitancy, Leila answers, "Well, that is possible but unlikely. There aren't many with my level of interest in travel and observation. I believe Clive was speaking about owners and servants. Servants are everywhere and often not conspicuous. But they won't be able to see you. There should be no danger."

Glancing toward Leila, Clive says, "Yes, servants are certainly an unlikely danger." As an afterthought, he adds, "But I worry about other time travelers, whoever they may be. Please, be careful." His eyes search my face intently until he is satisfied that I have paid attention. Mortimer and Leila ignore his comment.

I would soon learn that ignoring him was a big mistake! I take heed; my salvation!

Mortimer rolls his eyes at Clive's comment about time travelers. He looks at me with interest, until he finally murmurs, "An interesting mind." But Mortimer says nothing more.

I wasn't sure if he meant my mind or Clive's. I later decided he meant mine. If he had meant Clive's, he might have paid more attention to Clive's concern and saved me a lot of grief.

Clive seems very knowledgeable. His mysteriously dark eyes focus on me as he adds solemnly, "Try to stay to the main areas. Otherwise, you might become lost. Ordinary folk will not see you. Only another time traveler could see you and raise an alarm." I can tell he is worried. This is the second time he has directly mentioned other time travelers.

What does he know that I don't? Do Mortimer and Leila understand what he knows? I'm just a kid. It's all way over my pay grade.

More brightly, but still with a matter-of-fact voice, Clive continues, "You will get in by the kitchen. Find the stairs from the kitchen area to the main floor. That will get you near their dining room. From there, you can find the main stairs located in the central hall, which is two floors high. The main upstairs hall has a balustrade that surrounds and looks down into the central hall below. This means you can be seen easily from upstairs if you become visible."

"What's a balustrade?" I ask, slightly overwhelmed with too much stuff to remember.

Clive smiles at my question. "A balustrade is a fancy word for a fancy rail or banister with fancy spindles."

I nod that I understand. I ask timidly, "When do I go there?"

Clive answers, "After dinner tonight. Barbara and James are at home tonight without guests. They will have the opportunity for discussion. I hope you overhear plans for the robbery, which will occur in less than a week. Her Ladyship mentioned the future date to me today." Clive glances at each of us.

Trust Her Ladyship Leila to keep the dates in mind! Does she ever forget anything?

Leila smiles at me, and her head bends forward in my direction.

What if her tall hair falls over as she tilts her head?

Leila suppresses a giggle. Busted again!

The day drags with inactivity. I wander in the house seeing the great public spaces, the family's private rooms, and the tiny servants' rooms, which are very shy on comfort.

The house is fascinating! The kitchen is both exciting and gross, since birds are brought in dead, feathers and all, and then gutted right there in the kitchen before they are cooked! Not so clean!

The smells everywhere are strong. Hygiene is poor, and even my nine-greats have significant body odor, which their perfume fails to hide!

But their smell is fainter than their servants'. The servants work hard, sweat, and still have no bath or shower to clean themselves. Bathing is considered a health hazard, and no one wants any part in that. I am developing a keen awareness of the hardiness of my ancestors and their tolerance of ugly smells!

After a late-afternoon nap and then my dinner, Clive appears. "It's time," he says.

I follow Clive. He walks briskly. I have to concentrate to keep up. We exit by the servants' hall, and walk through dingy, unlit streets. We walk over brick or cobblestone roadways, not a sidewalk in sight.

"Aren't there any sidewalks?" I ask.

Clive answers, "No. While the ancient Turks, Romans, and Greeks had pedestrian walkways, Europe does not. Sidewalks will be accepted as a necessity for pedestrian safety only after Baron Haussmann and his patron, Napoleon III, renovate Paris in the nineteenth century. We have over a hundred years to wait."

Clive tells me this as part of history, history that will occur in a hundred-plus years after his death. Wow! It seems odd to get a history lesson from the future. More wonders!

I ask, "Do you seep out to travel like Leila does?"

Half smiling, Clive answers, "Yes. I often accompany her for her safety if Mortimer is unable to attend to her, and sometimes I attend them both. Each trip is always instructive."

"So you keep learning?" I ask.

Clive answers, "Oh yes, I do. I try to better myself even though I am dead."

I can't think of anything to reply. His comment sounds ridiculous but maybe not in the circumstances!

For many years, I have thought about Clive's statement. Like Leila, here was a person with a fine mind from humble beginnings. He has worked his way up to the esteemed position of earl's valet. Yet he still wants to increase his knowledge, even if only he notices. I still respect that ambition and drive. He is a fine example for any person, young or old.

We reach an enormous house, set far back from the road. The building and its land are surrounded by a thick stone wall with a high fence on top. There is a gate that allows access to the courtyard, which is surrounded on three sides by the building. A stately main door looms ahead in the dark.

"This way," says Clive, motioning us to the side.

I exclaim, "This place is huge!"

Clive replies, "After Mortimer dies, this will become the Earl Poppycock's residence. It is larger than the present home where Leila and Mortimer live."

I follow along beside Clive. We look an unlikely pair. One is a sturdy man in mid-eighteenth-century clothes, the other a beanpole

American boy in fleece slippers and red-and-white vertically striped pajamas. We are walking together, one visible but the other invisible. Both are talking, but only one can be heard. To an outsider, Clive might appear to be talking to himself. Fortunately, it is so dark no one can see.

We reach the kitchen wing, nearer to the road on the back side of the buildings. The streets are narrower there; and across the road, the houses are close together, mean, and dilapidated.

"This is closer to the road behind the house. Why didn't we come from the other side?" I ask.

Clive replies offhandedly, "Because I want to live till tomorrow. You take your life in your hands going there, even in daylight. Do you see that stone wall with the fence atop running all around? That is not for decoration."

I think about the smells of the city, the bad personal hygiene with chamber pots, no showers, limited handwashing. The poor-quality drinking water is contaminated with sewer water and used only by the poorest.

Leila recited tales of poverty and crime. I am not in the least surprised that my eight-greats-grandparents live in an enormous palace with a highly dangerous slum out back, separated only by a great stone wall with its fence on top.

"You don't want to be a weakling and live in 1742 London," I say.

"Right on, kiddo," Clive says.

I do a double take when I hear that. The reply makes me think of Marjorie and Bertie. With increasing admiration, I ask, "Have you done some twentieth-century time traveling?"

Clive replies, "The 1920s were fun. And I liked the clothes, very flattering to the substantial male figure! And so very unlike the clothes of the 1960s. Too tight!"

From a man living in London in 1744, this seems a very odd thing to say. Even more odd, I understand completely!

We reach the kitchen door in what an American might call the basement, although the windows are well above ground level. The stairs down to the kitchen door are unlit and dark. The door is unlatched. Clive opens it and quietly makes sure we both are inside. He motions to me to say nothing.

A voice from the dark says, "So you have finally decided to pay a call." The voice is young and female.

"Eliza, you got my note?" asks Clive.

"Yes, I did. That's why I'm here," comes her somewhat flirty reply.

"I thought we should arrange a time when I could call," responds Clive.

"Coy one, aren't you?" she asks.

Clive answers, "Just a respectable gentleman, wanting to call on a respectable lady."

Eliza says, "All right then, tomorrow at 4:00 p.m. or a little after. Not too long after, mind. Milady will have finished her breakfast by eleven, had her late-morning stroll, written her letters, and be dressed for tea. I will have an hour to myself before dressing her for dinner."

"Tomorrow it is, early afternoon, at four. Shall I present myself here?" asks Clive.

"Yes, this entrance will do," she replies. "Now, aren't you staying just a little while?" she asks, her voice shifting to a very encouraging tone.

"Alas! I must do things for my master. I shall see you tomorrow," is his terse reply. He nods to me. That's my cue it is okay to stay.

And with that, Clive disappears up the stairs.

Eliza murmurs something under her breath. What a bad word! The young lady appears a lot put out.

I don't understand. Exactly what did she expect when she was alone with a suitor after dark, in a poorly lit hallway with only a few candles burning, near an empty kitchen with a big table? Being ten is difficult! I miss a lot.

I don't dare move. Eliza looks right through me as she blows out the candles and walks away. I am about to get out of her way when she walks right through me.

With a giggle I say, "Guess she doesn't know I'm here."

I seem to have the house to myself. The servants' quarters are quiet. Curious, I poke my translucent head through walls and doors to look inside rooms. Some servants are sleeping, some talk to one another, and a few are in the middle of their nightly prayers before bed. One man is…well, what *is* he doing? Never mind! How would any of them ever know anyone peeked in on them? More importantly, how would I ever know someone peeked in on me? I don't like *that* thought.

I go upstairs. Eventually, I find the enormous dining room with its paintings and tapestries on the walls around a long central table surrounded by ornate chairs.

Staterooms nearby have chairs and settees lining the walls, which provides space to walk in the center. Carved and painted woodwork throughout indicates wealth and taste. Paintings line the walls, all to suggest education and refinement.

The central great hall is open to the upper hallway all the way around on the second floor. Bright colors on the ceiling's plaster moldings pull the eye ever upward.

I walk on stone, but no sound comes from my feet. Apparently, I am invisible and inaudible as Leila's mind reading keeps me safe. I climb the most monumental and impressive staircase I have ever seen and admire the ornate balustrade that is indeed as impressive as Clive said. I can look down over the balustrade onto the main hall from anywhere on the second-floor hall. I crane my neck to see the fancy painted ceiling way, way up. Wow! This is like a fancy hotel!

I head to where Clive said Barbara and James might be. I seep through a door and find myself in a huge bedroom with a gigantic four-poster with fancy draperies around the bed. There is a fireplace of ornately carved marble. On each side sit matching chairs with a small candle table. Chests dot the walls, each with fancy inlaid wood and gold metalwork on the legs and near the top.

This bedroom connects to a sitting area through an archway. Voices come from there. Barbara is talking to James.

Just in case, I stay hidden. I don't really know why staying hidden is a good idea since I am invisible and inaudible. Maybe Clive's concerns rubbed off on me. Anyway, hiding saves my life!

"I know how you feel, James. But something must be done," says Barbara.

"Why is that?" asks James.

Barbara continues, "Edgar may have wonderful ideas about the management of the estate. But all that could be yours. Think on that." She pauses for a breath, while James ponders.

She presses on, "While I still have plenty of my money, as time passes, my money will not be enough. I refuse to reduce expenditure. There is style to be maintained. I have a title. I had it from Father, before I met you. You do not. You will remain without title and perhaps low on funds at some future date. Action has to be taken. This is not our first discussion."

James says, "Your suggestions have worried me. I am fond of Edgar. He is my brother. And there are risks. We are good enough."

I peek around the corner. Barbara sits on her chair, turned away from me. James faces my direction, slouching on a small sofa, his muscular legs wide apart.

"Good enough!" Barbara's voice rises. Her brown eyes flash with anger. Her thin lips tighten as she barks, "You sound like a weakling, a true weakling. I didn't marry a weakling. I married a man!"

James sits up straight and demands in an angry, nasty tone, "What is your plan?"

Barbara speaks slowly and clearly, "If Edgar is accused of a robbery, he could be jailed. He might be disinherited. Then the money and title will come to you. He might stay in jail, in which case, you win again. He ends with nothing; but you are more worthy, my dear husband, my dear sweet."

James pays keen attention, greed in his eyes. Still listening, I slowly move safely back out of view behind the archway, barely peeking around the corner.

Barbara's hand carelessly runs along the inner part of her thigh over and over as she continues, "I spoke to your valet, Emmett. He knows someone who can arrange a robbery. It will happen while the owners are safely out of town. You can plant evidence, and Edgar will be convicted."

James's anger seems to melt away. He asks quietly, "Whom do you suggest be robbed?" His eyes seem mesmerized as they follow her hand as it traces her thigh.

"Edgar's friend Walter Johnson," says Barbara, speaking casually, without concern for the victim.

"But he is a fine person," objects James with his eyes still on the hand now moving along the inside of her upper thigh.

Barbara replies, "He won't be hurt. He has plenty of money. He won't miss some silver from his vault. I have dined there with you. Abigail treasures their frog and rabbit figures made from silver—silly, sentimental fool that she is."

Barbara leans toward James and says, "Presently, Abigail is preparing to visit her grandchildren. She leaves in the morning. Walter is to follow later, in less than a week. The robbery will occur the night after he leaves, but only if you agree, my sweet." Her hand now touches his thigh. He slouches again, legs spread wide apart. Her hand moves all the way up, gently massaging his inner thigh muscles, and sliding across from the top of one inner thigh to the next. Their eyes are locked.

"But if you agree, then you must visit Walter with Edgar after Abigail's departure. Arrange to excuse yourself so that you can find the figures, which are in her reading room. Steal one of them, and then put it in Edgar's possession, perhaps in his library where it can be found. With Abigail away, no one is likely to notice the missing figure." She pauses to let James catch up with her plan. Meanwhile, both her hands methodically continue to rub his upper inner thighs.

James asks, "How do you know so much about their household? We are social with them but not close."

Barbara moves from her chair. As she sits beside James, she turns toward him. Fortunately, her face is still directed away from me. Reaching forward to touch her fingers affectionately to the side of James's face, Barbara replies, "At my direction, my lady's maid, Eliza, has made a new friend in the household." Barbara smiles knowingly at James.

In a quieter and lower-pitched voice, Barbara continues, "Eliza says that the silly girl talks and talks if she is given a little treat and a sympathetic shoulder. She tells Eliza everything that is occurring in the household. The gullible idiot doesn't even know that she is being used. She thinks Eliza has become her new best friend. The fool!"

226

Barbara laughs and then leans forward to kiss James on the mouth. James seems to like this. The kissing takes too much time.

What's going on? Why is her hand strongly rubbing James's upper leg again? Is he itchy? Why is he sometimes moaning? Is he in pain?

Barbara continues softly, "After the robbery, we will hide the rest of the silver in the attic. A small trunk in the attic or extra silver in the vault will never be noted. The inventory checks missing silver, not silver that has been added. The police will not expect to find it and certainly not at my residence in modern London."

With quick breaths between kisses on Barbara's lips, James asks, "Why not let the thieves…sell it…as part of their payment?"

Again, Barbara kisses him on the lips. Then he kisses her on the neck, over and over. She finally answers, "That is fine if they are never caught. But if the stolen merchandise surfaces, the police might discover who the robbers are. If caught, the thieves might talk, and the trail might return to me. It is far better to buy the silver from them. They have their payment, and we keep the evidence under control. No reason for anyone to talk to another person, ever."

James straightens his back and shifts slightly, looks directly at his wife, and says, "I'm impressed! You have really thought this through. You are thorough. How long have you schemed this plan?"

She kisses him on the mouth again and then replies flatly, "That does not matter. Do you see a fault?"

"None whatsoever," James replies.

Between kisses, Barbara asks, "Are you willing?" My, she has a busy tongue even when she's not talking!

While James returns her kisses, he murmurs, "I have reservations…about Edgar. He is…so earnest. He loves Jemima, and…they have a child." James seems uncertain, at least about his brother. On the other hand, his tongue seems to know exactly what to do! Busy, busy!

Barbara pulls away slightly as she emphatically says, "We will have children too. Ours will need provisions as much as his." Her hand runs along his thigh, up and down, rhythmically.

"There is logic in that," James agrees with a moan. His free hand straightens something big in the front of his breeches.

My inner voice asks, *What did Mortimer say?* My head hears Mortimer's voice, "James never did anything that was not for his own benefit."

Yes, that is what Mortimer said!

Barbara moves closer to James. Her fingers slide through his hair. Her mouth is on his again. Her hand is busy doing something with his upper thighs again, or at least, I think it's his thighs. Why? Does he have a pulled muscle that needs massage? What's going on? I wish I could see better, but peeking around the corner doesn't provide much of a view.

I am horrified at Barbara's plan as she leads James to her side, against all morals, against all instincts of love for his brother. James's response sickens me. And these are my eight-greats-grandparents! Yuck!

They are breathing more quickly, with the occasional moan from each. What are they are doing now? Oh, my goodness! That's something I truly don't understand. Enough already; I can't look anymore. They have stopped talking. What will they do next? Scary question!

It's time to scram.

Besides, I have learned all I need to know about poor Edgar. As I step away, my foot makes a sound. Darn! I have become audible. What about visible?

Get out of here, idiot!

Moving away from the archway to stay hidden, I dash to the door.

"I hear something," says Barbara as she looks around.

"I heard nothing," responds James as he waves his hand in dismissal.

Barbara repeats, "No, someone is here. I definitely heard something."

I hear her dress rustle as she stands.

My mind is spinning as I panic. *What to do?*

At the door, my hands look solid! I cannot seep through. I open the door a crack. Glancing back, I see Barbara standing in the archway.

She yells, "Stop!"

Oops! She has seen me!

I race through the now-wide-open door, grab my slippers in my hands so I don't fall, and take the stairs two at a time. Once, I almost do topple as I race to the dining room to get my bearings. I glance back.

From the upstairs hallway, Barbara glares down at me from over the balustrade. She screams, "Bloody hell!"

No question, she has seen me!

Racing to the kitchen stairs, I run a new speed record! When I'm one floor down, Barbara's bedroom door slams. Busted! She must be mad knowing she cannot catch me. Wow, my terrified heart is racing!

The servants' kitchen stairs are steeper and narrower than the grand stair ascent to the upper floors. But only servants use these. They don't matter in this society. They don't need to be impressed.

At the kitchen door, I hurriedly put on my slippers. I can still hear the noise from my steps, but the noise is quieter than when I was near Barbara. Once I am past the outside gate and on my way to my nine-greats-grandparents' house, I make no sound even when I try.

I remember clearly that Leila said, "My mind reading will keep you safe! But if you are thought-connected to anyone else, you will be visible and audible to that person, real flesh and blood as it were, but only when you are near!"

Thank heavens Barbara sees me only when I am nearby! However, I do not yet feel safe! And Clive was very right to worry about my being seen by other time travelers.

Two men across the street are lounging against a building. They seem sinister, but they don't look at me. My hands now appear translucent to me. I hope that I am invisible to them.

I have a scrap of paper with a map. I follow it carefully until I seep back into my nine-greats-grandparents' house. I head straight to

Mortimer's dressing room. Clive is waiting for me. 'Cause I'm near when he looks at me, I am solid again, fully materialized.

Clive looks concerned as he says, "You are sweaty and flushed. You look like you had a fright. Tell me what happened."

Collecting my thoughts, I calm down slowly and recount everything that happened. I breathlessly spit out, "Only a robbery is planned when Walter and Abigail are away. But the plan is to destroy the reputation, or the life, of Edgar for the purpose of gaining his inheritance and his title. Barbara is the leader and organizer!" After pausing to catch my breath, I add more calmly, "They even plan to buy the stolen silver and hide it in their house so nothing surfaces." I tell him what Barbara and James were doing to each other. "What was that about?" I ask.

Clive responds quickly, "That explanation may wait for another day!"

I'm so upset that I don't push for an answer. Finally, I say, "But something is wrong, Clive! Barbara heard me. She saw me, which made her swear and then slam her bedroom door when I was already one floor down.

"I made no sound that anyone could hear when I was in other parts of the house. Eliza didn't see or hear me. She even stomped right through me as she walked along the hallway. James didn't hear me, but Barbara did."

Clive responds, "I was afraid something like this might happen. Barbara is a smart one, she is. And she is a schemer. I suspect she traveled back in time from her trunk, just like Leila, just like Mortimer, just like me. She is Barbara present and Barbara future, playing out the planned role with her husband, who is James in the present only, at least for now." Pondering, he adds, "Yes, that is what must have happened." He pauses while he thinks.

Clive continues, "You had to open the bedroom door when you were escaping because Barbara's thoughts made you materialize completely. When you were away from her thoughts and influence, you could seep through doors and walls again." He looks very worried. "Do you understand all that I have said?"

My impolite thoughts say, *I've already figured this out. That's why I'm in a panic.* Instead, I reply calmly, "Yes, Clive, I understand."

Clive seems lost in thought as he says, "Barbara is the type to slam a door or throw something when things don't go her way. I'm not surprised you heard her swear and her door slam. I'm glad she couldn't catch you and do something worse!" After a slight pause, Clive advises, "We will need to be very careful."

Ya think so? I'm glad Leila isn't here to read my sarcastic thoughts.

I feel sick in the pit of my stomach. Suddenly, I feel very cold with rising panic. What if she caught me? I might be dead now, and no one would have known to help me! I hear Barbara's voice. I recall her plans. She has no morals. She is capable of anything, capable of destroying anyone who gets in her way!

Clive asks, "Do you understand that both Barbara and soon James will be as they are in their trunk, with knowledge from the past and the future? Soon James will travel back through time to join Barbara."

I'm too frightened to reply because I really do understand, far more than he realizes. I nod my head and fix my eyes on Clive.

He continues, "They have nothing to lose and everything to gain. Eternity in their trunk is better than what they fear is their final destination. To save themselves, they will block us all. They can deny everything that you overheard."

I stop myself from saying what I think Barbara is capable of doing.

After pondering for a moment, Clive continues, "We must get proof. We will need to see them planting the evidence and confront them when they hide the rest of the silver. Then we will have something to work with, something that Saint Peter and the courts will understand."

I nod that I understand. I do, in part. But the thought of staying any longer terrifies me!

Clive says, "I shall tell the master."

That seems an odd name for my nine-greats-grandfather!

My eyes flash toward Clive. "Make sure Leila knows too," I suggest.

Clive says, "That goes without saying." He winks at me. "She may know already."

I look confused. Clive says, "Tell me she has not read your thoughts. Tell me you missed it when she did." He laughs.

I begin to laugh. I need humor now! I laugh louder and feel less scared.

I hope no one sees how very scared I am!

Chapter 17

Barbara's Plan Revealed

Leila arrives in the dressing room moments later. She asks me to repeat what I told Clive. I am just about to begin when Mortimer arrives. After they settle, I tell everything again.

Both Mortimer and Leila are astonished that Barbara overheard me. Mortimer mutters, "Oh dear! Oh dear! I didn't anticipate this!"

Yup, true statement! And you rolled your eyes.

They come to the same conclusion as Clive. Barbara is Barbara present and future, and present James will be future James very soon.

Leila says, "Barbara must have suspected that Mortimer and I are back in the past. Our trunk has been too quiet. She knew, they all knew, that you and Susanne asked about help for your investigation. Soon both of them will know that Jeremiah is here. They are extremely dangerous." Leila looks as worried as Clive.

When I ask them to explain what Barbara and James were doing to each other, Mortimer looks at Leila. She fixes her gaze on him with a question in her eyes. Faint red creeps under Clive's dark skin.

I ask again, "What were they doing? What does all that mean?"

"That can wait for your father to explain," says Mortimer tersely. "No more about that now."

"Okay!" I drop that topic as ordered. Three adults sigh in relief.

Mortimer looks pensive before he adds, "There is nothing we can do to affect what has already happened. There is nothing we can do to prevent the murder or the robbery."

I demand, "Why not? It hasn't happened yet. We still have time. Why not stop it from happening?"

Mortimer looks at me sympathetically as he says, "Remember, we have returned to the past. The robbery and the death have already occurred in the past...just not yet. We can only observe in the past, and we can act only when we are back in the present. Each of our actions, for good or ill, has consequences; and the ripple effect carries far out. Altering the past is too complex to do." He sees my confusion. "Let me explain."

I nod as my shaky voice says, "Yes, please."

Mortimer begins, "Suppose someone dies in an accident. No one is to blame. Nobody wants the accident to happen. The victim may have a spouse who is devastated. However, because that person died, the spouse may eventually remarry and have more children." He pauses and waits to see that I understand.

I nod and say, "Yes, so far so good."

Mortimer continues, "The natural desire is to go back to prevent the death in the accident. That interference, if successful, will prevent the second marriage and will thereby prevent the birth of all the progeny, meaning all the children, born of the second marriage. This will have unintended results for generations."

What a concept! My brain imagines, *So here I am, talking to someone who suddenly disappears, midsentence, because he or she no longer has been born after a time traveler and fixer saves a life four generations before!*

Leila quietly giggles, as she nods yes and gazes approvingly at me.

I say, "In other words, you may really muck things up if you try to fix something in the past, to correct an already completed action."

"Yes, Jeremiah, that is the gist," Mortimer replies and nods sagely. "We can only shape the present and the future. There has been universal agreement in the netherworld on this with severe punishment for attempting to alter the past."

"What?" I exclaim.

"We have courts, and we have the ultimate tribunal. Whatever the motive, eternal damnation for breaking that law is an awful thing. And once condemned, there is no escape and no appeal," replies Mortimer in a matter-of-fact voice, "and no leniency, even for justifiable and altruistic motives." Mortimer stares directly at me and states flatly, "Don't ever get charged with that crime!" Then he starts a different discussion amongst all three adults.

I am overwhelmed by this information as the three talk about what to do next. Still shaken by my encounter with Barbara, everything seems unreal. This time related past and present stuff leaves me exhausted and mentally overloaded. I am desperate for sleep.

Leila sees my eyes closing as I stand. She says, "Let's get Jeremiah into bed and get him some rest. We can figure out more in the morning."

Clive helps me into bed, his powerful arms lifting me. The feather bed is wonderfully soft and comfortable. I don't hear them leave the room.

In the morning, I am ravenous. I wake up early, long before the rest of the household.

I see servants stoking fires, sweeping floors, polishing brass. Two look familiar, but I don't really know who they are. Hours later, the family gets up.

I devour my breakfast when it arrives. Fortunately, the door is open when I go into Leila's room. She is still in her nightclothes, talking to her maid and drinking chocolate, probably cacao, dissolved in warm milk. She sits on the bench in front of her dressing table, the morning mail beside her.

She appears anxious and distracted as she and her maid make conversation. Leila sees me in my striped pajamas, surreptitiously wags a finger in greeting, but says nothing to me.

I remain invisible to Marie and silent. I don't touch anything. I don't want Marie to see solid objects moving on their own. The explanations would never fly! Leila asks Marie to run a small errand for her. Her task sounds like a lame excuse to buy an hour. But Marie readily agrees and disappears into the hallway, closing the door silently after her.

I stand behind Leila. She can see my reflection in her dresser mirror. As soon as Marie leaves, Leila says to my image, "There is another problem. Barbara has invited herself and James to dinner tonight. There is a standing agreement that they may dine anytime. I have replied yes. But why does she want to be here tonight?"

She thinks for a moment. She turns on her bench and looks at me directly, commanding my attention. "You came here on my thought contact. If that mental contact is broken, you will need to establish contact with Clive or Mortimer immediately. Do you understand?"

"Yes," I reply. I sense the fright, the intensity, and the urgency in Leila's voice.

Leila continues, "Barbara had thought contact with you last night, which made you visible and audible to her. That thought contact caused you to materialize.

"You and I have a strong thought connection so that away from me, you can seep through walls, be inaudible and invisible, and still safe. That is because of my mind-reading ability. Not so with others."

She pauses and looks at me sternly. She almost pleads, "Like I said before, if you and I lose thought contact, you must make immediate contact with Mortimer or with Clive. Otherwise, you will fall into the time abyss!"

Alarmed, I ask, "What is the time abyss? What's an abyss anyway?"

Her eyes never leave my face as Leila answers, "An abyss is defined as a chasm, a rift, or a hole. It means you could fall into a hole where there is no measured time." She pauses and fixes my gaze to see if I understand. "The time abyss is an eternity without time. It is very difficult to return from there." Her face is very somber as her eyes now focus on the floor.

Trying to understand, I ask, "You mean that it's the end for me if I fall into the time abyss?"

Leila is near tears as she states, "Yes." Her chin jiggles just a little.

I quietly say, "We didn't talk about this before."

Leila replies, "I didn't anticipate the need."

"Is this part of the 'much' you didn't tell me?"

Leila looks embarrassed. "It would seem so. Frankly, I had forgotten. It came to me last night after I realized Barbara is future Barbara as well. That fact changed everything!"

I swallow hard and quietly ask, "I could die?"

Leila looks at me sharply as she responds, "We shall not let that happen." She seems angry, an emotion I have not seen in her before.

Later in the morning, Clive and Mortimer are with Leila in the dressing room. Once alone behind closed doors, they begin discussions again. Watching everyone, I sit quietly scared.

Leila tells everyone else what she told me in the morning.

Mortimer says, "I don't think Barbara is capable of using the time abyss. Adding that to her sins would make her unredeemable."

Leila replies far too sweetly, "I don't think redemption is one of her priorities, Mortimer." She looks resigned, her face sad and grim. Mortimer looks as if he realizes for the first time how truly evil Barbara really is.

Clive nods in agreement. "She knows no bounds. We must be very vigilant." Clive pauses for a minute and then continues, "I suspect Barbara has some plan of action for tonight. Don't leave her alone for a moment."

Leila says, "I shall seat her to my left with James on my right." She smiles. "That way, she is always at my side."

The room is suddenly silent. Everyone looks downcast.

In the quiet, my overloaded mind starts to wander. I wonder if time in the past and time in the future move along at the same rate. If it does, my body has been sleeping for almost two days, and someone may have noticed that I am a sleepyhead. I am uncertain what to do.

Anxiously, I speak out, "Does time pass at the same rate in the past and in the future?" I am thinking about everyone at home as I speak.

All three look at me, surprised.

"Does time what?" asks Mortimer.

I ask again, "Does time pass at the same rate in the past as it does in the present and future?" I look from one to the other, inspecting all three. They seem confused by my question, even Leila.

"I ask because I came here two days ago in the evening just before supper, and this is morning two days later. Phoebe put me to bed at home on Tuesday night. Is it still Tuesday night at home?"

They gawk at my anxious face as I say, "If I have slept at home for two days, someone will have noticed." I stare back at their quizzical faces.

Clive answers in a kindly voice, "Oh, I do understand what you mean. All time passes at the same measured rate." He looks at me, sensing my concern.

He continues, "They have yet to discover the reason you are deeply unconscious. They have noticed. Medical authorities have been notified." He looks at me steadily.

"Oh!" I think for a moment. "I can figure out how long I have been asleep in the future by the amount of time I have spent here?"

Clive responds in a matter-of-fact voice, "Correct."

Mortimer asks, "Are you concerned the family is worried?"

"Yes. My actions have probably caused needless worry to my family," I answer truthfully. "I regret that. It was a selfish choice to come here without anyone knowing except Susanne."

I'm mad at myself for being so thoughtless.

Leila regards me with pity and moves slightly closer. She mouths, "Oh, my poor child!"

My anxious eyes glance at her and then fix on Clive as he clears his throat and says, "Taking a liberty, I have introduced myself to Susanne and told her you were safe. She was uncertain what she should say to the family. I suggested she say nothing at the moment." Clive's dark eyes penetrate mine as he inquires, "I hope Master Jeremiah agrees?" He tilts his head slightly to the side as he speaks, his eyes still on mine. His coarse features soften with empathy.

I think for a moment before I respond limply, "There is nothing they can do. You gave her the right advice, Clive. Thank you." What else can I say?

Leila touches my hand briefly as she says, "Let us concentrate here so we may have you safely returned." She looks at me sympathetically as she finishes.

As much as I like Leila's sentiment, it's not helpful. Again, she regards me with concern.

I spend the remainder of this day in the past resting, eating, and wandering inside. I am fascinated by the number of people involved in the day-to-day care of the house. The work of many people is required to keep this one house running to order for its owners.

I think about each person needing food, clothing, and a place to sleep. Room and board is what Leila calls it when I ask. I learn that the day-to-day expenditure of money from the family is enormous. And this happens in every house of its kind in London, all over the country for that matter. The concept is staggering. Then I think of the palace that James and Barbara have. No wonder Barbara is so greedy!

However, there are other solutions besides robbery and destruction. Her plans are hideous. I am angry my eight-greats-grandfather is so weak he follows the lead of his evil wife. I am horrified that I am related to Barbara, or either of them!

When Clive returns from his appointed meeting with Eliza, I ask him, "How was the visit?"

Clive answers, "She has more interest than I do. From our conversation today, it is clear Eliza has no morals. Like her friend Emmett, James's valet, she most certainly has criminal ties. While that's probably useful for Barbara, and for James, I found out nothing. I hope never to see Eliza again." His hand motion is dismissive of the topic and the lady.

Eventually, Leila and Mortimer dress for dinner and then gather to talk in the closed-door dressing room. I'm sitting on the bed, eating my early dinner from a tray. Leila is clearly anxious, although she is trying to hide it. She says bravely, "I will keep a close eye on that Barbara. I wish I knew her plan!"

"Leila, you said that you got sick a week before the robbery."

She nods, "Just so."

I ask, "What happened? Does that illness occur tonight?"

She looks at me closely and says, "They said that I fainted at dinner or just afterwards. I was out of sorts for days. It was never clear what actually happened. But I recovered without incident. No matter."

She cups my chin in her hands as she says, "You don't miss details, do you? Not to worry! I recollect my illness occurs a few days from now, but I'm not certain. For some reason, the time frame is blurry in my mind. That's most unusual for me."

Mortimer mutters to himself, "I wish I were better with dates. Things sometimes run all together after the passage of so much time."

Leila shrugs her shoulders and once more mutters, "No matter. No matter at all."

My later comment? Wrong! Utterly wrong! Her illness nearly costs me my life.

She steps away, all business, as she says, "You must keep out of sight. Barbara may see you. Plan on staying here in Mortimer's dressing room."

"Sure thing, Leila," I reply insincerely.

Again, she looks squarely at me as she sweeps out of the room, her gown almost trailing on the floor. She is trying to hide her worry and concern over Barbara's schemes, but it shows through. Looking concerned, and furtively casting anxious glances toward his wife, Mortimer follows after her with a clean waistcoat, no food spots yet. Their harried faces wear different expressions when they reach the top of the stairs. As they say in showbiz, "The show must go on." These two are definitely now "onstage."

I hurriedly finish eating my supper from its tray. Why do I have a really unhappy feeling about tonight?

Noise and clatter increase as guests arrive. Ignoring Leila's directive to stay put, I creep out of the dressing room, walk down the hall, and peer down to the floor below. I try to remain hidden.

I see Leila smiling broadly, chatting to one or two guests, and then talking to James and Barbara. As Leila moves on to other guests afterward, Barbara scans with her eyes, looking for me, I'll bet. She looks up in my direction, smirks to herself, and abruptly turns her head to Mortimer to engage him in conversation.

Suddenly, I feel afraid.

After his chat with his mother, James wanders the room, chatting and drinking wine. He makes eye contact with his wife. She makes a small hand gesture and slightly tilts her big hairdo in my direction. He looks toward me and smiles to himself.

Now, I feel very scared!

Wine flows freely. People talk. Some retire to the drawing room. Others keep circulating. There are about ten extra people Leila has invited for the occasion of her son's visit for dinner.

Eventually, they all go into the dining room. Something tells me that I must observe that meal, no matter how scared I am.

I go down the main stairs quietly. The door between the busy serving area and the dining room is open. I perch unseen behind the open door while servants bring in food to the serving area for the footmen to dispense and carry empty trays away, all within a few feet of me. I notice that serving a dinner and clearing away is a real production involving many people.

By gazing directly into the dining room through the crack made by the hinges of the open door, I see James sitting to the right of Leila, facing toward me. I see the back of Barbara and have a side view of Leila, sitting at her end of the table. Mortimer is the host, and he is at the other end of the table, out of view.

Banter is shared, and stories are told. It is a lively group, and Leila keeps the conversation going. In different circumstances, I would love to be a guest at that table!

The butler fills the wineglasses as dinner begins. Footmen troop through my door to serve soup to each guest as a first course.

For the main courses, footmen pass close by me as they carry multiple platters, each laden with one type of the various vegetables or meats on the menu. Each footman displays the platter to each guest who then may decide what he or she wants and how much. The array seems endless. Will the serving platters ever stop?

Each footman serves from the left. The first footman starts with the person seated to the right of the host. Another footman begins to serve the person to the right of the hostess, just to speed up the serving process, I guess. As the large and heavy-laden platters empty, more appear magically, only because of the labor of the servants slaving beside me. There is always plenty of each item for any guest no matter where they sit at table.

Do the servants enjoy such plenty?

I see that Barbara is fiddling with the large ring on her hand. I strain to see. As Leila turns to the right to address a footman regarding a problem that she has noticed with one of the platters, Barbara's ring pops open above a small compartment. Immediately, her hand with its ring waves over Leila's wineglass. With horror, I watch as powder falls into Leila's glass and disappears. Barbara taps the ring closed immediately.

A poisoner's ring! I have read about them. Barbara has just used a poisoner's ring on Leila! What to do? I was told I must not interfere, just observe. I must remain quiet. I cannot raise an alarm. I feel frantic, but what can I do? Mortimer was very clear. We cannot change the past! My knees bounce with anxiety.

Leila finishes her wine and is served a fresh glass. She seems to be enjoying her meal when she says, "My, I suddenly feel exhausted but…for what reason? It has not been a strenuous day."

Barbara smiles at James and at Leila. James nods back to Barbara and smiles at his wife. He looks hard at the spot where I am hiding. He taps an index finger against his nose and smiles at Barbara again. Her head nods abruptly; she got his message.

I know he has seen me. As I come away from my hiding spot to head back to the dressing room, a busy servant girl carrying away dirty dishes walks right through me when I accidentally step ahead of her. Surprised and beyond tense, I mutter, "It's okay, miss. I didn't feel a thing."

Too bad humor is not helping my anxiety!

On my way upstairs, I see Clive. As we speak, I fully materialize. Since I am now visible, he looks around the bedroom hallway to make sure we are alone and that no other time traveler is watching.

"Come with me," I demand. "There is a problem."

We enter the dressing room and close the door. I'm agitated and upset as I recount what I have seen. Clive listens intently. He whistles when I exclaim, "Barbara is wearing a poisoner's ring." He whistles again when I emphatically declare, "I saw Barbara use it!"

Clive says, "Stay here out of sight. I will be back." Clive returns downstairs.

After dinner with its fanciful desserts, the men withdraw to the library and the women to the drawing room. As the ladies are chatting, Leila says, "Oh dear…I must retire…I feel a little unwell."

Mortimer is notified, and Clive appears, concerned. He looks at Leila and then glances at Barbara. Barbara does not know he is Clive present and future. He keeps it that way.

Leila seems weak. Guests cluck concern and good wishes, while bewigged heads, above full bellies, bow and scrape to their hosts before their departure.

"We shall leave and let you rest," rises like a chorus. Barbara comes over and kisses her mother-in-law's cheek. James kisses his mother's hand, the hand he has helped poison. The guests depart, supervised by Mortimer. Clive helps Leila upstairs. She is too wobbly to manage on her own.

Barbara takes her time preparing for departure home. In fact, with James, she is the last to leave. She is still present when Leila reaches the second floor. Once outside, James assists Barbara into their waiting carriage. Barbara tells the driver to stay.

By the time Leila is upstairs, she is almost asleep. She rests on her bed. Mortimer is soon at her side, talking to her and holding her hand. Clive is at the other side. I appear through the dressing room door and stand at the foot of the bed.

I exclaim, "She has been poisoned!" I tell Mortimer what I have seen.

"Probably something to make her sleep deeply," says Clive. He seems quite certain.

Genuinely anxious, Mortimer asks, "Why do you think that and not something else?" From under his heavy brows, his fearful face looks down helplessly at his unconscious wife. He looks close to tears, every unsaid fear rising!

Clive's eyes fix onto Mortimer's face as he replies, "Remember, we know she does not die. We remember her falling ill sometime before the robbery, nothing else." Clive pauses, waiting for Mortimer to respond. Mortimer does not respond. Helplessly, the poor man stares at his wife, strokes her arm, and holds tight to her hand. He pleads, "Please awaken, Leila, my dear. Please open your eyes. Mortimer loves you. Look and see." There is no response from Leila. She is deeply unconscious.

After giving Mortimer enough time, Clive continues, "And later, we who are alive now do not remember anything about Jeremiah. Despite what has happened, he is our only concern now." Clive's eyes are violently pulled away from Mortimer. Suddenly, he stares wide-eyed at me. His face looks like he is seeing his first horror film!

As they were talking, I felt something repeatedly grabbing at my legs. My arms lock on to Leila's bedposts, but I am forcefully pulled away.

"What's happening?" I yell.

Both Mortimer's and Clive's eyes are helplessly transfixed upon me in terror. Suddenly, I am whirling and twisting. Everything around me moves quickly, distorting my vision. Objects appear twisted. I cannot control my movements.

I am no longer in the bedroom. Clive, Mortimer, and Leila have disappeared. The house is gone. I am surrounded by coldness and blackness, broken by streaks of distorted and illuminated objects as they race by.

My thoughts desperately reach out to Clive and Mortimer, but something blocks me. My mind becomes black and empty. I am cold and nauseated from spinning.

Barbara's face appears briefly, smirking and chortling. "Welcome to the time abyss. I hope you enjoy your eternity in nowhere." She cackles. She laughs and laughs until she almost coughs. Then she disappears.

The sense of free fall continues. I twist, then twirl and twirl, becoming colder and colder until my teeth chatter. My stomach heaves, eager to vomit.

What can I do to save myself? Is anyone thinking about me? Am I lost forever?

Loudly, I cry out in desperation, "Help me! Please, help me!"

Chapter 18

JEREMIAH'S SALVATION

I don't know how long I spun out of control, cold, and nearly sick to my stomach. It seemed forever. Even years later, I still shudder with the vertiginous nightmare of that spin in the vortex of the time abyss.

I land with a thump, clutching my queasy stomach! My teeth chatter from the cold, and I'm missing a slipper. It lies on the floor beside me.

Edgar is beside me, disheveled. I quickly learn that he has arrived with me in what appears to be a closed carriage! His wig is twisted partway around over his face. His breeches have pulled up very far. Ouch! He fixes his wig. Next, he sits up tall and raises himself off the bench seat to fix his wedgie. Then his hand rights himself.

My five-greats-grandparents, Marcus and Beatrice, are on the opposite bench seat in the carriage. At least, they look like Marcus and Beatrice, but there is something different about them. Well, Marcus sports a top hat; that's different from the attic. But there is something else. What is it? I am so confused!

"What are you wearing, child?" asks Beatrice, as both of them inspect the two new arrivals.

I put on my slipper. I gulp, swallow saliva hard, and try to answer Beatrice's question. In a frail voice, I squeak out, "My pajamas and my slippers. I hope… I hope… I don't vomit."

"Sweet child, you look like a peppermint stick," says Beatrice with a smile.

In greeting, Marcus removes his top hat briefly. "He looks like a nearly sick, very cold, and very frightened peppermint stick," chortles Marcus, trying to make light of the situation. The top hat returns to his head.

Bewildered, I ask, "How did you find me?"

Marcus speaks slowly and clearly but quietly, "Let me tell you everything I know. The night before the dinner party, Clive warned us that Barbara had spotted you, Jeremiah. With her up to no good, we figured you might need help. Clive also wanted witnesses present to testify when the time comes to clear Edgar."

He adds, "Clive told us he presented himself to Susanne and told her you were safe so she could remain calm at home. Ironically, he didn't want her to raise an alarm, which might warn Barbara!" Quietly, Marcus almost mutters, "Perhaps it was already too late to worry about that."

He looks out the carriage window as he pauses to let everything sink into my mind. *Clop, clop* go the horses' hooves. That's a comforting sound.

Marcus continues, "We three, meaning Edgar, Beatrice, and I, were in Mortimer's house the night before Leila received Barbara's dinner request. Jemima remained behind to observe activity among the trunks. Beatrice and I dressed as servants who do not interact with family. Invisible and inaudible to the living, we had free access to the house in the early hours. If anyone from the future saw us, we hoped not to be recognized. We succeeded." Marcus seems content with what occurred.

"Did I see you?" I ask.

"You did, but you didn't realize who I was." Marcus looks at me and laughs quietly.

Beatrice says, "I was a chambermaid. I stoked your fire this morning, and as it should be, you didn't notice. Of course, I used a very different age!" Beatrice laughs.

I am appalled that I am so callous and unobservant. But could I have recognized either of them at a much younger age?

Marcus says, "This morning, Clive told us about the intended dinner party." He stops to gather his thoughts.

In the momentary silence, my mind flashes to the answer for my confusion about the appearance of my five-greats. Of course! The difference is not the top hat. Beatrice and Marcus are twenty or more years younger than the final age they chose for their residence in their trunk. No wonder they look different!

Both have smoother skin without wrinkles. And when Marcus took off his hat, I saw that he has slightly darker hair, and lots more of it. He is less portly. But he already sports those sideburns!

Beatrice has a slightly fuller figure. She is still thin but not so skinny that she looks like she could blow away. Her face is long, and her chin is pointed, but she is far prettier with the little extra fat. Her eyes are still full of curiosity! And I like her bonnet; it's rather pretty.

After his brief silence, Marcus looks at me steadily and solemnly asks, "You saw the poisoning?"

"Yes, I did," I reply. "How is Leila? She was really weak and wobbly before she lost consciousness. I am worried about her. What was she given?" I inquire anxiously.

Marcus replies, "It was a sleeping medication that Leila received. She will sleep deeply and awaken with a little confusion and probably a gap in memory. In no time, she will be back to normal. Future Mortimer, Leila, and Clive have returned to their trunk. Mortimer said the trip was a bit of a chore with Leila so floppy."

Crazy rag-doll images flip through my mind!

He adds, "The persons presently living in 1744 have no recollection of your visit. They only know that Leila became ill after a dinner party. They called it fainting." His eyes dart side to side as he decides how best to proceed.

Slightly more animated, perhaps with anger, Marcus continues, "Beatrice noticed that Barbara waited in her carriage when Leila was taken upstairs. Barbara's closed carriage hid her as she departed from her living self to sneer at you in the time abyss. Along with James, she has returned to the attic." Marcus looks disgusted as he mutters, "She seems very satisfied with herself."

This fascinates me in a sick sort of way. Then I ask, "How did you save me from the time abyss?"

"With the information we had, Edgar figured out what would happen," Marcus says. He glances silently toward Edgar.

In surprise, I stare intently at Edgar, his neck twisted uncomfortably to the side, so thin, so frail, and so very tall. He seemed timid, damaged, and frightened when I first met him. I am amazed he could do anything. I wait.

Edgar begins, "I tried to figure the worst thing she might do. It didn't take much to decide that putting someone in the vortex of the time abyss was the worst. She did what I expected." He swallows hard.

After pausing in disgust and anger, he continues, "You needed mind connection with future Leila to keep safe. She kept that mental contact with you even as she took over Leila the living. After that, her mind reading allowed you to safely separate from her, to seep through walls and doors, and to be safely invisible and inaudible.

"But when she was drugged by Barbara, the drug affected both living and future Leila. The mind contact was severed, which put you at risk to be pulled into the time abyss." He pauses again, this time to let me understand.

Edgar continues, "I was not involved in what you, Mortimer, Clive, and Leila were doing. Staying invisible, I observed while Marcus and Beatrice became spies as servants. I didn't want to be recognized as the son of the house or to interact with the living Edgar. And I was careful to stay away from James and Barbara."

While he pauses, once again I notice the *clop, clop* of the horses' hooves. The sound calms me. My stomach settles.

Edgar continues, "I stayed invisible and inaudible even from all other time travelers. Hiding near you, I also witnessed the poisoning. As I heard you tell Clive about the poisoner's ring, I became very certain what would happen next."

I look at Edgar with new admiration. Previously, he seemed so weak and afraid, a real Caspar Milquetoast. Perhaps I am starting to see the man that Jemima loves so deeply.

Edgar resumes, "Timing was the issue. Too soon and Barbara would know I was interfering. Too late and you would spend eternity spinning in the cold."

Edgar appears angry as he adds, "I saw Barbara as she blocked mental contact from Clive and Mortimer, just as the drug stopped mental contact between Leila and you." With a shudder, he adds bitterly, "When you saw Barbara laughing at you, I saw her too. She was really enjoying herself! But her comment to you kept mental contact. Accidentally, that kept you closer to me. She released you from her thoughts, thinking you were lost in the abyss."

Taking a deep breath, Edgar continues, "With all my might, I concentrated my thoughts on you alone. I nearly lost you, but I did catch your thoughts. I heard your cry for help!" He looks down at me, starts to smile slightly, and proclaims with a fake drawl, "And you said please! Therefore, I had to help." Everyone else also smiles as Edgar chuckles quietly at his attempted humor.

In his normal voice, he continues, "Somehow, I managed to land you in the closed carriage that Marcus arranged ready to receive us. It was a near thing, but we succeeded." He sighs with relief as he thinks about what he has just done.

Edgar's glistening eyes look at me carefully. He seems to understand my thoughts. We both fight tears—tears of relief, anxiety, and gratitude.

When I am able to speak, I say truthfully, "I am very grateful to you, Edgar." Another terrifying thought crosses my mind. Fearing the answer, I ask, "Could you have been pulled into the time abyss too?"

"Yes," he replies simply.

My eyes become very big. Breathlessly, I almost whisper, "Thank you, Edgar. Thank you for saving me. Thank you for taking that risk to yourself!" I lean against Edgar's lengthy torso. He wraps a long arm around me and holds me tight. Edgar can feel my shivers. He holds me tighter. That feels good.

I have never forgotten his brave actions. I have never forgotten that he said, "It was a near thing." That's British-speak for "You were nearly killed, kiddo."

Marcus glances away as he clears his throat and declares, "We are now heading to our residence. We will be there soon."

Beatrice reviews the passing scenery and adds cheerily, "Just a few minutes more."

"This sounds foolish, but what year is it?" I ask.

Together, Beatrice and Marcus answer, "It's 1839."

"Okay." I shrug my shoulders. I remain thankfully snuggled in Edgar's warmth.

My head is frantic to make sense of everything, including time. "I left home on Tuesday," I state. Once again, I listen to the *clop, clop* of the horses' hooves. The regular rhythm of the sound helps me to make sense of my surroundings. I ask, "What day is it now at home?"

Edgar's arm holds me tighter as he replies, "Thursday."

"That's kind of what I figured," I reply. "And it's Thursday evening here?"

Edgar glances down at me and replies, "Yes. It's early evening on Thursday." His face shows understanding and empathy as he adds, "It must be hard to keep everything clear." He returns my nod while his arm tightens around me, just for a moment. What a comfort!

We sit quietly and comfortably as I stare out through the carriage window at the passing trees and then houses. Our horse guides the carriage along the once-dangerous back road to the same house where Barbara and James lived. As we pass, I realize the slums on the back of the house have been cleared away, and some rather fine new homes have replaced them. The streets are all wide but littered with mud and horse droppings. A ditch runs along each side. The ditches collect rainwater and sewage, which smells.

Inside the property gates, the air smells cleaner, and the noise level drops off. I notice that the old wall and a newer fence enclose the property, ninety-five years after my first visit.

The butler, standing straight and tall, opens the door. He sees only Beatrice and Marcus. He says, "Good evening," to his master and mistress, and takes the hat Marcus hands to him.

I stand silently in front of Edgar. His hand remains on my shoulder. While standing in the hall and looking pensive, Beatrice mechanically requests, "Tea in the library, please."

The butler glances at the bonnet Beatrice is wearing, says nothing about it, nods, and replies, "Yes, ma'am." His eyes flash to the bonnet again, but he still says nothing. He tries to get the eye of his mistress, but she is gazing straight ahead, lost in thought. After glancing at the bonnet one last time, his figure, with straight, almost military posture, disappears silently and efficiently toward parts unknown, probably the kitchen.

Marcus guides us as he states, "He only saw Beatrice and me. He did not see Edgar. Nor did he see you, Jeremiah."

I am relieved. The close call in the time abyss has left me shaken. Leila once said, "Details matter." I need details to put things into order in my mind. Otherwise, everything is too confusing! I miss the calming sounds from the horses' hooves.

Inside the library, I am very surprised to see Jemima pacing beside her chair. She is with Bertie, Marjorie, Joshua, and Penelope, who are seated in various chairs around the room. Like us, they are fully materialized as we exchange greetings and wave.

"We were so worried about you both," says Jemima anxiously. She hugs Edgar and kisses his cheek. She enfolds me, hugs me tight, and then returns beside Edgar.

Beatrice sits at a tea table with four empty chairs, absentmind-edly motions to us, and quietly commands, "Please, sit." As we do, Marcus sits opposite Beatrice. Jemima returns to her chair, near Edgar's, clearly relieved to see that her husband is safe. I get a full view of everyone from my side of the tea table.

Apparently distracted, Beatrice unties her bonnet and places it beside her. She mutters to herself, "I should have removed this in the hall. I wasn't thinking. My thoughts were much too perturbed that you two might be observed. And I was trying to figure tea for nine, when only two can be seen. No explanation came to mind that would suffice. Sometimes I'm such a fool, too easily distracted. No matter." She looks annoyed at herself.

Ignoring the comments from Beatrice, Bertie jokes, "What a spin you had!"

"Are you glad I left you my handkerchief and cigarette holder?" inquires Marjorie with bright eyes full of mischief. She stands and advances toward me, after a glance to her perturbed hostess.

I reply, "Those gifts convinced me that meeting all of you was not a dream, not a nightmare, and that you are real. But it has become a nightmare since!" I shiver as I speak.

"My poor boy! But you are here! All is okay," quips Marjorie cheerily. She tousles my hair, pats it back in place, and then returns to her chair.

No tea and sympathy here! Just tea.

There is a knock on the door, and the butler enters. Everyone except Beatrice is silent.

Back still straight, the butler bends at the waist to place the tray on the tea table. Beside the steaming pot, there are two cups only. Beatrice tries to hide her irritation. She still cannot think of an excuse to order tea for nine!

"Thank you," she says, looking grumpily down at the tea tray. She hands her bonnet to the butler, clearly frustrated that she forgot to remove it in the hall. Her gaze is locked on the two cups she has when she wants nine. Without eye contact with him, she commands irritably, "Kindly take care of this for me, please."

The poor butler senses her annoyance and looks at Beatrice anxiously. I think he wants to ask, "What did I do wrong?" The poor man leaves with bonnet in hand, military posture forgotten as his shoulders slouch. He closes the door silently behind him.

"You need this, dear Jeremiah." She pours tea into one of the cups. "Milk and sugar?" She looks at me with a slight smile.

"Yes, please," I say.

I hold the cup in my hands, ignoring the saucer. The warmth feels good, for I am still shaking from the cold. Marcus wraps me in a throw that is lying on a bench beside the fireplace.

Beatrice says, "Edgar, you need tea as well. You look pale. Are you still cold?" He nods yes. "Both for you too?" she asks, nodding toward his cup.

"Yes, please," he replies.

When Beatrice apologizes that there are only two cups, everyone else says, "None for me."

Beatrice states, "I wanted tea for nine but couldn't think of a reason my poor butler would understand. My apologies for being a poor hostess."

"Nonsense," is the loud and universal response, which improves her mood dramatically. Everyone looks on as we finish the warm beverage. Both of us hold the cup in our hands for warmth.

"We must plan our next action," says Marcus. "We must keep ahead of Barbara and James."

I interject, "Do they think they succeeded in killing me in the time abyss?" My stomach heaves as little as I ask this.

Edgar says, "Yes, I believe they think exactly that."

With an angry edge to her voice as she speaks, Penelope adds, "They seem very self-satisfied just now."

I exclaim somewhat sharply, "I thought we could not change the past, alter what has already happened?" I look around as I speak. My eyes are blurred by tears.

"That is true," answers Edgar.

Furious, I say, "Well, they did. So far as they know, they killed me. That is changing what happened in the past."

"Actually, that is not what happened," says Edgar.

I am shocked. I look at Edgar in disbelief and loudly exclaim, "You mean they didn't try to kill me?" A few angry tears fall.

Edgar responds, "Yes, they did try. James and Barbara are both dead. By murdering you, they did not change the past. You live in the future. They reached out from the past to alter the future. Fortunately, they failed." Edgar looks at me sympathetically.

I think I understand his meaning. To be certain, I ask, "Although no one can go back to alter what has already happened, the past can reach out to the future to alter future events?"

Marcus replies, "That is correct. The present and the future are both built upon the past." Edgar nods agreement.

I deliberately try to calm myself. Otherwise, I won't understand what has been explained. Marcus remains silent, I guess to give me some recovery and think-time. Small talk begins as Bertie and Marjorie chat with their son Joshua and his wife, Penelope. Edgar is seated near Jemima and talks with Beatrice, who is all agog to know the grizzly details of his trial and execution. As a Victorian matron, she sure likes to know the gory details.

At some point, Joshua says, "Mortimer and Clive hurriedly got all of us up to date when they returned to their trunk." He looks toward his wife.

Penelope chortles. "Leila is still half asleep from the drug. I suspect she won't remember much from this trip or the timing. That was a strong knockout drug she got! Her soul is still snoring."

Finally, Marcus declares to the group, "We really must start a plan."

Marjorie answers brightly, "Bertie and I have been scheming together for some time." Completely surprised at the source of this announcement, everyone pays attention in utter silence.

Marjorie looks around at the quiet group before she continues, "From circumstantial evidence and Barbara's overheard plan, we suspect that James hid the rabbit in Edgar's secretary." She scans the group for nods of agreement.

Satisfied, she adds, "Bertie agrees that those two would not want the rest of the stolen silver to surface. And this is also what Jeremiah overheard as Barbara's plan. Presuming that Barbara actually *did* buy the stolen silver to prevent the robbers from getting caught while selling it, where is it? Well, Bertie thinks the silver is presently in the country house where we have our trunks."

Everyone looks at Marjorie in astonishment. "Really? How could that be?" asks a chorus of voices. Marjorie sees their reaction and looks to her husband for support.

Bertie answers, "James and Barbara could not put it there. The country house was built in the nineteenth century, long after James and Barbara were both dead.

"But think about it. Getting the silver into their London house would be sufficient. Boxed or crated, maybe mislabeled, left in the attic, it would be ignored for decades. And if found generations later, it is just old silver that has come to light in a very prosperous household. Obviously misplaced, but no one would think of stolen property as they look at the loot." Self-satisfied, Bertie looks around at everyone. Marjorie smiles at her beau.

Bertie continues, "But the loot probably moved to the country house when the London house was sold." Again, Bertie looks around the group and adds with a sly smile, "Just like a few of you did."

The older generations gasp and then look at Bertie in astonishment. In unison, Jemima and Beatrice utter, "Of course! Bertie, you *are* clever."

News flash!

Proudly taking over from her husband, Marjorie says, "Now, we need to divide and conquer as we search. If we find the silver, and especially if we find the frog that goes with the rabbit, that will badly incriminate James and Barbara." She looks triumphant.

There is a repeat chorus, "What a clever idea!" Marjorie does a curtsy, left hand under right elbow, right arm up with index finger pointing to her chin, fifth finger up. It is a silly gesture that makes everyone laugh.

Bertie takes a simple bow to polite applause.

Suddenly, I feel much better, and a bit warmer! *I'm also relieved that Grandpa Bertie is not actually the village idiot! That role is already played by typecast Humphrey.*

Bertie adds, "We two have decided to search the attic. The more joiners, the merrier the welcome. After that, does anything else need to be done?" He looks around expectantly.

Marcus asks, "How will you prevent James and Barbara from knowing what you are doing?"

"Quiet in the night." Marjorie giggles. She looks at Bertie in an odd way, as if they are sharing a joke between them. Suddenly, I remember *the look.*

"We can help you," says Joshua as Penelope nods in agreement. "And we will not discuss plans in our trunk, in case we are overheard."

"Help accepted!" exclaims Bertie.

Edgar says quietly, so quietly that everyone stops to pay attention, "While you search, I suggest Jeremiah stay here. If he returns, James and Barbara will know he is not dead. If he continues to remain asleep and cannot be awakened, they will believe that they have succeeded. They will think that nature is just taking its course."

This suggestion from Edgar surprises me. He has thought far ahead! "Won't my family be worried about me?" I ask anxiously.

Marcus says quietly and sincerely, "For the greater good, we must make sacrifices sometimes."

"I want justice for Edgar," I state firmly as I look at Edgar with admiration and sincere gratitude.

Everyone is silent for a moment. Marcus coughs slightly. By contorting his broken body, Edgar's shiny eyes look straight at my face. He says, "Thank you, Jeremiah." Once again, silence descends after his words.

After a moment, I break the silence when I look at Marcus and say, "I have a question." Marcus and Beatrice both gaze at me expectantly. "Leila tells me it takes energy to materialize. Does it take much energy for your future self to enter your living mind?"

Marcus answers, "It requires effort. But once the living mind is asleep and the future self is in control, the process is self-sustaining. One is no more tired than after a busy day."

I look at Marcus as he answers, and then ask, "And you and Beatrice are future selves occupying your living body and mind?"

"Yes, dear," answers Beatrice. "Fortunately, when my future self has gone, I will have no recollection of my visit."

This sounds like idiocy until I realize it summarizes the situation nicely.

Beatrice continues, almost as if talking to herself, "I could not bear to recall the Boer War, the First World War, the Second World War, the Holocaust, the Blitz of London, the wars in the Middle East, the many assassinations, the racial unrest, the political turmoil on a day-to-day basis—the weight of all those recollections! So many tragedies!" Beatrice looks sad and then brightens. "I am glad that I will never know those things during my lifetime." She looks around to the others, satisfied that she is safe and secure in early-nineteenth-century England.

My word, that speech sounds foolish! But it is correct.

For some reason, my brain wants to sarcastically say, *There will always be an England.*

I keep quiet about that but continue my quiz. "What about the rest of you? No one else is in their living self. Does materializing for this meeting require a lot of energy?"

Penelope answers, "Yes, it does. It is less than materializing alone since we are with others doing the same energy expenditure. We share costs, as it were. We link thoughts to each other, as you did with Leila to go back through time. This saves some energy. But the effort is exhausting eventually, and I for one will soon need to return to my trunk."

There is general discussion of fatigue and the need for a nap.

Beatrice offers Edgar and me another cup of tea. We both accept. After the second cup, my hands are finally warm.

"We cannot talk about anything in the attic," Marjorie says. "Let's develop a plan here."

At length, they discuss various ideas for the search, how to divide up the labor, suggest various assignments, and decide who will be on watch in case someone else not in the group becomes nosy or gets suspicious.

I suddenly realize that all these people are usually very active, even though they are all dead and residing in a trunk. I listen as they describe nosy neighbors and gossips, all related!

Eventually, the ancestors decide to meet again the following day. They say their goodbyes with comments about plans for a quick, deep sleep followed by an after-midnight search. They repeat how they plan to discreetly rouse one another from sleep to begin the search without attracting attention from the others.

"Just like a game of spies," says Bertie. Clearly, he is enjoying his adventure!

After they each say good night, I hear six pops, as one ancestor after another disappears into another time. I am left alone with Marcus and Beatrice.

Dare I ask what happens now?

Chapter 19

THE NEXT DAY

Beatrice smiles at me and says, "According to our calculations, we are your five-greats-grandparents."

"Yes, okay," I reply uncertainly because I sure don't know.

Beatrice says, "I do so love that American expression 'okay.' So very useful!" A moment later, she continues, "I have watched all the family as they grew. I remember your mother playing on the lawn and in the woods. She was a bit of a tomboy, always in trouble."

Marcus laughs to himself as he hears his wife speak. He watches me closely while Beatrice talks.

She continues, "Constance always did whatever Ian, her older brother, was doing. They were not quite two years apart. She was his shadow and wanted to be just like him. Neither of them had much patience for poor Brian, their younger brother. Despite being about five years younger than your mother, he was always trying to keep up. But early on, the age difference made it difficult for him."

Beatrice muses almost to herself, "I could often see Brian's frustration and hurt when he was left behind. I sometimes wonder, what effect did that have? But Ian and your mother behaved as normal children. Without knowing any difference, children are often very thoughtless and unkind."

My interest is piqued. "Brian is my middle name," I say.

"Yes, it is," responds Marcus cheerily.

Beatrice continues, "Before his teen years, one of Ian's friends was killed accidentally by an older brother who was cleaning a shotgun. The poor brother didn't realize the gun was still loaded. The death affected Ian badly and devastated the brother. Ian became more aloof, afraid to let anyone become close, even though he had many friends. He developed an emotional wall separating himself from others. While avoiding personal attachment may have been his way of protecting himself from further emotional pain, that action left him lonely and disconnected." Beatrice looks sadly at the floor. "And emotionally very vulnerable," she adds quietly.

I glance toward Marcus. His face appears quiet and grave.

Then Beatrice brightly focuses on my eyes again as she says, "Your mother tried to reach out to Ian. It didn't work. As a result, your mother and Brian became quite close." Beatrice smiles as she adds, "She loved him enough to have you carry his name." She pauses, still smiling.

The smile fades as she quietly continues, "I never thought Ian made the best choice with Evelyn as a wife." Almost whispering, she finishes with "But I do worry about Brian."

We Americans in the clan all know Uncle Ian's family and Uncle Brian, so I declare, "Mom says Uncle Ian is to inherit the title. He and his wife are stuffed shirts, according to Dad. I suspect Mom silently agrees because she never contradicts Dad when he says this. She never says anything bad. She only says that Ian is so very unlike Papa."

Marcus adds, "Yes, indeed, Ian is very unlike his father."

I pipe up, "Mom sometimes says that she feels sorry for Brian, who has had multiple jobs and never seems settled. He has been divorced twice, but no children."

"That's right," agrees Marcus as if he has just been reminded of something. "Indeed, that's right," he mutters pensively.

"But Uncle Ian has two sons," I add.

"What are they like?" asks Marcus offhandedly.

I reply, "I really don't know."

"Have you ever met them?" persists Grandfather Marcus.

I reply, "They were at Uncle Brian's first wedding when I was about four and a half."

"Tell me about that," he insists, while Grandmother Beatrice gives me encouraging glances and a smile.

Dredging up old wounds, I begin, "Dexter is a year older than me, and Collin is two years older than his brother. We were with Uncle Ian and his family sometime after the wedding, but I don't really remember why. For some reason, I was given a bright-green balloon. I was thrilled, like any four-year-old would be.

"Collin, who was seven or thereabouts, told me to put the balloon on the ground so he could show me a trick. I loved my balloon, but I was over the moon when he told me that my balloon could do tricks. Expecting to see something marvelous, I happily did what he asked. Collin stomped my balloon and laughed hard when it burst. I guess he thought his trick was funny. I remember I cried when my balloon went pop, which made Collin laugh even harder. I think Collin was the really mean one and the ringleader. Dexter laughed, but only a little."

"Crushing your balloon was a cruel thing to do to a child," says Beatrice sympathetically.

I reply, "You are right, Grandma Beatrice. It was cruel. Dad hopes Collin will grow out of his mean streak. I've met them a few other times when they were Stateside. They are full of themselves and like to brag about their fancy school chums."

"That doesn't sound very interesting," says Marcus.

"Right on, Grandpa Marcus! We don't find their fancy friends' names interesting at all. Collin is the leader, and Dexter is a follower. At least, that is what Susanne says." To get off the topic, I add, "But they are okay, I guess." My shoulders sort of shrug as I finish.

With interest, Marcus asks, "You and your sister are not in close contact with them?"

"No, we are not," I exclaim. "Susanne calls them snobs," I add honestly and emphatically, "and we are not interested in snobs."

Marcus glances toward his wife, who smiles in return. They appear satisfied, as if they have answered a question. But what question?

I'm curious. Why the interest in the cousins and our relationship? I was a little older when I discovered why several ancestors had reasons to watch some members of this generation closely, very closely indeed.

Beatrice continues, "Your mother has done so well. Middle child, independently minded, she struck out on her own and moved to America." She pauses for a moment and then says, "I watch you and Susanne occasionally, but I find it harder to get over to America." Her eyes flit to her husband. I see him smile back.

She rambles on, "Leila has the knack down easily. She has tried to explain how to do so without expending too much energy. I always fear losing energy mid-Atlantic. I do not want to end up with the passengers of the *Titanic*." She laughs uneasily.

I ask, "How do you know about the *Titanic*? I read about the sinking on April 15, 1912. That was after you died."

She smiles. "I do seep out and watch, listen, and learn. Leila taught me how. I just don't seep out as much as Leila."

I exclaim, "She is a real ringleader!"

She disagrees, "I don't know if I would say that. She has a keen and inquiring mind, always wanting to learn. That desire has not stopped with death. When she reaches heaven, Saint Peter will have his hands full!" She laughs out loud.

With a laugh, Marcus says, "No wonder Saint Peter wants the family to solve the murder. It causes a delay, at least, before he must cope with Leila!"

Beatrice glances toward her husband with affection, as she laughs heartily. Afterward, her eyes return to me as she demands, "Now tell me all about you." She smiles and flutters her eyes momentarily in anticipation. Marcus listens intently and awaits my reply.

I outline the basic facts, talk of Susanne, Phoebe, how hard my parents each work, and the change in Dad after Papa's last visit to New York three years before. I talk a lot about Phoebe.

"But your mother is often away, isn't she?" Beatrice asks.

"She has to work," I say.

"Of course, dear." Beatrice nods in understanding.

Both ask me about school, about my reading, my hobbies, and my interests. I answer, despite getting sleepier and sleepier. Both listen attentively.

When Beatrice notices I am falling asleep, she says, "Oh, my dear, your eyelids are falling shut. We must get you to bed."

I say good night to Marcus and follow Beatrice upstairs to a guest bedroom next to the one she shares with her husband.

The furniture is carved beautifully. Even those who like plainer styles must admire the workmanship. The bed is comfortable. Despite my curiosity and fascination with everything around me, in no time I am deeply asleep.

I wake rested and starving! Soon after, Beatrice knocks. Once inside with the door closed, she asks, "What would you like for breakfast?"

I reply, "Anything. I am starving."

She says, "I will need to do a tray. Oh dear, the servants will wonder." She waves her hand and quietly disappears again.

After a short time, Beatrice returns with a picnic basket. "I took this basket and went into the larder myself when Cook was shopping and the others were elsewhere in the house. What fun to steal from oneself!" She giggles like a schoolgirl conspiring with a friend.

Inside is a bottle containing cold milk, pieces of cooked chicken, cold potato salad, scones, butter, jam, a plate to put it all on, a glass from which to drink, a cloth napkin, and cutlery. While Grandmother Beatrice sits on a side chair, I devour everything except the bones as we chitchat on and on.

She's a talker!

Afterward, my granny stands and then walks over to a cupboard to show me a pitcher with water, a washing bowl, a chamber pot, and towels. "It is not like a modern shower. That is something I do wish I had lived long enough to use. But it is better than what you've had for the last few days in the eighteenth century. Welcome to the nineteenth!"

As I say, "Thanks," she turns to leave me alone. The door closes softly behind her.

In the first half of the nineteenth century, people wash at least sometimes. Certainly, Beatrice and Marcus smell better than the living Leila and Mortimer did. I am glad those body smells disappeared when the nine-greats began residing in the trunk! No body, no smell!

Not long after I have cleaned up, there is a knock. Marcus and Beatrice enter my bedroom, along with Bertie, Marjorie, Joshua, and

Penelope. I notice they are all fully materialized as they extend morning greetings.

Searching for places to sit, Bertie and Marcus alight on chairs either side of the fireplace. Joshua and Penelope sit together on the window seat overlooking the garden. Beatrice sits on the desk chair. Marjorie bounces and then settles on the bed beside me. The amount of the bounce surprises me. Like the rest, she has fully materialized. That means she has her usual body weight. She is a bigger girl than I realized.

"Edgar and Jemima didn't come back?" I ask.

Marjorie looks at me and says, "Edgar is still exhausted from his work yesterday and the search during the night. Jemima stayed with him. They both know you are fine, so there is no need for them to be here. I'm sure you understand."

"Of course, I do," I reply.

Penelope interjects, "Their presence at the trunks allows Barbara and James to think Edgar did nothing and that their plan succeeded. Edgar and Jemima send their best wishes."

I answer, "I am grateful to Edgar. He is my hero."

Joshua says, "Mortimer is still tending to Leila. She is awake but rather confused about recent past events. The drug has muddled her recent memory, and that upsets her. The memories related to the trip may never be righted."

Looking toward Joshua with concern, I ask, "Will Leila be okay?"

"She will be fine. It will take a few days to completely clear her system of the drug. Her mind is already tracking new information well. She seems back to normal in that regard," he replies. "And she knows all about what happened."

I say, "I'm glad she will be fine. Before the dinner, Leila said that she remembered getting sick with a fainting illness, but she wasn't sure when exactly. She said she thought that it would occur in a few days, but she wasn't certain of the date. You are right that the drug mucked up her memory. Her memory is usually right on."

Joshua adds, "As I said, some of her memory of this episode may be confused forever. But new memories will be just fine."

All are silent, each registering concern for Leila and quietly wondering how Mortimer will cope, even with Clive's help.

I'm surprised that even a phantom can be drugged up till stupid. Who knew? Oops, that didn't come out quite right. I say nothing! And Leila can't read me just now. *Sliding by!*

After the momentary pause in the conversation, Marcus breaks the silence, "Any news?"

"I'll say," says Bertie.

"The cat's pajamas!" exclaims Marjorie.

"Things went well," adds Joshua.

"We had a bit of luck," quips Penelope with a smile.

Bertie looks like a happy schoolboy as he says, "We decided to look in the unused attic room to the east. Leila and Clive have never cleaned in there because it's storage only. Before Jeremiah's visit, I don't remember the last time a living person inspected the area."

He continues, "Marjorie and I, mostly Marjorie, thought that would be the best place to start." He looks at his wife and smiles broadly. "Smart girl, my Marjorie!"

"But the prize goes to Penelope," Marjorie exclaims as she points to her daughter-in-law. "She is quiet, but she is a thinker. She figured out the puzzle in no time."

All eyes turn to Penelope, who glances at Joshua and touches his hand. Penelope begins, "It wasn't that difficult. We figured that James and Barbara purchased the stolen silver from the thieves and probably kept it in their attic for safekeeping.

"The house in London was sold decades after our present house was built. After the sale, attic boxes from the London house came to our attic, moved at the same time as any number of our trunks." Penelope pauses momentarily. She glances from person to person as she speaks. She adds, "Just to be clear, the ancestors' trunks didn't get shifted by the movers. The ancestors and their trunks came all on their own." She pauses to glance at her audience before she finishes, "But what I mean is, *everything* from the London attic emptied into the country one, most things without a second glance." She checks faces to see that her point is clear.

Marjorie interjects, "If you've checked any dates or time periods on your calendar, you must realize that Bertie and I completed the house sale in London. The sale was a financial necessity. I was the one supervising the move."

"And a fine job you did too," flatters Bertie with a wide smile. "Hear! Hear!"

Marjorie glances at her husband, smiles sweetly, otherwise ignores her husband's buttering as she rolls her eyes, and states tersely, "To be frank, at the time I had no interest in old boxes in either attic! None were inspected, guaranteed."

Penelope drops her eyes momentarily, smiles knowingly, glances up and around, and pushes on by saying, "While curious later generations might discover and open a box labeled silver, could there be any reason a box would never be opened for inspection? Then yesterday, Bertie mentioned that the box could be mislabeled. That got me thinking."

Penelope appears at odds and frustrated. She is not expressing herself the way she wants. Finally, she asks, "What I mean is, was the box labeled as something else other than silver, something that would go from the London house to the country attic and likely remain unopened?" She pauses and looks around.

Penelope continues, "Anyway, we were busy putting our phantom heads into box after box. It takes energy to seep into a box and look inside. We knew we had to inspect all the containers in that room, all storage trunks, and all the boxes. It's a big room! And it's full!" She stops to breathe, then exclaims dramatically, "It was taking forever!"

She pauses again before she says, "Then I thought about what a detective might do. Have a theory. Run a hunch. Thanks to Bertie, I read labels looking for something that could have been in James's attic, something that might never be opened when it was transported to the country."

Marcus and Beatrice are sitting on the edge of their seat. Marjorie bounces slightly on the bed. She is obviously having fun.

Penelope says happily, "There was a large heavy wooden box marked 'Schoolbooks, James Wadsworth, Earl Poppycock' in a back corner." She stops for a moment as she looks around.

Penelope continues excitedly, "Having 'Earl Poppycock' on a box of schoolbooks struck me as odd. His name at school was James Wadsworth, not the Earl Poppycock. There were no dates on the lid. That was also odd. The label should have been his untitled name and the years covered by the books. I became suspicious and even wondered if Barbara did the labeling—she is such a snob. She's the sort to include the title." Dislike echoes in Penelope's voice as she almost snorts the word "snob." She pauses and looks at each of us in turn. We all remain on the edge of our seat.

Finally, Penelope says, "I stuck in my head, and there was the silver. The box contained candlesticks, plate chargers, and a silver frog. I checked for an inscription. It reads, 'To Walter from Abigail,' with the same bit about their anniversary. That ancient labeling snobbery saved us all a lot of work! And we all got some extra sleep!" She raises her closed fists high with open arms and shakes them twice as she exclaims, "Triumph!"

When Penelope's arms relax, she appears very pleased at her accomplishment. She blinks repeatedly with pleasure over a smile that is almost ear to ear, showing off her perfect teeth. My word, she is pretty! She looks toward Marjorie.

"Wow!" I exclaim, as I bounce up and down beside Marjorie. She holds my hands so I don't go flying off the bed.

"Good job!" Beatrice is beaming.

"Well done!" Marcus shows a wide smile.

Marjorie states emphatically, "No one would ever open a box of old schoolbooks. Later, James became an earl, so no one would toss them either. Why bother to open the box during the move? It looks like it was tied up in 1744 and remained untouched. Of course, that is difficult to know with certainty." Then she mutters to herself, "Guaranteed I didn't untie the string during the move." She laughs a little.

Bertie adds, "Penelope says the silver is wrapped in kitchen linen to prevent rattling. The wooden box is heavy, but so are books. A perfect foil." Bertie looks pleased with his summary.

I whisper to Marjorie, "What is a foil?"

Marjorie pipes up, "Something that stops something else from happening. It is a perfect disguise to prevent discovery of the silver." She bounces on the bed again. Her weight puts me into motion too.

A chorus exclaims, "What a brilliantly simple plan! Who would have guessed? Congratulations, Penelope."

I'm confused about the word "chargers." Then I recollect that Nana recently talked about a fancy dinner she and Papa attended. When she was talking about the meal, she mentioned plate chargers. I knew about my phone battery and its charger, but I was baffled about a plate charger and foolishly asked why a dinner plate needed a battery. After she stopped laughing, Nana explained to Susanne and to me, "Plate chargers are often made of silver with a fancy edge and a flat central area. They are designed to sit under a fine china plate. Their purpose is to show the good taste and wealth of the host and hostess."

"To show off?" I asked.

"Right you are," Nana replied with a knowing smile. "Their only purpose is to show off."

My recollection finishes at the same time as the chorus of congrats, so I ask, "Where is the silver now?"

Penelope replies, "The box is untouched. I didn't touch the string ties, remove the lid, or shift the silver. It is in the far corner, and on top of it, there is a box of real school papers belonging to James Wadsworth that is dated, but no title."

Looking at each person, I ask, "Now what do we do?" I badly want an answer.

"We six have discussed this," says Bertie, looking at the three others who searched with him and giving credit to Jemima and Edgar who also helped. With sympathy in his eyes, Bertie says, "We need to get you home. After a rest, you need to tell the family what has happened. Susanne can back you up. As you know, Clive kept her informed. She has not told anyone of your time travel. That is for you to do."

Bertie looks at me keenly and says, "You have two lawyers in the family, your mother and grandmother. Leila can act as judge. The other ancestors can act as jury. It is time to seek justice for Edgar."

"There is something else you should know," says Joshua as he looks directly into my eyes.

I stare at Joshua anxiously, waiting for whatever is next.

"At present, you are in the hospital," he says kindly.

"What?" I exclaim. That caught me off guard!

As I look around the group of ancestors in the year 1839, I recollect that I am living in two different centuries—at the same time!

Joshua repeats, "In the hospital."

I ask stupidly, "Why?" Muddled, I glance around and ask, "What happened to me at home?"

Joshua continues, "You have been unconscious for days. You left home Tuesday night and arrived before dinnertime here. Right now, it's Friday morning back home. You have had medical evaluations, and you are receiving intravenous hydration. The doctors are baffled. Your parents and grandparents are all there."

"My poor parents! No one except Susanne knows what has been happening." I exclaim, "I'm such a selfish idiot!" I look round at concerned faces and say anxiously, "Mom must have flown over from America! She is not due in England for another month because of work. That means I mucked up her office as well! And both Papa and Nana returned from London? Nana wasn't due till Friday evening."

Marjorie is the one who says, "Her child is ill. Your mother has to be with you. She loves you." She tousles my hair and then pats it back. "Same rules apply to your grandparents."

I gulp. I look at Marjorie with new respect. She is a deeper person than she lets on. Why is she afraid to show it?

"Everyone must be worried," I say. "I am sorry I caused them grief. I should have told them what I was doing."

Marjorie strokes my hand once, in reassurance, and then she laughs brightly. "We will get you back so you can wake up and tell your story."

Once again, I rehash, "I didn't tell anyone but Susanne what I was doing. And she was told to keep quiet. I have worried them all. That was selfish of me."

"They will understand when you tell them," says Marjorie patiently. She smiles at me, touches my shoulder, and says, "Truly, they will understand, not to worry."

I look around. "I don't know what to say. I want to thank you all for saving Edgar."

"Nonsense. It was you who saved Edgar. Others have failed," declares Joshua as he looks at me proudly.

"Stuff and nonsense. It was you who solved the puzzle and saved Edgar." Bertie laughs.

"It was all you, with backup from Susanne," states Penelope.

"Poppycock, if they say it wasn't you," claims Marjorie as she laughs and laughs.

They all laugh.

"Poppycock indeed," cheers a chorus of ancestors who all have shared a title called Poppycock. They all laugh again. Bertie laughs so hard he coughs.

Marjorie commands, "Gather 'round and hold hands." When everyone complies, she adds, "Now touch foreheads as best you can with the person beside you." She waits for everyone to do as she commands. "Now think about arriving in the attic. Think of your comfortable trunk. And, Jeremiah, you think of a comfortable bed."

Marjorie looks at everyone, then at me, and declares, "Jeremiah, you are odd man out. No forehead to touch. Put your forehead against my arm. I have enough energy for us both!"

That I truly believe! I hear pops all round. There is a flash of light. Then there is nothing but the silence of sleep.

Chapter 20

After Jeremiah's Return

Light intrudes through the gap between my eyelids. Bed is so comfortable. Just five minutes more! I make a sleepy-pleasure sound, move a little in my bed, and close my eyelids tight again.

"He is moaning," Mom says. The slits between my eyelids open just enough to see that she looks at me anxiously.

"He seems comfortable," says Dad's anxious voice beside me.

Is it five minutes already? But bed feels so good! Why are Mom and Dad talking in my room? I'm trying to sleep. And I know Mom is in the States. Clearly, this is a dream. I'm so very comfortable after a little shift toward my side. More sleep? Oh yes please.

"He moved and shifted in bed," says Mom. Her voice sounds funny, weak, or something. Why is her voice right beside me?

Okay, I'm up. I open the eyelids.

"Wait. His eyes are opening," exclaims Dad excitedly.

Why does Dad make this sound like a big deal? I look around with a start. This isn't my room! Wait, I remember. Joshua said I was in the hospital. Wait, Joshua, two greats, no, one great, but… he's dead…wait, did I meet dead ancestors? Wait…this is a hospital room, right? I'm confused! Well, if nothing else, the bed felt good, at least while sleep lasted.

My parents are beside me. Susanne sits in the corner, next to Phoebe. I can see Papa through the doorway, and I can hear Nana talking to Papa.

"Where am I?" I ask as I try to sit up.

"In the hospital," Dad answers.

"Over here, they call it an infirmary," adds Mom. Her hand absentmindedly pushes against my shoulder. I stop trying to sit up.

"Oh, a hospital room. Okay…why?" I ask stupidly.

Phoebe is suddenly tight beside Mom. She gives my forehead a kiss. Some wet drops land on my face—is she crying? With a shaky voice, Phoebe exclaims, "You have been unconscious for days." She kisses my forehead again. "I was so frightened. Thank heavens you are talking," she says and moves back to her chair.

Some memories suddenly flood back. I did indeed meet dead ancestors. I remember that now.

My mother's hand touches my face. Her strokes on my forehead feel wonderful. "How are you feeling?" she asks quietly, now mucking with my hair.

"Hungry," I reply.

They all laugh.

Looking at Mom, I ask, "When did you get over from Stateside?"

She responds almost mechanically, "When you didn't wake up and were taken to the hospital, I got the first available flight." She looks at me searchingly. She nearly cries.

"What day is it?" I ask.

"Friday, in the morning," replies Dad.

"Wow!" I look at Mom and ask, "Do you have jet lag?"

"I'm just tired and worried," she replies tearfully. "You were found unconscious Wednesday morning when you missed breakfast."

"Really," I exclaim, "that's a long time!" More memories are flooding back. *Gotta be careful.*

I look around from my adjustable hospital bed, the head elevated slightly. I have a tube going into my left arm and a clear liquid slowly dripping into the tubing.

There are flowers on the windowsill. Susanne smiles at me very happily. Phoebe has a hand before the lower part of her face and tears in her eyes. She waves at me until I wave back. Her eyes are red.

"Welcome back," Susanne says knowingly. "Did you have a successful time away?"

Her comment triggers recollections of all the details of the time travel with Leila, the time spent in 1744 London, and the plans made with ancestors in 1839. I ponder for a moment before I smile at Susanne and say, "Yes, it was very successful. I will tell you later."

Susanne nods. The adults don't understand.

Dad says, "You didn't take a drug, did you? What did Susanne mean?"

Looking right at him, I answer, "No, Dad. I will never do drugs. Reality is too much fun all by itself!"

If only you knew how much fun, and how much danger!

My father looks confused and maybe not reassured.

Papa sees that I am talking, tells a nurse, and comes in with Nana. Nana smiles and comes over to me. She hugs me tight.

"How are you?" Nana asks.

"Okay," I answer.

She asks, "What happened?"

"Dunno," seems my safest answer.

Papa gives me a big hug. There is a quizzical look on his face, and then resolution, as if suspicions have finally been confirmed. But he says only, "I love you." He looks as if he wants to say more, but doesn't. Walking toward his chair, he turns to me again with lips apart to possibly say something, stops, closes his mouth, and returns silently to Nana.

When the doctor arrives in a few minutes, he says cheerily, "I understand we have someone waking up." The doctor asks how I feel. He asks more questions—have I suffered a head injury, taken drugs, had a fever, do I hurt anywhere? Then the kicker, "What is the last thing you remember?"

Thinking fast for that one, I answer, "Not sure." It is not right to lie to a doctor or to anyone else, but I do. The truth will not fly. The doctor will not understand!

He examines me head to toe.

With my eyes fixed directly on the doctor, I say, "I'm hungry." He smiles down at me. "Really hungry," I repeat emphatically.

"Best sign possible. We will get you a sandwich and a drink. If that stays down and you survive hospital food, off home you go."

"Thank you," I say enthusiastically.

He says to my parents, "I want to see him again in a few days."

Dad replies, "Of course, sir," as the doctor leaves.

After a few short hours, I am without the intravenous, fed, showered, and in clean clothes. Ever the optimist, Phoebe apparently insisted that clean clothes must be ready for me at the hospital, all prepared for a trip back home. Surprise! They are needed!

Never do I want to see that pair of pajamas again! They make me look like a giant walking peppermint stick. Will they ever scrub clean? If they do, I vote that they go to Goodwill or the Salvation Army! Someone else may do peppermint stick imitations with red-and-white striped pj's!

At home, everyone hovers as we cluster together in the sitting room. "But I feel fine," I say when adult eyes repeatedly glance at me. Apparently, watching me will keep me awake!

Mrs. Stewart is a woman of very few words who rarely leaves her kitchen. She usually pays attention only to her food preparation. Imagine my complete surprise when she comes into the sitting room to briefly see me and loudly say, "Hello, Jeremiah. I hope you recover quickly." What an honor! With her hands pulling at her apron, she nods at the family and me. Then she's gone.

Nigel and Mr. Brown also appear. In normal voices, both of them express good wishes for a speedy recovery. Nigel is so relieved to see me doing well that he bounces off his toes twice like a choir-boy who cannot laugh out loud. His brilliant smile shows repeatedly when he and Mr. Brown chat amiably with me and the family for a few minutes before they leave to continue their duties. But then they usually talk and visit more than our wonderful cook.

Phoebe gets me a Mrs. Stewart sandwich, and then another, each with a tall glass of milk. I can tell Mrs. Stewart is glad I am safely home. Her sturdy sandwiches are even thicker than usual! She must be glad I am here to eat them.

Mom says, "You were unconscious, and we don't know why." She appears very tired. She still looks anxious. Of course she would; she doesn't know what happened.

After my visitors leave, Phoebe and the family remain with me in the sitting room. I can tell that they are anxiously bored while vigilantly guarding me from falling unconscious again, or so they think.

Susanne glances at my parents, at my grandparents, and at Phoebe. She looks squarely at me before she asks, "Do you feel up to talking?" There is a commanding tone in her voice.

After speaking, she stands up and gazes round at the family. Turning her face directly to me alone, she inaudibly mouths, "Stop their misery." Susanne walks past me and disappears up the stairs without any explanation.

As she leaves, I quickly glance from person to person and clear my throat. "There is no time like the present," I begin. "You all need to know what happened."

Motionless, they stare at me as I say, "Please, get comfortable so that I can explain. At least, I hope I can explain." They look far too surprised to say anything for a few moments.

I add, "You will all need to help."

In unison, Mom and Dad say, "What do you mean, Jeremiah? What has happened?"

Nana, our granny lawyer, looks at me with wide-open baby blues and asks, "What have you done, young man, that you need our help? What trouble are you in?" My goodness, she sounds stern!

Deep in thought, Papa looks at me intently but says nothing once again. His face looks like a mixture of anxiety and relief.

As they finish their questions, Susanne returns, covering her skirt pocket. As she sits near Mom, I feel eyes intensely focused on me. Quietly, I say, "Let me begin to explain. But first, I must apologize. I never intended to cause you such anxiety. That was thoughtless and selfish."

Now everyone is really wondering what I have done. They all look at me with silent question marks for faces.

Papa clears his throat, looks at me knowingly, and says, "I think everyone is too confused to know what to forgive. Secrets are such heavy burdens. I think you need to explain so everyone may know what you did, no secrets kept. Don't you agree? No one, not one person in this house, should have secrets anymore." He looks resolute with one thumb pointing to his own chest.

It was then that I realized he was talking about more than *my* secrets. His words and his thumb gesture were giving me an all-clear signal to spill all the beans because he has figured that Leila told me about his trip to the attic and his time travel.

I reply, "Yes, Papa, I agree. You are right." Some in the group twig that Papa's words might have a double meaning. They look at Papa and then at me in confusion. I mutter, "Let me see, where to start?"

Dad exclaims ominous words, "Start explaining, Jeremiah. Let's hear it now, from the beginning."

As I look at their perplexed faces, I mumble almost inaudibly to myself, "How can others understand? After all, even I can scarcely believe what happened."

Dad tersely commands, "We cannot hear you, Jeremiah. Start again."

Swallowing hard, I begin clearly and audibly, "On Monday, I met Nine-Greats-Granny Leila and the other ancestors who reside in the attic."

Mom, Phoebe, and Dad exclaim, "What?" Mom looks terrified. She grabs Susanne's arm and holds on for dear life as if Susanne were suddenly in danger.

Nana almost shrieks, "Who is in the attic? Did you say ancestors, or bodies of ancestors?"

"Ghosts of ancestors, no bodies, Nana," I quickly reply. You can tell she's a lawyer.

Susanne sits beside Mom quietly, a slight smile on her face. She sometimes likes to play uproar by shocking our parents. I can tell she is silently having a good time, even though her arm is tightly squeezed by one scared mom.

Papa has a slight smile too, and a slightly self-satisfied look on his face. Suddenly, I realize that he should have easily guessed what I had done, especially since he did the same thing himself. Now I'm wondering why he didn't say anything to anyone. Instead, he acted as if he was as much in the dark about my illness as the rest. That confuses me.

After the commotion settles, I tell everything I know regarding Edgar's troubles from the first day's visit. I finish by admitting, "I was confused when I found the brightly colored handkerchief and cigarette holder. Until then, I had decided it was all a bad dream. After all, it's difficult to believe that a crowd of ancestors reside upstairs."

After the first day's details, I continue, "Susanne came with me to meet Leila in the attic on Tuesday. As it happened, she ended up meeting all the ancestors as well."

I am interrupted by another storm. All adults except Papa exclaim, "Susanne, you knew what was happening and said nothing!"

Poor Susanne looks like a caged animal in distress. At first, Mom clutched Susanne like something was going to whisk her away. And now, Mom holds Susanne by the shoulders, looks really angry, and curtly demands, "Why did you not say what was happening?" Mom looks as if she might wallop her daughter!

Finally, Susanne pulls her arms and shoulders free from Mom and says, "It was Jeremiah who insisted on making this trip. I told him he shouldn't. It was his job to say what he was doing. And a servant of an ancestor told me that Jeremiah was safe and for me to stay quiet for his own protection. There was nothing we could do anyway, so I stayed quiet like I was told to do." Her face is scarlet with embarrassment, and her chin jiggles wildly.

"Oh please, don't cry," I mutter under my breath. No one hears me. Almost silently, I mumble, "I've been thrown under the bus. There must be tire tread marks on my back." Again, fortunately, my words are not heard. Oddly, I wonder, *Is Leila around to enjoy a good eavesdrop?*

Papa opens his mouth to say something. His eyes dart side to side as his mouth closes again, without saying anything.

To calm Mom's fury, I say, "In Susanne's defense, the ancestors told her to say nothing because they thought that silence might protect me from another ancestor. The intentions were good. Sorry about the results."

After the storm passes, I continue, "It was Mortimer's sincerity that convinced Susanne that the ancestors were real, wasn't it, Susanne?"

I can tell that she is relieved that the attention is back on the story. With emphasis, she says, "Instead of being translucent, he almost materialized fully to solid appearing flesh and blood as he spoke. He was very sincere as he asked for help." The chin settles. No tears.

I exclaim, "We both decided to try to clear Edgar's name." If she is throwing me under the bus, she's coming with me.

Susanne nods vigorously again as she says, "Oh yeah! And when Phoebe showed us the rabbit she purchased, we both realized it was the rabbit used to convict Edgar!"

I guess she is willing to take the blame right alongside me. Besides, what else could she say before—everything she said was true. *Let's forget about the bus and the tire marks.* Relieved, I take my turn to nod vigorously and say, "Oh yeah!"

I describe the trip through time to London 1744. My report of my initial scary panic trying to make contact with Leila creates another small panic, here in the sitting room. When that settles, they hear about the visit to James and Barbara's house with Clive, and the conversation I overheard between Barbara and James. I say emphatically, "I heard Barbara outline her plan to destroy Edgar to get the title and his inheritance. But she heard me as I listened, because she was also a time traveler."

After I describe Barbara's yelling at me during my escape from her house and why she could see me, there is another uproar. Mom and Phoebe both say, "You might have been killed if you had been caught!"

When things settle again, I continue, "And then Barbara acted to shut me up. The next night, she poisoned Leila with a sedative at dinner," I exclaim, "which drove me into the vortex of the time abyss." I describe that terror!

Mom, Dad, and Phoebe look horrified as they stare at me. Mom starts to cry. This gets Susanne's chin going again. Oh dear! Poor Nana looks overwhelmed while Papa is anxiously silent and biting his lower lip.

I quickly say, "It's all okay. Edgar saved me! We landed in a closed carriage with Marcus and Beatrice in 1839." I fill in the details, including the meeting that occurred this morning with generations of ancestors.

I continue, "Clive was the dutiful servant who didn't want to make the family aware of what was happening, all in case Evil Barbara might be tipped off that I had time traveled. He was afraid she might do the same. As you can guess, she figured it out anyway all by herself." As I talk, I check that I have given credit to all the ancestors who helped.

"Our ancestors found the stolen silver in the attic here, which incriminates Barbara and James." I look at Papa and say, "But, Papa, it was your mother, Penelope, who figured out how to find the silver more quickly by looking for a mislabeled box."

Papa turns his eyes from the floor and fixes them on me. "How so?" he asks.

"Everyone realized that when the London house was sold, attic boxes were all moved here. She noticed a wooden box labeled as the schoolbooks of James Wadsworth. There were no dates, which is unusual, and the box had the title Earl Poppycock. He wasn't the Earl Poppycock while at school. Those were her clues."

Papa smiles sadly but proudly with bright eyes and replies, "She always was one for noticing details, often to my detriment." He chuckles slightly.

I add, "All those who helped me return to the present now hope all of you will assist with a trial."

Everyone looks at me in astonishment, except Papa, who is somber and quiet. He looks away. Afterward, he looks at me and at Susanne, and then down again at the floor. The rest remain over-whelmed and speechless.

I finish with "I regret I didn't tell Clive to let the family know what was happening. We all thought keeping my trip a secret would protect me. Anyway, there was nothing you could do. Sorry!"

Susanne stands and says, "Clive was our nine-greats-grandfather's valet. He's the one who returned from the eighteenth century during the last few days to keep me informed about Jeremiah's progress in 1744 London."

That sounds like a silly sentence, but it's right!

Everyone, except Papa, stares bug eyed and open mouthed at Susanne as it finally sinks in that she has been kept up to date by a spook visiting from the eighteenth century, not just by a ghostly servant who resides upstairs.

"More of them were coming into my attic?" shrieks Nana.

"No, Nana, Clive resides upstairs. But he traveled back through time to 1744 London and then did a return trip to talk to Susanne," I reply. "That took a lot of effort on his part," I add.

"Several return trips, actually," mutters Susanne.

I exclaim in surprise, "Several? That really took effort."

As I'm talking, Susanne produces the handkerchief and the cigarette holder from her pocket.

"What are these?" demands our mother. She grabs the objects from Susanne and inspects them closely. She notices the perfume on the handkerchief. "That's expensive perfume," is all she says. She looks befuddled.

Meanwhile, Papa sits bolt upright. Nana's surprised eyes stare at Papa. He says, "That is the handkerchief and the cigarette holder used by Marjorie Wadsworth, Countess Poppycock, my grand-mother." Papa looks around to the others, nods his head as he makes a resolute decision, and states, "I saw them when I was in the attic and met everyone myself. I was a few years older at the time than Jeremiah is now." Papa's bright-red face appears sad as he says, "I tried so hard to help poor Edgar, but I failed." He looks embarrassed and maybe angry as well as sad.

That confession cost him!

There are gasps from Nana and my parents. Phoebe's mouth is wide open. Her teeth click loudly when her mouth snaps shut.

Dad looks bewildered as he fumbles for words. "You mean… this nonsense they say…is real?"

Mom looks from me to Susanne, and then to her father. From her appearance, my guess is that she can't decide if what she hears is real or if each of us has lost our marbles.

"Yes, Jeremiah's tale is very real," says Papa. He looks at Dad first and then each adult in turn.

The adults, especially Dad, seem confused. Nana and Phoebe look stunned.

Suddenly, Mom's eyes flit side to side. A thought has just crossed her mind, and she looks furious. I see a similar expression on Phoebe's face, but she is not in a position to say anything. But I see her nod as Mom demands, "Do you mean to tell me that you went back in time yourself, Papa, with the same results, so you knew what was happening, and you said nothing? Why would you keep such information secret?"

Papa turns pale for a moment, collects his thoughts, and finally says, "As a teenager, I tried to help Edgar, and I failed. I regretted the attempt and tried to forget all about it. I never returned to the attic, even for a visit to my ancestors. You know me well enough to know that I have difficulty accepting failure.

"When I time traveled, I was unconscious for days, just like Jeremiah. With two exceptions, I never told anyone about my time-travel trip. I kept the cause of my apparent illness a secret even from my parents. That was wrong, for it worried them to think there might be a recurrence. For years, I hoped never to need to explain anything at all."

Papa stops to glance at Mom who is still glaring at her father. "I never suspected that the children would go to the attic, so I wasn't certain what had happened to Jeremiah. If I said that I suspected he was time traveling, and he wasn't, then I would have exposed my secret failure for nothing. And if he was time traveling, there was nothing we could do anyway. I didn't know what to do. For the first time in my life, I didn't know what to do. Please, Constance, forgive me. My fear of exposing my failure won over common sense. I was uncertain and foolish." Papa's face has gone from pale to bright red again.

Mom looks at Papa, shrugs her shoulders in annoyance, and mutters, "Papa, you are sometimes a silly old fool. No one cares that you once failed at something. I understand why you acted as you did, and I love you regardless, but you are a silly old fool." She almost smiles as she wipes away her tears, muttering, "I forgive you, but I'm still mad."

"Thank you, Constance," he replies, "I think."

Papa smiles at me and at Susanne. "I am so glad Jeremiah and Susanne have succeeded. A great day for Edgar!" His face shows relief. He smiles briefly. He turns solemn again. With deliberate speech, Papa says, "We will need to see… What next to do?"

Nana's eyes are flitting side to side. She is obviously thinking through something. With a faltering voice, she interrupts, "John, do you mean to tell me that we have had phantoms residing in the attic all these years, and I…didn't…know?" I hear the same *tone* I sometimes hear from Mom.

Trouble! Deep trouble! Again!

Helplessly, Papa shrugs his shoulders as he ponders what to say to his wife. In a quiet voice, Papa says, "Yes, Iris, that is so. Left undisturbed, they are harmless. We had no power to evict them. What was the value of raising an alarm?" Papa looks at Nana anxiously.

I hope he is not in deep trouble!

My parents and Phoebe look anxious. What might happen next?

The room is engulfed in silence for a very long time. Nana appears lost in thought. Eventually, she quietly and slowly enunciates, "Well, John, perhaps it is just as well I didn't know. Nigel would have gone mad at the prospect, and I dislike keeping secrets from Nigel. He is such an extension of the family."

Saved!

"Hear, hear," replies Papa with a sigh of relief. He glances with real affection toward his wife.

Nana and Mom look at each other. Mom shakes her head as if waking up from a nightmare and says, "Nothing Jeremiah has said makes any sense. Susanne and Jeremiah say this story is real. And you, Papa, you are backing them up?"

Despite everything she feels, she is still questioning if anything of my story is real. That's her lawyer's instincts at work. In my head, I hear her say, "Trust, but verify."

Papa says, "I most definitely am backing them up, to the hilt! They have succeeded when I did not. I am grateful to them."

With an uncertain and doubtful voice, Dad says, "Then I guess that I believe them." Poor Dad has looked like a lost soul during most of this.

Mom still appears skeptical and confused, but her anger has gone. She looks from me to Susanne to Papa and then to Nana. She glances at Dad who still seems befuddled. I can tell she is summarizing the situation in her mind. She smiles ever so slightly as her eyes flit back at me.

Phoebe remains quiet, looking very uncertain indeed. She will follow Mom's lead.

Eventually, Mom says, "I guess I need to go with the flow. Majority rules!"

Nobody said anything about a majority opinion. Where did that come from? I guess Mom wants an excuse so she can believe her son and daughter!

Mom's shoulders shrug almost to her ears, cartoonish. She glances toward Nana, who nods back. Nana now looks like she has made up her mind. She is no longer befuddled or stunned. She looks ready for action. Mom and Nana both speak together, one voice crowding over the other. "There will need—"

"Continue, Nana. You go first," Mom says graciously as she looks at her mother.

Nana nods in response to Mom's words and says, "There will need to be a trial. Our ancestors are right. We have two lawyers. The ancestors can be the jury. Leila will make an excellent judge by all accounts of her personality. Justice must be done, and the situation in the attic must be settled."

She shudders slightly at the thought of phantoms residing in her garret. She's too polite to say, "The phantoms need to move away, out of my attic!" I think for a moment and realize that, as a Brit, Nana would more probably say, "The phantoms need to shove off."

"I agree that justice must be done," says Mom. "Nana, will you be the lawyer for the prosecution? I shall be for the defense. I was born a member of the family. You married into this tribe. I should defend members of the family, even if they appear wicked and cruel."

Nana says, "Yes. That is a good plan. Thank you for taking the harder role."

Phoebe looks anxiously at Mom and Nana. She looks totally bewildered. A few years ago, she once joked with Papa about working here. I'll bet she's now glad to live Stateside. Susanne goes over to sit near poor, confused Phoebe.

Mom fixes me in her gaze and says, "Thank you for your earlier apology, by the way. It's just as well you didn't tell me about your planned trip. I would have said, "No. Too dangerous."

Dad, Nana, and Phoebe all echo Mom's words.

Phoebe says, "You were almost killed, maybe twice. I just hope that risk was worthwhile."

Papa says nothing. Time passes in silence.

Eventually, Susanne says, "I feel bad too. We didn't think about anything except clearing Edgar's name. Neither of us thought about the effect on the family. I contributed to the anxiety. I apologize too."

There are murmurs among the adults. Nana looks at the others and says, "I'm sure the others agree with me that you should have told us what was happening. We understand the reasons for your actions. But your time travel was a terrible experience for us. You were unconscious here with no apparent reason. It was terrifying."

Then Mom interjects, "While I would have said, 'No, stay put, too dangerous,' I am very proud of you both. You two had the guts to defend someone against a wrongful charge. That takes courage! Like Papa said, it is a great day for Edgar."

"Hear! Hear!" Dad and Nana say together.

Papa states, "I am grateful I did not know what you were doing, although I sort of guessed. It was foolish of me not to say what I suspected, and I sincerely apologize for that. But I am glad you succeeded. You both sought true justice, not just the rule of law. The rule of law convicted Edgar wrongly."

Papa pauses for a moment before he continues, "I still feel frightened when I realize what nearly happened to you. You came too close to a very different outcome. I am grateful you are safe, glad you succeeded, and terrified you might do something similar again!" He smiles through a very solemn face.

Phoebe says, "Jeremiah, you could have died. That scares me so much that I don't know what to say. I love you both. Thank heavens each of you is safe here." A tear falls down her cheek, which she wipes away awkwardly.

Nana adds, "Considering these results, I am glad you did what you did. True justice is often hard to obtain. Its pursuit takes courage. We are all very proud of both of you."

Finally, Dad says, "If I may be allowed, I'll speak for everyone." He pauses till he sees all their heads nod. "You worried us sick. I mean not only Susanne and Jeremiah—I'm including you, Papa. We accept your apologies because we know you all mean it. We are glad you are safe with us now. We love you all, and all are forgiven." After a brief silence, he adds, "Now, let's move ahead."

Everyone nods in agreement. All quietly utter, "Hear! Hear!" Susanne and I receive heartfelt hugs.

Phoebe holds me very tight and says, "All is forgiven. Please stay safe!" Her eyes are wet.

Shortly afterward, Nana suddenly says forcefully, "I feel like storming the attic and chasing those old intruders away. I trust you three, so I *do* believe we have phantoms in residence."

Mom and Dad both say, "We're with Nana." I see Phoebe nodding in agreement.

Oh dear, Papa has a rebellion on his hands.

Papa replies, "I understand that sentiment entirely, especially since Leila's desire to clear Edgar's name nearly killed our grandson. I'd also like to see each one in their final resting place and the attic empty of ghosts. However, it doesn't work that way. An authority higher than any earthly power allowed them to delay their final destination to heaven or wherever. That same authority gave them permission to stay in our garret after they were moved from the London house when it was sold decades ago. We need to work together with the phantoms who helped Jeremiah. Once Edgar's name is cleared, they will all leave, with permission from above, and the attic will be empty."

Nana opens her eyes wide and exclaims, "You mean if we wanted to evict them, we would be fighting the ultimate City Hall!"

"Saint Peter himself. He's the one who bargained first with Edgar, then Mortimer, and lastly with Leila and the rest," says Papa.

I pipe up, "That's what I was told too."

Nana nods and indignantly declares, "I understand, but I wish that Saint Peter, or his boss, had cleared things with me!" Her eyes flick side to side, and her tone softens as she realizes who is the boss and how unlikely he was to give her a call to get her permission. Then she adds, "But for now, we'll simply do what needs to be done."

The other adults laugh out loud at Nana's silly tantrum and then agree to follow her lead. "Yes, let's do whatever needs to be done," they say.

Following Papa's statements and Nana's outburst, an awkward silence returns to the gathering. I'm not exactly sure that I understand everything Papa said, but the adults seem very thoughtful. Susanne looks solemnly at the floor.

Finally, Papa says, "We all need to figure how best to exonerate Edgar's name so the phantoms can clear out from the attic. That's the way it works. We need to follow the rules from a higher authority, far beyond our earthly control. Let us recover overnight. We will sleep soundly, now that Jeremiah is safe. We need to think about our duties and how best to proceed. We can convene in the attic tomorrow after some planning."

With everyone finally in agreement that clearing Edgar's name is the only sensible way to empty the attic, the adults begin to discuss multiple plans of action, without consensus. Finally, Papa again patiently says, "We need to sleep on this. Let our minds forget about this topic during the rest of the day, and wait for tomorrow. There has been too much new information. Processing takes time. A sensible plan will be obvious to us in the morning, after a day at rest and a good night's sleep."

"Agreed," says Nana. She glances at all the heads nodding yes. "We accept Papa's proposal."

As my eyes scan my relatives, I say, "I must tell Leila that I'm safely home."

"No need, dear. I am right beside you," whispers Leila in my ear, "and fully recovered, thank you very much."

Papa looks at me and winks.

Susanne giggles quietly, hand to mouth, suppressing a laugh.

Papa says, "I think that can wait until tomorrow."

Papa knows Leila is here, as does Susanne. Just the three of us got the invitation to hear! We three laugh.

Everyone else looks puzzled. They heard nothing, so why the laughter? With so much new and strange information, and so much speculation about action plans, they have systems overload. They look at each of us but ask nothing. Dad still looks befuddled.

Leila whispers again, "I will listen for the morning's plans so that I can tell the others upstairs. Goodbye for now, dear boy. And welcome home." I feel a touch against my ear as she disappears.

Susanne smiles knowingly in my direction.

Papa looks at me and winks again.

I can't wait for tomorrow. I'm excited, but also scared. What will happen when we see that wicked Barbara again? Even with others around, I am not sure what she might try. But I need to keep a lid on my boiling emotions and pretend everything is smooth sailing.

Oblivious to my inner feelings, Susanne talks with me happily and decides an afternoon of board games is in order. Everyone, including Phoebe, our parents, and our grandparents, joins in. We laugh and joke at our silliness. Tension and anxiety about the next day dissolve for the moment.

After Mrs. Stewart's specially prepared dinner, I get a nudge and knowing wink from Nigel. Was he ever in the attic with Papa? Uummm? Or is he just giving me support, telling me that he is a friend? I don't know what he knows, and finding out may be difficult. He keeps secrets far too well. He calls it discretion.

After supper, I want to talk to Papa alone, not just because I'm scared about tomorrow. I have a question that I could ask Dad, but he might tell me, "Your mom will answer that."

If I ask Mom, she probably would say, "Later, dear," or "Phoebe and I will talk to you later."

Phoebe's first response will be "Let me check with your parents." All others eliminated, Papa it is! Besides, there's another question that is for him alone.

Eventually, I find him by himself reading the newspaper in the sitting room on the sofa, the chesterfield, as the Brits say.

As I sit near, facing toward him, I ask, "May I ask you a question?"

"Of course you may," Papa replies. He puts the paper aside.

I stare at him as I ask, "Does Nigel know you went to the attic when you were a teenager? Did he go with you?"

Papa looks up at me, snorts, and says, "No. Nigel wasn't working here yet. He was still a young schoolboy when I voyaged from the attic. But then I was just an older schoolboy, not yet seventeen."

Aha! Nigel is younger than Papa.

Something must be really bothering Papa. Without my asking anything more, he rambles, "But I thought I was the smartest one who didn't need help. That was stupid arrogance! Trying alone, by myself, caused me to fail." He stops speaking for a moment. He looks at me steadily, locking my eyes with his. "I cannot tolerate my own failures. But that episode taught me that we all need help. Remember and learn from that!

"I learned a life lesson about needing help, but still, I tried hard to pretend it never happened. That was another mistake. Accept all your mistakes, and learn from them all by facing them directly. Hiding is useless." His keen eyes still focus directly on me. "I should know," he adds sadly. His gaze slowly drops to the floor.

Papa pauses before he glances in my direction and says, "Now, back to your question, which is really asking, 'How many knew, and how much did they know about the phantoms and time travel?'"

He waits till I nod and affirm, "Yes, Papa, I suppose that is the real question."

"Let's start with Nigel. Later, when I had the chance, I never told him about the trip nor that he had phantoms residing in his garret." He rubs his hands over his forehead as he continues, "While I never wanted to tell Nigel anything of what happened, I might have told him if he had asked. But like Nana said, that information would have spooked him!" His eyes almost close as Papa laughs at that silly joke. "But he never quizzed me. He knew about my teenage illness but never made the connection." He laughs again as he says, "Discreet Nigel never pries!"

When Papa recovers from laughing, he says, "My cousin Emma Winter was a number of years older than me. She was visiting one summer when she was in her midtwenties. That's when she tried to help, about a decade or more before I did. I was just a kid, about six, and my mother was still alive. The servants saw her going to the attic regularly. Rumors started when they overheard her as she told my parents, within my earshot, that she wanted to help salvage the reputation of an ancestor. But that was all that she said. She never said how she wanted to help. And she never said anything to anyone then about persons residing in the garret." Papa laughs as he says, "So far as my parents knew, she could have meant helping an ancestor by placing an advertisement in the local paper."

When he stops entertaining himself, Papa continues, "I've discovered over the years that servants' gossip is never-ending. Anyway, Nigel may have learned about her desire to help through servants' gossip. Like them, he had no hard facts to know much of anything. Neither Nigel nor my parents ever knew she met ancestors upstairs." After a pause, Papa repeats, "In their lifetimes, my parents never knew that they had resident guests resting directly above their bedroom, one floor up."

Papa looks at my face and says, "Emma never time traveled, by the way. That I do know with certainty because she told me when we talked several times, just before and then after my time travel trip. I thought I was safe to share my plans with her. She seemed the sort who could keep a secret. She was a smart girl who was never bothered by anything.

"I had overheard her conversation with both my parents and heard the servants' gossip too. After my teenaged self met Leila, I called Emma and asked her probing questions. By the time I petitioned her, she was a young woman in her midthirties, and a mother herself." Papa stops talking for a moment and then adds nostalgically, "And such a lovely person. I was very fond of her. My cousin was both beautiful and smart."

Moments later, he continues, "Emma was generally reluctant to share information about the phantoms in the attic, but she did tell me everything she knew when I revealed Leila and I planned to time travel. I was one of the few people she ever told. Imagine my surprise when she said she already knew not only Leila and Mortimer but had met everyone else in the attic gang. And no one else knew! That was proof she could keep a secret very well. Years later, she quietly informed me when she purchased the rabbit."

Papa seems lost in memories, until he adds, "As with you, time travel caused the same physical results. I was unconscious for many days here. The doctors thought I had suffered a stroke." There is a lengthy pause. Papa's eyes move to the floor between his feet. He is recollecting. I remain silent, waiting patiently.

His eyes return to mine as he says, "Besides Emma, the only person I ever told about my time trip was Mr. Brown. He never gets fussed about anything. And I told him a long time later. Neither of my parents knew what I did. They never knew why I spent several days unconscious."

Papa's face becomes very sad and full of remorse as he adds, "I know that their uncertainty about my illness worried them. They were afraid of a recurrence, which was not in the cards. But I just didn't know how to explain. And I didn't want to admit the reason I failed... My arrogance and my stupidity. That was wrong!"

He pauses again and then quietly says, "Keeping that secret from my parents was an even bigger mistake, bigger than my arrogant know-all attitude. Like any lie, the secret became a burden! Lies and secrets are heavy weights to carry. Added to that, my failure angered me. I wanted no reminders, so I never visited the ancestors ever again, all of a few floors up. That is another regret; but you, my dear fellow, have saved the day! Years of regret are leaving me because of your success." Papa suddenly smiles brightly.

"Oh," I say. I look down and to the side. I am not sure how to proceed.

We sit together silently for a while until Papa inquires, "Do you remember the trip to the Statue of Liberty during my visit when you were seven?"

"Yes, I do," I reply emphatically.

"Do you remember when I seemed to be getting sick?" he asks.

"Sort of," I honestly reply, "but I was only seven at the time. There was a lot I didn't understand then."

Papa smiles and says, "Maybe so." He makes no other comment about my lack of understanding. "Have you guessed what really happened?" he probes.

"No. I was too young to understand," I say quietly.

"You may not remember, but your dad said that I made history so alive and realistic that it seemed as if I had been there. My guilty secret of knowing dead ancestors personally made me afraid that he had magically figured out that I had indeed met ghosts of ancestors. Thinking I had been discovered terrified me so much that I got quite sick to my stomach."

Papa silently stares at me so intently and for so long that he is actually slightly scary. He eventually continues, "Does that give you any insight into how bad guilty secrets can make you feel? Lies and secrets are heavy burdens indeed, and they want to come out at the worst times!" Papa is lost in thought again. He stares at the floor, until he finally looks me square in the face and says, "Jeremiah, remember this. Don't gather guilty secrets. Their weight will break your back."

When he said this, I didn't know what to say. After a time, I muttered lamely, "Okay." We sit in silence again.

I hesitate and then ask, "May I ask something else?"

Smiling slightly, Papa replies, "Of course you may. Fire away."

I sigh and then ask, "Papa, was your Grandfather Bertie in the navy?"

Papa looks utterly surprised by the question. He answers, "Good heavens, no! Bertie had no discipline. He was a party boy!" He looks at me keenly, his eyes inquisitive. Amused, he questions, "Why do you ask?"

"Oh, nothing," I reply.

Papa briefly stares at me, and then his eyes glide away. He rubs his chin with his hand, glances at me again, and asks, "Was it something someone said?"

He knows something!

"Well, yes, I guess it was," I reply truthfully. I say nothing more and stare at my shoes.

"Was it something Marjorie said?" asks Papa.

Surprised, I glance at Papa and answer directly, "Yes, it was. She said, 'Hello, sailor,' to Bertie." After pausing for a moment, I ask, "But if he was never in the navy, why did she call him that?" Looking at Papa even more intently, I query, "And how did you figure that I asked because of something Marjorie said?"

"Because I heard her say the same thing to Bertie," replies Papa. He pauses and then suddenly appears sad as he states, "It was at the time I was trying to help."

Again, he stops speaking for a moment. The sad look disappears. More cheerfully, as if he is remembering something quite funny, he adds, "But when I was talking to Marjorie and to Bertie, I was somewhat older then than you are now." He looks at me as if this is significant.

I don't find this particularly helpful!

"If Bertie was never a sailor or an officer in the navy, why did she call him a sailor?"

Papa looks at me with a wise smile and says, "It's a code."

To hide my confusion, I smile back. I think that Papa believes I understand him, maybe because I smile. Very wrong assumption! My smile is a cover. He nods slightly, as if the topic is resolved.

He is clueless that I do not understand anything. Why do Bertie and Marjorie need a code? They can talk anytime. They reside together in a trunk—you don't need a code when you are that close together! He thinks that I know something that I don't. Dang, I'm only ten years old, but I feel embarrassed! I let the matter drop. Maybe I will ask again later.

He thinks we have finished, so Papa picks up his paper to read again. I sit still, but he ignores that. He's back with his paper.

For some reason, I suddenly recall what Barbara and James did together as I eavesdropped. Maybe talking about Bertie and Marjorie triggered my memory. I don't know why their peculiar actions slipped by me or came to mind now. Anyway, since I still don't understand, I decide to ask.

"Papa, may I ask another question? Sorry to be a pest."

"You are never a pest. Ask to your heart's content." Papa laughs. Down goes his paper again.

"Well, do you remember that I said I eavesdropped on James and Barbara in their house?"

"Yes, indeed. That is how you learned of Barbara's plans," says Papa with interest.

"Well, I saw something I don't understand," I murmur.

With a twinkle in his eyes, Papa inquires innocently, "What did you see, Jeremiah?" I don't think he is really ready for what I am about to ask.

I describe the thigh rubbing, her fingers in his hair, the kisses, the moans, and everything else. I honestly say, "I don't understand what they were doing."

Papa flushes slightly. He tries to be sedate and serious, but the twinkle in his eyes becomes more intense. A hand in front of his mouth suppresses a slight cough. He looks out through the window for a moment, as if searching for the best response out in the yard. Or is he planning an escape route? Long moments pass in silence.

Papa sighs deeply once and then says quietly, "Well, Jeremiah, let's just say that Barbara was using her feminine wiles to warm up her husband so that he might go along with her plans. Do you understand?"

I don't know what "feminine wiles" are, so I feel at a loss. This is something else I am supposed to understand, but don't. Too embarrassed to ask if men have wiles too, I dishonestly say, "Oh, okay, got it."

That's a lie!

Papa chuckles. I keep smiling. I leave the room as soon as possible. I don't want Papa to know that I'm an idiot. I hate not knowing something that I should. Ugh!

As I leave Papa, the only thing I understand is that Papa also heard Marjorie call Bertie a sailor even though he was never a navy man. And I haven't got a clue why James needed warming up. He didn't say that he felt cold. And why kiss someone if they are cold? That's not helpful. They need a blanket, not kisses. I am lost!

At bedtime, I am surprised how tired I am. Time travel requires more energy than I imagined. The ancestors say it takes too much energy to materialize; now I am beginning to understand what they mean!

Susanne gives me a big good-night hug and says, "Welcome back, traveler." She turns as she is heading to her own room. She states, "I have more questions. I'll catch you later, okay?"

I nod. I want to ask Susanne the same questions I asked Papa, but I am too tired. She'll tell me if she knows, but maybe later.

Phoebe gives me a big good-night hug and kisses my forehead a little harder and longer than usual. She says, "I worried so much. You frightened me. I do love you so." She gives my forehead another peck.

Phoebe continues, "I was concerned when you and Susanne were horse riding. I had no idea you were fighting dead psychopathic ancestors in the attic. I will relax when you are on a horse again instead!" She laughs nervously.

I give her another hug. She kisses me hard on the cheek.

She repeats, "Good night," and disappears to check on Susanne.

I feel comfortable with Phoebe near, but I am too tired to ask her about sailors and *the look*, or about warming up. Later, there will be time to figure out all this stuff. Mostly, I am too tired for the answer.

I stretch in comfort. Bed never felt so good! I am soon deeply asleep.

Chapter 21

THE FACTS OF THE CASE

During and after a good breakfast, the family weighs the pros and cons of several action plans until they agree on one. Afterward, Papa insists that Nigel, Mr. Brown, and Mrs. Stewart be included. Papa says, "They have worked here loyally for years. They need to know all that has happened. No more secrets."

"And there is safety in numbers," Nana adds quietly in an uncertain and tentative voice. She sounds like she is trying to convince herself as much as the others.

Clearly, Nana is as scared as I am! I keep my fears to myself.

When all three of the staff join the family in the sitting area by the kitchen, it takes a while to get them up to speed, especially Mrs. Stewart. She's not fond of new ideas, and everything has to be repeated louder, what with her hearing problems and all.

After Papa's first try, she utters, "Posts in the attic? You've got posts in the attic! That's foolishness unless you were planning on building something. Whatever made you put posts in the attic?"

"Ghosts, not posts," says Papa louder.

"I heard you the first time. And why are your posts any of my concern? Any laborer could fetch them out for you," she says, sounding very annoyed. "I can't be expected to hoist them anywhere."

She still looks baffled when Papa patiently yells, "Not posts, we have ghosts!" No success, so he tries a different word. "We have phantoms in the attic."

She looks at him like he's an idiot as she says, "Well, I can't fathom it either. How can I help you fathom why you put posts in the garret?" Bewildered, she looks at Papa and shakes her head.

Her gaze shifts to Dad as she asks, "Do *you* know why he can't fathom putting posts in the attic?"

Poor Dad doesn't quite know what to do, and he is trying so hard not to laugh. Mrs. Stewart's eyes focus on Dad as he shrugs his shoulders.

"You see. Foolishness!" she says to Dad in a quieter voice than usual.

Is that her version of a whisper?

Mrs. Stewart looks directly at Papa and exclaims loudly, "Utter foolishness!"

Hapless Papa runs one hand through his thinning hair. He looks almost defeated.

The women are trying to suppress laughter. Phoebe becomes very busy bringing breakfast debris in from the morning room. We must have used more plates and glasses than usual because she's been in the morning room for a very long time, with the door closed. Maybe the door is stuck? Nana gazes out the kitchen window as she fusses with cleanup, occasionally putting a dirty dish into the dishwasher. Even more dishes? Mom heads to the bathroom, probably to laugh unheard.

Now I truly understand why Nana always writes out the day's menu.

Nigel and Mr. Brown stand by helplessly. Nigel bounces on his toes, up and down, over and over. Mr. Brown quietly and discreetly smiles.

Finally, Dad asks, "May I try, John?"

Smiling with relief, Papa says, "Yes, please, Sam, have a go. God bless."

Using his deepest voice, Dad projects operatically, "We have spooks in the attic, the ghosts of dead people."

Mrs. Stewart turns pale and seems upset. She quietly asks, "You've found dead bodies in the attic?"

Dad sits on a chair directly in front of hers. Even sitting, his height looms over her. He touches her face slightly to make her look directly at his mouth as he says, "The spirits of dead people, their ghosts, their phantoms."

"Oh, you've got phantoms in the attic, the ghosts of the dead," she says, sounding annoyed. She shrugs her shoulders. "Well, why didn't you say so?" She looks relieved as she mutters to herself, "You had me rather scared."

Dad's success makes him smile, perhaps prematurely. Poor Papa grits his teeth. Mrs. Stewart anxiously asks again, "And there are no dead bodies?"

"None," booms Dad.

"Well, that's a relief. You had me quite at odds. And I'm not bothered about anyone's ghost. I'm sure they are all harmless. After all, they have been here since Methuselah was an infant, or so I'm told. And all that time without incident."

No wonder she was scared about bodies but not ghosts in the garret! Old news.

Dad's smile withers while everyone does a double take when she says this. Dad sees Papa's keen glance and asks operatically, "What did you say? You knew about the ghosts? And that they were harmless?" It takes a few tries, but she eventually hears. Papa and Nana are both looking at Mrs. Stewart with keen interest. Nana's cleanup is forgotten. Phoebe emerges from the morning room to listen and watch. Mom is back from the bathroom. Even Nigel and Mr. Brown appear interested in what next she might say.

Mrs. Stewart's eyes dart side to side. She appears anxious about how to answer and mutters, "I'm not sure it is my place to say."

She glances at Nana who says, "It's all right to tell the truth."

She takes her cue and responds, "It was Old Cook who reported tales to me a while before she left, that be twenty years ago, or thereabouts. We worked together for a few years before she told me what had happened when His Lordship was a youngster, not yet seventeen. It was just a little while after some form of illness Master John had, well before my time. Master John lay unconscious here for a week and was thought to have stroked, or so Old Cook declared. But

I don't know myself. Like I said, it was well before my time. Anyway, Old Cook saw someone in old-fashioned clothes snooping around and asked him what he was about."

Nana, Papa, and now the rest of us are staring wide-eyed at Mrs. Stewart, mesmerized. Nana says, "Continue, please."

"The old codger said, 'Master John was ill for a week, while his mind traveled.' Old Cook told me she decided that 'the traveling mind' was the old codger's way of saying, 'While he was unconscious and out cold,' since that had been Master John's illness. Apparently, she replied, 'Well, he's mended now.' The old codger was pleased to hear it, and said so." She pauses for a moment to decide what else to say.

"Keep going," insists Nana.

"All right, then, at your insistence," she replies quietly. Then she states, "Old Cook demanded, 'Where are you from?' and the old codger replied, 'I'm a former Earl Poppycock as what was, and my spirit resides upstairs with some others waiting to clear the name of my son Edgar.' And she said his first name sounded half dead already, Mortimer or some such like, but she couldn't recall for to be certain." She pauses again, trying to recollect distant conversations. "Old Cook thought he was a daft homeless one and told him straight, 'You go back where you're from and stay there, no problems, see.' He agreed easy enough, said he and others resided upstairs in the attic, all as ghosts of the dead, but asked her not to raise an alarm, since he only came down because he was worried about Master John. She said, 'Mum is the word, if you are never seen again.' I was hired years later, but a few years after she got to really know me, she told me. She said, 'I'm telling you in case the old codger comes snooping around again, and especially since he said he was a former Lord Poppycock who resides upstairs in the garret.' That's what she said. I never knew what to believe, so I nodded and smiled and didn't pay her story much heed. But now, you say she had it right."

Nana asks her question in writing, "Why didn't you say something?"

"Well, Lady Iris, I did know that Old Cook often held odd ideas, really odd ideas; and I thought this was one of her fancies.

Personally, I never saw anything to make me think otherwise. And she said she never saw the old codger again. To my mind, if he was really a former earl come down to visit, well, he was from a good family and therefore harmless. No alarm needed for that. And if he was only a passing fanciful idea, why raise a false alarm about her passing fancy? She had lots more of them, and none ever needed an alarm. And it was no one else's business either. I didn't want gossip. That's why I always kept my trap shut, discreet-like, respectful. Besides, I'm the cook, here to prepare good meals, not the local rumormonger."

We assumed bad hearing doesn't mix with new and strange ideas! We assumed she had nothing to share. And now, without knowing, she has shown that she was always way ahead of us, both with information and in management! Again with the assumptions!

We are all dumbfounded, especially Phoebe, who peeped out of the morning room early into the saga about Old Cook. Both Nigel and Mr. Brown do repeated double takes during her story as she sits babbling away without concern.

Our recovery time is not immediate!

When the family does recover and finally has a plan, Papa writes it out for Mrs. Stewart. Her eyes are fine. She reads Papa's note and understands immediately. She says, "If you don't mind, Your Lordship, I'll just watch."

Papa nods vigorously and yells, "That's the best idea!" Then he writes "yes" on her paper.

She nods back in agreement and exclaims, "Imagine that! Old Cook didn't have a silly fancy. She did indeed talk to the ghost of one of the Lords Poppycock. Well, I never!"

We never did either!

All this takes forever!

After a short break, both family and staff seem ready for a trip to the attic.

I know Leila listened to us. I heard her laughter, a comment about hearing aids, and a sweet comment about Old Cook. She also grumbled that Mortimer shouldn't have come down and materialized to check on Papa as a teenager. "I checked on John ever so easily," she muttered, "with just a quick mind read. But Mortimer was attached to the lad and ever so worried." I also overheard her make comments under her breath on some of our initial plans before she scampered upstairs to share with a few. My, she can give candid appraisals!

In a morning stuffed with unusual occurrences, Susanne then states the oddest thing, "Edgar came to visit me last night and borrowed my cell phone. He quizzed me about how to use it, especially the camera. We went over a lot of details so he could use it easily. I hope I get it back! But why is he calling someone?"

Papa says, "I think I know why he needed it. He will take great care. He is a good soul." After a pause, Papa continues, "I helped him connect the phone with the printer very early this morning."

Susanne and I are both utterly surprised. Susanne mutters, almost to herself, "No wonder he asked about using the camera. He must have photographed something important. What's he up to?"

As arranged, Papa goes up the attic stairs first. I tag after him while the rest of the family and staff are still organizing themselves. The top step hides me, almost out of sight and watching, while he opens the west door and knocks three times at Mortimer and Leila's trunk. Promptly coming out fully materialized, they both give Papa a big hug and kiss on the cheek.

Leila says, "John, we are so glad to see you again." Her hand touches his arm and holds him close for a moment.

Perhaps a little tactlessly, Mortimer adds, "You have changed a great deal since your first visit."

"Indeed, I have. I was a teenager then, and now I'm a much older man. After all, that was over fifty years ago. I am very glad to see you both." Then he whispers, "Thank you for keeping Jeremiah safe."

Mortimer looks at Papa somewhat anxiously and whispers back, "Things didn't go exactly as planned, but all ended well, thanks to Edgar with help from Marcus and Beatrice."

Leila's own worried appearance disappears as she listens to Papa and Mortimer while they continue an exchange of morning pleasantries. Her anxious look returns as Leila quietly says, "John, please accept our thanks for your attempt to help when you were a teen, so many years ago."

Papa stares at her in surprise and sharply exclaims, "You must be joking! You want to thank me? Why? I failed." Both Leila and Mortimer appear very startled at the force of Papa's reply, and saddened at his obviously painful regret.

Leila's eyes are full of sympathy and pity. She glances at her husband, then fixes her eyes on my grandfather as she says, "John, you didn't fail. Remember, I pulled you back. I called a halt for your own safety."

Papa looks away from Leila and past Mortimer, stands resolutely tall, and quietly utters, "I was no use at all to either of you." Papa seems bitter. He looks like an elderly child with a chip on his shoulder!

At his words, Mortimer appears crestfallen while Leila's face looks almost stricken. Her tears form. She glances at her husband and then places her hand on Papa's arm. She quietly says, "But, John, you tried. You tried your best, and most importantly, you cared. That gave us hope. I held that hope close to my person so that one day Edgar's name might be cleared."

My grandfather's eyes brim with tears. Full of affection, they focus on Leila, surprised at her candid words. Fiercely blinking, he glances down at her hand resting on his arm. He remains silent as his free hand firmly covers hers.

Leila's eyes search each of his while she declares softly and clearly, "And the hope you gave us has sustained me for over fifty years. I count that as very useful, John, very useful indeed."

Papa's intense regret at his perceived failure almost visibly lifts. He sheds a few more tears along with Leila as she leans close and towers over him, their hands still locked together on his arm. They remain silent, linked together for a few minutes. Papa sighs so deeply he almost shudders, the way a toddler sometimes does after tears.

Mortimer stands behind them. One of his hands rests on Papa's shoulder in silent gratitude. He looks down sadly, recognizing the burden of regret his grandson has secretly carried. Finally, Leila moves her hand away and dabs her tears.

Mortimer's quiet voice says, "I have always been grateful to you, John. And I even came downstairs hoping to see you as you recovered from your journey, but Old Cook told me that you had mended, and she warned me away." His hand slides down Papa's shoulder to his arm and then falls away.

Papa whispers, "Thank you, Leila. Thank you, Mortimer." He wipes his face. They all stand silently side by side for a moment more, remembering. Papa's voice falters as he whispers, "Thank you both for speaking up." He pauses and then says, "I would have remained silent and let it be."

Her expression is sad as Leila says, "Yes, dear boy, I know." Then her face suddenly brightens with the mischief in her eyes as she murmurs, "Your silence? Not the best plan. And so unnecessarily British."

Even Papa has to smile, just a little. Eventually, Papa clears his throat and says, somewhat formally with a louder tone, "I have come for the business of the day."

Mortimer says, "Shall we wake the others?"

Eyes twinkling, Leila replies, "Shall we indeed?"

While Papa was talking to Mortimer and Leila, the rest of the family and staff were still climbing stairs, unaware of their intense discussion. That spared Papa. Their conversation remained a secret I easily kept without any weight upon my shoulders.

Papa and my nine-greats continue to chat as the rest gather like ducks on steps, all in a row. The two lawyers, Nana and Mom, are at the very top of the stairs, looking through the open door, to get the best view and to hear everything that is said. I head down to the bottom, on the landing, just behind Phoebe.

"All up! Come out! We have matters deserving our attention!" Leila is not sparing the horses on volume.

Edgar and Jemima appear quickly, as do Bertie, Marjorie, Joshua, and Penelope. Jemima holds Edgar's arm as they amble from behind the west door into the main room. Marcus assists Beatrice, who seems a little tired. The other ancestors appear. They are all translucent, floating a little above their trunk. Most look at Papa, wondering what he wants.

With languid vapor, Cybil and Humphrey appear. "Oh, what does the upstart want this time?" demands Cybil, like usual.

"Be civil, Cybil," snaps Papa sharply.

Cybil is startled into silence. Humphrey, at Cybil's side, looks rather surprised. Then he checks his wig and his hose, and the buckles on his shoes, as both he and Cybil float above their trunk. Cybil is now clearly in a pout, again.

Soon, all the ancestors are translucently floating above their trunks—all except Barbara and James.

"Barbara, James! Rise and shine!" yells Leila. The windows rattle.

Languidly, Barbara and James eventually appear. They remain nearly transparent, as if showing is too much bother.

Leila glares at them. She crosses her arms in front of her. The fingers of one of Leila's hands beat slowly and rhythmically against her opposite forearm as she impatiently waits. "Barbara! James! Show yourselves properly," demands Leila gruffly.

Surprised, Barbara looks at James and nods to him.

Finally, when James and Barbara are fully translucent, Leila announces to the masses, "You met Jeremiah when he visited here. Papa has some news he wants to share." Leila remains standing beside Papa.

Barbara sneers and almost laughs to herself as she says, "Some of us have heard about him. We are all so sorry that he died." She looks directly at Papa, who says nothing. Papa looks inscrutably at Barbara. "So sorry to preempt you," she adds.

Leila looks surprised by what Barbara has said. She mutters to herself, "She must be feeling very sure of herself, indeed."

James adds, "Yes, so sorry. Our condolences. I know you were quite attached to the boy." He tries to seem sincere.

As the news spreads among the ancestors, there are murmurs of sadness, condolences, and disbelief. Surprisingly, all who helped solve the mystery actively extend condolences, and some look positively grief-stricken. They all seem very sincere. What good actors!

"How did you learn that he died?" Leila asks Barbara directly.

Not anticipating the question, Barbara has not thought the answer out clearly. She stammers breathlessly, "I seeped out and heard it on the news, I believe."

"Quite so." Leila gives her enough rope to hang herself.

Cybil looks over to her mother-in-law. Barbara smiles back. Humphrey looks at his reflection in a windowpane.

Leila sees the exchange between Cybil and Barbara. Papa hears Leila say almost inaudibly, "Birds of a feather in life and after death. Barbara is a killer. She cares for no one. Cybil has never cared for another human being in her lifetime and not after death. No wonder she resides in a trunk close by Barbara and spends so much time finding amusement with her."

Leila becomes quiet. Her face looks like she is deep in thought. Papa can barely hear her words as she mutters, "I wonder, does Cybil know that Barbara believes she killed Jeremiah?"

Leila scans the crowd of ancestors. Papa looks them over too, paying attention to each. He pays particular attention to both Cybil and Barbara and their spouses. He turns to Leila and says under his breath, "I can't tell what Cybil knows about Jeremiah."

Neither has an answer. Leila shrugs her shoulders. Papa looks away.

Loudly enough for all to easily hear, Leila begins, "Jeremiah was a wonderful boy, very bright, always trying to do the right thing. That intent is something to be treasured." She looks at Barbara and James coldly. Barbara half-smiles back.

In a more businesslike tone, Leila continues, "That is not why we are here, however regrettable the events that happened. We have another purpose. Edgar is getting something. He will explain."

Edgar appears, fully materialized. He carries the wooden box marked "schoolbooks" that actually contains the silver. He sets the box down in front of his feet. A heavy brown bag nearly falls from his stretched-out vest pocket. He grabs it before it tumbles and sets it beside the box but says nothing about the box, nothing about the bag. His large right foot lands on top of the wooden box while he leans a hand against his right thigh. The bag falls to the side and hits with a hard thump against the box. By twisting his body, he scans the faces of the ancestors. He looks hard at Barbara. She stares at the box with uncertainty.

His poor broken neck makes me sad. He has to contort his body to look at anyone face-to-face.

On the stairs in front of me, Phoebe almost jumps when she hears the thump. She appears overwhelmed by the ancestral crowd.

Edgar says, "Before I begin, two other visitors are coming in. They are Jeremiah's grandmother and his mother."

Both appear on cue as the stair door swings slightly further open into the attic room. There are murmurs of sadness with words of condolence. An occasional eye is wiped to catch a tear. Once in the attic, Mom and Nana look straight ahead. Barbara glances from the box to Edgar and back again. She appears uneasy.

Edgar continues, "Both of these kind, grieving persons are lawyers. Should anyone raise a question, we have counsel here." He adds, "We have other visitors who will come in now." Dad, Susanne, Phoebe, Mrs. Stewart, Nigel, and Mr. Brown all appear. They stand near the staircase entrance in the middle of the attic, behind and off to the side of Edgar, who faces the crowd of translucent ancestors.

Phoebe is a little frightened. I can tell because she separates further off to the side. Is that spot any safer?

Before we came up, Dad said, "I will stand near the door."

"Will that protect me from a crowd of spooks?" I teased.

Dad replied helplessly, "It's all I know to do."

Dad intentionally keeps the door at the top of the stairs half open as he stands in front of it with his left hand on his hip. Hopefully, no one asks him why. I ascend the stairs quietly to peer in through the slit along the hinges on the left side of the door. The idea is to hear everything, and observe all that I can, unseen. I can see through the gap in Dad's left armpit! For a view, it's the pits!

Edgar looks from living person to living person. He says, "They want to hear my story. Nothing more for now." His gaze returns to the ancestors.

As Mrs. Stewart looks at all the translucent figures, she exclaims loudly to Nigel, "I once heard servants' gossip that there was something funny in the attic. And Old Cook told me her fancy, which was real as it turns out, and not a fancy at all. Well, I never!" Her eyes continue their scan from one translucent figure to another.

Nigel looks around as if he were in a dream. He appears startled by Mrs. Stewart's voice. He replies to her, "I also heard something all those years ago. It was servants' gossip that Emma Winter tried to clear the reputation of an ancestor. I never knew what she did. Do you know if she met these phantoms when she tried to help clear that ancestor's name?"

Mrs. Stewart doesn't respond. I suspect she didn't hear him. He looks upset. He wants to know who had information when he didn't. Nigel gives her a sidelong glance, moves closer to Mrs. Stewart, and says in a louder voice, "I thought it was just a tale."

If he thought talking slightly more loudly would make her answer his question about phantoms, well, he was wrong. If he thought moving closer would help, well, wrong again. She still doesn't hear him, period. I don't know how much of the proceedings she will actually hear. For her, this must be like going to see a mime show; no words, only gestures.

Nigel gives Mrs. Stewart another look, shrugs his shoulders in annoyance, and then ignores her. But he can't stop gawking. All pretense of butler's dignity is lost.

Mr. Brown appears rather uncertain. He looks to Papa, who nods back with a reassuring smile. Like Nigel, Mr. Brown is always discreet. He says nothing.

Edgar starts speaking again. "Some of you decided I was a black sheep. You never bothered to find out what happened. I was dead and could be ignored. I was old news.

"But after death, you decided to stay here to help solve the mystery of the suspected murder and the robbery of which I was wrongly accused. Some tried actively. Others just gave verbal support." Very tersely, he declares, "And a few wanted no resolution, all for their own good." As he looks pointedly and coldly at Barbara, Edgar says more clearly, "Some of you stayed here to avoid your final destination. Residing eternally and comfortably in a trunk is far better than fire and brimstone." He next turns his gaze to Cybil.

Cybil looks down. James turns slightly pale. Humphrey squirms. Barbara looks away, trying to ignore him.

Edgar says distinctly, "There was a robbery in London in 1744. Walter Johnson and his wife, Abigail, were victims of theft. The house should have been empty the night in question.

"But Walter was detained in London on business, and so was in the house." He pauses and then continues, "He died during the robbery." He pauses again, to let that sink into the onlookers' noggins.

Edgar continues, "I visited Walter two days before his death. My brother James asked to accompany me. Why did he do that?" Edgar pauses for effect.

"Why indeed?" continues Edgar. "James was not interested in the things that entertained Walter and me. He removed himself from us for a time. It is my contention that he stole something from Walter's home for nefarious purposes."

"This is nonsense," says James. "I just went along to keep you company."

Dad is in front of the door. Needing his attention, I whisper as loudly as I dare, "What is nefarious?"

Dad hears my question. He turns slightly toward the door hinges. "Evil, wicked," his twisted lips quietly answer from the corner of his mouth to the crack made by the partly open door.

Edgar resumes, "Walter was killed during the robbery. There was evidence against me. Walter's wife, Abigail, had a silver statue of a rabbit with an inscription that read, 'Abigail from Walter.' Above that was 'On the occasion of our first wedding anniversary 1716.' It is such an endearing sentiment." Edgar's voice is flat and cold as he finishes the last sentence.

"The rabbit was found among my books in my library, in my secretary. I did not put it there. I did not steal! But the courts used that evidence to help convict me." Edgar pauses and looks at the crowd of ancestors.

Edgar says more loudly, "I think that you, James, stole the rabbit when you absented yourself during our visit to Walter. I believe it was you, James, who placed it in my secretary, where it was found by the police."

The ancestors break into confused murmurs. They look at Edgar, animated, eyes flashing. They look at James, the younger brother, visibly shrinking and pale.

With a steady voice, Edgar starts again, "The silver rabbit was from a pair of statues. Bunny was Abigail's nickname, used only by Walter. That is why she was given a rabbit.

"Walter had a statue too. His statue was a frog. That served as a reminder for a young lady that there are frogs to be kissed before she finds the one who is truly a prince."

There are many murmurs among the ancestors. There is laughter and nudging of ribs between some of the men.

Edgar says, "Both were engraved with names and the anniversary date. The rabbit was purchased on the open market multiple decades ago after it was taken from police evidence. It changed hands a number of times until it was purchased by Emma Winter, who owned the rabbit for many years.

"Emma was a cousin to Penelope Winter Wadsworth, the wife of Joshua Wadsworth, also known as the Earl Poppycock, until his death." He continues, "You may remember Emma. She visited us several times. She knew the rabbit's significance but could prove nothing."

There are murmurs of, "Pretty girl she was, but so long ago. How time flies away."

Interrupting the murmurs, Edgar continues, "When she died, it was sold to a dealer in the Silver Vaults, as part of the distribution of her estate. Jeremiah and Susanne's nanny happened to purchase it recently."

Edgar reaches for the bag beside him and pulls out the rabbit. There are gasps of amazement.

Cybil speaks loudly and emphatically, "What are you on about? This is all gibberish. The courts said you were guilty. That is enough for me!" She looks annoyed as she shrieks, "Stop accusing James."

Barbara emphatically adds, "This is too much! We cannot be expected to waste the day listening to this. Go away, Edgar. Stay in your trunk and be quiet." She musters as much dignity and importance as she can.

"Silence!" booms Edgar's voice.

Several ancestors wince at the sound. A few look a little alarmed. Leila smiles. She is happy to see a glimpse of Edgar as he was before his trial and execution.

Barbara looks visibly shaken. She is a spoiled child at heart, accustomed to demanding her own way, with a tantrum if needed. She does not know how to deal with a force such as Edgar's. Like most bullies, she is a coward.

Edgar starts speaking. "The robbers who committed the theft and who caused the death of Walter were never caught. The items stolen, all silver, were never retrieved." He pauses for effect.

Slowly and emphatically, he repeats, "The thieves were never caught." He pauses and then asks, "Did they have a buyer for the stolen goods?" He pauses again. His eyes scan the ancestors.

"Here is a copy of the list of items stolen. It is from the police notations in 1744," Edgar says coldly. He hands a paper to a phantom near him and commands, "Circulate it, so you may read."

Hands materialize, hold the paper for inspection, pass the paper, and become translucent again. These hands appearing and almost disappearing are very disconcerting to watch!

Leila looks at her son with admiration. Edgar has been very busy returning unseen to the past to get that list.

Leila turns to him. She speaks from the corner of her mouth. "How very clever of you! How did you get that?"

Edgar looks at his mother, winks, and lifts the edge of a cell phone out of the pocket of his breeches. It is Susanne's phone, which she told us she lent to Edgar. I could not imagine why he wanted it. Now I realize that he time traveled last night, photographed evidence on Susanne's phone, and returned very quietly. He printed the images besides! All right, he had help from Papa. Regardless, he is a quick study!

"How did you get this?" Barbara demands loudly. She sounds scared.

"I seep out. I travel. I look. I listen. I learn." Edgar glances in Leila's direction and winks at her. He turns toward Susanne, swivels one of his long arms, and hands Susanne her phone.

Edgar glances again at Barbara and James. Cybil, next to them, also starts to look anxious. Humphrey seems a little confused, but complex thoughts are probably rather foreign to him. His confusion is understandable!

Very slowly and distinctly, Edgar says, "The robbers were never caught because they did indeed have a client to buy the stolen merchandise. That stolen silver has remained hidden…until today." He sweeps his foot off the box as he declares loudly, "This wooden box is labeled 'Schoolbooks, James Wadsworth, Earl Poppycock.' You see it is dirty, untouched, probably as it was the day it was packed."

Edgar looks at the box with intense curiosity till he says, "The wood of the box is old, but the paint markings are still easily visible on the lid. It seems odd that there is no date for the schoolbooks. Equally odd, the title is printed, but the schoolboy didn't yet have a title. That makes me wonder, when was this box packaged? And who packaged it?" Edgar looks hard at Barbara.

Murmurs already begin to circulate before Edgar rips open the ties, pulls on the wooden lid, and lifts it off. He passes the lid to the nearest spook. Arms and hands again materialize in excitement as the box lid passes from one person to another. Once the lid passes further along, arms and hands become translucent again.

Again, this spectacle is very distracting!

In the back, a male holding the wooden lid bitterly complains, "Foolery! I just got a sliver!" as he passes the lid to the next person. "Take care for yourself." Mutterings afterward are too soft to hear.

I am really glad I can't hear them!

We see nods and hear comments. A sort of buzz begins. The buzz of many conversations increases. The sounds all mix together, the buzz of curious wasps. Occasionally, we hear the words spoken, "One can see markings clearly. But it is for schoolbooks only. Why are we inspecting this? What is the purpose?" But the words overlap, increasing the buzz everywhere, like wasps everywhere.

"And inside, we should have schoolbooks, shouldn't we?" yells Edgar, over the noise of the buzz. He looks from person to person. The buzz dies out, with a few straggling wasp comments. Most everyone nods yes to his question.

He pulls out candlesticks. He requests, "Tell me. Are these on the list?"

"Two pair," says a male voice.

Edgar pulls out a second pair. He lines them up on the floor in front of him. There are gasps of astonishment. Barbara turns slightly green with anxiety.

He next pulls out twelve great plate chargers. "Are chargers on the list?" demands Edgar.

I think back to Nana's explanation of plate chargers. These are really beautiful ones and do indeed show off.

"Twelve," says a different and deeper male voice in response to Edgar's question. That deep voice pulls me back from my recollections of what Nana previously said.

Edgar stacks the twelve chargers beside the candlesticks.

"There you have it," exclaims Edgar.

Ancestors everywhere mutter with murmurs that applaud Edgar's display. There are episodic cries of "Shame! Shame!" directed at James and Barbara.

Barbara almost yells, "You have nothing. This silver could have come from anywhere. Your box is empty, and you have nothing that links James to the robbery!"

Cybil adds, "This is nothing. There is no evidence that any of this is related to anyone in this house." She clutches Barbara's hand.

Edgar says, "Let me see. We have a rabbit. I pulled it out of a bag. Can we find a frog? Shall I pull a frog out of my box?" he asks in a mocking voice.

Despite the tone of Edgar's voice, I suspect that he is enjoying himself, even if in a bitter sort of way.

When Edgar says "frog out of a box," I think of "rabbit out of a hat." I'll bet he is thinking the same thing too! I laugh out loud. Too late, my hand covers my mouth. Did anyone hear?

Edgar does indeed hear me. Apparently, he thinks like me. He chuckles quietly to himself despite his bitterness. He fumbles with his hand inside the box, hitting his hand against the wood in pretense that it is empty. "Let's get this linen out of the way," he commands. Rags fly onto the floor.

"What have we here?" Edgar tosses the last of the linen rags beside the candlesticks and chargers on the floor. "Is this a frog I see before me, its inscription toward my hand?" he asks dramatically. Triumphantly, Edgar holds up a silver statue of a frog, sitting firmly on a lily pad. Its head is slightly bent toward its right. Placed side by side properly, the two statues look at each other like lovers do.

There is uproar among the ancestors. They yell, "Shame! Shame! Shame on you, James!" The sound rocks the windows.

Barbara hisses, "You could have purchased this anytime." Her eyes are flashing with anger. She is so furious that her tears start to well up.

James looks stunned and helpless. He stands silent and motionless, head slightly down.

Barbara composes herself, straightens the sides of her dress with her hands, and says stridently, "You have no evidence to connect any of this to James. And…certainly not to me!" She could not be more emphatic.

James looks at her sharply. He looks at Barbara as if for the first time. He looks at his mother and back to his wife. His face appears horrified by what he sees. He realizes how he has been used and that he has been a fool! Too late now to fix anything!

There is stunned silence. The ancestors say nothing. Edgar says nothing. Eyes flit everywhere, full of questions. The quiet remains.

Edgar looks exhausted by his efforts. I think he is trying to prepare for what he must do next. Suddenly, he looks very sad and very tired. After all, he is accusing his own brother. Contorting his body to look at the crowd must be exhausting!

Breaking the silence, Mrs. Stewart loudly exclaims, "Well, I never!" Her eyes are transfixed by all the translucent figures. She is fascinated to see Edgar standing so tall, fully materialized, his neck at such an angle. Her sturdy frame looks tiny behind him. Some of the ancestors gawk at her.

Nigel looks around. He too is transfixed by the proceedings. He tries unsuccessfully to regain the dignity of a butler. Failing!

Looking at Mr. Brown standing beside him, Nigel whispers, "A few years after I started working here, I heard gossip that Emma

Winter tried to clear an ancestor's name for a crime he didn't commit. You knew about that too, didn't you?"

Mr. Brown glances toward Nigel. "Yes, my friend, I knew Emma tried to help," he says as quietly as he can, "but I knew no details."

Nigel whispers again, "I was told she tried, but I never knew how. I didn't know she met phantoms in the attic. I didn't know the attic was inhabited by spooks." Somewhat anxiously, Nigel questions, "Mr. Brown, did you know? Did you know that we had spooks?" Nigel's face looks very worried.

Mr. Brown turns slightly to Nigel. "Yes, I did," he replies in a very quiet, matter-of-fact voice, "but I did not learn that from Emma."

Nigel looks flustered. Suddenly, he looks very thoughtful. He recalls being told about Papa's unusual illness as a teenager. He turns directly to Mr. Brown and asks, "Did His Lordship come up to the attic as a teenager?" His voice whispers slightly louder, "Did Papa meet these phantoms?"

I can tell Nigel is flustered because he called my grandfather Papa.

Mr. Brown looks squarely at Nigel. He replies, "Yes, he did. He's the one who told me about them." He pauses and then repeats, "John Wadsworth, not Emma, let me know."

Nigel says in a louder, anxious voice, "His Lordship and Emma knew all this, and His Lordship said nothing to me! And you knew as well, Mr. Brown?" Nigel looks flustered. "I'm the butler. I should know everything about the household!" Nigel looks so angry that he doesn't know what to say.

Papa would call this a true fracture of the dignity!

Nigel eventually demands, "How could you leave me uninformed? And why would Papa, I mean His Lordship?" Nigel almost sputters as he speaks.

Mr. Brown replies, "I did not know Emma Winter met ancestors here until His Lordship—I mean John Wadsworth told me. That was long after his illness but before he took over the reins of the estate, before he became Lord Poppycock."

"He told me that he was unconscious for almost a week here at home because he was investigating the crime in the past." Mr. Brown looks at Nigel whose face shows utter confusion. Clearly, Nigel does not understand time travel!

Mr. Brown continues, "Yes, Nigel. I did know about these ancestors who reside here. And I knew that John Wadsworth—now His Lordship—traveled back in time with Leila. He told me in confidence before he became Earl Poppycock. It was a secret I have never betrayed."

Poor Nigel doesn't know what to do. He probably feels betrayed; he certainly looks bewildered. His face turns a little red as his eyes turn away from Mr. Brown and glance down to the floor. He shrugs his shoulders sadly and then looks straight ahead, stone-faced.

The whisperings of Mr. Brown and Nigel fade away. The silence resumes. The living all stand slightly apart from Edgar. He towers before them as he looks down at the box with its lid, and at the silver and the rags. The living group looks at the ancestors.

The ancestors look back at the living mostly clustered near the entrance door, with a stray Phoebe who stands out of the way, behind and to the side of everyone. She looks afraid of what might happen next. As an ancestor returns the police notation paper, it floats down beside the silver. Frightened by the unlikely group before her, Phoebe jumps when the paper lands. The room remains silent.

As he recovers, Edgar looks around. He appears both sad and angry. Eventually, with eyes fixed on the ancestors, he begins again forcefully, "You see the deformity of my neck. I was hanged. I was hanged for a crime I did not commit!" Edgar glares at everything before him, grabs the police report, and tosses it into the box. Obviously, his anger is building.

His voice rises in volume as he continues, "James had the opportunity to plant evidence. He was absent part of the time when we visited Walter. He had enough time to steal the silver rabbit.

"He was in my house and briefly alone in my library the same day we visited Walter. That was one of his many opportunities to plant evidence of theft onto me, to put the rabbit into my secretary." Edgar's furious voice is loud.

After a pause to regain his calm, Edgar continues, "James had motive. I was to inherit the title of Earl Poppycock. I was to inherit my father's land and his money." He pauses to breathe and looks down sadly at the floor.

Suddenly, looking directly at the crowd of ancestors, he continues, "James, with Barbara, wanted the title, the land, and the monies." Edgar's eyes blaze while his voice declares, "Barbara wanted a titled husband, and I needed to be out of the way for that to happen!"

There is a clamor among the ancestors. They express shock, disbelief, surprise, and horror. A few look bored, as if they might say, "We expected this from James and Barbara! Whatever! It doesn't affect us."

As the uproar settles, Edgar continues, "James and Barbara bought the silver from the robbers. The thieves didn't intend to murder Walter. He surprised them. In the dark, either he fell or someone pushed him down the stairs. All we know is that he died from the fall."

James stands sullenly, head down. Suddenly, he says, "Murder was never intended, I am sure."

"Silence, James!" screams his wife.

"I agree with that supposition," says Edgar. He looks sadly at his brother, and at Barbara with contempt.

Edgar continues, "But a short time ago, a brave young man stumbled upon the attic. He met Leila and Mortimer. When we met, and he saw my broken neck, he even asked why I had not chosen a different self, in the way each of you have been able to choose the age of your features. He was saddened when he realized that as part of my punishment, I have no choice. I must look as I did at my death. With the help of his sister, Susanne, they devised a plan to assist me."

There are cries from here and there. "Poor Jeremiah!" "Kind Jeremiah!" and "Such a loss!"

Encouraged by these sentiments, Barbara starts to relax a little. A faint smirk crosses her lips. She squeezes Cybil's hand.

Edgar speaks clearly. "With Leila, he traveled back in time, back before the robbery occurred in 1744."

There are gasps everywhere.

"I should like another visitor. Clive, if you will," says Edgar.

Clive appears from the nine-greats' trunk with a swoosh and a pop. "At your service, sir." Like Edgar, Leila, and Mortimer, he has fully materialized to give his testimony.

Edgar declares, "This is Clive. He is my father's manservant, his valet, and his friend."

Again, there are gasps. Among the unhappy murmurs, we hear, "I didn't know we were allowed our servants. I should have enjoyed mine!"

Ignoring the grumbles, Leila asks, "Clive, will you answer with the whole truth, under oath, with penalty for perjury?"

"I will," he responds eagerly with a willing half-smile.

Edgar says, "Clive, tell us what you know about Jeremiah's trip into the past." Edgar lets him gather his thoughts.

Clive describes the details of his involvement in time travel. He explains, "This phantom here before you controlled my living body while my living mind slept. Mortimer and Leila did the same thing to their own living body so that each could interact with Jeremiah in the past." He pauses to give people a chance to understand.

He continues, "Jeremiah traveled back with Leila. His safety in the past depended on thought contact with Leila or someone else from the attic who also returned to the past.

"As it turned out, when we thought we were the only ones who had done this, we were wrong. Barbara, and then James, did the same thing as well." Clive pauses to let this sink in. He glances from one ancestor to the next to see the impact of his words.

There is a clamor, the buzz of wasps all asking, "To what purpose? What was there to gain?" The words die away with an occasional straggler.

Clive spells out clearly what he saw and states what we did after my arrival in the city of London in 1744. He recounts the events I witnessed, describes the conversation I overheard between Barbara and James, and then adds, "When Jeremiah returned to Mortimer's home, he was still in a panic because he materialized when Barbara heard him. She gained thought contact with him as he eavesdropped.

That thought connection made the child materialize." Furrows appear on Clive's brow.

He continues, "We did not know till Barbara heard Master Jeremiah that she had also time traveled to occupy her living body and mind, thereby making Jeremiah visible and audible to her!" The frown furrows are deepening, and his mouth is downturned.

Remembering is making him angry.

Again, there is a buzz, a shocked chorus of disbelief from the ancestors, a chorus of surprise that Barbara had also time traveled.

Many of my ancestors must be a very tame group! Have none ever gone back to any previous time? Have they never done anything since they died?

Edgar asks, "Can you describe what happened the night of the dinner party held for James and Barbara at Barbara's request? This was the same night that Leila presumably became ill."

Why did Edgar use the word "presumably" with the illness?

Clive reports, "Jeremiah watched the dinner and saw the poisoner's ring, the one Barbara wore and used." He keeps to the facts as he states, "Leila's illness was the result of a poisoning with a sedative, not a natural illness. Leila felt unwell at dinner, worse after retiring with the ladies to the drawing room, and then, after we helped her upstairs, she fell into a very deep sleep."

Edgar asks, "What was the purpose of putting Leila into a deep sleep?"

He answers, "She was future Leila, the phantom Leila you see before you now, controlling her living body while her living mind slept. Jeremiah's safety depended on thought contact with Leila. With that connection severed, he would fall into the time abyss and spend eternity spinning out of control in a cold, dark, timeless universe. A horrible form of damnation." Poor Clive almost spits out the last sentence.

The murmuring buzz mounts, "Astounding! I cannot imagine!"

He continues, "Both Mortimer and I tried to grab thought contact with Jeremiah when Leila lost consciousness, but our thoughts were blocked." The olive skin of Clive's brow is now deeply furrowed. With his angry, coarse features, and his huge and powerful muscles, he is one scary-looking dude. With purpose, his eyes are drilling into Barbara.

Left alone with Barbara, what would he do? Stop thinking like that, Jeremiah!

Initially pale green and clearly shaken as Clive began to speak, Barbara is now a normal color, languidly smirking, head tilted coquettishly to one side.

What devious scheme is she hatching?

Edgar creates a pause and then asks, "Is that what happened? Did Jeremiah fall into the time abyss?"

Clive answers in a carefully controlled voice, "So far as I know, yes. Mortimer and I were with Leila, putting her into bed. Mortimer was on one side, I on the other, Jeremiah at the foot. Jeremiah suddenly yelled that something was wrong. He grabbed the bedposts, but he spun out of the room through the walls and disappeared. We never saw him again."

His dark eyes slowly and meaningfully scan the crowd of ancestors, intent on each one. He slowly articulates, "It was horrible! And it was Barbara and James who put him there." He glares at Barbara and then spits on the floor. His eyes then fix on James, and he spits again.

The room is silent in shock.

Shock at the story recounted? Nah, probably not. But a servant spitting at a peer? Now, that's a headline! It took guts for an earl's valet to spit at a lord and a countess. Clive still looks angry enough to kill those two ghosts!

Finally, he gazes down in resignation. Returning his eyes to Edgar, he breaks the stunned silence with a bitter voice, "Mortimer and I tried to make thought contact with Jeremiah, but our thoughts were blocked. We could only gaze in horror as he disappeared." As his eyes glance to Barbara, he notices her smirk. Again, rage consumes his features. His shoulders sag as he stares down at the floor, a powerful man, sad, angry, and crestfallen.

Murmurs of pity arise from the ancestors, along with cries. "How hideous for that poor child." Then the room is silent before the buzz begins again. Stray voices say, "This cannot be. It is unimaginable. Horrid!"

"Thank you for your testimony," says Leila. Clive stands off to the side and becomes translucent.

Edgar and Clive both note the smirk on Barbara's mouth.

With now-rosy cheeks and a brilliant smile, Barbara declares in a loud, clear, and commanding voice that silences the buzz, "Too bad Jeremiah died. He could have cleared up this misunderstanding. He just needed to be questioned, and soon all would realize that there is nothing in what you are saying." She sounds confident.

Cybil adds, "He was a child and a commoner. How could he reach such conclusions about a ring? Barbara likes large gemstones so her ring may have been large, but a poisoner's ring? How fanciful!" Cybil laughs nervously. "And his father is from Brooklyn!" She is the only one who laughs in the stony silence.

Edgar declares, "Barbara, it is interesting that you already knew Jeremiah was dead." He pauses dramatically, then emphatically speaks slowly and clearly, "The story of Jeremiah's death was *never* on the news!" He bellows, "You, Barbara, are a liar!"

Barbara turns deeply green.

She keeps changing color like a chameleon.

Within moments, sweat beads form on her upper lip.

She's really frightened.

And now, it is Edgar's turn to smirk.

Leila calmly says, "I think we have enough evidence to go to trial."

Chapter 22

THE TRIAL

Leila repeats, "Yes, there is enough to go to trial. I shall appoint myself as judge. Jeremiah's mother will defend you, James and Barbara. Nana will be the prosecutor."

"Are you mad?" shrieks Barbara.

"On what charges?" demands James with alarm.

"There is the robbery in 1744, allegedly arranged by you two. There is a death in 1744 as a result of the robbery. There is withholding evidence resulting in the execution of an innocent in 1745." Leila pauses before she continues more forcefully, "Now, there is the suspected murder of Jeremiah Wadsworth in the time abyss, arranged by Barbara with help from you, James, present date." She pauses briefly. "Is that enough?" queries Leila rhetorically.

"Hear! Hear!" yells a chorus of ancestors. The men now pound on their trunks. Some of the men almost materialize in their enthusiasm. Why are they pounding?

I flash to a conversation I heard between Dad and Papa as they talked for a long time about political systems on each side of the Atlantic. That's how I know that these titled men, lords all, were once appointed to the upper chamber in Parliament, called the House of Lords. It functions somewhat like the American Senate. Each had a desk in the Lords' Chamber, which they thumped for emphatic political comment during debates. Now, they are thumping their trunks here, just like they once thumped their desks in the House of Lords!

As the noise settles, the men become translucent again, some almost transparent.

Once there is quiet, Leila continues, "And the others here will be the jury, the jury of your peers." Her hand gestures to the ancestors, mostly former earls and countesses. She laughs at her own joke.

I am a little confused. Then I remember what Mom said last night, "A jury is composed of people equal to you, each person called a peer. This is not to be confused with a titled person, also called a peer. To help you with the meanings, remember that Papa, the Earl Poppycock, is a peer."

It is a good pun—especially when the men act like peers in Parliament! Her joke helps me, just as intended.

James and especially Barbara continue to object. The other ancestors, earls or countesses most everyone, overrule them.

"You shall stand trial!" comes as a united chorus.

"Does the prosecution have any witnesses?" Leila asks.

Nana answers, "Five more. Clive has already answered under oath."

"Call the first witness now," Leila commands.

Every ancestor moves to see and strains to hear. Barbara and James look very anxious. After the previous uproar, there is a curious quiet.

"I call Edgar Wadsworth," says Nana clearly.

Edgar is sworn in under oath and agrees to tell the truth, the whole truth, and nothing but the truth.

Leila asks, "Did you consider yourself under oath during your previous statements?"

Edgar replies, "I did consider myself under oath and spoke only the truth."

Leila nods to Nana and says, "Proceed."

Nana quizzes him about his return to London in 1744 as the ghost of Edgar and his role at Leila's house during my stay.

Edgar tells the court, "The night before Leila's illness, Clive came to our trunk and warned us that Barbara was up to something." He describes which people became prepared for action. Edgar states clearly, "I did not inhabit my living body. Instead, I remained invisible and inaudible, watching and deciding what to do. However, Marcus and Beatrice decided to disguise themselves as servants in Mortimer's house the night before Leila became ill. They both wanted to be eyes on the ground, to observe, and act if needed."

Some ancestors murmur, "They dressed as servants. How extraordinary!"

What snobs some are! I am embarrassed for them. They don't comment about remaining invisible or the time travel. All that seems more extraordinary than changing clothes and pretending to be a different person for a few hours!

Nana asks, "How did you think you could help as an invisible phantom?"

Edgar replies, "I tried to think like Barbara. I realized she might try to sever the mental connection between Leila and Jeremiah. With that severed and without another person in the past having mental connection to him, Jeremiah would fall into the time abyss."

Uproar returns. The buzz is back! Various stray voices exclaim, "How can this be? She is his eight-greats-grandmother. She would never do such a thing! Horror!"

Edgar waits and then says, "That *is* what happened. Jeremiah saw her place a powder in Leila's wine. Leila fell deeply asleep, very fast. And before Clive and Mortimer could act or overcome Barbara's thought block, Jeremiah disappeared through a wall and into the abyss."

There is quieter buzz as murmurs go through the crowd again. Murmurs of consternation, horror, and disbelief circulate. A few cry out, "Shame!"

The buzz stops as Barbara interrupts, "You know nothing. Leila became ill and fell asleep very deeply. Bad things happened after that, but all of that has no connection to James or to me! There is no evidence, only wild conjecture. There was no poisoning!"

Edgar looks at her, his face as cold as stone. He speaks very distinctly, "There is someone who may verify what I have said."

Barbara retorts loudly, "There is no one. We cannot rely on the testimony of servants, commoners that they are. And your prime witness is dead. You said yourself that he fell into the time abyss."

Barbara puffs up, trying to look commanding and regal. She demands, "It is time to call a halt to this travesty. Edgar, go away. Go back to your box! And take your sniveling Jemima with you!" She flushes red with anger as she loudly snaps, "You didn't get the title because you were never worthy! My James was the worthy one."

"Does the prosecution have another witness who can verify these statements about the poisoning?" asks Leila.

"Yes," replies Nana.

Leila looks at Mom and Nana. "If the defense and prosecution do not object, I should like to see the next witness in person before the present witness is dismissed. Does either object?"

"The defense does not object," says Mom with a quiet voice.

"The prosecution does not object," Nana says calmly.

"Bring the next witness before the court." Leila does not dismiss Edgar as a witness.

Nana declares, "I wish to bring in the person who may corroborate Edgar's story." Nana speaks loudly enough to make sure I can easily hear. "Will my witness please step forward? Jeremiah Wadsworth!"

Total chaos and uproar ensue. The buzzing wasps exclaim, "How can this be? No one escapes the time abyss. What has happened?" Peers thump trunks again. The buzz is deafening.

Barbara turns very pale and nearly loses her footing as her knees buckle beneath her. She catches herself from falling. She stares at me in terror.

James, pale and shocked, fixes his eyes on the floor, as his shoulders visibly sag. There is nothing for him to say. He is as guilty as Barbara.

Barbara looks at Cybil in desperation. Cybil's face shows confused anxiety. Humphrey fiddles with his wig.

I leave my hiding spot, walk up the last step into the attic, and stand in front of Edgar. He looms over me, making me look very small and vulnerable. One of Edgar's big hands rests on my shoulder. It covers almost half my upper chest.

"May I address the court still as a witness?" asks Edgar, looking expectantly at Leila.

"You may," she answers.

Edgar says, "This young man attempted to clear my name and to save us all from eternity in our trunk. As a youngster, at only ten years, he didn't need to try. But he is a wise and kind soul, who likes to solve puzzles. He took pity on me." I feel a single tap on my shoulder.

Edgar adds, "I hid but watched everything that Barbara did. No one knew I was in the house as future Edgar, an invisible ghost, ready to act. I saw the poisoning too. I saw the poisoner's ring used by Barbara to drug Leila into a hopelessly deep sleep." He pauses to let the significance of his words be understood, and looks into the faces of the crowds of ancestors before he slowly articulates, "I saw Barbara poison Leila."

He continues, "As Leila fell unconscious, Jeremiah was pulled into the time abyss. Barbara blocked the thoughts of Mortimer and Clive. They couldn't save him." He pauses and looks at the other ancestors two by two before he eventually continues, "But she couldn't bear to let him go without sneering at him. That sneer created thought contact. Accidentally, she provided me enough time to act. I had to wait till she was finished. Otherwise, she would know I was interfering.

"When she broke off thought contact, thinking he would die in the abyss, I concentrated on him with all my might. I heard him cry out for help!" He pauses before he says quietly, "My thoughts pulled him from the vortex in the abyss. Together, we landed in the closed carriage of Marcus and Beatrice who were prepared to meet us." He pauses for breath.

Again, Edgar quietly states, "I witnessed Barbara saying to the helpless Jeremiah, 'Welcome to the time abyss. I hope you enjoy your eternity in nowhere.' Then she laughed and laughed. She thought she was safe by murdering her eight-greats-grandson!" Edgar looks at Barbara with anger and disdain.

There is buzzing and howls of "Shame! How could you do such a thing? You are a wild beast, not a human!" The howls are directed at Barbara, who looks around helplessly, pale, and trembling. Her sweaty face is a peculiar green color.

Each of the lawyers asks Edgar a few questions for clarification before he is dismissed as a witness. I am sworn in under oath.

Afterward, Nana directs, "Please, tell the court your entire story."

I tell everything of the time travel back with Leila. I recount how Clive took me into James and Barbara's home. I repeat the conversation I overheard in their residence.

"Who was the brains behind the plan?" asks Nana.

I quietly state, "Barbara was the ringleader who arranged the robbery. Her agent was James's valet, named Emmett. Barbara did not intend the death of Walter. That was an accident, but it happened as a result of her actions."

"Who decided to plant evidence?" she asks.

"It was Barbara's plan to plant evidence. After slight hesitation, James agreed to her plan," I reply. Heads nod as they recollect that this fits nicely with Edgar's statements of James's absence during part of the visit to Walter.

"How could Barbara know you traveled back in time?" asks Nana pointedly.

"All the ancestors knew we children were investigating. And the trunk of Mortimer and Leila was too quiet," I state.

Nana asks, "So do you think that Barbara decided to act to protect herself because she figured out that something was afoot?"

"Yes," I reply.

"How do you know Barbara went back in time?" asks Nana.

After a moment's pause, I continue, "After I listened to the conversation between Barbara and James, Barbara heard my slipper make a noise as I tried to leave. When she saw me, she swore and then slammed her door when she couldn't catch me. In order to hear me or see me as I eavesdropped, Barbara living also had to be future Barbara, the phantom. Only future Barbara could hear or see me or cause me to materialize."

Nana guides my testimony by asking, "What did you see at the dinner party?"

I pause and swallow hard before I say, "From the serving area, I peeked into the dining room when the guests were seated. James was facing me. Barbara's back was turned to me, and Leila's sideview was directly in front of me. Through the crack between the open-door hinges, I saw Barbara use her poisoner's ring to put a powder in Leila's wine when Leila turned to her right to address a footman about a problem that she noticed with one of the serving platters. James intently watched the door where I was hiding, which made me suspect he was future James and knew I was there. I saw James's nod to Barbara as he watched his wife poison his own mother at the dinner table. Very soon, Leila began to feel tired."

"What happened next, Jeremiah?" Nana asks. "Please tell us, even though it may be difficult."

Speaking slowly, I say, "Clive took Leila to her bedroom. Mortimer and Clive desperately tried to help her, but she became so deeply asleep that she and I lost thought contact.

"I tried to make thought contact with Mortimer and Clive, but the thoughts were blocked. I fell into the time abyss," I say with a cracking voice. "It was awful. I spun around and around in the cold and dark. I almost vomited from the spinning."

While Nana looks directly at James and Barbara, she asks, "When did you last see Barbara before today?"

"I can tell you exactly," I say firmly. "Barbara's face appeared in the time abyss vortex. I saw her face clearly as she laughed and said, 'Welcome to the time abyss. I hope you enjoy your eternity in nowhere.' It was an awful thing to do to someone," I state with a wobbly voice. Tears nearly fall.

When I say this, there is an appalled silence. Moments later, the buzz begins and soon becomes a chant, "Barbara, shame! Barbara, shame!"

Barbara looks around desperately for support and finds none. I look hard at her, but she's all fuzzy because my eyes are full of tears. I am trying not to cry. She still scares me, even with people around to keep me safe.

Cybil steps away from Barbara, holds her hands against her own person, looks frightened, and stares intently at the floor. She glances back briefly. For the first time, she sees the true Barbara. Cybil's gaze returns regretfully to the floor.

"Well, maybe she didn't know what Barbara had done," mutters Leila almost inaudibly to herself.

"What happened next?" demands Nana. "Let's keep on track."

I wipe my eyes and continue, "As Edgar said, we arrived with a thump inside the carriage of Marcus and Beatrice in 1839. We went to their residence and laid out our plans." I name the people involved.

Nana asks, "Now, Jeremiah, do you know who found the box that was labeled 'Schoolbooks, James Wadsworth, Earl Poppycock'?"

I reply, "Penelope said she followed up on a comment Bertie made. His comment suggested that the box of silver might be purposely mislabeled. She used detective reasoning to find the silver hidden in a wooden box labeled 'schoolbooks.' That was clever." As I look around, I see a few people smile slightly as they nod in agreement.

"The label on the schoolbooks was funky," I add. "It included the title, but James didn't have the title when he was at school. And there were no dates on the box. Penelope said that the undated 'schoolbooks' label with the title made her suspicious. Then she said, 'Barbara is such a snob. She's the sort to include the title.' That's when I knew Penelope suspected Barbara had packaged the loot."

Nana asks, "Why would anyone want to label the box as schoolbooks?"

"Marjorie said that if the box were discovered as schoolbooks, no one would bother to open it. Since it was a titled person's schoolbooks, the box would not be tossed away either. Bertie said it was a perfect foil. I learned a new word when he said that."

Nana is almost laughing as she queries, "What new word?"

"Foil," I reply. "Bertie said, 'A perfect foil.' I asked Marjorie, and she said, 'It means something that stops something else from happening. It is a perfect disguise to prevent discovery of the silver.' That's how 'foil' became my new word!"

I hear laughter and chuckles all over the place. Nana and Mom both have a hand over their mouth, as if they were about to cough.

It takes a moment before Nana can ask, "Do you know why Barbara wanted to hide the stolen goods?"

I reply, "I overheard Barbara answer that question herself. James asked, 'Why not let the thieves sell it as part of their payment?' And Barbara replied, 'That is fine if they are never caught. But if the stolen merchandise surfaces, the police might discover who the robbers are. If caught, the thieves might talk, and the trail might return to me.' She hid the goods so that nothing would lead to James and Barbara. All they had to do was store the silver in their house."

"Did you hear Barbara say what she would do with the purchased loot, Jeremiah?" asks Nana.

"Yes, I did," I reply.

"What was her plan?" Nana smiles as she asks me the question.

"She planned to put the box in the attic or the vault where no one would look," I answer.

Nana's eyes focus on the ancestors as she says, "Thank you, Jeremiah. In summary, we have a box labeled 'Schoolbooks, James Wadsworth, Earl Poppycock.' Essentially, they are of no value. But they are the schoolbooks of a titled aristocrat. Therefore, they were kept but never unwrapped when the London house was disbanded and the contents moved to the country home. The box just found a new home, undisturbed, in a country retreat, where it stayed for another hundred years or thereabouts."

Nana looks at me as she asks, "Do you think that is what happened?"

As my thoughts become clear, I slowly reply, "Well, when I eavesdropped, I overheard Barbara tell James her plan for the silver. Penelope found the silver in our attic after the box was moved here when the London house was sold. I guess that plan worked!"

I look around slowly. Eyes are intently focused on me. Some are still smiling. A few are trying not to giggle. *Glad to amuse!*

Nana looks at the ancestors as she says, "But the clincher is the pair of silver statues, the rabbit and the frog. There is an inscription on each, 'Walter from Abigail' and 'Abigail from Walter.' Above that, each carries the inscription 'On the occasion of our first wedding anniversary 1716.' The silver in front of you has those inscriptions." Nana's eyes scan the crowd of ancestors.

Nana pauses before she asks, "What does finding the second statue here mean to you, Jeremiah?"

I'm getting tired and a lot befuddled. I stare hard, directly at Barbara and James. This helps me. When I see my enemy and then see my friends, I'm not so frightened anymore. I focus my thoughts as I say, "The police had the rabbit because it was stolen property discovered at Edgar's house. I heard Barbara tell James to steal one of the statues and put it in Edgar's house. I guess he must have stolen the rabbit. I heard her plan storage of the stolen goods. We know that when the London house was sold, the contents came here."

Pausing to gather my thoughts, I finally continue, "If James did what his wife demanded, then he put the rabbit in the library at Edgar's house. We know he had the chance to do that. It makes sense that whoever put the rabbit in Edgar's house was involved with the robbery. We know why they hid the rest of the stolen loot, including the stolen frog. And all of it ended up in Papa's house in a box marked schoolbooks belonging to James Wadsworth. It sure sounds like James and Barbara were responsible for the robbery."

Barbara yells, "You admitted Phoebe purchased the rabbit just a few days ago! She could have purchased both!" She is desperate. Her voice rises as she speaks.

A male voice asks, "May I have leave to speak?" Everyone turns their gaze to Joshua, quietly off to the side with Penelope.

Leila replies, "Yes, Joshua Wadsworth, formerly the Earl Poppycock, you may…but in a moment. First, does the defense have questions for Jeremiah?"

Mom looks at the ancestors, at James, at Barbara, and then at me. "No, Your Honor," is her reply.

"Does the prosecution have further questions?" asks Judge Leila. Nana replies, "No, Your Honor."

"Jeremiah, you are dismissed as a witness," says Great-Granny Leila.

I move away to lean against my dad. One of his long arms wraps over my shoulders and holds me tight. That feels mighty good!

Leila looks toward Joshua and says, "Please begin. Consider that you are under oath and must tell the whole truth."

"I do consider myself under oath," he replies earnestly. He fully materializes as he speaks.

Joshua pauses briefly and then says, "The rabbit remained in police evidence when it was never claimed by the Johnson family. Eventually, it was found in the evidence boxes, old and unwanted, long after all the people involved in the case were dead."

Joshua continues, "Leila followed its path on her many times seeping out to travel, look, listen, and learn. That is how she knew it was taken from Evidence and sold for a profit. It traded hands several times until it was purchased by Emma Winter, who knew its significance. As we learned earlier, she tried investigating during a visit here as a youth. But she was not successful."

Again, the crowd murmurs about Emma. The ancestors keep mentioning that she was good looking and smart. Clearly, she made an impression.

Joshua says, "After my arrival here, I tracked the rabbit. It was not a difficult task. Emma kept it in a place of honor. After her death, it was sold to a dealer. I found it and kept it hidden in the dealer's store. The proprietor in the Silver Vaults may have forgotten about the purchase.

"I materialized and went to the shop in the Silver Vaults to sell the rabbit to Phoebe." He glances fondly toward our nanny. After a moment, his eyes return to the group of ancestors as he says, "At home, Phoebe even commented how much the proprietor looked like me in our portrait. I can vouchsafe the provenance of the rabbit. And we all saw the frog leave the box."

Leila asks, "Are there questions for Joshua?"

Both Nana and Mom say no.

"Thank you for your testimony, Joshua. You are dismissed."

As Joshua moves back toward Penelope, he becomes translucent again.

I nudge Dad and whisper, "What is provenance?"

"The history of something so you know where it came from," he whispers in return.

"Thanks," I reply.

Edgar says, "May I have leave to speak?"

"Yes, indeed," replies Leila.

Edgar begins, "The box was unwrapped in the view of all here. The frog came out of the wrappings in the box. For the skeptics here, we have two guests who can answer questions about the frog and the rabbit. May I introduce them, Leila?"

Barbara is still green. She looks like her stomach is heaving in a most unfamiliar way. She looks like she might get sick.

"You may introduce them," replies Leila.

"Enter, please," says Edgar. Two people suddenly appear. "Let me introduce Walter and Abigail Johnson," he says with a smile.

There are audible gasps from some ancestors.

Our visitors appear immediately. They seem very solid, not translucent at all. Where did they come from? Did they come out of the ether?

James turns pale. Barbara looks really sweaty, and the armpits of her dress are now stained.

Leila says, "Do you consider yourselves under oath?"

Two voices reply, "We do regard ourselves as under oath and must tell only the truth."

"You are husband and wife?" asks Leila.

"Yes, Leila, we are. You were at the wedding," Abigail replies.

"So I was!" Leila giggles.

"Walter, you were killed by robbers, were you not?" asks Leila.

"Actually, Leila, I heard the thieves. I came down the stairs to investigate. In my haste and without a candle for illumination, I fell, landed at the base of the stairs, and remembered nothing more till I was addressed by Saint Peter."

"I see," says Judge Leila. Then she asks again, "Are you saying you were not murdered?"

"No. I fell during a robbery at my house. Had the robbers not been there, I would have had more years with my beloved Abigail."

"Quite so." Leila doesn't know what next to say. Walter's comment is so sad.

Nana asks him questions about the visit of James and Edgar two days before his death. He answers, verifying that Abigail had already left for her visit to their daughter and that James was absent for a significant portion of the time he and Edgar talked together.

"Walter, from what you have said, James could have been anywhere in the house?" Nana inquires.

"Yes. He had freedom to move about, even in Abigail's absence. We trusted him," he answers.

"Now, please examine these," commands Nana and points to the silver rabbit and frog.

"With pleasure," he replies while he gently handles them. "I remember these gifts so very well. Abigail received the rabbit, because my private nickname for her was Bunny." He glances affectionately at his wife and giggles quietly. "It is inscribed 'Abigail from Walter.' The frog was mine, from Abigail, as a reminder that I am Abigail's true prince. It has an inscription 'Walter from Abigail.'" He adds, "Each also has the inscription 'On the occasion of our first wedding anniversary 1716. As you can see, placed side by side, the two animals gaze lovingly toward one another." He deftly places them side by side. The animals do indeed gaze longingly toward each other.

There are murmurs among the crowd.

"There is no doubt that these are yours?" Nana asks.

"Let Abigail look also," replies Walter.

She does. Her early-eighteenth-century dress lets everyone see her catch her breath as she handles the two objects. "Walter, I never thought we should see the two together again." She starts to quietly cry. He wraps his arm about her shoulders and holds her tight.

"Is that sufficient for the court?" Prosecutor Nana asks.

Leila says, "The court is satisfied."

Defense Mom says, "No further questions for these witnesses regarding the statues."

The ancestors murmur, "Enough. It is true. No more is needed."

Leila says, "Thank you, Walter. Thank you, Abigail." Leila looks at both fondly.

As she points at the silver figures, Abigail asks, "What happens to them now?"

Leila looks back at Phoebe, who nods approval.

"You may have both, should you wish," Leila replies.

Walter and Abigail confer. "We have a different wish," says Walter.

Abigail asks, "Is Phoebe here?"

"Yes," says Phoebe, as she steps forward from far behind and to the side of Edgar, where she was partially hidden and out of the way of the family.

Abigail continues, "You were attracted to the figure of the rabbit. And with that, you helped solve the mystery of Walter's death and Edgar's wrongful execution. Our pleasure is to give both to you in thanks, from Walter and from me, on behalf of Edgar." Walter smiles broadly at Phoebe as Abigail hands her the figures. Edgar beams with pleasure.

Phoebe's eyes well up with tears as she accepts their gift. "I shall treasure both," she states quietly. "Thank you." She looked frightened during the proceedings. Now she appears overwhelmed with gratitude. She places the figures near the other silver for safety.

I'll bet she is still wondering what will happen next.

Walter and Abigail look around the room. Walter says, "You will soon be making a decision. I know you will be fair, merciful, and just. Thank you." He looks at each and every person, but he deliberately ignores Barbara, James, Cybil, and Humphrey.

"Jeremiah, you deserve our special thanks," says Abigail. She feels like real flesh and blood as she embraces me. Likewise, Walter feels very solid as he leans down to kiss my forehead, one hand on my shoulder.

Walter says, "You are a kindly lad and a good soul. You and your sister deserve special recognition."

Both reach out to Susanne and give her a hug and kiss.

All the ancestors, with the exception of four, cry out, "Hip, hip, hurrah! Hip, hip, hurrah!" They clap their hands in approval for a very long time.

James and Cybil stare sullenly at the floor. Barbara is white with rage. Humphrey looks confused. Poor old Humphrey!

Embarrassed and bright red, I look toward Susanne. I see her red face smiling back.

Walter and Abigail turn to Edgar. Walter says, "You are to be congratulated. You were wronged. We hope you soon shall be pardoned."

Edgar shakes Walter's hand and holds it tight for a moment. He kisses Abigail on the cheek and holds her briefly as they say goodbye.

"May we leave now?" asks Abigail.

Leila asks, "Does the prosecution have any questions for Walter and Abigail?"

"No, Your Honor," replies Mom.

"And the defense?" Leila inquires.

"None," replies Nana, "their testimony has been quite clear. No further questions."

Leila answers, "Yes, my dears, you may leave. But visit when you can. I so love your company." Leila kisses them both on the cheek.

"Perhaps you will be able to visit us," suggests Abigail.

"Oh my. I hadn't thought of that. Mortimer and I should like that. Let's see what unfolds," Leila giggles.

"Yes, we would like to visit," says Mortimer. He moves to shake Walter's hand and kiss Abigail on the cheek.

Both visitors wave to the crowd, wave vigorously to Jemima and blow her a kiss, look back at Susanne and at me, touch Leila's shoulder, and wave goodbye to Mortimer.

"Walter, my prince, come along," says Abigail.

"Coming, Bunny."

Hand in hand, they both vanish. There is a hush over everyone.

My mouth moves as I mutter inaudibly to myself, "How did such solid persons disappear so quickly? Does heaven have different rules or different energy levels than the attic phantoms have?"

A long silence follows. I'm getting as anxious as Phoebe. What happens next? How do these ghost trials work?

Chapter 23

Verdict and Sentencing

At last, Leila breaks the long silence by asking, "Is the prosecution ready for final arguments?"

Nana steps forward and summarizes the case and the charges against James and Barbara. Both hang their heads, James in shame and Barbara in fury.

"The defense may proceed with their final arguments, if ready," says Leila.

Mom summarizes the case against James and Barbara. She tries to make it less horrible than it is and tries to introduce doubt, which doesn't really work very well.

When she finishes, Leila looks at Nana and Mom.

"Do either of you have any additional things to say?"

Nana repeats, "The prosecution rests."

Mom takes a deep breath, looks hard at the livid Barbara, and says, "No. The defense rests."

"Now it is time for the jury to deliberate," instructs Leila.

There are murmurs from various groups. Some remain quiet and pensive before speaking to their neighbors. Some have strong opinions. Surprisingly, not all are uniform. Gradually, they all look solemn, and a hush ensues.

"What does the jury say in the case against James and Barbara Wadsworth, once known as Earl and Countess Poppycock?" asks Judge Leila. Speaking clearly, she continues, "On the charge of arranging the robbery of Mr. and Mrs. Johnson?"

With a single voice, they all shout out, "Guilty!"

Leila states the second, "On the charge of withholding evidence during the trial that led to the execution of Edgar Wadsworth?"

Again, they shout in unison, "Guilty!"

Leila states the third charge, "On the charge of attempted murder of Jeremiah Morris?"

"Guilty!" This is very loud, in unison, with no stray voices.

Leila continues, "On the charge of the murder of Walter Johnson?"

There is a slight pause. Mostly in unison, the voices speak more quietly, "Not guilty."

"We now must proceed to sentencing." Leila's voice is wavering. She is near tears. Barbara is not her kin. She is her son's wife and deservedly not a favorite of Leila's. But James is her own flesh and blood, her own son. She has trouble continuing.

The room brightens as sunlight streams in, making the brass nameplates glow. A deep and authoritative voice booms, "Sentencing is beyond your powers. That is for me to decide."

Everyone searches for the source of the voice.

"Who speaks?" asks Leila as her eyes search everywhere.

"I am Saint Peter. I shall decide from here forward," says the voice slowly and deliberately.

There is a giant buzz again as individual voices mix together. The wasps are back, and the sound is bigger! There are stray comments about judgment day. The ancestors each agreed to stay to help clear Edgar's name and find the guilty parties, knowing they will go to their final destination when the mystery has been solved and Edgar's name exonerated. All have had a very long time to ponder what clearing Edgar's name actually means. For them, this truly is judgment day. There can be good news or very bad news, and today's decision lasts forever. Some stray voices sound a little nervous. Some phantoms start to fidget. Others appear totally relaxed and accepting.

Saint Peter's voice continues, "I have waited a long time for a resolution of these matters. Jeremiah, I thank you for your bravery, your courage, and your kindliness toward Edgar." The voice pauses briefly and then says, "Susanne, I thank you for supporting Jeremiah. You helped him plan and understand enough to be safe."

Susanne blushes as much as I do.

After another pause, the voice continues, "Edgar, your name is cleared forever."

Edgar's relief is visible. Tears well up in his eyes. He looks to Jemima, who comes to his side. They embrace tightly. Jemima gives him a long kiss on his lips. Side by side, they look very happy.

There are murmurs. "Well done!" "Congratulations!" "Good job, all!" I'm too overwhelmed with happiness and gratitude at Saint Peter's decision to say anything. I give a thumbs-up to Edgar and Jemima, to Susanne, and to Papa.

The voice continues, "Phoebe, I thank you for your great help in raising such fine young people. Your love for them is noted. Sam and Constance, as parents, you have done well."

Each person smiles. Phoebe blushes and looks around uncertainly. Dad looks as if he doesn't know what next he is expected to do. Mom's eyes are bright as she holds Dad's hand in hers. Most ancestors nod in agreement with Saint Peter's words.

The voice adds, "John and Iris, as grandparents giving your living example, you have had a profound influence on these young people. Thank you both for what you have done in your lifetimes."

Our grandparents look around at the ancestors and at the living. Papa smiles and Nana's eyes become bright. She mouths, "Thank you, Saint Peter."

There is a pause, and then the voice summarizes, "You have all done well, with notable exceptions." After another pause, Saint Peter seems more businesslike as his voice says, "Now to the matter at hand." There is another pause, a forever pause. The room is as quiet as a tomb!

Eventually, Saint Peter breaks the silence. He speaks crisply. "Barbara Wadsworth, once known as Countess Poppycock, you have been found guilty of arranging the robbery which resulted in the death of Walter Johnson, guilty of withholding evidence in the trial of Edgar Wadsworth that ended with his wrongful execution, guilty of the attempted murder of Jeremiah Morris, your eight-greats-grandson.

"During your lifetime, you have been arrogant and selfish. You have never helped others. Instead, you exposed the weak and helpless to ridicule. You have never been repentant. You are damned!"

There is shocked silence at Saint Peter's harsh words, followed by a slow murmur of agreement.

I mutter cynically under my breath, "I guess the title of countess doesn't much matter to Saint Peter." I feel Dad's arm tighten around me for a moment. I guess he agrees.

In response to my words, Mr. Brown nudges my ribs. I guess Papa heard me too. He turns slightly toward me, waves, and smiles.

The voice continues, "James, like your wife, you spent your life indulging yourself without a thought to others in need. You have no moral fiber. You agreed with your wife in committing horrible crimes, all without remorse. You are damned!"

Leila bursts into tears. "My son! My son!" she sobs. Mortimer holds her shaking shoulders. Jemima moves close to Leila to comfort her with her presence.

The voice continues, "Cybil and Humphrey, I have considered you two for a long time. You both were arrogant and mean-spirited in your lifetimes. Cybil, you lead by example, showing arrogance and a lack of concern for anyone who wasn't directly useful to you. Calling Leila 'the upstart' did not endear you to me. And I witness all!

"Humphrey, you were too self-absorbed to notice anyone except yourself. I have no use for either of you."

Cybil looks at Humphrey, searching for solace and help. He looks stunned and absentmindedly fiddles with his clothes.

The voice adds, "Your sins are not so egregious as those of Barbara and James. But you will not be happy where you are going."

Saint Peter's voice pauses. The whole crowd remains silent, somber, and solemn.

The voice softens. "Now for the rest of you. You have all been sinners of varying degrees. Some have deeply repented and are forgiven. All of you showed a willingness to stay and help Edgar. That is worth much. Soon, you shall all come with me."

There are sighs of relief, smiles, and then a quiet "Hear! Hear!" from a few.

Without warning, the room darkens quickly and deeply, almost to blackness. All sunlight vanishes; coldness fills the air. Have hopelessness and despair consumed the room?

A brilliant flash of fire surrounds Barbara. She screams, "No!" and disappears with the flames.

James is silent. He looks sadly toward his mother and father. Wordlessly, he disappears in a flash of fire the same way as his wife.

Leila sobs uncontrollably, "My son! My son!"

Cybil looks to Humphrey, but she's not finding much comfort there. She is terrified and ready to accept assistance from any commoner who is able to help her, even someone from Brooklyn! With Humphrey, she disappears in a puff of smoke.

"My grandson! He is a fool, but he is my grandson," sobs Leila.

In utter darkness, we all wait. We are horrified, shocked into silence. Huddled against my dad, I shiver with the cold!

Chapter 24

THE FINAL GOODBYES

Intense sunlight returns; the room glows. During the blackness, I felt cold and sad. The warm sun makes me feel hopeful.

Despite his booming voice, Saint Peter sounds like a kindly and gentle person as he says, "It is time to say your goodbyes. I shall give a little extra time to the ten who helped Jeremiah. The rest will come with me now."

The ancestral crowd waves to Nana and Papa, Mom and Dad, Phoebe, Mrs. Stewart, Mr. Brown, and Nigel. I move near Susanne as the ancestors cheer us and exclaim expressions of thanks and congratulations on a job well done. They say special thanks to each of the ancestors who helped us.

During the chaos, Clive races over to us to declare, "Miss Susanne and Master Jeremiah, I must say it has been a pleasure." His dark eyes focus intently on each of us as he shakes our hand. His coarse features are beaming with gratitude, and his dark eyes are shiny with tears.

"I was lost without your help, Clive," I honestly say. "And I paid attention to your concerns about my possibly being seen. That saved my life in Barbara's house. Thank you, Clive. I owe everything to you. And again, thank you for talking to Susanne. Those extra trips across the centuries must have exhausted you."

He replies, "It was all for a good cause, to help a good family, and to help you. Thank you for what you have done, and the family honor that you have restored. You both have my everlasting gratitude."

I shake his hand again, and Susanne gives him a hug.

I ask, "Do you understand that you are really a part of this family, Clive?"

His face registers surprise. He responds, "I work for the family, sir, and for the benefit of the family."

I reply, "After a few hundred years, I think you are truly part of this motley crew we call family." I see Leila nearby and recognize what she has been doing. I turn my head to her and ask, "Don't you agree with my thoughts?"

Suddenly at my elbow, she exclaims, "Clive, I saw you spit at Lady Barbara and Lord James."

Suddenly nearly ashen, Clive stammers his interruption, "But, milady, you know…you know what…Barbara did." When he notices Leila's mouth beginning to smile, his confusion stops his stammering. His head swivels back and forth between Leila and me.

Just then, Leila interjects, "Oh, dear one, I had no intention of creating an upset." After he calms, she continues, "That spitting was only one of the many loving things you have done for us over many years. As judge, I wasn't allowed to spit at her. Thank you, my dear friend, for doing what I was forbidden. You truly are our friend, our helper, our guide. Your advice was Jeremiah's salvation in that house. We are forever in your debt. When we meet on the other side, you must join with our family because you are indeed part of our family." She smiles broadly and holds his hand.

Overcome, Clive utters, "Oh, milady, thank you. An earl's valet accepted…," but his voice fails for anything further.

"Accepted? It's rather more…perhaps the word is 'adopted' into the family," she finishes for him. Her hand touches his face briefly in a grateful caress.

Since he doesn't have his own trunk, he waves goodbye in a daze and walks unsteadily over to the trunk where he has served for centuries. Looking so happy he must be dizzy, he stands and waits, his dark eyes bright and blinking fiercely.

Then each pair with their trunk disappears with a pop, one after another. Pops are heard all over the attic. Susanne and I notice Clive's muscular figure still standing by Leila and Mortimer's trunk.

A few moments later, he vanishes with a faint sound. Finally, only ten ancestors remain. They all fully materialize to say their special goodbyes.

Leila reaches for me, kisses my cheek, and hugs me tight. Then she holds Susanne. With her arms around us both, she says, "I love you both beyond description."

Mortimer shakes my hand and gives me a hug. He kisses Susanne and holds her tight. "Thank you both," he says, eyes glistening.

Edgar enfolds Susanne and me in his enormously long arms. "I am grateful that my name has been cleared. Thank you both."

When Edgar releases us, Jemima gives each of us a long and heartfelt hug and kiss. "We waited so long for some very special people. You were worth the wait." Her intensely green eyes glisten with tears of gratitude.

When Susanne looks at Edgar, he is different. She points to him rather impolitely. I look where she points. His neck is straight, and his face is fuller. He looks like he could conquer the world. Even his hose fit his fatter legs.

We look at the new clothes he has, fashionable for his time. And they fit! Despite his teeth, I see why Jemima was attracted to him! He cleans up nice!

"Now you have a choice in how you look!" Susanne exclaims, looking at both Edgar and Jemima. They nod yes.

Edgar replies, "I am as I was the day after my marriage to Jemima—ready to face the world unafraid." His arm goes around his bride's waist and holds her.

She leans against him with happy smiles. Jemima's figure is slightly fuller. Her skin is smoother, without lines. She looks like a lovely young bride. Her beautiful green eyes show her love.

She wears a new deep-green dress, with lace at the square neck and at the sleeves. The top is tight fitting and low cut; the skirts below the fitted waist are full. The dress flatters her figure and brings out the color of her eyes. Her large emerald pendant shoots green flares, and the surrounding diamonds flash. She is lovely to see! I feel such happiness for them.

As I look at them, I feel confused. My spinning head asks, *How did they get new clothes so quickly? What is going on? I am lost again! Does just making a choice create the difference?*

Marcus and Beatrice come over to Susanne and me. Beatrice holds us tight as she says, "I am so proud of you both. You have moral backbone. I will always watch over you. Remember that you both are loved."

Marcus shakes my hand and states, "Well done, brave lad." He gives Susanne a kiss on her cheek and hugs her briefly. "You are a good and smart young woman. I love you." He looks at me again. "I love you both."

Bertie says, "What a rip we had! A little time travel and a scavenger hunt. I haven't had such fun since our heyday. Well done, all of you." He looks at all the living.

Marjorie adds, "You two really are the cat's pajamas. And, Jeremiah, you wore pajamas for much of the time!" She laughs.

Susanne reaches into her pocket. Out come Marjorie's handkerchief and cigarette holder. "These are yours," she says as she hands them to Marjorie.

"Thank you," says Marjorie. "I will take the cigarette holder. I don't want you to pick up that bad habit! But keep the handkerchief. It will remind you of our adventure."

With a hug and an air kiss, she says, "We will meet again much, much later. I look forward to that time." Marjorie smiles a brittle smile. Clearly, she doesn't want to say goodbye, but I suspect Marjorie never cries, ever. She looks away, eyes bright. No tears!

Bertie looks at me and shakes my hand. He pecks Susanne on the cheek and says, "Well done," to both of us.

He reaches for Phoebe to give her a peck on the cheek. He says, "Thank you for buying the bunny. It was the cornerstone."

Phoebe flushes and says, "I could not have done that without Joshua." Phoebe looks in his direction. "Joshua, you make an excellent salesman." She laughs nervously.

Joshua says jokingly, "As the interim proprietor in a Silver Vaults shop, I am flattered." He bows in a pretend eighteenth-century bow to a lady. They all laugh. He kisses Phoebe on the cheek.

Joshua turns to Susanne and me. His arms reach around us both. "Know you are loved, not because you succeeded, but because you tried." He hugs us again.

Penelope comes to us and says goodbye with hugs and tears. "I love you both. Always know that."

Then Joshua and Penelope, both nearly in tears, turn to Nana and Papa as they say almost in unison, "We miss you every day. We will keep watching over you, trying to keep you safe."

I see that Papa has tears. He says, "I miss you both. I especially regret that our time together was cut short, Mum."

Penelope's breath catches as she says, "It was a stupid thing. I avoided an animal in the road. The accident that ensued cost me my life, my time with you, and Joshua. It was a sad accident, but you are stronger because of it."

Penelope holds Papa in a tight hug for a very long time and then kisses his cheek. Afterward, she gives Nana a long hug and then says, "Keep well, my dear. Look after your charge." Her eyes look down slightly as she points past Nana's arm to Papa. Penelope's chin jiggles fiercely as she tries not to cry. It's the same thing Susanne's chin does before she bursts into tears. *So that's where Susanne gets it!*

Joshua says to Nana and then Papa with a big hug, "Take care, both of you. Goodbye, Iris. Goodbye, son. You both are well loved." Nana has tears. Papa's sigh is audible.

After the departing ten have all doubled down on our parents and grandparents, they say their goodbyes to Phoebe, Mrs. Stewart, Mr. Brown, and Nigel, with murmured thanks for looking after the family.

Leila approaches my mom and dad. Leila says, "You two nearly lost Jeremiah, you know. Maybe on two occasions this trip. Think about that. Take time with your children." She adds, "They will be grown and away soon enough. Don't miss the opportunity that you still have." Leila touches Mom's cheek with real affection. "They both are special people, like their parents."

Mom is near tears. She hugs Leila tight, as does Dad. They both say and Mom repeats, "I understand."

Mortimer kisses Mom and shakes Dad's hand as he says, "You two have done well by the children."

Leila reaches for me, pulls me slightly apart from the others, and whispers in my ear, "Jeremiah, my dear boy, don't worry about that Asperger's thingy. You thought the doctor said asparagus syndrome? Really? You are a funny lad. You are tall and skinny, but you'll never turn green." She laughs merrily.

My shocked voice asks, "You were with me in the doctor's office?"

"Of course, dear. I *do* need to know about your welfare. And that doctor was so nice and very competent. I checked. But when your mind said asparagus syndrome, I was very glad you couldn't hear me laughing. Anyway, in a few years, you will have conquered social exchanges as you surmount autism. But the benefit of your struggle is that you will be forever graced with an enviable memory and a surprising ability to process detail, something very useful to many good people. Use those abilities."

I whisper back, "How do you know what will happen?"

"I read minds. I know. Just wait a few short years and see." Then Leila flutters her long lashes, smiles warmly and lovingly at me, and adds, "Don't be fussed by autism, or me."

I'm confused, so I ask sincerely, "Why would I be fussed?"

She glibly replies, "Because I know firsthand the work you do to negotiate daily life. But it will get easier, just as the nice doctor said."

"You've been snooping inside my head a lot, haven't you?"

"Of course, dear. That's what grandmas are for. Not to worry. Grandma Leila will keep track of you, watch over you, and do her best to protect you," she replies in a businesslike, matter-of-fact voice.

My mind flashes, *That's what fusses me.*

She looks at me sternly till I think, *But my response is normal.*

Seemingly satisfied, she smiles and murmurs, "Yes, your response is very normal," and touches my face gently with her hand as her departing gift. Her eyes are very bright as she utters, "I love you deeply, dear boy."

I reply, "Love you too, Grandma Leila." Near tears, I give her a goodbye-forever hug. Eventually, she releases me and extracts herself from my grip, nods, and slowly moves away.

I'm almost too baffled by our conversation to notice another chaotic chorus of "Thank you! Love you! A job well done!" as these ancestors prepare for departure.

It's hard to imagine all the feelings Leila must be having right now. She looks in my direction and nods a vigorous yes.

All eyes are bright, but Leila now cries quietly. Her one son has been pardoned and his name cleared. That was her goal, and it has been achieved, but at what cost? Another son and a grandson have been damned. That's a lot to figure out in one's head, even for Leila. Mortimer is beside her, an arm about her shoulders, helping her stay calm.

Likewise, Mortimer must be in pain now too, just like Leila. But like a good spouse, he looks after his true love first.

Each pair slowly becomes translucent again and waits.

"Ready?" asks the voice of Saint Peter.

As each replies in turn, most say, "Yes, Saint Peter, I am ready."

Together, Marjorie and Bertie quip, "As much as we will ever be."

Leila glances at Mortimer and holds his hand. She looks over to Edgar and Jemima. "We love you both," she says. Mortimer waves his free hand to agree. Vigorous nods from Edgar and Jemima return the same message.

One after another, each trunk with its occupants disappears with a pop. Soon the room is empty of all trunks. The two trunks seen through the west door, Leila and Mortimer's and Edgar and Jemima's, are the last to disappear with pops. Suddenly, the attic feels very empty.

Papa and Nana, Mom and Dad, Phoebe, Susanne, and I stand almost huddled together while Mrs. Stewart, Mr. Brown, and Nigel look on.

I feel very lonely for a moment. I will miss the vivacity of Leila, and I regret not knowing the real Edgar better.

"Well, I never!" exclaims Mrs. Stewart loudly. "Who would ever have believed it possible? I should have given Old Cook better heed."

Nigel nods. The family gawks at each other.

Dad says, "Was this all a dream?"

Susanne waves the bright aquamarine handkerchief she has received from Marjorie. Dad stares at his daughter and at Marjorie's handkerchief. He nods silently while his eyes flit down, then sideways toward Mom. He appears confused, looks down again, shrugs his shoulders, and then glances back again toward Mom.

Mom gazes back at him. She sees his confusion and disbelief. "Believe it, buddy. What you saw and what you heard all really happened." She blows him a kiss.

Dad still scans the group around him in disbelief just as Mrs. Stewart again loudly exclaims, "Well, I never!" Dad involuntarily jumps a little and then glances toward Mrs. Stewart's figure when he hears her loud voice.

"You all need tea and biscuits," booms Mrs. Stewart. She stomps down the stairs muttering, "Well, I never!"

Mrs. Stewart has a very loud voice—always. I guess that's because she is hard of hearing. Later, I'll ask if that's right.

Mr. Brown turns to Papa. He says, "I remember what you told me about your experience years ago. I never mentioned it to anyone, partly because I was not sure what actually happened. Now I know everything you told me was spot-on! My hat goes off to Susanne and especially to Jeremiah." Mr. Brown looks at Susanne and at me. He smiles.

Mr. Brown adds, "Congratulations, young man. And congratulations to you too, Susanne." He turns to Papa, pauses before speaking, and then says with decided firmness, "I think the least said about this, the better."

Papa nods in agreement.

Mr. Brown searches to find Nigel nearby. He touches Nigel's arm and looks at him directly. Nigel looks back at Mr. Brown with conflicting emotions on his face. Our butler does not appear eager to talk. He still looks angry and hurt.

Mr. Brown begins, "Can you forgive me, Nigel? I could not say anything. I gave a promise. I gave that promise to John Wadsworth, now Earl Poppycock, our employer." I can tell Mr. Brown is afraid Nigel will remain angry with him or with Papa.

Nigel thinks for a long while in silence without any change in facial expression.

Mr. Brown becomes anxious. "Please, Nigel. You have a choice to make. We must all live with the consequences. Think carefully," he pleads.

Nigel recollects, "Lord John's visit to the attic was before I knew the family." After a moment, a faint smile returns to Nigel's face; his features brighten. He says quietly, "Perhaps it is just as well His Lordship didn't want me to know. Phantoms in the attic! I would have looked over my shoulder forever, always wondering who was watching!" There is new mischief in his eyes as he adds, "This is another time that even the younger Papa was right. Best not to know. Ignorance is bliss!" They both laugh. Mr. Brown sighs deeply. He appears relieved, as does Nigel.

Nigel adds, "All of them are shoving off now anyway. After they shove off, I don't need to worry about spooks anymore!" They laugh together again.

"Thank you, my friend," murmurs Mr. Brown so very quietly that he was difficult to hear.

Nana comes over to Mr. Brown and to Nigel. "Both of you were included in all this for several reasons. We were concerned about safety, and there is safety in numbers. We also wanted you to know the truth."

She pauses before she comes to the punch line. "But please, make sure that both of you and Mrs. Stewart respect the family's privacy." She stares both of them in the eyes, a little sternly.

Mr. Brown says, "Yes. Discretion always."

Nigel replies, "I understand the need for discretion. The situation is odd, to say the least." He pauses uncertainly, nods to Mr. Brown, and then adds, "I will undertake the task of speaking to Mrs. Stewart."

Mr. Brown's shoulders sag in relief as he whispers to our butler, "Oh, thank you, my true friend."

"Yes, thank you, Nigel." Nana adds with a little laugh, "Some days, speaking to Mrs. Stewart can be an exhausting undertaking. And like today, sometimes has shockingly surprising results."

Mr. Brown simply says, "Indeed."

Nigel chortles, smiles his brilliant smile, and points discreetly to his ears.

As her eyes sweep from Nigel to Mr. Brown, Nana says, "And thank you, Mr. Brown. I always know I can trust each of you implicitly."

Nana watches as Nigel and Mr. Brown walk down the stairs, side by side. They talk together quietly and amiably. Their voices are overshadowed. Floors below, Mrs. Stewart can still be heard muttering, "Well, I never!"

After I overheard Nana speaking to Nigel and Mr. Brown, I appear at her side as the two men leave. "Nana," I ask, "what does 'implicitly' mean?

Nana smiles down at me. Her hand reaches to muss my hair. "Well, curious cat, what does 'implicitly' mean? Implicitly means absolutely. It is a shorter way of saying 'completely and without question.'"

She stops mussing my hair and absentmindedly starts to pat it back into place. *Good luck with that!* She quietly says, "So now, my little eavesdropper, you have a new word." Her hand slips from my hair and closes under my chin, gently pushing my face up toward her. She gazes into my eyes while her thumb strokes the side of my cheek.

Nana says, "I am so glad my curious cat has nine lives." She pauses and then says, "Nana loves you."

"And I love Nana," I reply. She turns toward Papa who is now nearby.

Nana touches Papa's arm. His eyes are still moist. "Are you all right?" she inquires cautiously.

Papa says, "I now realize how much I missed after her death and how hard it was for my father. They were good people."

Nana takes Papa's hand and leans against him as they head for the stairs. Nana asks, "How did you manage knowing phantoms resided in the attic and could be snooping?"

Papa stops walking and thinks for a moment before he replies, "At first, I tried to pretend I didn't know. And later, I accepted what I could not change. I just carried on." He mutters as he starts to laugh, "That will be easier now." He laughs again.

"My smart man," says Nana as they descend the stairs, "and they have all shoved off, never to be seen again, at least in this lifetime."

That turned out to be a very wrong assumption! Again with the assumptions! But that is another story.

Mom turns to Dad and stares gently into his face while she declares, "You made adjustments after Papa's visit three years ago. I think I will need to speak to my company. Leila is right. It is time to heed her advice." She hugs her husband. She adds, "We are fortunate in so many ways. Let's not make more mistakes."

Both look at their children. "See you downstairs," they say.

Phoebe smiles when she hears all this. She watches as Dad and Mom head to the stairs.

All business, Phoebe says, "Come on, you two. Down we go." She begins herding.

Susanne says, "Don't forget the gifts you received from Walter and Abigail Johnson."

Phoebe appears surprised and exclaims, "Oh dear. So much happened that I totally forgot!" She returns to the box with silver piled before it. "Help me pack this up," she requests.

In a few minutes, all the silver, except the frog and rabbit, is back in the box, wrapped and sealed with the lid. "We can leave the box here for now. It's a reminder of what happened."

She picks up the frog and the rabbit. "These are beautiful. What a splendid gift! One with many memories." She laughs. "Maybe someday I will find my prince." Cradling her gifts, Phoebe heads for the stairs. Over her shoulder, she says, "So far, I haven't even found a frog."

All I can think is *If the men available are frogs, why bother?* But I know that Phoebe, like Susanne, would like her special man. Susanne drives me nuts sometimes with her speculation about one boy after another. Sometimes she seems boy-crazy! Yuck! They are both nuts. Wisely, I keep silent.

I look at Susanne and say, "Thanks for believing."

"Anytime," she says. Susanne thinks for a moment while her eyes spell mischief. She adds, "Well, anytime, maybe!"

Phoebe stops at the head of the stairs and looks back to scan the enormous room, empty except for one box. "Someone should write all this down," says Phoebe. She turns to go down the stairs. Her head swivels slightly back toward us while she adds, "This story would make a very good read!"

Susanne looks toward me as I walk beside her. She murmurs, "We had a real adventure. But I am not sure anything can be told to friends outside the family. The friends might think that the tale teller was nuts!" Susanne laughs.

She says, "I guess no one will ever know." She pauses, looks at me from the corner of her eye, and adds, "Unless, of course, someone does decide to write everything down." She giggles. "Will someone decide to write it all down?"

As we walk side by side down the stairs, I remain silent.

Chapter 25
THE PURPOSE OF OUR TALE

We descended those stairs almost sixty years ago. I still remember Phoebe's words about a good read and what Susanne said at the time. I kept journals of all our adventures, mostly outlines written at the time that were fleshed out later. As a child, I couldn't understand everything or remember all the details of conversations that were above my head. Those I filled in later, piecing together the probable things that were said, especially when I heard the same thing repeated many times.

I tidy up after breakfast and sip another cup of coffee. My mind slips back to the past, to good, happy memories and bad memories that still scare me.

I never wanted to write too soon—I could hurt someone's feelings unintentionally, something I would never do willingly. I'm not sure I wanted to write and share family secrets, ever. But Susanne is right. The story is worth telling and needs to be shared.

I think back to Papa and our visit to the Statue of Liberty when I was seven. He turned pale and looked ill when Dad joked that Papa's knowledge of history was so keen and realistic that it almost seemed as if he had met historical people from long ago.

Naturally, poor Papa turned pale. His actual meetings with long dead ancestors were mostly kept secret. After my later time travels, he felt that his story could also finally be told. But at that moment near the Statue of Liberty, he was afraid his secret might come out. None of us could have understood at the time, and he would have admitted a failure that he regretted. The guilt of that secret literally made him feel sick.

I remember when Papa said, "Lies and secrets are heavy burdens indeed, and they want to come out at the worst times!" He gave me good advice that I use daily when he said, "Jeremiah, remember this. Don't gather guilty secrets. Their weight will break your back."

But Papa learned much more than that when he met his ancestors. More than once he shared, "My meeting with ancestors made me realize the importance of knowing history, giving credit where credit is due, and not repeating the errors that our ancestors made before our time."

It was later that I was able to add to his conclusions and share my thoughts with him when he was very elderly and frail. When we were talking together near the end of his life, I said, "I now realize that a single version of history might not be the correct one, or the all-inclusive one."

"Perhaps that is the best history lesson of all," was the quick reply from his thin, gaunt face. And then he repeated, "Never gather guilty secrets. Their weight will pull you under. That's the evil of guilty secrets, even in a global historical narrative." I was glad we had that conversation even though it occurred very near his death. Papa was wise on many levels, even to the end! And I have paid heed to his words.

Now, so much time has passed that the people I might have offended by this tale are all dead, and hopefully at peace. No offense can be taken there.

There are others who would have been delighted by this story. Our parents, grandparents, and beloved Phoebe, God rest their souls, come to mind. They provided examples of lives well lived because theirs were lives filled with honesty, affection, and kindly love with respect for all. That is a large part of their true legacy.

So you see, that legacy is really the reason to share this story. They are an example of how persons can treat one another to create a wonderful life for all as a result. A kiss on the forehead every night is just the beginning.

Silently pondering my memories, I glance out the window as the doorbell rings. "Oh good, it's Susanne," I mutter aloud.

As I open the door, I see Susanne's usual bright smile and hear her say, "Good morning, Jeremiah. I'm here to work. I hope I'm not too early."

"Never too early," I reply.

She settles into a comfortable chair with a good light beside it, makes brief small talk about this and that, and then settles into reading the manuscript. Her red pencil is lethal!

As Susanne sits across from me reading the manuscript, I feed her coffee and treats. Many hours later, she finishes. She gets up and silently walks to stretch her legs. She comes over with the manuscript and sits beside me on the sofa. This will be the first time all day that she has spoken about the book. I don't know what she will say. Her silence has made me a little anxious.

She begins, "Yes, Jeremiah, I think you covered most everything that needed to be said." She pauses and looks toward me. "It must have been difficult for you to use the voice of a child. When you were seven, you spoke like an adult. Frankly, you were unbelievably precocious! I sometimes wonder if you were ever really a child."

We both laugh out loud. "Yes, Susanne, I do recollect that our parents, and certainly Phoebe, thought I was a somewhat strange, if pleasant, child. But you were the truly bright one. I just had a good memory."

"Your memory has served you well, Jeremiah. Well done."

We talk more, outlining a few changes, a few wording issues. We laugh at the occasional hilarious typo.

"Are you satisfied, Jeremiah?" Susanne asks.

"I don't know. We were always being taught facts so that it is difficult to know what the child remembered at one age without accidentally bringing in later memories. I do so wish my memory had a date stamp for each entry! Lord knows, I can't time travel anymore to verify anything."

"Silly you," teases Susanne. "You are always thinking the impossible."

"But it is finished, and soon out of my hands," I honestly reply.

Susanne hands back the manuscript and happily exclaims, "I vote yes! It does you proud. And it tells our story."

Outwardly, I blush with pleasure. Inwardly, I sigh with relief.

Susanne looks thoughtful for a time and then says, "You do realize how lucky we were, don't you, Jeremiah?"

"Yes, I've always thought we were lucky to meet so many of our ancestors. Very few people can honestly say they have had conversations with dead relatives!" I laugh out loud.

Susanne also laughs a little before she continues, "And you were lucky to have survived. You do realize you nearly lost your life?"

"Yes, Susanne, I do know. But I do not dwell upon that—too morbid."

She continues, "But we must not forget how lucky we were in being born into this family and lucky with the parents and nanny that we had."

She stops long enough to let me see the path she is taking before she continues, "It was our good fortune that Phoebe stayed with us as our nanny until we were nearly grown, and then remained as a family friend. Can you imagine a revolving door of caregivers, nanny after nanny, all with different behaviors or different expectations? We would never have known which direction to go. We might have never felt loved." She pauses to think for a moment. She looks somber and perhaps a little sad.

I wait for her to speak.

Susanne continues, "And if we ever had a rotten nanny, we could easily have learned never to be vulnerable by expressing affection. We might have become closed, mean, and selfish. Certainly, we might never have had the reassurance of unconditional love, the kind of love that Phoebe gave us even when our parents were absent, the kind of love that nurtured us."

I reply, "As you know, Phoebe kissed my forehead every night as she put me to bed, even when I was too old to need a kiss on the forehead. She did the same for you. Do you miss that, sometimes, just a little?"

Susanne looks directly at me. Suddenly, her chin jiggles wildly, and tears swell in her eyes just before she answers, "Sometimes I miss that a lot. And Phoebe is dead now. I shall never have that kiss from her again." Her voice breaks, and it takes a moment for her to recover.

Eventually, she says, with a slight quaver in her voice, "As an adult, I never doubted that our parents loved us. Early in my childhood, I was not so sure. It is hard for a child to feel love from absent parents." She pauses again. Her one hand is near mine.

She continues, "Remember, I am older. Dad changed his behavior toward us after Papa's visit when you were seven. Mom changed hers after she met the ancestors. That was ten years of age for you and almost thirteen for me. In those early years, it was Phoebe who gave me the love I craved." Her hand now grasps mine and holds on tight.

Despite her efforts, Susanne's tears do fall. I wait, unable to speak anyway. Finally, she says, "It was our nanny, the one constant in our life, who saved me by showing me love. I am so very grateful that she remained a constant for us. I loved her dearly and still do even though she is gone!"

"Me too," is my sincere reply. Now I shed tears that I do not wipe away. I don't care if Susanne sees my tears fall because I still miss Phoebe.

We sit in silence side by side, her hand held tightly in mine. She leans against me; that feels good! My sister is a good person, and I do love her dearly. She is my truest friend. As we see each other's tears, we giggle. Neither is embarrassed. We both wipe our faces with our spare hand as we stay clutched together with the other.

"We are a pair," says Susanne with a little laugh.

"Always have been," I reply glibly.

Eventually, Susanne sits up, releases my hand, pulls two tissues out of the box, hands me one, and blows her nose with a honking noise. She says, "We were privileged: grandchildren of an earl, children of a lawyer and a financier. But by example, the people who sculpted us, all of them, were down-to-earth people. Remember the context. Our grandparents were an earl and a countess who worked as a farmer and a lawyer! And Nana practiced till she was eighty! Yet they behaved like normal people, earning a living, never conveying an attitude of entitlement. That is not usual!

"They made demands of us, and they insisted that we fulfill our obligations. With our parents, they taught us that we must make our own way in the world. And all were fair and all were kind to everyone." She pauses to gather her thoughts.

Susanne repeats, "We were taught to make our own way in the world, but taught us to do so with kindness. Those were great lessons that we learned early on, painlessly. I have always been very grateful to them for that. Different attitudes from our parents or grandparents, or a different nanny, could have made us into demanding and entitled monsters!"

I am startled. I had never thought about this! Incredulous, I stare at my sister and say, "Susanne, you are so right. Indeed, we were taught to make our own way. Honesty, fairness, and kindness were learned by example. It was all done so simply and consistently that I've never thought about what a different upbringing could have done to us. Without thinking, I may have assumed it was the same for everyone."

"No, Jeremiah, we were very fortunate, and in the minority," my sister responds.

After a period of silence, I say, "Once again, I feel overwhelming gratitude to Mom and Dad, to our grandparents, and to Phoebe, our steady companion as we grew up. Yes, Susanne, you are very perceptive. We could have become very different people."

We sit close together in silence for a few minutes. Then Susanne says, "I've always thought you were a very special brother, Jeremiah, and very different from other people. I am glad we are still close."

My silent thoughts take over for a moment. I've been different from the rest because of autism. But my disability, my autism, has turned out to be a great asset in many ways. And best of all, Susanne has always loved me regardless of my social awkwardness. I don't want my voice to falter, so I clear my throat before I say, "You were a smart kid who grew into an astounding woman. You know that I love you deeply. Like you, I am glad that we are close."

She smiles her lovely smile, looks at me happily, and leans back on the sofa as we sit side by side.

Silence returns. Susanne takes my hand again for a few minutes more. We just sit, two old children together, holding hands.

Small talk eventually resumes. Susanne suddenly thinks of a few more minor changes that I make immediately as we recheck parts of the manuscript. Susanne says, "I'll proofread the finished copy."

Shortly afterward, my sister says she must leave, gives me a peck on my cheek, and says goodbye. Suddenly, I am alone. My solitary thoughts take over.

As I said before, it is nearing the end of my time. Too soon, I shall be at peace. Shall I perhaps have the pleasure of the company of all those wonderful souls I once knew? And shall I also have the company of the few true physical and passionate loves of my life? Will I have Leila's skills to guide the following generations? These questions I cannot answer.

In the meantime, I think over today's conversation and what Susanne and I have done with our lives. We have lived our lives to the fullest, pushed ourselves to achieve. We nurtured all of our talents as best we could. Both of us have tried very hard to be honest, fair, and kind. That can be difficult with some. We always show affection and love, no grudges, please.

And always, we have looked to the greater long-term goals, not the immediate gratification that most expect all too often. And we learn, always learn. Knowledge and education weigh very little; they are not heavy to carry. Mommy told me that! The weight of knowledge is so unlike the weight of guilty secrets.

So, dear reader, I hope you have enjoyed this tale of an old mystery with its adventures, narrated by a child, with comments from the old man he became, and all with a push to action from his sister.

Yes, it is true. It took a while, a very long while, before I shared the mystery surrounding Eight-Greats-Uncle Edgar. At last, I unraveled the tale and wrote it all down to share with you.

About the Author

Max W. Justus is on his second career. His first? Not important. But writing with purpose is now his passion. Think about it: writing with purpose—that's almost as important as reading with purpose.

He has written a series that follows the lives of Jeremiah and Susanne throughout their long and useful lives. The reason? He uses his characters to provide a glimpse into what kindness and fair play can do in society. Secondary reason? Let the reader romp through the book and then be inspired to lead by example.

Is Mr. Justus fomenting a cultural revolution? Not likely. Kindness and fair play are not truly revolutionary; they are ancient customs, almost a lost art.

When Mr. Justus tires of these characters, he writes the occasional whodunit, just for fun.

In real life, he's an ordinary bloke who earns a living, loves his wife and kids, and welcomes the grandkids home. Living in rural America, he feels blessed.

But not to worry; he's not slacking. His pen is still on paper.

CPSIA information can be obtained
at www.ICGtesting.com
Printed in the USA
JSHW051742100822
29116JS00001B/6